Chapter

I t had, Lauren quickly realised, been a spectacularly stupid idea to apply mascara in the back of an Uber on the way to a job interview at Buckingham Palace, especially when said Uber driver seemed to favour the brakes more than the accelerator pedal.

In her defence, though, the lighting in her tiny hotel room had been terrible, and there was also the small problem of having slept through her alarm, forcing her to get ready at lightning speed while puffy and jet lagged.

As far as omens went, it wasn't looking particularly great at the moment.

The picturesque sights of central London tinged with autumn colours flew past her as they drove down Park Lane, then stopped abruptly before disappearing once more. The towering parade of sycamore trees along one side of the road were shedding their final leaves as the nation's capital waved farewell to the final days of autumn. She knew little about the area other than it wrapped all the way around Hyde Park (thanks, Google Maps!), but the impeccably dressed men and women stepping out of luxury cars and into five-star hotels, including the world-famous Dorchester, made it clear this was a part of town that had a *lot* of money. The private-jet dealership they briefly braked in front of confirmed her thoughts.

Ever since Lauren had received news of her in-person interview at Buckingham Palace, she'd been replaying the moment of her grand arrival in her mind. She'd imagined gliding through its gates in a glossy black London taxi, sailing past curious tourists with an air of reverence towards the institution – and of course humility for the opportunity – before gracefully stepping out to ascend the ... steps? Runway? She had only been to London one time before, on a poorly chaperoned high school trip in which she spent most of her time hunting down One Direction merch instead of paying attention to the landmarks around her, but she vaguely recalled a grand entrance flanked by serious-looking guards in scarlet uniforms and bearskin hats *somewhere*.

The reality, however, was that she was showing up in a dented Prius that smelled like wet dog, with her feet throbbing in a pair of too-tight high heels (she had picked up some nude Prada pumps on sale at Nordstrom, but they had only been available half a size too small), and to top it off, she'd nearly been blinded by a mascara wand. The Palace had sent her a PDF map of the drop-off point where she should go, but the driver had waved it off when Lauren offered it to him, muttering that he knew the city like the back of his hand, and Lauren found herself envying his easy confidence.

She felt discombobulated and not like herself.

She hated it.

Her phone buzzed in her lap, and she picked it up without thinking of who it might be. Or more specifically, who it might not be. In the past six years that she had spent in

For Yoshi, Marnie and Hudson

ROYAL
SPIN

ROYAL SPIN

A Novel

Omid Scobie & Robin Benway

SPHERE

SPHERE

First published in Great Britain in 2026 by Sphere

1 3 5 7 9 10 8 6 4 2

Copyright © Omid Scobie and Robin Benway 2026
Title page illustration © Christian Coop/iStock

The moral right of the author has been asserted.

A CIP catalogue record for this book
is available from the British Library.

Hardback ISBN 978-1-4087-3457-5
Trade paperback ISBN 978-1-4087-3458-2

Typeset in Garamond by M Rules
Printed and bound in Great Britain by
Clays Ltd, Elcograf S.p.A.

Papers used by Sphere are from well-managed forests
and other responsible sources.

Sphere
An imprint of
Little, Brown Book Group
Carmelite House
50 Victoria Embankment
London EC4Y 0DZ

The authorised representative
in the EEA is
Hachette Ireland
8 Castlecourt Centre
Dublin 15, D15 XTP3, Ireland
(email: info@hbgi.ie)

An Hachette UK Company
www.hachette.co.uk

www.littlebrown.co.uk

DC working at the White House, her circle of friends had narrowed to just two people who also worked there: her boyfriend, Brian, and her best friend, Brooke. She hadn't noticed it at first, her days and nights so busy with work. And then once she *did* realise how anemic her social life had become, it hadn't seemed so bad. She had her best friend and her boyfriend! Who else could she possibly need?

A best friend and a boyfriend who didn't hook up behind her back for months before Lauren finally found out. That was who.

She glanced at her notifications and sighed before swiping up on her screen. 'Good luck!' the message read, accompanied by a custom emoji image that looked just like her mum.

'Thanks ☺,' Lauren texted back without thinking, which proved to be a mistake because her mother took it as an opening for conversation.

'Are you in the car now?'

'Yes, heading to the palace.'

'Is your driver being safe? I can see your location on my app. Is he doing the speed limit?'

'Yes, very safe,' Lauren, who had no idea what the speed limit in London even was, texted back as they came to an aggressive halt at a red light. *So safe. Safest ride ever.*

'Rosie next door said that there's a lot of crime and theft outside Buckingham Palace so BE CAREFUL. Lots of tourists means lots of pickpockets. And probably norovirus.'

Lauren suspected that her mum's next-door neighbour, Rosie, most likely hadn't left Atlanta in at least fifteen years, much less owned a passport, but she tapped on the message to like it because it was just easier that way.

Lauren had been sitting on the sofa in her studio apartment in DC when she was first contacted by a British-based recruitment agency about the deputy head of royal communications role at Buckingham Palace. At the time, she'd been surrounded by a half-eaten pint of Ben & Jerry's ice cream, a cashmere throw that she had spent way too much money on and the very specific despair that came from losing both your boyfriend and your best friend in one fell swoop. By the time the conversation ended, she hadn't known who to tell first. Buckingham Palace! London! Royalty! Her fingers had immediately tapped on Brian's contact info, where he was unfortunately still saved as one of her favourites. Lauren thought there should be an 'Unfavourites' list as well, a place where you could save all your shitty ex-boyfriends so that you would be automatically blocked from calling or texting them at three in the morning after drinking four margaritas with a bunch of friends who had just listened to back-to-back episodes of *Call Her Daddy*.

Ahem.

Her finger had hovered over Brian's number, Brian's name, Brian's photo. It had been taken at a wedding the previous summer at Martha's Vineyard where Lauren had known exactly one person: Brian. But if there was one thing Lauren knew how to do, it was integrate herself into a crowd, and by the end of the evening, she had become besties with half the bridal party, led a small but very raucous conga line and listened sympathetically to the groom's drunk aunt rant about her philandering ex-husband.

She very pointedly did not catch the bouquet. She had laughed off the idea and stood next to Brian while some of the younger women pretended to elbow each other out of the way, and he had put his arm around her and squeezed her close. Lauren thought at the time that she had something better than flowers, something strong that wouldn't wilt in her hands, and for that brief moment, she had felt like she truly had it all. An amazing job in the White House press office; a cute apartment in DC; Brooke, the bestest bestie who had ever bested; and Brian. Alex Cooper would have been so proud!

What an idiot she had been.

In an ideal world, after getting the invitation to interview, Lauren would have called Brian and then Brooke and screamed for a bit about what to wear, but that hadn't been an option anymore either. So instead, she had called her mum, and it was nice, but it wasn't the same. Afterwards she showered for the first time in three days, put more than a few empty wine bottles into the recycling bin, ordered sushi on Postmates and sat on her sofa in somewhat-clean sweats to research everything she could about the job, the British royal family and the Palace.

And fortunately, handling problems that took place in internationally famous landmark buildings was kind of her speciality. Or at least it was, until she'd found out about Brooke and Brian. Until she couldn't even step into the White House without feeling like she was going to dry heave. She had prided herself on being able to think on her feet in any situation, her days occupied by press releases, foreign dignitaries, global leaders and relentless demands from reporters and TV news producers. Sometimes it was glamorous and sometimes it was drinking cold leftover coffee with a Celsius energy drink chaser at three in the morning, eyes all blurry and red, but Lauren had loved it. She had loved being able to control the narrative, being able to handle anything that came her way.

And then the one thing that she couldn't handle completely derailed her.

Lauren glanced at her phone again as the Uber driver made a sharp turn that was definitely not at the speed limit, and opened up her calendar, which now contained nothing but empty white squares. She scrolled back a month to mid-September, when her boss had called her into her office and gently but firmly suggested a leave of absence, the tone in her voice making it clear that it wasn't really a suggestion at all. At first it had been a relief to leave her job, to cut off the limb rather than deal with the wound, but then Lauren's days – and the wine bottles and takeaway containers – started to stack up, all of them empty. The night before she got the call about the Palace position, Lauren found herself crying over a film that featured talking dogs.

Had it really been just three days ago that she got that call and managed to pull herself together, put on some Skims, and fly across an ocean? Time really had no meaning sometimes.

Her phone buzzed again. Mum. Who else?

'Do you have hand sanitiser?'

Sometimes having a mum who worked for the Centers for Disease Control and Prevention was great and sometimes it was . . . not. Time to engage Do Not Disturb mode, Lauren thought, and quickly swiped out of the app.

The Palace loomed ahead of her, surrounded by tourists (and criminals, according to Rosie, the world's least travelled person), and for a moment, Lauren felt the same rush that she often experienced whenever she'd arrived at the White House every morning for six years. The feeling almost took her by surprise, the way that it was both familiar and unfamiliar. Could she maybe start feeling that way about Buckingham Palace? Could she see such a hallowed building as a revered institution that perhaps—

'Fuck's sake,' the Uber driver fumed. *'Bloody tourists.'*

Lauren snapped out of her sentimental reverie.

As the full scope of the Palace came into view, it seemed both larger than life and more quaint in person than it had when she was sixteen years old and busy mourning Zayn Malik's departure from One Direction. She immediately pictured those iconic moments on its famous balcony in front of huge crowds – the big kiss after a royal wedding, waving to the people after a coronation. Could she help orchestrate those moments? Could she really be a part of this?

As her car approached the building, Lauren waited for the crowds to part, for the iron gates to open up and allow her driver to graciously pass through and coast up to the front door ... but then she watched as the driver went right past them.

'Um, excuse me?' she said, bothered by the timidity in her own voice. She was always extremely aware of being an annoying American whenever she visited a foreign country and took great pains to not be *that* person, but more often than not, it just made her a stranger not only in a strange country, but a stranger to herself, too.

The driver waved off her concern, hunching over the wheel as he navigated a little *too* closely around a group of schoolchildren. 'I know where I'm going,' he snapped, then jabbed a finger towards the printout of the map that Lauren was still holding on her lap. 'You want the side entrance.'

Yes, of *course* she did. The *side entrance*. The discreet, members-only entrance that was probably only for the most important people, like the pope. And Beyoncé. Lauren preened a little at that, smoothing her hands down her forest-green pencil skirt that she had paid a lot of money to have dry-cleaned in twenty-four hours, before picking at a thread in the hem. Damn. She wished she had seen that back at the hotel.

As she looked up, they were arriving at ... well, a rather normal-looking side gate on the pavement with two bored-looking security guards leaning against a patrol booth. They both glanced at her car with the same look that most people gave to squirrels: not thrilled to see them but resigned nonetheless.

Lauren climbed out of the Prius, wincing a little as the heels pinched her feet. She had planned to return the shoes once work in DC eased up a bit, but when her schedule suddenly became empty, she realised she didn't want to leave her apartment. And so the shoes continued to sit unworn in her wardrobe until three days ago, when she found herself tossing things into her carry-on suitcase like she was the best friend character in a rom-com movie, flailing and frantic.

And now, standing in a new city in front of one of the world's oldest institutions, Lauren wondered if this was just how it would be from now on, if she would soon be entering her thirties trying on new jobs, new relationships, and new locations, none of them ever fitting as well as the ones that got away.

One of the security officers checked her ID and credentials, only giving her a passing glance as he made sure that she matched her passport photo, then ushered her inside to another waiting area. Lauren smiled as she walked up to the tall security desk. The man asked for her details, proof of address, the purpose of her visit, and then proceeded to hold up a battered-looking webcam to take an extremely unflattering below-the-chin photo for her visitor's pass. Lauren hung the small lanyard around her neck and flipped the front side around so it wasn't visible. One eye shut *and* her embarrassing full name printed on the ID were not part of the cool Palace entrance she had envisioned.

In front of her, two rows of glass security doors awaited, and beyond them a courtyard that led into the Palace itself. She looked around and caught sight of a delivery trolley filled with boxes addressed to the office of the Princess of Strathearn, who, thanks to a Wikipedia deep dive, Lauren knew was fifty-two years old and currently the youngest of the working royals. She *casually* sidled up to get a closer look at the fancy brand names on the address labels before a man popped his head into the room and gave her a quick look up and down. 'You must be Bea—'

'Lauren Morgan,' she said brightly, offering her hand. 'And you must be James.'

He shook her hand in a way that made Lauren think he'd be applying hand sanitiser as soon as he could. 'James Colleran,' he replied. 'I'm the chief of staff to the principal private secretary to the Queen.' His glasses gave him a somewhat preppy, boyish look, but because of his tweed suit and neatly parted brown hair, Lauren wasn't sure whether he was in his thirties or fifties.

'It's really nice to meet you,' she said. 'Thank you so much for having me here today; it's such an honour to be at Buckingham Palace.'

James paused just long enough before speaking that Lauren wondered if it would be up to her to fill the awkward silence. The courtyard beyond the security office was quiet, and she was very aware of how loud her voice sounded. She had become used to speaking up at work, to make sure that she could always be heard over both the din of reporters at press briefings and the interruptions of some of her younger, cockier colleagues. If she looked, there were probably a few lozenges at the bottom of her handbag. She used to buy them in bulk.

9

She was about to open her mouth when James finally replied.

'Yes, well, thank you for coming.' His smile was somewhat friendly. 'Especially on such short notice, of course. I trust your flight was comfortable?'

She had been in economy in the middle seat, the person behind her grabbed at her headrest every time he stood up to use the bathroom, and somewhere on her plane was a toddler with a cough that could only be described as 'tuberculosis adjacent'.

'Oh, it was great, thank you,' she said. 'Piece of cake.'

James's right eyebrow twitched just a little. 'Well, excellent,' he said. 'I assume you got the briefing notes about the position that we sent you?'

Lauren patted her bag, gesturing towards the iPad inside. 'Right here,' she said. 'Thank you so much for sending them.'

James held open the rather unassuming door on the other side of the courtyard for her. This was it, she thought. She was about to walk into Buckingham Palace. Hours of Netflix binges had given her a vague idea of what was coming: antique furniture, sweeping staircases, ornate silk rugs, bitchy courtiers and, of course, the grand artwork.

So she was more than a little disappointed to be greeted by what looked like the service area at the back of a hotel: exposed pipework, battered walls, staff running back and forth and zero art. In fact, the only thing on the walls were ugly plastic bumpers to stop trolleys from causing further damage. It was a hive of important activity, but, as she caught sight of a vending machine filled with crisps and chocolate bars and a sticky-looking bank machine, it felt *far* from regal. *The Crown* it was not. This must be a special shortcut to get to the royal offices, she thought, like when the Secret

Service would take the president out of restaurants through the kitchen.

James began moving down the corridor at a much faster clip, and Lauren hustled to keep up with him, her strides matching his just like she had taught herself to do back at the White House. She weaved in and around those racing past – cleaners, kitchen staff pushing trolleys full of produce, gruff-looking men with deliveries, labourers carrying toolboxes.

'Of course, we're still interviewing for the position,' James said, gesturing to her to keep following him. 'We have a few candidates in the running, but we prefer to do interviews in person. It may be a bit old-fashioned—'

'Oh no, it's wonderful,' Lauren said, waving away his concern with her hand, and was glad she had managed to get a last-minute appointment for a gel manicure. 'Honestly, if I don't have to do a Zoom call ever again in my life, I'll be very happy.' That was a lie. Lauren would have killed to see a bunch of professional faces in a grid from the comfort of her own home. 'Plus it's nice to actually see where I could be working, get a feel for the office, meet people face-to-face.'

'—but we find that sometimes the old ways are the best ways,' James finally finished, levelling her with a cool gaze.

'Of course,' she replied. 'Why mess with tradition?'

'Exactly.' James glanced at his phone, then stopped in front of an office and poked his head in the doorway. 'Keep us updated no matter what,' he said to someone Lauren couldn't see. 'This is a priority.'

'Absolutely,' a voice said.

'I apologise, we're just dealing with a little … situation at the moment,' James said, continuing down the hall as he glanced at his phone again.

Lauren's ears pricked up. The word *situation* could mean a lot of things, especially in a thousand-plus-year-old institution. It could mean a toilet was blocked in the East Wing or it could mean someone was abdicating the throne and absconding to Europe with their divorced lover. 'Of course,' was all she said, though. 'I understand. I imagine working with such a wide variety of, um, *personalities* means you have to stay on your toes at all times.'

James put his hand on a doorknob and paused before looking at her. 'You truly have no idea,' he said, opening the door and ushering her in.

Now this was more like it! Huge pieces of art in heavy gold frames filled the walls and followed a giant, dark wood staircase up to where she assumed the private quarters for the royal family would be. The Queen's apartments, perhaps. It was impossible to understand the scope of such a space on a TV screen, or more accurately, on Lauren's iPad while Coughy the Baby hacked up a lung across the aisle from her. The ceiling was so high that they seemed to be almost floating towards the heavens, and the portraits on the wall dwarfed Lauren. Kings and queens from centuries ago, she assumed, looked down on her as she gazed in awe.

Her mum, she thought suddenly, would absolutely love this.

It was also, Lauren noted, pretty draughty there, with just a tiny plug-in heater on the floor keeping the entire area from freezing. She guessed that central heating hadn't really been a thing back when the Palace had been built in 1705. (Yes, she had looked up that fact. Her extensive research also taught her there were a total of 775 rooms, over 40,000 lightbulbs, and 350 clocks used in the entire building.) The cold made her think of her old office jumper, the one from Old Navy that had been more comfortable than 99 per cent of the overhyped brands she had been influenced to buy. Brooke would always tease her about that jumper, usually mimicking one of those WASPy women with a glass of wine that you find in American TV dramas set in the suburbs.

She felt a stinging behind her eyes and quickly banished Brooke from her thoughts. Romantic breakups were definitely difficult, but a best friend breakup could shatter the most tender part of anyone's heart.

Or at least, it had shattered Lauren's.

James didn't seem to be aware of the ostentation of the cavernous space or of Lauren's inner monologue. He kept up a steady pace, and Lauren adjusted her blazer and stood up straight, fully ready to walk into an even grander room.

Instead, he ushered her into a room that definitely would not be described as 'grand'. More like 'drab office space in a corporate park somewhere in Indianapolis'.

The comms office, Lauren noticed, looked a bit like *The Office*. (The American version, at least. Lauren had never seen the British version, which was something she realised she might have to fix soon.) Dust-covered fluorescent strip lighting hung in random stripes across the ceiling, there were a dozen or so pine-coloured Formica desks with industrial-looking legs scattered throughout the room and Lauren spotted several cardigans slung over the backs of chairs. The computers looked new, but the rest of the tech in sight was very much not – including the two yellowing fax machines next to the printing station.

Every head in the room swivelled to look at her, and Lauren waved a little, feeling like the new kid dropped into a class-room in the middle of term. 'Hello.' She smiled widely.

Already she could see more people leaving other office spaces with something in their hands – papers, a coffee mug,

13

an empty folder – in order to look busy while attending to the real business at hand: scoping out the potential newbie. She and Brooke had done that plenty of times in her old office, going back and forth with unimportant tasks in order to see if the new hire was cute or if Meredith (ugh, *Meredith*, she had been so annoying) had snuck out for injectables on her lunch break again. The day BTS came to the White House, Lauren had tracked nearly ten thousand steps without ever going more than fifty feet in any direction.

A woman emerged from a side office carrying an empty mug and wearing the exact kind of comfortable shoes that Lauren wished she had packed instead of the two (beautiful) traitors that were currently on her feet. Lauren smiled at the older lady, who immediately looked over her shoulder to see if there was someone behind her she was smiling at.

James, who seemed to be really trying to get in his own ten thousand steps that day, didn't stop to acknowledge the curious eyes or Lauren's cautious greeting. He led them into a separate space, shut the door behind them, sat down and immediately began tapping at a laptop.

'Is this . . .' Lauren glanced back at the closed door. 'A bad time?'

'It's honestly *never* not a bad time,' James replied, his eyes not leaving the screen. 'That's the first thing you should know about working here.' He hit the return key with more force than necessary, then sighed and glanced up at her. 'We're just managing a small situation to keep it from becoming a bigger . . . issue, and time is of the essence, I'm afraid.' He gestured to the chair across from his desk. 'Please, sit. Would you like anything? Water, perhaps?'

'No, thank you, I'm good.' Lauren perched on the edge of her chair and carefully placed her bag on the floor. 'And truly, not a problem. I understand situation – or issue, as you said – management all too well.'

'Yes, well, with *your* politicians.' James chuckled, his eyes flicking to the screen again. Whatever it was, it wasn't good, and he tapped out another forceful message before sighing. 'So as you know, we're looking to fill the position of deputy director of royal communications . . .'

Lauren nodded and started to speak before James cut her off.

'This is not an easy job; this is not a fun job. You won't be making DC money. The press will no doubt make your life difficult, especially as an American coming into the institution. But what this job does offer is . . .' James leant forward and looked over his glasses. 'Honour.'

'Honour,' Lauren repeated. She wanted to go back to the 'not much money' part, but James kept talking.

'Working for the royal family is one of the greatest honours in this country,' he said. 'You'll find that there are people here who have served Her Majesty for decades, and they do so because of a love of country as well as tradition. Esteem. *History.* And with all of that comes the deepest responsibility to—Oh, eff right off!'

Something on his laptop had grabbed James's attention again. 'Honestly,' he muttered, and began typing away. 'Do I need to do everyone's job around here?' He glanced at Lauren. 'Sorry, so sorry, just one minute.'

'Of course,' Lauren said. She was starting to get that adrenaline flutter in her stomach, though, that feeling born from the gap between imminent crisis and immediate solution, the knowledge that someone needed to solve the problem *now now now* and the understanding that she, Lauren Morgan, was the one who could do just that.

Her fingers itched to fly across a keyboard, too. She wanted to pick up a phone and sigh in disgust, just like James was doing now. She wanted to do something, get results and move on in a way that she hadn't been able to do since she saw Brian and Brooke kissing in his office, neither of them expecting her to show up and surprise Brian so late at night.

Before James could leave the room, though, a woman came bursting through the door, and apparently she hadn't got the memo about honour, esteem or history being some of the job perks.

She looked ready to burn the whole building to the ground.

'Amelia,' James said, standing up from his chair, and Lauren stood as well, nervously glancing between them. Amelia Adams was the director of royal communications – or comms, as they called it at the Palace. She would be Lauren's boss, the one Lauren would answer to, perhaps step in for occasionally, her workplace ride or die.

'We have Lauren Morgan with us,' James said in a tone that clearly meant *Don't say anything to scare her off.* 'I was just explaining to her that—'

Amelia and her heavily kohled eyes barely cast a glance in Lauren's direction, and Lauren felt grateful for that, the way one might be relieved to not fall into Medusa's direct line of sight.

'James,' Amelia said. 'I. Am. *Done.*'

'With what, exactly?'

'This!' she cried. '*All* of this! How many times, James? How many times do we have to do this?' Her energy filled the room, which made James seem intimidated in comparison, and Lauren felt that adrenaline burn get just a little bit stronger.

Something was happening. She could practically taste it in the air.

James blinked fast, which was the closest thing he had shown to panic so far. 'Amelia,' he said. 'We both know that these sorts of changes take time. We have a plan, we are executing it—'

'No,' Amelia said as another man suddenly showed up in the doorway, looking as annoyed as Amelia was furious.

This was seriously the strangest and best job interview Lauren had ever attended.

'Eugene,' James said, gesturing towards Lauren yet again. 'This is Lauren Mor—'

'What are we doing about this?' Eugene said to Amelia, not even sparing Lauren a glance. Bless James for even trying to introduce her, Lauren thought, and it made her feel a bit warmer towards him.

'Don't ask me,' Amelia said. She was wearing so much mascara that Lauren was worried her eyelashes would tangle together every time she blinked. 'I am officially done, Eugene. None of this is my problem anymore. I am *not* getting called in on my weekends and days off to deal with these ... issues that should have been dealt with a long time ago. I haven't had a deputy in nearly eight months and I'm expected to just put out every single fire that these pyromaniacs keep setting off!'

'We are *dealing* with it,' James insisted, but both Amelia and Eugene looked sceptical.

'Is "pyromaniacs" a metaphor?' Lauren asked, but nobody so much as looked in her direction.

'If this even touches Her Majesty and the Pearl Jubilee ...' Eugene said, leaving the warning unsaid. He must be Eugene Ainsworth, the Queen's principal private secretary, she thought, recalling all the names from her LinkedIn deep dive. Probably in his early fifties or so, with a few streaks of silver in his light brown hair, dressed impeccably in a three-piece suit. Lauren had never rarely seen a man who wasn't a groom choose to wear a waistcoat in real life.

Lauren was still standing, as was everyone else in the room. 'May I ask?' she said, and this time every head in the room swivelled viciously towards her. 'What is the crisis, um, I mean situation, on hand here?'

Amelia seemed to finally notice her for the first time. 'Lauren Morgan,' she said. 'You're here because you want the deputy position, yes?'

'Yes,' Lauren said. 'James here has been very kind so far—'

Eugene snorted in a way that wasn't flattering to either himself or James.

'Great, yes, wonderful, James is a delight,' Amelia said, resting her hand on the desk. 'So tell me, Lauren. Let's say that you come into work one morning and find out that one of the working royal family members—'

'By *marriage*,' Eugene interjected. 'Royal by marriage.'

'—decided to place a highly offensive, some might even say *racist* vase in the middle of a dining table at a private luncheon honouring the significant contribution of nurses and health-care workers from the Caribbean nations to the National Health Service, and when asked about said vase, claimed that it had been a wedding gift given to her many years ago by another royal. *Not* by marriage, this time,' Amelia added, giving Eugene a withering glance.

'Yikes,' Lauren said. 'I assume the press . . . ?'

'Already have pictures taken by our very own in-house photographer that will be on all the front pages when they go to print this evening, yes,' Amelia said. 'Not one person working at that engagement noticed the glaring problem in the middle of the room. Not one!

'I should also add that just one year ago this same individual was caught on CCTV telling a foreign shop assistant to "learn proper English".' She made finger quotes around the last three words.

'Oof. Who married this person, exactly?' Lauren asked. 'They sound like a nightmare.'

'They're certainly *causing* nightmares,' Amelia said. 'So tell me, Lauren Morgan, formerly of the United States White House, how would *you* deal with this problem?'

The adrenaline burn inside Lauren was now a wildfire.

It had been so long since someone had required an answer, a solution, a plan from her. She'd spent every day of the past month in her apartment, relating almost every tangible item to either Brian or Brooke, or them together, and that fire she'd always had for her job and life had been doused in depression and tears. So many tears. (She'd go to her grave before she would ever tell anyone about the one afternoon when she drank an entire bottle of wine and ugly-cried her way through a double feature of *Barbie* and *The Sisterhood of the Traveling Pants*.)

It had been so long since she had felt wanted or needed or even *necessary*.

And goddamnit, she was ready to work again.

'Okay,' Lauren said, automatically switching into her 'work voice'. Brooke used to always tease her about that and—Wait a minute, fuck Brooke. This was Lauren's time to shine.

'First,' Lauren said, 'get an official on-the-record statement out there before the press can write a word. 'Buckingham Palace does not tolerate racism in any shape or form ... The person in question' – whoever it is – 'blah blah blah, is deeply sorry and ashamed over the choice they made today and wants to express their sincere apologies for their action.' Do *not* say 'They apologise to whoever might have been offended,' that'll just make it worse. And then you put this individual on lockdown. They're taking time off from royal duties to reflect on their actions, to learn ... you can say that. And then they truly do need to go off and learn or this will be ten times worse the next time – because there will be a next time – they do something like this.'

The office was starting to feel a little warm, and Lauren shrugged out of her blazer, grateful that she had also taken her dark-green blouse to the express dry cleaner before she had left DC. 'Can I?' she asked James, gesturing towards the whiteboard on his office wall, and he nodded. 'Great, thanks,' she said, then grabbed a marker and wrote 'STATEMENT' on the board before circling it and drawing an arrow down.

'Next,' Lauren said. 'Do you have high-ranking royals on call or anything like that?'

Three pairs of eyes blinked at her.

'Well, get a senior royal, your most popular one, out there ASAP, and make sure it's one who hasn't done anything controversial for a while, if that's possible.' Lauren wrote 'UNPROBLEMATIC ROYAL' on the board, then drew an arrow to the right.

'Then have that royal carry out a private engagement at the British Museum to meet with curators and researchers to learn more about artwork and jewellry with ties to colonialism. She or he will then announce that the Palace will be working with this team to remove offending pieces from the Royal Collection and educating staff and family members about these items. And you get a crew of royal admirers lined up outside the museum entrance. I don't care if you have to bus them in, just get them there.' 'HISTORY MUSEUM' went up on the board, followed by 'FANS.'

'Then, whichever reporter is going to give you the biggest headache—'

'All of them,' Amelia muttered.

'—contact them right now and give them an early heads up because, and tell them this, they're so important. Spread out exclusive details for each of the other outlets as well. That'll move the story on and lessen the impact of whatever they're about to print; it could even change the direction of all the articles tomorrow.'

'And you truly think that offering up a statement on a visit that hasn't even been announced or planned yet will keep the wolves at bay?' Eugene smirked at her and crossed his arms.

So many men had looked at Lauren like that over her entire career. It never got less annoying.

'And as for *your* office,' Lauren continued, turning to look directly at Eugene, 'you do not say a word. Not one word. It can only touch you if you open the door and let it in, so you keep those wolves out, okay?'

Lauren paused, dry-erase pen still clutched in her hand. She felt hot, like she had just gone for a jog on a cold day, her cheeks flushed. 'Anyway,' she said. 'That's what I would do. And yes,' she said to Eugene, looking him in the eyes. 'It *will* work because flattery works on everyone, especially those who think it won't. Nice tie, by the way.'

Eugene glanced down and patted the red-and-blue-striped silk tie. 'Oh, thank you.' He beamed.

'See?' Lauren grinned.

There was silence in the room for a few seconds, and then Amelia smiled so wide that Lauren could see her back molars. 'Well, then,' she said. 'You're obviously hired.'

'I'm what?' Lauren repeated.

'You're hired.'

'You're hiring me as deputy?' Lauren said.

'Well, sort of,' Amelia said. 'Technically you would be acting director of comms until they find my replacement. I'm leaving today.'

'What?!' Eugene cried.

'Amelia, let's—!' James interrupted.

'No, that's it, I told you, I officially quit. I resign, I'm going out in a blaze of glory, whatever you want to say. But I am done and I think that you' – she gestured towards James and Eugene – 'will be in *excellent* hands.'

'*My* hands?' Lauren said. She was starting to feel like a parrot, repeating everything that Amelia was saying to her. 'Wait, I wasn't even interviewing for that position. *You're* supposed to be in that position!'

'Yes, exactly!' Eugene said, and even though he was agreeing with her, Lauren couldn't help but be a little offended.

Amelia just held up her hands. 'I'm sure all of you will work it out and come to an agreement. Lauren, it was a pleasure meeting you. I wish you well.'

Lauren was pretty sure that was the oral equivalent of signing off an email with 'Best'. It did not bode well.

'Oh!' Amelia said as she started to leave the room. 'Make sure you ask them about the diversity czar they've just taken on.' She laughed to herself as she disappeared around the corner, leaving a good amount of emotional chaos in her wake.

Lauren turned back to look at James and Eugene. 'What exactly just happened here?'

'Amelia happened,' Eugene said.

'And you've been hired,' James added. Lauren didn't think it was possible for him to look more pinched, but apparently she had been wrong about that. If he wasn't careful, he would hurt himself. 'Wonderful.'

'Back up a minute. Who or what is a diversity czar?' Lauren asked.

James placed his hands on his desk and sighed. 'When something like this happened last year we announced plans to hire a 'diversity czar' to help with our diversity, equality and inclusion efforts both inside and outside the Palace.' He didn't make finger quotes around the phrase, but Eugene did.

'You do realise that things involving czars tend to not end well, right?' Lauren said. 'Revolutions, false identities, families murdered in basements, animated films, the whole thing.'

'Well, after nearly a year of searching, we've found just the person for the position,' James said. 'Lady Cordelia Aspinal will be joining us after spending several years living and working in Tanzania in East Africa; her father, Lord Aspinal, owns a gold-producing mine there.'

'A white aristocrat with hands stained by blood money,' Lauren said. 'That's the lane you're choosing?'

James's mouth flattened into a thin line. 'Perhaps.'

'Yeah, you might want to rethink that choice,' Lauren said. She sat back down in her chair, trying to think through the events of the last sixty seconds. 'I can't even start tomorrow. I only packed a carry-on. I still have leftover takeaway in my fridge back in DC! I'm supposed to check out of my hotel by noon!'

'We can take care of that,' James said, and when Lauren looked at him, she saw a man who, if she didn't accept the job, was deeply, deeply screwed. 'Well, except for the leftovers, of course.' He attempted a smile, but it looked more like a grimace.

'I need . . .' Lauren started to say before realizing that the list of things she needed was way too long and jumbled. 'I need time,' she finally said. *And Band-Aids for my heels and a double espresso and some sort of simple carbs situation, stat.* 'I need time to decide.'

'You can have until tomorrow morning,' Eugene said.

'That's what I was about to say,' James said, then turned back to Lauren. 'You can have until tomorrow morning.'

Eugene scoffed.

'Tomorrow is Saturday,' Lauren pointed out.

'Clearly, time is of the essence. Otherwise we'll need to continue interviewing other candidates on Monday as well as find another Amelia. As you most likely have surmised, her job is not one that can go unfilled for long. Things tend to . . . unravel.' He stood up and did that same smile-grimace again. 'Any other questions?'

Lauren thought fast, but all that came to mind was Sheryl Sandberg's smiling face on the cover of *Lean In* that her mum had given to her when she graduated from high school. 'I want double the salary that Amelia made.'

'Absolutely not,' James said. 'It's a taxpayer-funded position, so there is no wiggle room. The Palace does not negotiate with job candidates.'

'Or terrorists,' Eugene added.

'All right, then.' Lauren reached for her bag. 'You'll have my decision tomorrow.'

In the black cab back to her hotel, it took Lauren all of twenty seconds to make her decision.

No way in hell was she taking that job.

What had she even been thinking? Moving to London on a whim for a job in a country that she last visited when she was sixteen? She'd have to break her lease, pack up all her things and finally clean out her hall cupboard, which was where she put everything that she didn't want to deal with.

Which, she realised, was a little *too* on the nose.

And besides, what kind of maniac would take a job that was given to her after a five-minute interview in which her prospective boss quit on the spot and walked out? That was one *major* red flag, Lauren thought to herself. And that wasn't even including the potential pay cut! Would Lauren have an assistant? Her own office? Or would she have to sit in the middle of the office at one of those worn desks that looked like stale slices of bread?

No thank you.

'Nope, nope, nope,' she said to herself just as her phone buzzed. She half hoped it was the Palace calling her so she could just tell them no now and be done with it, go back to the hotel, get some room service chips and enjoy an afternoon in the city before heading home. Maybe she could even go to a museum, see what exhibit was at the Tate Modern or something.

She picked up her phone and saw a Google News notification. Half the time she just swiped them away, but this one got her attention.

'Is Brian Martinez the Next DC Wunderkind?' the headline read. There was a little photo of Brian, too, and before Lauren's rational, logical brain could stop her, she was opening the *Atlantic* article.

It was a really good photo of him. Obviously posed and with the faux-humble smirk that Lauren used to love before she hated it. Fuck.

She couldn't bring herself to do anything more than skim the piece, scrolling fast enough to catch keywords but not context. *Rising star. Moving up. In demand.*

Lauren's phone rang, a picture of her mum coming up on the screen, but she ignored the call, not in the mood for more true crime warnings from Rosie. When she went back to the article, she saw another keyword, and this time she closed the app altogether, a lump in her throat.

Brooke.

She had just enough dignity to not start sobbing in front of the cabdriver, but still.

But still.

London passed in a blur, feeling more grey and unfamiliar with each street that flew by. It was awful to be homesick for a person rather than a place, Lauren thought to herself, but she supposed that was what happened when you fell out of love with someone who used to feel like home.

A voicemail notification popped up and Lauren opened it, wanting to hear her mum's voice, if not necessarily her words.

'Lauren!' her mum chirped. 'I thought you should know that there's an article about Brian and it mentions you. I wanted to send you a screenshot but I don't know how to do that so I thought I would just read it to you. Where did it go? Ah, got it.'

Lauren put her hands to her eyes. Forget the painkillers. It was officially time for tequila.

Her mum cleared her throat.

'"Martinez declined to comment on the matter, but several sources confirm that his relationship with Brooke Geary – a staff assistant at the White House Office of Digital Strategy – has swiftly become the talk among influential circles in DC. Martinez's former girlfriend, White House press assistant Lauren Morgan, has moved on to explore freelance opportunities, according to a spokesperson."'

'Freelance opportunities?!' her mum said. 'What the heck? They should have called *me* for a quote! I would have told them everything they wanted to know about that . . . that bozo! Anyway, honey, I love you and I'm very proud of you. I mean, my daughter interviewed at *Buckingham Palace* today! I told the ladies in my cardio drumming class. And I'm sure it went great and you impressed the hell out of them. Oh, and use those mini wipes I got you to clean everything in your hotel room because trust me, you don't want to know what I know about how the *E. coli* virus travels. It's ugly. Call me when you land tomorrow, okay? Love you.'

Lauren didn't know how it was possible to say both the exact wrong and exact right things in one short message, but her mum always managed to do just that.

When she went back to the article, Brian was smirking at her again, only this time, it felt like he was mocking her, like he was daring her to do something about the article, his relationship, his success.

The taxi drove past a traditional-looking pub just then, complete with tiny square windows and ivy. A group of people who looked to be about Lauren's age were meeting up outside, laughing and drinking. It was Friday, she realised. One of the couples outside looked at each other and kissed, and Lauren found herself glancing away, tears filling her eyes.

Yes, she would leave London and go home to DC. But what was waiting for her there? No friends, no boyfriend, no other job offers. Just an ugly sofa she never got around to replacing and leftover takeaway that, if she was being honest, had been in her fridge for a little too long before she even left. It was sad. She was sad.

But in that cramped office in the back of a legit palace, Lauren had felt alive. Smart. Quick. Maybe even happy, just for a second? It wasn't going to be perfect or easy, and Lauren had no idea what the road ahead of her could possibly even look like, but one thing she knew for damn sure was what it looked like behind her, and in the moment, watching the world pass her by one pub and person at a time, that was enough for Lauren to change her mind.

Also, wunderkind? Please! Brian was *thirty-four*!

The cab turned the corner, and Lauren's brain refused to stop her hands from flying across her phone's screen and jabbing at a number.

'James?' she said once he answered. 'It's Lauren Morgan. Let's do this. I accept.'

Chapter 2

Lauren had to admit that she had been just a *smidge* dramatic about her grand announcement. In the moment, she had felt powerful! Independent! Free!

The reality was a little bit different.

For starters, she had accepted on a Friday afternoon, which meant that she would be starting on Monday, which left her with only two days to start moving her entire life across the Atlantic Ocean. Lauren had begged her landlord to let her break her lease. It was equally surprising and depressing how a call and an exorbitant payment to a relocation company could remove her DC life in a single weekend. They had promised she'd have her belongings in six to eight long weeks and apparently that was the good news. 'One guy who didn't fill out his customs forms properly had to wait for six months!' the manager told her. Lauren hoped that in those weeks she could find a place of her own in London, though the Palace had agreed to pay for her hotel room until she did.

On Monday morning, Lauren skipped the rush hour metro crush (*tube*, she kept reminding herself), and the ridiculous surge prices on Uber, and walked twenty-five minutes from her temporary Marble Arch digs to Buckingham Palace, ready to begin the next chapter of her life. The October air was crisp, and thanks to more comfortable shoes, she practically skipped through her Hyde Park detour feeling both anxious and excited about the journey ahead.

And bonus! She had brought a giant box of Krispy Kreme doughnuts to break the ice with her new colleagues.

'Good morning!' she said to the security guards at the side entrance, who seemed as thrilled to see her as they had the last time. Inside she picked up her new staff pass from the security desk.

'Oh, I was wondering if I could have one with just my middle name and last—'

The security guard at the reception desk interrupted, his patience as thin as the strands of hair on his shiny head. 'We can't reprint them.' He slid it back across the tall reception desk, her awkward webcam photo staring back at her. She reluctantly hung it around her neck and flipped it around.

'Well, please just call me Lauren,' she said, smiling. 'No formalities here!'

The man chuckled dryly. 'I think you'll find *here*, there are.'

As Lauren shuffled through the two glass security doors holding a dozen doughnuts in one hand and her bag in the other, she felt herself get flustered. She was nervous, damn it. She hadn't felt anxious at work in a long time.

'You have two minutes before your very first meeting,' James greeted her as she stepped into the office.

'Thanks for the welcome. Great to see you, too, James,' she said, heading to the empty office that James pointed to without looking up from his laptop. Nobody else seemed to pay any attention to her, which was fine. She was fine. No big deal. She set down the doughnuts and shrugged out of her long overcoat.

'Do I have to do any intake paperwork or anything?' she asked.

James looked up and blinked at her. 'We've already done a thorough background check.'

'Oh,' Lauren said, then wondered how *thorough* thorough was. 'What about anti-sexual harassment training? Do I have to do a webinar?'

She hadn't thought it was possible for James to look even more puzzled, but she was wrong. 'Do you plan on sexually harassing anyone?' he asked.

'Of course not.'

'Good, then you've passed. Congratulations.' James stood and gathered up his laptop and several folders before gesturing to her. 'No sitting, we're moving. I assume you brought your—What is that?'

Lauren looked at her empty desk. The only things on it were her new work laptop and phone, her handbag and the green-and-white doughnut box. 'Oh, I brought doughnuts for everyone,' she said. 'A little first-day treat. Look, they're Halloween-themed!'

James looked at the box as if it contained snakes instead of baked goods. 'Doughnuts,' he repeated. 'You really like to lean into that wholesome-American experience, don't you.' It was not a question.

'I think liking fried sugar is a near-universal experience, regardless of one's country of origin,' Lauren said, picking up the box and scooping up her own laptop and a yellow legal pad out of her purse, along with her lucky pen. 'But if this is your way of declining, I understand.' She smiled at him. 'Which way to the conference room?'

*

Even more drab than the main office, the 'conference room' was just four desks pushed together, surrounded by chairs that looked like they were straight out of a classroom. The fluorescent lights overhead gave the blank, dingy walls a sterile glare that made Lauren think of a hospital's emergency room. On one wall was a framed portrait of the the current reigning monarch of thirty years, Queen Rowena, staring serenely down upon them, and Lauren nodded her head as she walked past it. James laughed at her gesture.

'Everyone else should be arriving momentarily,' he said. 'Our alignment meetings take place once a week and are an opportunity to make sure everybody is in sync with the work being done. We start on the dot whether or not everyone's here, you should know. It's a tight ship because even a few minutes could cause a delay in the schedule and—'

'And Eugene would have an aneurysm?' Lauren interrupted, remembering the Queen's private secretary all too well.

James cleared his throat and shuffled his stack of folders again. Who even brought folders to a meeting these days? Lauren wondered. Wasn't everything digital? Did the Palace not use Google Docs or at least an encrypted server?

'Yes, something like that,' James said, wiping at some invisible dust on his chair before sitting down. 'Also, you should know that we hired a different diversity czar over the weekend and she's starting today as well. She was previously at Scotland Yard, the headquarters of the Metropolitan Police, and is familiar with the Palace and its, um, culture.' *Unlike you* were the unspoken words in the air.

'Wonderful,' was all Lauren said, desperately wanting to gloat that they had taken her advice about not hiring some blue blood whose father owned an African gold mine. She sat down a few chairs away from James and watched as several staffers entered the room, along with Eugene, who seemed a little flustered and out of breath but recovered quickly under James's frown.

'Thirty seconds to spare,' James told him as the rest of the chairs were quickly taken, and Lauren got that same feeling in her stomach that she had had on the first day at a new primary school after her mum moved them to a new neighbourhood. Would she have to say a few fun facts about herself like she had had to do when she started at the White House as an intern? She did a quick mental roundup just in case: Her favourite karaoke song was 'Party in the U.S.A.' by Miley Cyrus (what she lacked in talent she made up for in enthusiasm), she had double-jointed elbows, she knew all the words to 'Jabberwocky.'

'Thirty seconds?' Eugene replied to James as he sat down next to Lauren. 'So I'm early, then.'

A woman sat across from Lauren at the table. She had on a maroon jacket and skirt with a silk blouse underneath that looked as if it had been perfectly tailored to her body. Lauren was no slouch in the dressing department, especially on her first day working at the Palace (in a Veronica Beard suit jacket and cropped trousers that she had put on her credit card during an emergency shopping trip at Selfridges over the weekend), but this woman seemed immaculate, down to her perfectly sleek long bob.

'Well then,' James said as the eighth and final person scurried into the room. 'Just down to the wire, Harriet. Lucky for you.' Harriet, a soft-faced older woman in a twinset and pearls blushed as she took her seat, and Lauren quickly set a mental reminder to never, ever be late for any meeting from this point onwards.

'Good morning. So first order of business, we have two new

faces here,' James said. 'After Amelia decided to take a leave of absence to focus on, ahem, some personal issues, we have a new deputy director of communications, who will cover both positions in the meantime.' It was clear from the tone of his voice that James equated 'focusing on personal issues' with 'dealing with a termite infestation'. 'This is Lauren Morgan; she comes to us straight from the White House press team, so rest assured she's used to a good amount of chaos.'

'Hi, everyone,' Lauren said, starting to stand up from her seat. 'I'm Lauren, and—'

The new hire sitting across from Lauren gave a barely imperceptible shake of her head. Lauren got the message and immediately sat back down. So much for fun facts. Not that it mattered anyway. It felt as if people were actively not looking in her direction, afraid of paying too much attention.

'Lauren,' James added, 'has brought us *doughnuts*.'

A few eyebrows went up, and Eugene hid a laugh behind his fist. Lauren shot him a glare and cleared her throat. 'Just a little hello gesture from the American,' she said.

Several people were already reaching for the box, including a young blond woman who had, so far, been glued to whatever was happening on her phone screen. Lauren sat back in her chair and looked smugly at James, who mostly seemed annoyed that he had had to introduce her in the first place.

'We have also filled our diversity role. As you may know, Lady Aspinal had to unfortunately turn down the position at the last minute due to a scheduling conflict—'

The woman across from Lauren smirked a little.

'—so we are indeed very pleased to welcome Joy Hamilton to the position of diversity czar instead. We know that she already has several plans in place to help with, uh, certain aspects of Palace life.'

34

The stylish woman Lauren now knew to be Joy looked up from her laptop just long enough to give an acknowledging nod to the room before going back to her typing. 'Honoured to finally be a czar,' she said. 'Rasputin says hello. And yes, as James said, we've already put several steps in place to help mitigate the effects of the Countess of Lancaster's latest actions.' She glanced up again. 'Credit, I must add, should also go to Lauren for mapping out this plan a few days ago, or so I've been told.'

Lauren sat up a little bit straighter in her chair. Solving problems *and* bringing doughnuts. (Which, she noticed with some satisfaction, were quickly disappearing.) 'That's the job,' she said.

'Indeed it is,' Joy said. 'So we have the countess reflecting on her actions and taking time to "listen and learn". In the meantime, the Princess of Strathearn has graciously agreed to liaise with the British Museum and the Royal Collection teams as they pull out more offending items from occupied royal residences. There will also be an educational document for other family members and household staff on why those items are offensive in the first place, in case they've somehow missed the cumulative effects of one thousand years of British colonialism.'

'Well, thank you, Joy—' Eugene started to say, clearly a little uncomfortable with the subject.

'You're very welcome. In addition,' she continued, 'there are several reporters and photographers accompanying the princess during her museum visit this morning, which will help stem the tide of negative coverage in the press. But again, credit goes to Lauren.' Joy smiled at her, and it seemed sincere. 'Although I have *zero* doubt that there will be future opportunities to put out more of these fires. Hopefully we can even start preventing them.'

Eugene *also* had a sincere look on his face – sincerely annoyed at the doughnut that had been placed on a napkin in front of him. He poked at it with his pen, and Lauren fought the urge to snatch it away. Those orange and yellow sprinkles were completely wasted on him.

'Thank you, Joy,' James said, this time standing up. 'Your presence at the Palace will be most valuable. I'd also like to introduce the rest of our team here to our new faces. Harriet Parker is our communications secretary, which of course means she will be working with you on the majority of media efforts, Lauren. Harriet has been with the royal household for coming up to twelve years and has worked closely alongside a number of our late members of the royal family.'

Lauren and Joy both gave her a little nod. Harriet nodded back, aiming for an expression of over-the-moon pleased yet deeply serious. But instead, she just looked like she was having a muscle spasm.

'And this is – Violet, *please*, if I could have your attention – Violet Broughton, our head of digital engagement. From the official website to the social feeds, it's all in her hands.'

Violet, who appeared to be barely twenty-two years old and made Lauren feel like it was time to take retinol seriously, glanced up just long enough to say hello, the way one would say hello to their old aunt Clara at Thanksgiving, before going back to her phone. 'Sorry, I'm tracking real-time engagement on our latest post,' she said by way of explanation, which was exactly what Lauren would have said if she was head of social media and wanted to avoid being part of the meeting.

'Now, Lauren,' James continued, 'I appreciate you have only just joined us, but I think we'd all like to hear your initial thoughts on the next few months and what efforts you might be thinking of to improve public image, trust and the royal family's connection with the public. We can't afford more negative press, especially with the US state visit less than five months away.'

Violet and Harriet looked especially weary at that last sentence.

'A US state visit?' Lauren repeated.

'I'm sure Amelia put the details in her handover notes,' James said with a wave of his hand. 'Anyway, please continue.'

'Yes, of course,' she said, adding *US state visit?!?!?!?* to her mental list of Things to Deal With – Amelia most definitely had not left handover notes. 'As these, um, unfortunate situations continue to pile up, the image of the monarchy continues to suffer as a result. What I propose is something that I learnt the power of during my six years at the White House.' She glanced at Eugene as if to say, *You're not the only one who's worked in an esteemed institution, pal.* 'I suggest we begin hosting weekly in-person media briefings.'

James choked on the sip of tea he took from his travel infuser flask.

'Let me get this straight,' Eugene said, not even trying to hide his smirk this time. 'You want to bring the press – the same organisations that work around the clock to cause absolute mayhem for the monarchy, that we so carefully try to keep at arm's length while still providing necessary access – *into* the Palace? Every week?'

'I do,' Lauren said cheerfully, then stood up so she could start pacing around the room. She always thought better when she was moving.

'The latest polling numbers don't lie,' she began, '"Never complain, never explain" doesn't cut it anymore in this age of transparency, especially among the younger generations. Being secretive and mysterious just leaves the press to fill in the gaps, the public becomes confused and we're no longer in charge of the narrative. Waiting for them to approach us for a comment in the final hour of a story puts you – well, us – at a disadvantage every time. We're living in a twenty-four seven news cycle, and social media, along with an entire circus of talking heads, shapes the conversation around everything. I looked through several years' worth of coverage and it's pretty obvious that attempting to cover things up, create distractions or hide behind anonymous source quotes in newspapers isn't working so well.'

'We are absolutely *not*—' Eugene started to say, but Joy held up a hand.

'It would be nice to hear her out,' she said. 'This could be good for everyone.'

Lauren fought the urge to take Eugene's doughnut away from him and put it in front of Joy instead. 'Thank you, Joy,' she said. 'By doing a weekly press briefing, we can help shape any stories, show we are accountable for our words and actions, and also give a timely heads-up about any upcoming events and points of interest, so they're not filling the gaps with gossip.'

'Plus,' Lauren continued before taking a deep breath, 'I also downloaded some recent polls from a few different agencies on how the British public feels about the monarchy.'

Both James and Eugene sat up like a current of electricity had run through them.

'They're not great,' Lauren said, 'and I suspect I'm not the only person in this room who knows that. So I've mapped out a tentative five-month plan that can help us improve those numbers ahead of the state visit.' Her 'plan' was really some arrows on a legal pad pointing to the words *BAD POLLS*, but she'd come up with something more substantial in the next few days.

There was a snicker at the table, but Lauren couldn't tell where it came from. '*So* American,' someone muttered.

'So what if it's American?' Lauren retorted. 'I can tell you that it works. It'll let us curry favour while also keeping them at bay. Think of it this way: We're giving the press a steady stream of glances into the royal institution, but we decide which windows they get to look in and when.'

Violet grinned. 'Sounds a bit lecherous.'

'Okay, that wasn't my best metaphor,' Lauren said. 'But you understand where I'm going with this, right? And I think our first media briefing should be this Friday, introducing Joy as the Palace's first diversity chief, which is a huge moment for us, along with talking points and the chance to ask a few questions. We couldn't come out of this looking bad.'

Eugene just shook his head. 'They are going to eat you alive,' he said. 'This lot are a different breed to the US press; some of them are absolute animals.'

'Maybe so,' Lauren said. 'But my job isn't to protect myself, it's to protect all of *this*,' she said, dramatically gesturing to the entire room. 'And this is an excellent way to do just that.'

There were a few beats of silence.

'I like it!' Joy said. 'What's the harm, Eugene? Are you afraid they'll storm the building?'

Eugene paled slightly. 'N-no,' he said, making clear that was exactly what he worried about on a daily basis. 'I just feel that Her Majesty has managed to steer this ship for the past thirty—'

'With all due respect to you and Her Majesty, Eugene,' Lauren interrupted, 'we also need to move with the times.'

She half expected a sniper to burst into the room and take her out for even suggesting such a thing, but instead the room was quiet.

'One month,' James finally said. 'That's four briefings. If all goes well, we'll continue with them. And if it all goes wrong, and I do fear it will, it'll be your head and not ours.'

'Ah, love a good guillotine reference,' Joy said. 'Probably best not to reference the French Revolution while sitting in a palace, though, yeah? Didn't end too well for them.'

James cleared his throat. 'I ask that you send me an outline of the first conference by Wednesday morning,' he said. 'We'll need to approve the topics and list of outlets, and we also need time to get the room ready by Friday.'

Lauren suspected that 'get the room ready' meant 'find an actual room that we can use,' but that was fine. 'Great, absolutely,' she said.

Eugene laughed dryly and shook his head. 'Next order of business, please,' he said. 'I have a stroke scheduled for ten thirty, don't want to be late.'

'So needlessly dramatic,' James muttered as Lauren sat back down. She caught Joy's eye and gave her a 'thanks for backing me up' smile, which Joy returned.

She was pretty sure she had just made her first friend in a very long time

The rest of the day was an experience in diminishing returns.

Nobody was outright mean to her, but they weren't exactly friendly either. When Lauren went into the office's small communal kitchen to make herself a pretty awful instant coffee, conversation wilted away until she was the only one in there. Setting up her Palace-issued iPhone had been a challenge since nobody was answering the IT number, and when she finally got it up and running, she was immediately inundated with spam emails, including one that cheerily began, 'Hello Pervert!' The phone, she was later warned, would be wiped every fourteen days for security reasons, so if she wanted anything saved, it needed to be stored in the cloud. (The same cloud where Amelia had hopefully saved a folder titled something like 'State Visit: Everything You Need to Know!' because there were certainly no documents left on her desk.)

At least one productive thing came from that afternoon: a tall whiteboard that Lauren had wheeled into her office and set to work covering in Post-its with the names of all the royals who were even remotely related to her new job – past, present; working and nonworking. It was a very colourful family tree in more ways than one, and Lauren just hoped that the extensive British monarchy Wikipedia page would not lead her astray.

James was ensconced in his office for most of the day, either loudly tapping on his keyboard or quietly talking on the phone behind closed doors. Which was better than Eugene, who seemed to have come up with a thousand reasons to walk past her office door, sighing every time he did so.

At first, Lauren did her best to ignore him by focusing on her project. She made it through the Prince and Princess of Strathearn and their teenage twin son and daughter. Everything after that got a bit . . . crowded. But when Eugene walked past and sighed again, Lauren put down the Post-its. 'Eugene, can I help you with something?' she asked. 'My office doorway seems to have a magnetic pull on you.'

There was a pause in footsteps, then Eugene doubled back. 'Yes,' he said tightly. 'It feels as if you've accepted this job with little to no regard for the history of the institution or the family.'

Lauren just nodded. 'Yes, I got that impression from you several times today.'

'This job is not a game or a chance to show off to those back in the States,' he continued. 'Bribing us with sweets, initiating all of these American concepts.'

'I suggested press briefings,' Lauren said. 'I didn't say that we should stage the Super Bowl halftime show on Palace grounds.'

'What you don't understand,' Eugene said, ignoring her, 'is that discretion and decorum are at the heart of this institution. It's not about *access* or seeming more *friendly* or *accommodating*. It's bad enough that some of the family have been forced onto social media. But you want to set up a stage like they're here for entertainment, and I want you to know that I will do everything I can to protect Her Majesty from any . . . any crassness.'

'Well, since that is your *literal* job, then okay,' Lauren said. This wasn't the first time a male coworker had tried to mansplain her job to her, but it was the first time it had happened in a foreign country where she had jet lag, no friends and all of four outfits.

'You do what's right for your job, Eugene,' she continued. 'And I'll do what's right for mine.'

Eugene sputtered as Lauren sat back in her chair. 'Fine,' he said. 'But when this whole plan of yours collapses, I'll be the first one to point out that I was right.'

'I have no doubt,' Lauren said, turning back to her laptop like she had several important emails to send, instead of deleting more spam.

She did have a doubt, though. She had several, and glancing back at her Post-it tree, she felt some of her confidence collapse. It wasn't just Eugene's criticism of her plans or the hushed silence that met her in the communal kitchen. What really rung in her ears was James's tone when he talked about

42

Amelia's 'leave of absence' for 'personal issues.' It made her feel like someone was pressing on a bruise that she thought had healed, and she couldn't help but wonder if someone back at the White House was talking about her in the exact same judgemental way.

And then she wondered if anyone was even talking about her at all.

An email popped up from Sarah Collins, the head of human resources, with a number of admin-related forms attached. 'Hope you're settling in well,' it read. 'Just wanted to add that, while there isn't a written dress code, it is advisable that you always keep a black outfit in the office or with you on travels (in the event of tragic news) and pair your skirts with tights.'

Lauren glanced down at her bare legs. As she thought about it, she realised that every other woman, Joy included, was wearing them.

Damn it. She loathed tights.

She sat down at her desk, ready to respond to Sarah, when she found herself looking at her personal phone and logging into Facebook. She didn't have many notifications, just a few birthday reminders for friends she no longer kept in touch with, and she deleted them before moving up to the search bar and typing in 'Callum McConnell.'

Her father's profile came up right away, probably because Lauren had searched for it a few times over the past month. She had recognised the old photo as a handful of the ones her mother hadn't destroyed after he had left when Lauren was eight years old. She hated that the old photo made her feel a bit sad. Had no one taken a photo of him since then?

His location was still the same: Aberdeen, Scotland. It hadn't changed ever since the first time she had looked him up years ago. She had tried to explain it to Brian once, why after everything she still felt drawn to her father, but she couldn't translate her feelings into words and Brian was a man who dealt in facts.

'Who gives a shit where he lives?' Brian had said. 'He left you and your mum when you were a kid. Fuck him. You should just block him.'

'Yeah,' Lauren had said, and then never brought it up again.

Her fingers hovered over the phone, and just as she was about to take the plunge and begin a message to Callum, the sound of heavy rain began to batter the glass of the French doors in her office. Despite the bare surroundings of her empty white office, the tall doors behind her heavy oak desk framed the perfect view of the Buckingham Palace gardens. She had debated opening them earlier to step out and have a closer look but feared that royal security detail would swoop in out of nowhere and tackle her to the ground. Just like the White House was in DC, Buckingham Palace was probably one of the safest buildings in the city to be in—

But security, Post-its and her dad all left Lauren's mind when the doors suddenly slammed open, letting in heavy rain, a gust of wind and a tall Yeti of a man with a bicycle.

Lauren shrieked and wished she hadn't bailed on that self-defence class Brooke signed them up for last year.

The raincoat-clad sasquatch came to a halt, bright blue eyes wide as water dripped off his hair and unkempt beard. He had a bagel clamped between his teeth. He started to say something, then paused and took the bagel out of his mouth. 'You're not Amelia.'

'I-I've taken self-defence classes,' Lauren managed to stammer.

'Definitely not Amelia,' the Yeti said, with the slightest hint of an Aussie or South African accent. 'Where's Amelia?'

'I'm the new Amelia,' Lauren said, 'For now at least. And you can't come bursting into someone's office like this and getting water – oh, will you shut the door? You're ruining my work! Damn it,' she sighed as another gust of wind sent an entire branch of her royal family tree to the floor.

'Apologies, apologies,' he said, pushing the doors shut with one of his muddy boots. 'Amelia let me cut through her office so I don't have to go all the way around. Probably should have knocked first.' He glanced at Lauren's family tree project. 'Well then,' he said. 'Forgive me, but shouldn't you have already learnt all of this? Or are you just trying to bankrupt the monarchy via their office supplies?'

'I'm a visual learner,' Lauren shot back. 'And the royal family tree is more like a forest.'

'Very fair, very fair,' the man replied. He stood back from the board for a moment, sizing it up, then bent down to retrieve a fallen Post-it. 'May I?' he asked.

Lauren just nodded.

He reached forward and swapped the Earl of Winchester with the late Earl of Lancaster. 'There,' he said with some satisfaction.

'Oh.' Lauren stood back.

The Yeti smiled. He really was a mass of wet hair and ugly cycling gear. He laughed. 'I was just cutting through and forgot about the regime change entirely.' He picked up his bike and his bagel. 'I'll have to find a new secret passage.'

'Wait,' Lauren said. 'Which department do you even work in? What's your job? If it's in the mailroom, I need to drop this off, actually,' she added, holding up an envelope.

Lauren saw what she thought was a smirk behind that

unruly-looking beard. After a beat, he turned to the white-board and pointed towards the Post-its. 'Pick one,' he said, then nodded at her as he took the envelope and wheeled his bike out of the room.

Lauren looked at the whiteboard, covered in names and titles of very, very important people. *WTF.*

Lauren made her way to the office kitchenette, hoping there would be some doughnuts left. She could use a sugar fix after that embarrassing encounter. She spotted the box, and luckily there was one left. She was about to bite into it when she had an idea and grabbed a plate.

She knocked on Joy's office door. 'Come in!' Joy said, sounding as chipper as Eugene had sounded irked. 'Well, hello you. How's the first day?'

Lauren just held up the box. 'A Yeti broke into my office and got water all over the place and I think he might be one of the royals but he also might just have been a sarcastic bike messenger. Doughnut?'

'Who says no to a sugar rush?' Joy replied. 'And yes, Americans aren't that well-versed in sarcasm. He was proba-bly just one of the courier guys messing with you.' Joy picked up the glazed ring with a napkin and split it down the middle. Lauren gratefully took her half.

'James acted like I brought anthrax to work, but look, this was all that was left,' she said. 'So take that, James.'

'Mmm.' Joy chewed for a bit, her eyes rolling in enjoyment. 'You do realise,' she said as she finished chewing, 'it'll take more than these to win that lot over.'

Lauren sagged in her chair. 'Probably.'

'Definitely,' Joy corrected her. 'Still, can I request churros for your next gesture of goodwill?'

Lauren tittered, feeling some of the tension ease from her

shoulders. She had missed this, sitting after hours with a work friend, gossiping and talking plans. It almost felt like home, and at this point in her life, that was no small thing.

'Maybe one of those big coffee urns from Starbucks,' Lauren said. 'Or a cake for James's birthday.'

Joy laughed. 'Definitely,' she said. 'With confetti and streamers, of course. Oh, by the way, I have something for you.' She reached into her desk drawer and pulled out a package that she slid across her desk.

A pair of opaque black tights.

'I brought extra pairs to keep here,' Joy said, her voice less boisterous and a little bit kinder.

Lauren took the tights from her. 'Eugene probably had HR email me about it,' she muttered.

'Eh, don't worry about him,' Joy said, waving the thought away like a pesky fly. 'I suspect he's one of those that's not great with change. Most of them in places like this aren't.'

'But he doesn't hate *you.*'

'Yes, well, it's probably bad form to outright hate the Black diversity "czar". But also, I know how to play the game. This is not my first position like this. You're just . . . oh, help me out, there's probably a good American sports metaphor for this.'

'Throwing a Hail Mary pass?'

Joy snapped her fingers. 'Sure, that one, if you say so. You'll learn, you'll figure it out. And the next time you pass a Marks and Spencer, you'll stock up on tights. Make sure to get the ladder resist packs, though. Otherwise they'll run in minutes.'

Lauren took a deep breath, rubbing her temples with her fingers. 'I just don't want this to be a mistake,' she said. 'Because I can't go back home. I just can't.'

Joy was quiet. 'Let me give a piece of advice,' she finally

said. 'You know that saying about how you can catch more flies with honey than vinegar? Here, it's the opposite. You need to be a little sour, a little spiky, if you want to earn their respect. More lemons, less lemonade. But that being said, you can *always* bring me sweets. My door is open to you.'

Lauren smiled. 'You got it,' she said. 'So how was your first day? What made you move here from Scotland Yard? That seems like it would be a lot more exciting.'

'Sure,' Joy said. 'Especially if you want to never have a decent night's sleep or vacation for the rest of your life. I just got back on the dating apps, and it's hard not to look at every guy with suspicion, knowing what I know about people.'

'You're single, too?' Lauren said.

'Divorced,' Joy replied. 'Three years now. One kid, Theo. He's eight and already campaigning for a phone. Which, ha, dream on. One day you'll be trying to figure out how to get rid of the thing.'

'It's hard being a single mum,' Lauren said.

Joy raised an eyebrow in response. 'You have a kid?'

'No, I was just raised by a single mum. My dad split when I was eight, so it was just her and me.'

'Ugh, what a bastard. And yes, it's bloody hard. His dad and I are still good friends, we're fifty-fifty parents . . .' Joy trailed off with a shrug. 'It's not easy, but it's easier than being married to the wrong person for the rest of my life, I can tell you that. So do you plan on including all of this in the first press conference starring me?' Joy asked.

'I'm not sure yet,' Lauren said. 'I'll probably need something more scandalous, if I'm being honest. I feel like the press here has high standards for drama.'

'Ha! I'm too busy trying to keep grown adults from drowning themselves in a racist lake.' Joy sighed, about to say something else, when the sounds of Eugene and James floated down the hall.

'It is a terrible idea, James!'

'Have you considered maybe loosening your waistcoat a bit, Eugene? That vein in your forehead is starting to get a bit too prominent.'

'Fine, have it your way—'

'I will, thank you.'

'Enjoy burning the monarchy to the ground.'

'I will, thank you.'

'Will you *please* take this seriously, James?' Eugene said as the voices faded down the hall and behind a closed door.

Lauren and Joy looked at each other, waiting for the other to speak first.

'Do you sense—?' Lauren started to say.

'*Incredible* sexual tension,' Joy finished.

'Right?!' Lauren whisper-screamed.

'Do you remember *Beauty and the Beast*? It's like Lumière and Cogsworth, but they're going to bang,' Joy added, which made Lauren laugh harder than she had in a long time. 'I'm just saying!'

'Well, good, maybe it'll keep Eugene from trying to manifest failure for the press briefings.'

'Speaking of!' Joy said. 'Go get your laptop and let's brainstorm a few things. Can't have you ruining my big debut with all your fanciful American ideas.'

Lauren grinned, then dashed off to grab her computer.

It was the first time in months that Lauren had been grateful to work late into the night.

Chapter 3

By Thursday, the day before her first press briefing (and, presumably, the day before Eugene planned on gloating at her first failure), Lauren was worn down. She'd spent the past week meticulously memorising the royal family tree; finding a black dress to hang in a garment bag on the back of her door, which really felt like a bad omen to Lauren, but hey, it hadn't been her idea; and reading through scads of articles, tabloid and otherwise, written by the royal correspondents and news reporters attending the press conference.

'Demand is high,' Lauren had pointed out to Eugene when she passed him in the hallway Wednesday afternoon.

'Of course it is,' he replied without looking up from his phone. 'Everyone loves going to the circus.'

'Ooh, not me, I'm afraid,' Harriet said. She had a way of sneaking up when you least expected her, Lauren had discovered. 'All of those clowns and the way they look at you as if they might be about to do something sinister, it's actually really quite terrifying.' She shook her head sadly. 'Much prefer a bit of Cirque du Soleil.'

Eugene and Lauren had both politely smiled and then quickly gone their separate ways.

It wasn't just navigating the Palace, though, that was exhausting. It was navigating London. At first Lauren had thought it wouldn't be too difficult since there was barely a language barrier, but everything had happened so fast that she hadn't taken time to think about the culture barrier. And as the October nights started to get colder and her soulless hotel room got lonelier, Lauren found herself looking for familiarity wherever she could find it. She dropped way too much money at Whole Foods on Kensington High Street because it looked just like the shop back in DC, got coffee at Starbucks even though the little independent spots scattered around London were probably far better, and even ordered her food from Uber Eats instead of the far more popular Deliveroo service because the app reminded her of Postmates, which didn't work in London.

But by midmorning, she perked up. She had scored her first major victory.

She had found a place to live. An actual apartment.

She had seen it online on Wednesday afternoon, and while she didn't know a ton about London neighbourhoods, a lifetime of watching rom-coms had taught her that Notting Hill and Hampstead were where the magic happened. And this spot in a converted Victorian town house, on a leafy side street near Hampstead tube station, looked *perfect*. The rent was reasonable, the pictures were gorgeous – high ceilings, original mouldings around built-in bookshelves, a little Juliet balcony, big windows that let in bright sunlight – and there were even a few pieces of furniture included by the landlord. It was a studio with the tiniest kitchen space, but Lauren thought it looked so cosy. She practically ran there after work,

51

dodging the crowds of people who were presumably all going home to their own cosy apartments, and when she arrived, there were already four couples eagerly waiting outside to view the space at the same time. Competition for rentals in London, she had been warned, was fierce – especially one that was available to move into immediately.

'Oh, hello,' the leasing agent said as she offered Lauren a card before she put her key in the building's front door to let everyone inside.

'I'll take it,' Lauren said breathlessly, winded from having power walked across half of London.

The others all looked at her in surprise.

'Do – do you want to at least look at it first?'

Lauren shook her head, gasping for air. 'It looks beautiful. I love it. I'll take it right now.'

And it *was* beautiful. After the losing couples shuffled away, Lauren stood in the room and felt very proud of herself. A warm orange glow from the leafy street's tall lamps shone through the huge arched windows as she transferred a holding deposit from her bank app before signing an initial lease agreement with a pen borrowed from the agent. Lauren added a little flourish to her signature as she decided that this was a sign that everything was going to work out in London, that her press briefings would be a spectacular success, that she would—

'I have to say, not everyone was open to the idea of a shared bathroom, but you young ones always seem game for anything!' The leasing agent beamed at her.

Lauren paused. 'I'm sorry, the what?'

'The shared bathroom,' the woman said with a smile. 'It's only with the neighbour next door and the door is right outside your own door. You'll both have your own keys for it.

Some of these old buildings have been converted weirdly, but you'll get used to it.'

Lauren sighed. *Nothing is perfect, I guess,* she thought to herself, before looking down at the still-drying signature on her lease, then back at the apartment. It really was beautiful. 'That's okay, I can make it work!' Which, Lauren realised, was quickly becoming the theme of her new life in London.

Back at work the following day, she tried to convince James to let them use any room other than the one he had reserved for the press conference, which had walls that looked like they belonged in a detention centre and absolutely no space for a podium.

'James,' she said, the moment she spotted him on her way through the maze of corridors that led to the office. They stopped near the grand staircase just before the comms office entrance, right next to the space heater, which was on full blast. (Lauren hoped that these tiny things dotted around the offices were not going to be their primary source of heat in the coldest winter months.) 'Please. There has to be another of the, what, eight hundred rooms in this building—'

'Seven hundred and seventy-five, actually,' James replied.

'I knew that. Can we please use one of the other seven hundred and seventy-four instead? The room you picked is giving *interrogation room*. It doesn't look very' – Lauren waved her arm around to indicate the room's dire state – 'Palace-y.'

'Palace-y,' James repeated. 'That's the word our acting head of comms has chosen to describe Buckingham Palace.'

Lauren could feel a tension headache starting to bloom behind her eyes. 'What I'm trying to say,' she replied, 'is that photographers and, maybe in the future, TV cameras will be at these conferences. This is the first time you're letting the press show this side of the Palace. People beyond just us will see it. And when these people think of Buckingham Palace, they want to see splendour and tapestries and gilded walls.'

'Perhaps they should just go to Disneyland, then,' James said.

'Isn't there a room with at least *one* chandelier?' Lauren protested. 'A big window maybe? Some drapes?'

'Fine,' James finally said. 'I'll see if you can use the screening room in the Queen's Gallery.'

Lauren quickly Googled it on her phone. No windows or velvet draperies, but it did have chandeliers and pillars. 'Perfect!' she said.

Eugene peeked over at her shoulder. 'Indeed,' he said. 'A cursed room for a cursed conference.'

'A cursed – what?' Lauren asked. 'Wait, are you messing with me, Eugene? James, is this room cursed?'

'Best not to speak of it,' Eugene said as he disappeared around the corner. 'Wouldn't want to upset the spirit of the chained monk.'

Lauren turned to James. 'The chained what-now? Did you just give me a haunted room?'

'Ignore him,' James said. 'That monk is harmless. The room's biggest problem is that the roof has been leaking. Better hope it doesn't rain.'

'Yes, because it never rains here.' Lauren sighed.

'I would say focus on handling the press instead of the weather forecast,' James said. 'Rain is the least of your problems for tomorrow.'

Lauren was about to Google 'Buckingham Palace ghosts real?' when Eugene suddenly reappeared alongside a tall man dressed in what she could immediately tell was a very expensive bespoke suit. His hair was expertly cut, his face clean-shaven, shoes polished, a jawline that could cut glass and, oh my God, this Hemsworth brother of a man was the bearded Yeti who had blown into her office with his bike and bagel—

'Lauren,' Eugene said, 'I'd like to introduce you to the Duke of Exeter. As I'm sure you're well aware, we've been fortunate to have His Highness return to our shores after a long stint in New Zealand.'

Lauren did some quick math, picturing her Post-it tree. The Duke of Exeter was the Queen's *nephew*.

Fuuuuuuuuuuuck.

'It's, uh . . .,' Lauren was absolutely *not* well aware of this, but she quickly paused the mini-heart attack she was having and remembered to curtsy. 'It's a pleasure to meet you, Your Highness.'

'Lauren Morgan is our new acting director of communications,' James said. 'She comes straight from the White House, so we have very high expectations.'

That was news to Lauren. Both James and Eugene often seemed like they didn't expect her to know how to tie her own shoes.

'It's lovely to meet you,' the duke said. 'For the very first time, of course.' He gave her a small smile that clearly said he remembered everything about their first encounter, and Lauren felt a brief urge to either punch him or make out with him, she wasn't sure which.

'Likewise,' she replied. 'I hope my role here at the Palace can serve your family and the institution, um, well, Your Highness.'

Eugene blanched as the duke just looked amused. 'Please, call me Jasper,' he replied. 'Eugene, we better get going, but—'

'Of course, of course.' Eugene started making his way up

the staircase, but when his back was turned, the duke leant down to Lauren with a smile.

'Let me know if you'd like any more help with your family tree,' he whispered.

'Thank you, Your Highness,' Lauren said. 'But I think I can take it from here.'

'Of course,' he said, that handsome, slightly smug smile still on his face, then jogged up the stairs two at a time.

'James!' Lauren hissed as soon as he was out of sight. 'What's he doing here?'

'Do you have amnesia?' he said. 'Eugene literally just introduced him to you. He's the Duke of Exeter.'

'No, I know *who* he is.' And she did, that was the thing. Lauren had read a whole host of articles about this duke while assembling her wonky family tree. She had learnt all about his parents' decision for him to not take on a life of royal duties after they were subjected to nonstop hounding by the press throughout the course of their marriage and how his mother desperately wanted to make sure their son lived a 'normal' life. Which led to his decision to study in and then stay in New Zealand as a civilian, how he took over a small sheep farm there and turned it into a huge business producing wool, his marriage to university-sweetheart-turned-tech-entrepreneur Jessica Wu – who had left him two years ago for another tech billionaire. Lauren knew the full story, just not the part about growing a giant beard, moving back to the UK and storming through people's unlocked office doors. 'But why is he *here*?'

'Well, I shouldn't be the one telling you this, but his return is probably going to be one of your responsibilities,' James said, looking both smug and excited to be the messenger. 'Right now, the world still thinks he is in New Zealand, but Her Majesty has been worried about him since his divorce and, after hearing about the collapse of his business, and' – he lowered his voice further – 'his *finances*, she suggested it might be time to take on a role within the family. But for that to work, he's going to need serious media training and a little image rehabilitation, which would, of course, would be up to our acting director of comms to spearhead.'

'How bad is his image?' Lauren asked.

'Oh, not good!' James said brightly. 'His ex-wife, Jessica, became a billionaire after selling her AI startup, but none of it ever entered the duke's pockets because of the prenuptial agreement he was made to sign in order to protect the Crown. So over the past two years he has borrowed obscene amounts of money from banks and investors to keep his own fledgling business and investments from going under and, you didn't hear this from me, he's basically on the verge of filing for bankruptcy. So the Queen encouraged him to return, and he's just moved into one of the BP apartments. His rent is a steal, I've heard.'

'He has to pay rent?!' Lauren said.

James looked shocked. 'Of course he does,' he replied. 'They're not running a shelter here. So expect Eugene to come to you with this very soon. I'd start sketching some plans now, if I were you. And act surprised when he tells you!'

Lauren sighed and wondered if the expired painkillers at the bottom of her handbag would at least be somewhat effective. 'Of course,' she said. 'Thanks for telling me.'

'Telling you what?' James laughed, heading down the hall. 'Have fun planning your little press party!'

'Nooo!' Joy said, covering her mouth with her hand. 'From the way you described him that day, you made him out to be Hagrid!'

Lauren was working on getting the childproof cap off her painkillers. 'So yeah,' she said. 'Not a bike messenger, not some rando, just the beloved nephew of the Queen.'

'Here, let me help,' Joy said, taking the bottle from her. 'I feel like Theo picks up some new lurgy every week at school. I could open these in my sleep.' She popped the lid and passed it back to Lauren. 'So. Was he as handsome as the photos?'

'Unfortunately,' Lauren replied, and Joy squealed in delight. 'What am I even going to do with him? If he's going to become a working royal, he'll need an entire press plan and a host of engagements.'

'Didn't you have to make some of the worst people look decent in DC? This will be a walk in the park,' Joy said. 'I'll tell you what, though. He better not steal my thunder at the press conference tomorrow.'

Lauren swallowed two pills dry. 'Are you ready for your big debut?'

Joy scoffed. 'I'm always ready. That mob doesn't scare me. A lot of them knew me or knew of me back when I was at Scotland Yard, they wouldn't dare.'

'But they'll mess with the American,' Lauren replied, saying the quiet part out loud.

'Oh, absolutely,' Joy said. 'But you can handle them. You've got this.'

It was so sincerely said that Lauren felt tears prick at the backs of her eyes. 'Yeah, I do,' she said. 'I *really* think this is a good idea. Seriously. The best.'

The shower at her new apartment building did have spectacular water pressure, as Lauren discovered on Friday morning. It had taken her all of fifteen minutes to move herself and her one suitcase in on Thursday night after work, after a stop at

John Lewis for sheets and some towels that were on sale. As she was brushing her teeth at the shared bathroom sink that morning, a tall woman about her age with big, bouncy blond hair waltzed in wearing a slinky black dress that had a strange duality of looking both high fashion but also fast fashion. Lauren wasn't sure which it was. She had a pair of heels slung over one finger, and with her free hand, she leant towards the mirror and began pulling her false eyelashes off. 'Una,' she said to Lauren, who had paused mid-brush to stare at her.

'Lauren,' she replied. 'I'm the new—'

'I guessed,' Una replied, widening her eyes even more as she successfully tugged one lash off. 'These buggers. I've got to start getting extensions again.' She glanced at Lauren in the mirror as she went to work on the other eye. 'You work?'

'Doesn't everyone?' Lauren said, trying to make a joke.

Una just shrugged. 'Depends what you count as work, babe.'

'Um, yes, I do. At Buckingham Palace, actually.'

'Ooh, fancy,' Una said in a tone that implied it wasn't that fancy at all. 'I slept with one of the royal guards once. You know, the ones tourists are always trying to make smile. He fainted during a parade one day and quit right after. Poor boy went viral. Wonder what ever happened to him.'

Lauren just stared at Una. 'Wow,' she finally said, since that seemed to be the most polite and truthful response.

'I know, right?' Una tossed her lashes into the trash and grabbed a pack of makeup wipes. 'Fuck it, I'll wash my face later. Gotta go to bed and get some beauty rest.' She waggled perfectly manicured fingers at Lauren as she left the bathroom. 'Good luck at the Palace, neighbour. Try not to go viral.'

It wasn't the worst piece of advice Lauren had been given

59

so far. She just hadn't expected it to come from the walking Sephora that was her new bathroom mate.

Lauren was still feeling unnerved as she jumped on the tube to make the thirty-minute journey to work, using her brand-new Oyster card that she kept referring to as her SmarTrip card. Old habits died hard, and Lauren was feeling the struggle.

At least her outfit was on point: an Aritzia trouser suit she'd bought last weekend, paired with a J.Crew wool overcoat to brave the colder weather.

'What, no blueberry muffins today? A case of Pop-Tarts?' Eugene said when he saw her, but she ignored him in favour of shrugging out of her coat and flinging it on her desk before heading outside of the main Palace building to the haunted room James had reserved for her in the Queen's Gallery. It was pitch-black until she found the switches on the wall, and she was relieved to see that both chandeliers were in perfect working order and the two buckets that had been positioned to catch rain were bone-dry. According to her weather app, at least, no rain was expected that day.

She spent the next two hours supervising a few maintenance workers as they set up a small podium, a microphone and speakers, her arms crossed in front of her as she paced back and forth, checking her phone every fifteen seconds for … well, she wasn't quite sure. At this point, she was ready for anything from a last-minute abdication to a zombie outbreak.

She was expecting twenty-five reporters, and she had done some intense research on all of them, staying up until 2:00 a.m. reading their articles on her phone because the Wi-Fi in her apartment had yet to be connected. They were from Britain's top broadcasters, the sleaziest of tabloid newspapers and the few publications that were firmly anti-monarchy. She'd kept the list varied, not wanting to be accused of liberalism, conservatism or favouritism, despite the fact that Eugene said that, privately, the Palace preferred to only work with outlets that were favourable to the monarchy.

One thing she hadn't considered, though, was that in her quest to find the perfect room for the press briefing, she had sacrificed size for style, so as reporters, photographers, and broadcast journalists and producers filed into the space, haphazardly printed badges around their necks and bemused smirks on their faces, Lauren realised that it was going to be a packed house.

'Better crowded than empty,' Joy whispered as she sidled up next to Lauren.

'Yes, you're right,' Lauren muttered, glancing at her press list and trying to match the names with faces. One by one they trickled into the room until all six rows of chairs were full, a few latecomers standing off to the side.

The butterflies in Lauren's stomach spontaneously doubled.

'How many of these have you done before?' Joy asked her.

'Participated in? Hundreds.'

'And run?'

Lauren swallowed.

'Forget it,' Joy said. 'Forget Eugene standing in the back there – oh, you hadn't seen him. I'm sorry, my bad. But forget all of them. You're the one in charge here. And if you need, just throw it to me and I'll charm the absolute hell out of everyone.'

'Lauren,' James said quietly, gesturing at the riser, and Lauren nodded and gathered up her notecards as she stepped towards the podium.

No time for nerves anymore.

'Good morning, everyone,' she said into the mic, and felt grateful when it didn't squeal with feedback. 'For those of you who don't know me yet, I'm Lauren Morgan, the new acting director of communications at Buckingham Palace. Thank you so much for coming today, we're grateful to have your presence for what I hope will be the first of many productive weekly media briefings. Today you'll have a chance to hear about some of the measures we're taking in order to promote diversity both inside and outside of the institution.'

She knew what to do at this point: Find three people in the room – left, right and centre – and keep her eyes shifting between them. It gave the impression that she was speaking to the entire room, and it would make her look less like a robotic mannequin.

She found her three targets easily: David Bellow from the *National Echo*; Laura Slater from *BBC News*; and Oscar Mason from the *London Tribune*. Fortunately, all three of them looked fairly open to this new experience, unlike the guy from the *Daily Dispatch*, who somehow managed to look annoyed, bored and smarmy all at the same time.

'Today we have something we're very proud to announce a new role, and we wanted to make sure that you all had a chance to ask questions, get more information—'

'Lauren! Adam from the *Daily Dispatch*!' a voice shouted, proceeding to talk without waiting for a response. 'Do you have any comment on the rumours that the Duke of Exeter's business has gone bust?'

Everyone in the room tittered, and, back against the wall, Lauren could see Eugene cover his mouth with his hand awkwardly.

That *jerk*.

'I do,' Lauren said, giving Adam a serene smile. 'The Palace is not in the habit of commenting on the private lives of the family, especially nonworking members. I would think that someone who's been around as long as you have would know this.'

Some of the other reporters chuckled, and Lauren could feel the swell of the room swing back her way.

'Now, before we move on to other questions—'

'Why did you leave the White House?'

'Is it true that you were paid a taxpayer-funded bonus to join the comms staff?'

'Are you able to confirm that the Countess of Lancaster is vacationing in Majorca?'

'Any comment on the recent *Atlantic* article about Brian Martinez that also mentioned you and Brooke Geary?'

'Who's standing next to you?' Oscar, who was sitting in the back, asked the last question, and Lauren felt instant relief.

'Thank you, Oscar. He has asked by *far* the most important question of the day, so, Oscar, please collect your medal on your way out.' The room laughed again and even James, whom Lauren could see out of the corner of her eye, looked slightly amused.

'This fabulous woman next to me is Joy Hamilton, and the Palace has the privilege of being able to welcome her as our very first diversity chief.' Lauren absolutely refused to use the Palace-preferred title of 'czar' on record. 'Having spent the past seven years at Scotland Yard, Joy brings an incredible amount of experience, enthusiasm and professionalism to this role, and I know I can speak for the entire household staff and family when I say that we're looking forward to working with her and improving efforts not only within the Palace but outside of its gates as well.'

'Is it true that you had already hired a—'

'Thank you once again, Adam, for your extreme profession-alism and not interrupting,' Lauren quickly added, stepping aside to let Joy take over the podium.

'Moving forward, questions will be asked in an orderly fashion after we have finished speaking,' Joy said in a no-nonsense yet agreeable voice. 'I'm not as patient as our American friend here.' And indeed, the whole room seemed to settle a bit. Lauren took note. 'Oscar, your question again, please?'

'Yes, how did it go unnoticed by not just the hosts but also aides that the Countess of Lancaster had displayed such an insensitive item in the middle of the room at an official engagement?'

Lauren felt all her goodwill towards Oscar dissipate.

'Thank you for your question,' Joy said, sounding more brusque this time. 'While I can't speak for the choices of others, I can speak to a systemic issue – the lack of diversity and awareness within this institution – that has allowed over-sights like this to occur and excluded other perspectives for far too long. My role is to ensure this changes. As you have seen with the princess's recent visit to the British Museum, some work is already underway, but this is not just about removing offending items or issuing apologies; it is about transforming the culture within the royal institution so that diversity, equality and inclusion are baked into every level of decision-making. This was a distressing and disappointing incident for everyone here, but I believe this is also a turning point, and I am committed to ensuring future actions reflect the values of inclusivity and respect moving forward.'

Lauren nodded along with her before stepping up to the podium next to Joy. 'In the coming weeks we'll be revealing future steps and actions,' Lauren added. 'Joy has already been

64

an imperative addition to the royal household, and we're very grateful to have her expertise as we move forward.'

'Is it true that the Prince of Strathearn got hair plugs?' one of the reporters called out.

Baby steps, Lauren thought with a sigh.

By the end of the day, Lauren had her heels off and a Diet Coke firmly in hand. Aside from the rocky start, the press conference had gone with so few hitches that Eugene couldn't pick at her about it, and James even seemed moderately pleased. She'd spent most of the afternoon scanning social media, news sites and her Google Alerts, relieved to see that the news of Joy's hiring seemed to have landed generally well.

'I am,' Joy announced as she came into the room, phone in hand, 'and this is from a social media post with over three thousand likes, mind you, a "much-needed and very overdue addition to the Palace".' She beamed as she collapsed into a chair across from Lauren. 'Should I get that tattooed somewhere, do you think?'

'Absolutely,' Lauren said. 'Maybe like a chest piece, right over the collarbone?' Joy laughed. 'Something subtle, of course. You don't want to look like you're bragging.'

'Well, well done, you,' Joy replied. 'Seems like today was a success, right? No major gaffes, you got the message across and filled some headlines, and even that sweaty little shit from the *Dispatch* shut up after a while.'

Lauren smirked as she reached into her desk drawer and pulled out a Diet Coke for Joy. 'I've got a whole stash, by the way,' she said. 'This drawer is always open to you.'

'You're doing the Lord's work,' Joy replied, and opened the soda. 'So what's on the agenda for the next press briefing?'

'You tell me,' Lauren said, then leant back in her chair and pressed her fingertips to her temples. The mattress at her new place was in desperate need of a topper to make it comfortable, and it was cutting into her sleep. Unfortunately the La Mer eye cream she had bought on a whim two months ago when she was still receiving a decent salary wasn't doing much to hide the effects. 'I'd love to get to the point where we're proactive instead of reactive, you know? Focus on the work the Palace is doing instead of the mistakes.'

'Well, good luck with that.' Joy took a sip of her Diet Coke just as Lauren's email pinged.

'So much spam,' she sighed, then leant forward and squinted at her screen, scrolling through the thirty-odd emails that had come through in the past ten minutes. 'Oh wait, one of the reporters emailed.' She clicked on the message. 'He wants to go to lunch?'

'Who does?'

'One of the reporters from this morning,' Lauren replied. 'What do you think his agenda is? What's even the rule here about meeting reporters?'

'Which one is it?' Joy asked.

Lauren typed 'Oscar Mason' into her search bar, then turned the laptop so Joy could see it. 'Oscar, from the *London Tribune.*'

Joy leant forward and peered at the screen. 'Oh *hell* yes, you are absolutely going to lunch with him.'

'*Joy.* Okay, yes, he's moderately handsome—'

'This man looks like a young Henry Golding, and if you say otherwise, you are the biggest liar and I'll be forced to renounce our newfound friendship.'

'He's a reporter!'

'And you run comms! Your entire job is maintaining relations with the press! You don't want to upset him by refusing a lunch invitation.'

Lauren paused. 'I don't like the way you just said "maintaining relations".'

'You shouldn't. There was nothing decent about it. But I stand by my point that if he wants to go to lunch, especially on his paper's coin, then on behalf of the Palace, you have a royal duty to say yes.'

Lauren glanced at her laptop, then at Joy, then back at her laptop again. 'What if it's just coffee?'

'If you're paying, then sure, coffee. But if his paper is picking up the tab, then go big and bougie.' Joy sat back in her chair and crossed her arms over her chest with a grin. 'Lauren has a *daaate*.'

'Lauren has an extremely professional potential lunch meeting with a member of the press, and it is going to be very *platoooooonic*,' Lauren sang back as she started to reply to Oscar's email. 'Hello, Oscar,' she narrated as she typed. 'Thank you so much for the invitation to lunch. I would be happy to meet and discuss some of the Palace's long-term plans—'

'Boring!' Joy declared as she stood up. 'Dusty and dry.'

'Professional!' Lauren shot back. 'And I take it back, your rights to my stash have been rescinded.'

Joy just shrugged as she waggled her eyebrows. 'Worth it,' she replied. 'But in all seriousness, be careful. It's all well and fine at first, but hooking up with a reporter would actually get messy fast. And trust me, I've seen more than a few messes over the years.'

'Yes, yes, noted,' Lauren said as she finished her email.

A few minutes later, Oscar replied. 'Wonderful, thrilled to hear of it. The Goring Hotel Monday at 1:00 p.m.? You can text me at this number if it's easier.'

Lauren quickly typed the number he provided into her phone then texted: '1pm is great. See you then.'

*

At 1:01 p.m. on Monday, Lauren felt like she had made a mistake.

Yes, she was meeting with a member of the British press for the first time in her new role. Yes, she had read as many of Oscar's articles as she could to prepare for it.

And sadly, yes, this was the first time she had been out with a man since she had broken up with Brian.

She knew that her posh restaurant meeting with Oscar wasn't an actual date, but still, she felt out of sorts, like she was trying to sing along to a song that she hadn't heard in years. Brian hadn't liked fancy restaurants, had always preferred dive bars, roadside diners, the McDonald's value menu. At first Lauren had loved that about him, the Ivy League guy who was rising through the ranks at the White House and yet still preferred places with pleather booths and sticky tables. But over time it began to annoy her, the way he used his privilege to coast through places where others could often get stuck. He had never had to eat off a dollar menu because his dad left and that was all his mum could afford before she got paid. Lauren had. She never forgot.

And Brian could never remember.

'So,' Oscar said as he shuffled his chair closer to the table. Lauren snapped herself out of her thoughts and sat up a bit straighter. The Dining Room at the Goring Hotel felt classy and intimate, with tall draped windows, high-backed dining chairs with wooden arms and heavily starched linen table-cloths. For someone who had eaten many dull Pret A Manger lunches since arriving in London, Lauren felt her stomach growl as she glanced at the refined menu.

'Thanks so much for meeting with me,' Oscar said.

Goddamnit, Joy was right, he *was* cute. Lauren gave herself three seconds to inwardly swoon over his floppy dark hair, sharp nose and eyelashes that almost looked like they had been AI generated. Why did men always get the good lashes? It seemed very unfair.

His shirt and suit were neatly cut and fitted to him in a way that made Lauren think he probably had a tailor and definitely worked out. Did he have family money? she wondered. Many of the reporters she had seen at the briefing were a bit rumpled and wrinkled, more concerned with landing the story than how they looked, but Oscar seemed different.

'I sort of felt like I was shouting at you during the press conference, so it's nice to be able to talk properly here.'

'Well, you had to shout to be heard over Adam from the *Dispatch*,' Lauren said, spreading her napkin in her lap and very grateful that she had chosen to re-wear her wide-legged trousers that day. Joy had given her a thumbs-up when she had arrived at the office, which Lauren took as a huge seal of approval, given Joy's exemplary fashion sense.

'Adam,' Oscar chuckled. 'He's what you'd expect from that place, but I wouldn't worry much about his type.'

'I'm not worried,' Lauren replied. 'I can handle difficult characters.'

'Good to know,' Oscar said, then placed his own napkin in his lap before steepling his hands together and looking at Lauren over the table. 'So how's the job going so far, Bearnas?'

She dropped her butter knife, creating a clatter that she barely heard over the ringing in her ears. 'Excuse me?'

The soft smile on his face now seemed sharper. 'That is your name, right? Bearnas Lauren Morgan? Or did I get it wrong?'

She had been so, so stupid.

'Okay,' she said. 'What do you want?'

Oscar blinked. 'What do I want?'

'You asked me here under the pretense of talking about

69

future engagements, of getting to know the comms team, and this is how you start the conversation? Acting like James Bond because you found out my full name? I'm sure the Pulitzer already has your name on it.'

Oscar only looked more amused, which was infuriating. 'So I take it you don't like to go by Bearnas, then?'

Lauren pulled her napkin to the side, ready to stand up, but Oscar reached across the table before she could leave. 'Okay, okay. I'm sorry, I got too clever for my own good. *Lauren.*'

'You know, *Oscar,*' she said as she placed her napkin back in her lap, 'Adam might be a loudmouth jerk, but at least he wears it openly.'

Oscar held up his hands as if pleading for mercy. 'Point taken. I just thought it was interesting that you don't go by your full name.'

'I mean, would you?' Lauren shot back. 'My father followed a tradition. The firstborn girl was named after the father's mother, and it was both my and my grandma's bad luck that we got saddled with that name.' She reached for a roll, stabbing her knife into a pat of perfectly salted butter. Anger always made her hungry. 'Anyway, why do you care?'

'Honestly? It sort of makes me wonder what else you might not be talking about.'

Lauren rolled her eyes and bit into the bread. This lunch was already going downhill, but she was definitely going to eat her weight in warm sourdough to make up for it.

'So how did you get a working visa in a matter of days? Did the Palace get you fast-tracked?' Oscar asked, not reaching for a roll until Lauren had set her butter knife down.

'Surely your "sources" already know that,' she said. 'I have dual citizenship. My dad's Scottish.'

'Interesting,' Oscar replied.

'Not really,' Lauren said. 'What's your plan here? Are you writing a story about me?'

'Well, now that you mention it,' Oscar said, 'that doesn't sound terrible.' He smirked a little. 'Thanks for the good idea.'

'No comment,' Lauren shot back. 'On anything to do with me.'

'I'm only joking. My editor says you're not that interesting, but I don't agree. Anyway, I just thought that it'd be good for you and me to go to lunch, get to know each other better as reporter and Palace comms director. Mutually beneficial, as they say.'

Lauren adjusted her napkin in her lap and tried not to think about anything that could be seen as mutually beneficial. 'So this lunch is purely transactional, no story involved.'

'No story. As long as you don't do anything newsworthy, that is.' He smiled at her again across the table.

'And just to clarify further,' Lauren continued, 'your paper is paying for this lunch, yes?'

'Yes,' Oscar replied before adding on, 'within reason,' but Lauren was already flagging down their waiter.

'Do you eat oysters?' she asked Oscar, then continued before he could answer. 'Do you have one of those seafood tower things?' she asked the waiter. 'Great, we'd love one. And a glass of champagne as well.' She adjusted her napkin in her lap as the waiter disappeared to place her order. 'Just so you know, I'm also getting steak.'

Oscar's look was half fear and half admiration. 'And if I told you I'm allergic to shellfish?'

'Then you'd have a great last meal.' Lauren smiled at him. 'So. What do you want to know?'

*

71

After nearly two hours, a lot of questions about her time at the White House (six years, she was ready for a fresh start and a new adventure), where she went to college (Sarah Lawrence 4 lyfe, baby!), what she hoped to accomplish during her tenure at the Palace, if she planned on bringing democracy to the monarchy (Lauren was somewhat sure that Oscar was kidding with that last question), two more glasses of champagne and an absolutely incredible amount of protein consumed, Lauren made her way back to the Palace on foot. Oscar had offered to share his taxi, but she waved him off. She needed the fresh air and the exercise, she had said.

But also, she didn't want to find herself in the back seat of a car with him. Two hours of looking at his face, his broad shoulders, the Windsor knot of his tie had made her not trust herself.

Fresh air. Exercise. Maybe a coffee. Yes. That was what she needed.

Her work phone vibrated as she walked, and Lauren dug it out of her handbag, glancing at the text. 'Hi. Adam from Dispatch,' it read. 'Is it true that the Queen has been taken ill and is cancelling next week's engagements?'

Lauren scoffed and started typing. Eugene had sent a memo that morning that the Queen's private physician had visited due to seasonal allergies, and while it had seemed like an overshare in the moment, she was grateful for it now. 'Off the record, it's allergies, Adam,' she texted back. 'It's not like she has pneumonia. HMQ's work continues as usual.'

Sixteen minutes later, her phone started to buzz again, this time with a breaking news alert. Followed by another. And then another.

The Palace Refutes Claims that the Queen Has Pneumonia!

Doctor Visits Queen amid PNEUMONIA Fears

Does the Queen Have Pneumonia? What You Need to Know

Lauren felt a chill go through her body.

By the time she got back to her desk, James was already waiting for her.

'I think I messed up,' Lauren said, tossing her handbag onto her desk. 'Okay? I know I screwed up.'

'Oh, you're saying this to *me*?' James said with exaggerated naivete. 'You should save those excuses because Eugene is – '

Eugene suddenly burst into the room, and Lauren knew it was bad because his waistcoat was only half buttoned. 'Did you talk about Her Majesty and *pneumonia* in the same sentence?!'

'It was sarcasm! And it was supposed to be off the record!' Lauren cried. 'It was stupid, I was just responding off the cuff to a reporter who messaged me—'

'There is no such thing as sarcasm in this job!' Eugene cried. 'You put it in writing to some arsehat at the *Daily Dispatch*, who now gets to have his "exclusive" and that's all that matters! Half this country is about to think that the Queen could be on her deathbed right now, thanks to you.'

'But she's not!' Lauren paused. 'Wait, is she?'

Eugene balled his hands into fists and bit his knuckle.

All their phones went off again, and Lauren opened her laptop as James became even more pale, which Lauren had not thought was possible until that moment. 'Oh dear.'

Eugene looked at his phone, then at James. 'Well, it's been a good run, old chap.'

73

Lauren clicked on the message. 'Who is the Lord Chamberlain?' she asked.

'Only the most senior official in the royal household,' James said tightly. 'He oversees every royal ceremony, all protocol and, unfortunately for you, the entire operation of BP's staff and administration.'

Lauren glanced at the message again.

SEE ME IMMEDIATELY.

Fuck.

Chapter 4

Lauren felt somewhat like Dorothy and her ragtag friends walking towards the fearful Wizard of Oz as she, James and Eugene entered the Lord Chamberlain's ornate office in a much more grand part of the Palace. (Or as the comically long brass name plaque on his heavy oak door read: The Right Honorable Lord Buxton Chamberlain of Thimbleby GCVO.) Lauren had hoped that James and Eugene were just trying to intimidate her by making him sound like a gatekeeper from hell, but judging by the look on the lord's face when they entered his office, especially as he snapped his laptop shut and then folded his hands under his chin and levelled his gaze at them, Lauren realised that they – well, *she* – were in deep shit.

'Well,' he said. 'Ms Lauren Morgan. It appears the rumours that you might be a bit of a troublemaker appear to be true.'

Lauren gave a quick glance at Eugene, fairly certain that *he* was the one who had spread the false rumour the lord had heard about her.

'I would have thought that coming from the White House you would have a basic understanding of how easy it is for one's words to be twisted into a salacious headline. It is comms that you specialise in, no?'

Lauren felt her mouth dry a little, like she was back at school about to be sent to detention. 'I should have handled the situation better. In my defence, I did state to the journalist that my response was off the record, but he completely ignored it,' she replied. 'That's never happened to me before!'

'You seem to be under the impression that I'm a collector of excuses,' he said, the lines in his forehead crinkling as he raised his wiry grey eyebrows. 'I can assure you, I am not.'

She was about to continue her defence when she spotted a framed photo of a dog on the shelf behind him.

'I'm sorry, Lord Chamberlain, I don't mean to interrupt at all, but I just have to ask, do you have an Irish setter?' she asked.

His face immediately softened as he turned to look at the photo. 'Rosewood,' he said. 'My pride and joy. She's quite the legacy, bred from three lines of Westminster Kennel Club champions.'

'I can tell,' Lauren said, even if the dog looked as sweet and dumb as candy floss. 'Her colouring is gorgeous. Irish setters were the only kind of breed my grandmother ever had. Brandy was her last one and *such* a good girl, rest her soul.'

'Oh my God,' Eugene muttered behind her, just close enough to her to hear.

'You can always tell the true champions,' Lauren said, ignoring Eugene's comment. 'Sweet Brandy, she just didn't have the temperament for competition, but I bet Rosewood is—'

'At the top of her agility class,' the lord finished for her, just as Lauren was hoping he would. 'Her time to beat is unmatched, and we could not be more proud.'

Lauren chuckled. 'Dogs, am I right? We just don't deserve

them. Anyway, I'm very sorry about the mix-up today. I spoke out of turn and should have known better than to trust that a reporter would truly keep something off the record.' Her brain briefly flashed to Oscar, but she brushed it off.

The Lord Chamberlain just waved her words away. 'Well, the papers do tend to be rather sneaky at times. We'll let it go this once. Now,' he added, pulling out his phone, 'you have to see this video of Rosewood's latest agility course showing. Seventeen obstacles and she didn't miss one!'

'We would love to,' Lauren said, gesturing for James and Eugene to come closer. 'You can't have too many dog videos, right, James?'

'Never,' he said with all the enthusiasm of a person who was just told they needed a root canal.

'Well, I don't know *what* the fuss was all about,' Lauren said as they left the Lord Chamberlain's office ten minutes and five Rosewood videos later. 'He was absolutely delightful. I feel kind of bad that I didn't bring him doughnuts on that first day. Or a squeaky dog toy.'

She glanced at James and Eugene, who looked as dishevelled as she had ever seen them: the top button on James's starched shirt wasn't entirely through the buttonhole, and Eugene's receding hairline was showing just the slightest peep of nervous sweat.

'I would like for that to never happen in my lifetime again,' Eugene said, pulling out a perfectly pressed handkerchief (*Because of course he has a handkerchief,* Lauren thought to herself) and dabbing at his brow.

'I fully acknowledge that it is still working hours,' James added, 'but I need a drink.'

'You know the rumours about Marion's desk drawer, yes?'

Eugene muttered under his breath as he tucked his handkerchief away.

'Not rumours,' James replied.

'Oh, really?' Eugene said, raising one eyebrow.

'Wait, what?' Lauren said. 'What desk drawer? Who's Marion?'

They both immediately snapped to attention. 'Never you mind,' James said. 'And you should consider yourself very lucky that the Lord Chamberlain didn't destroy you.'

Lauren rolled her eyes. 'Please. He's a human being who graciously acknowledged that we are *all* human beings and that sometimes human beings make mistakes.'

'And sometimes those mistakes can lead to an international incident.' Eugene glowered at her.

'I don't think three web headlines from the British tabloids constitutes an "international incident",' Lauren scoffed. 'Has anyone ever told you that you're very dramatic, Eugene?'

James snorted, and Lauren filed that piece of information away so she could share it with Joy later.

'I have to ask,' James said as the three of them headed back to their respective offices. 'Did your grandmother really have an Irish setter named Brandy?'

Lauren just kept walking. 'Two words, James,' she said as she turned the corner. 'Crisis. Management.'

A few days following her successful first press conference, in the name of research and being well-prepared and a consummate professional (and also not wanting to give Eugene the upper hand), Lauren sat in her new apartment with takeaway for dinner. Her only furnishings aside from her bed were what had been left behind by the landlord, which included a little dining table, a small sofa, an absolutely massive TV stand and no TV. It wasn't exactly cosy, but it would do as she dug into her poke bowl and did a deep dive into every single thing ever written on the internet about Jasper, the Duke of Exeter.

Everything was as James had said to her at the Palace staircase: New Zealand, tech billionaire who divorced him, sheep. So many sheep. Fortunately there wasn't anything in the press yet about the whole bankruptcy-and-borrowing-money thing, and Lauren planned to keep it that way. But a handsome heir to the throne (even if he was ninth in line) who spent his days with baby lambs and seemed to do little else? If they made him a working royal, then this was going to be the easiest job she had ever had. She was going to crush it.

That was, if the press didn't crush her first.

She woke up the following morning to a flurry of front-page headlines:

ROYAL FAMILY'S POPULARITY DETHRONED

GENERATION GAP: YOUNGSTERS GIVE ROYALS COLD SHOULDER

ROYAL PAIN! CROWN'S POPULARITY SEES BIGGEST DROP EVER

'Ugh,' she muttered, running a hand over her eyes as her phone buzzed. It was a text from Joy with screenshots of more articles saying the same thing, followed by a message: 'Good luck with this today. Want anything from Pret? Had an early meeting at Theo's school so I'm running ahead for once.'

'Almond croissant and a latte PLEASE,' Lauren wrote back. 'You're the best. One day people will write songs about you.'

'They already have,' Joy wrote back, followed by the winking emoji. 'See you soon!'

'Well, the optics aren't ideal,' Eugene announced as he hustled into the meeting room, and even from a distance, Lauren could see his right eyelid stress twitching. Not a great sign.

'I'll say,' James muttered, and even Harriet had to bite back a smile.

'As you may have seen, we are on the front page of every single newspaper in the country, and it's not exactly good news.' He looked over at Lauren. 'I hope you're ready to start really working today.'

'Always,' she replied, trying not to take offence at his shady comment. Lauren reached forward and started combing through the newspapers that Eugene had fanned out on the conference table. 'So this stems from just the one poll, right? One single stat repeated in headlines over and over and over?'

'Not helping,' Harriet whispered.

'No, I just mean that it needs only one solution.'

'Which we still don't have,' James pointed out, widening his eyes dramatically at Lauren. *You don't know anything*, he seemed to be saying, a silent reminder to keep her mouth shut about their secret conversation about the Duke of Exeter. She gave him a very fast nod just as Eugene's phone began to ring. He answered it with his standard greeting of 'Yes,' then paused before leaving the room.

'Okay, I've got to ask, but why do you think that so many young people are either not interested or are losing interest in the royal family?' Lauren began.

'Oh, Lord.' James sighed, rubbing his forehead.

'Out of touch? People don't understand what they do? Has this actually ever been discussed here?'

The entire room looked at her.

'To find a solution, you have to discuss the cause of the problem,' Lauren added.

'Well, we might have something of a youth problem,' James said. 'Currently, all the working family members are, well, maturing.'

'They're *old*, James, you can just say it,' Violet said, then tossed her phone onto a tabloid. 'I'll spare you all the memes and comments I see about the ageing lineup, but trust me, they're rarely flattering.'

'Our only young royals are still too young for public appearances or duty, they're still at school, bless them,' Harriet added.

'How old are the twins now?' Joy asked.

'Sixteen.'

'Remember the photos of them at Legoland?' Joy said. 'They were barely tall enough for the rides.'

'So adorable!' Harriet said. 'Now they're almost taller than the Prince and Princess.'

'I hate to ruin this nostalgic reverie,' James said, 'but if we don't have any ideas' – he looked pointedly in Lauren's direction – 'by the time Eugene comes back into this room, I fear for all of our lives.'

'Wonderful news!' Eugene sang out as he practically bounced into the room. 'This wasn't something I was allowed to discuss before, but Her Majesty has requested that we accelerate plans to bring the Duke of Exeter into the working fold. Some of you, and certainly the press, are unaware of this, but he's already returned from New Zealand and is staying here at the Palace.'

'Literally everyone knows that,' Violet said. 'He's been riding his bike around the gardens for weeks.'

'He held a door for me just the other day,' Harriet added.

'Before I met him, he came into my office and I didn't know who he was because of the beard,' Lauren said, instantly regretting her overshare.

Eugene closed his eyes briefly. 'Of course you didn't,' he said with a sigh.

'I haven't seen a single bit of him!' Joy said. 'But I'd like to.'

'Has he ever done a royal engagement?' Lauren asked.

'He has not,' Eugene said. 'But he's still very much a member of the royal family – and at thirty-four, he potentially has the ability to appeal to both younger and older members of the public. That being said, we have to brace ourselves for the fact that he could bring in as much negative publicity as positive, at least in the beginning. He has a few . . . financial issues, and the press might try to suggest that he's only here to fix that with the help of the public purse.'

'I mean,' Lauren said, 'we all have that one family member, right?'

'*We* do not,' James said. 'But Eugene does have a point.'

'Regardless, this is not even up for discussion,' Eugene scoffed. 'This is the result of months of conversations. Her Majesty and the Lord Chamberlain have agreed to support the duke's return from New Zealand, where he has just been through an extremely amicable divorce—'

Joy huffed out a laugh. 'That'd be the first royal one.'

'—and is currently looking to take on public and official royal duties as a working member of the royal family.'

'So, I have an idea,' Lauren said as she opened an email. She had actually had the idea yesterday in her apartment while researching the duke, thanks to James's tip, but Eugene didn't need to know that. 'Remember the announcement we got from Great Ormond Street Hospital for Children? And how we weren't able to make any schedules work for an engagement because it was last minute?' She paused as everyone else pulled up the email. 'They're unveiling these incredible new murals and artwork throughout an entire floor of the hospital, to create a less stressful and more safe-feeling space for the young children there, and I think we should send the duke for the unveiling. A chance for the public to see his potential.'

'Ooh, I like this,' Joy said.

'I do, too,' James added, and Lauren appreciated the vote of confidence.

'Think of it as a soft launch, not an official engagement,' Lauren said. 'We could have one of the reporters there, maybe see him speaking to a few children, talk to some of the local artists involved. Do it embargoed, so the whole thing can play out in private before the world knows he's been out. Violet can take video. Just something where he's forward-facing but it doesn't feel like he's in front of a firing squad. He's new; we don't want to scare him off or give the papers a chance to cook up their own nonsense.'

Eugene looked at the email again. 'This unveiling is happening next week.'

'From what I understand, the duke has no upcoming plans. This is why he's here: to represent the royal family. This is *why* you brought him here, Eugene. And it's a *children's hospital*. This is, like, the best possible way to introduce him. He smiles at a few kids and everyone will fall in love with him and these poll numbers will soon be a thing of the past.'

'Well, the good news is that social media has *always* loved him,' Violet said, holding up her phone. 'Those old videos of him riding a horse still make the rounds online.'

They all peered in to see a slo-mo fan edit of the duke riding on horseback across a field. 'Oh, that jawline can't be real,' Joy said. 'You sure that's not AI?'

'That is *very* much the real deal,' Violet said.

The video slowed down as the duke looked up, presumably spotting the paparazzi lens, then shook some hair out of his eyes just as the video's music slowed down. 'Classic thirst trap,' Violet said.

Lauren, Joy and Harriet just kept watching. 'Could you, um, restart it?' Harriet asked. 'I missed the beginning.'

'Excuse me,' Eugene said. 'We are here to solve a problem, not watch poorly edited videos.'

'If that's poorly edited, God spare us the well-edited ones,' Joy said.

Lauren was still watching, though. In jeans and a white tee he looked more like a classic movie star than blue-blooded royal, but there was definitely something about him that stood out. 'This man,' she said, 'might just be the best thing to happen to the British monarchy in years.' She sat up, a huge smile on her face. 'I can absolutely work with this, Eugene, don't worry.'

'I wasn't,' he replied. 'And wonderful, because that *is* in fact your job.'

'Lucky Lauren,' Harriet murmured.

'This all feels a bit ridiculous,' the duke said the next afternoon, holding his arms out to his sides as a seamstress expertly nipped and tucked the wool material around him. 'I have other suits that fit just fine. Why do we have to create a brand-new one?'

'You'd have to ask Eugene, but I'd imagine it's because the event at the children's hospital is your debut,' Lauren explained. 'Your chance to make a first impression, and the press will be paying attention to every single detail.'

The duke's head snapped up. 'I was told that the press pack wouldn't be there.'

'They won't be.' Lauren was quick to fix her error. 'It's just one reporter filing back information to the other royal correspondents. There won't be any gotcha moments, I promise. Just you raising awareness for the good work that Ormond Street does.'

That seemed to appease him for the moment. 'Fine,' he said, wincing a little as the seamstress made the material even tighter. 'I suppose my main concern,' the duke continued, 'is that your little team of Three Musketeers just want to make me look as wealthy as my ex-wife and her new boyfriend, who conveniently is also a tech billionaire. Funny that, hmm?'

'What a coincidence,' Lauren said, looking down at her phone. 'They must have met at the monthly tech billionaire ice cream social.' She regretted the words as soon as she said them, worried she'd been too flippant, but her nerves settled when the duke snorted a quiet laugh. Lauren watched him from the side as he turned again. She wasn't sure what she had been expecting, seeing as how this was her first time working with an actual duke, but he had a sense of humour and a quick wit and wasn't afraid to say what he thought. It was refreshing.

'Wait a minute.' Lauren looked up. 'Who are the Three Musketeers?'

'You, Eugene and James, of course.'

'Oh, no no no, *no*,' Lauren said. 'No, we are not a team in any sense of the word, and certainly not some swashbuckling trio. We work together because we're contractually required to do so, and that's it.'

The duke turned to the left and looked at himself in the mirror, frowning slightly. 'And I suppose your presence today has nothing to do with the fact that reporters are no doubt sniffing around, asking about my life in New Zealand and my business affairs?'

Lauren could tell from the tone of his voice that it wasn't a question, and she thought back to the very first comment at last week's press conference, Adam from the *Dispatch* asking about the very thing that the duke was mentioning now.

'You think I don't know that everyone at the Palace is talking about me behind my back?' the duke continued. 'Bringing me here just to placate my aunt, who also happens to be the Queen?' He turned again, this time to look straight at himself in the mirror. 'It's a little humiliating.'

There was something in his tone that got under Lauren's skin. She knew all too well what it was to feel humiliated. She knew what it was like to move across an ocean and feel like she was starting from square one every single day, proving herself over and over again to people who didn't even want to like her in the first place.

'I think,' she said gently, 'that everyone deserves a fresh start. And that sometimes things don't work out the way we would like them to, but that doesn't mean they won't in the future.'

'That must be that famous American optimism at work,' the duke said.

'Well, you can take the girl out of America,' Lauren said, smiling at him in the mirror, a gesture that wasn't returned. 'Now, I've printed out and emailed you the info packet for the engagement on Thursday with some facts about the hospital, their new murals, some important names. Eugene will also go over it all with you beforehand.

'And, of course, I'll be with you throughout the engagement, so if you have any questions—'

'I'm sure I won't,' he said, looking at himself in the mirror again. 'I know how this works. They bring you in, build you up, then offer you as a sacrifice when someone with a higher rank makes a mistake. It's the playbook that works, and they use it every single time.'

'It's a visit to a children's hospital, Your Highness,' Lauren said.

'Just wait,' he replied. 'Whilst I may have been gone for a while, nothing has changed around here. You're new, but you'll learn.' The jawline that Joy had mentioned was still as prominent as ever, and Lauren didn't like the way her stomach flipped when she saw him gazing at himself.

'I do have one question, actually,' he said.

'Of course.'

'Are we *sure* that this isn't about just showing that I've moved on from my my ex-wife?'

Lauren paused before replying, 'Your Highness, if this trip on Thursday goes as planned, nobody's going to be thinking about your ex-wife at all.'

The duke paused, then turned and gave her a small smile. 'Finally. An answer I like.'

'First engagement today!' Joy proclaimed the following week as she strolled into Lauren's office, where she had been busy going over the minutes from her last press briefing and sipping a very hot and very strong tea she had made for herself in the office kitchen.

'This tea,' Lauren said by way of response, 'is kind of making me want to forsake coffee, which is a sentence I never thought I'd say.'

'That's how we get you,' Joy said, plopping down into a chair. 'First coffee, then you're forsaking your country. All part of the master plan.'

Lauren grinned as she turned back to her laptop. 'What's up?'

'Aren't you excited about your first engagement?' She made grabby hands towards Lauren, who immediately slid over the open bag of Maltesers she had on her desk.

'Yes, my first engagement. Yay. Woo. So excited.' Lauren glanced down at the itinerary she had printed out just in case she lost connectivity on her phone. She had triple-checked all the addresses, phone numbers and confirmations the night before, but she still worried that something could go awry. 'Did you hear that they're sending James to escort me?' she asked, reaching for the bag of chocolates.

'Noooooo,' Joy said. 'Why? They don't trust you?'

'Eugene doesn't want me to go alone,' Lauren said, brushing her chestnut brown hair out of her eyes and regretting the fringe that she had cut herself right after she left the White House. At least it was finally long enough to tuck behind her ears. (And never again would she take fringe-cutting advice from an eighteen-year-old TikTok influencer.) 'I can tell you James isn't happy about it either.'

Indeed, he hadn't been. 'What?!' he had screeched as soon as it was suggested in their weekly alignment meeting. 'What is the point of hiring someone, Eugene, if I have to do their job along with mine?'

'I never thought I'd say this, but I agree with James,' Lauren had replied.

Eugene had just shaken his head. 'Lauren's too new. We need someone who knows the ins and outs of these things. Imagine something going horribly wrong and we don't have boots on the ground?'

'You will have boots on the ground!' Lauren had protested. 'Me, you have me. And I have boots. Beautiful ones!
There hasn't even been a single crisis from my very first press
briefing.'

'You will find,' Eugene had replied, 'that being with a
member of the family outside of these walls can sometimes
be a little . . . unpredictable.'

Harriet had leant over towards Lauren, smelling like a
blend of fabric softener and Vicks VapoRub. 'He's thinking
of the runaway alpacas,' she'd whispered.

Lauren had blinked. 'The what nows?'

'Two years ago. Alpaca farm with the Duke of Hereford,'
Violet had said without looking up from her phone. 'There
was a jailbreak. Fur was literally flying. There aren't enough
lint brushes in the world for something like that.'

'Were the alpacas okay?' Lauren had asked.

Violet had shrugged. 'Guess so. We were too busy trying
to shield poor Hereford. He has terrible allergies to, we discovered that day, alpaca fur. Ugh!' she muttered as she tapped
angrily on her phone. 'All these people commenting "FIRST!"
on every post. You can't *all* be first, bloody imbeciles.'

Eugene had just raised an eyebrow at Lauren, who had
enough self-awareness to know that avoiding stampeding
alpacas was not on her list of skills and talents. 'Fine,' she'd
said. 'Me and James, joined at the hip.'

'Always carry some Claritin, just in case.' Harriet had
smiled at her, then patted her arm. 'Never hurts.'

Back in Lauren's office, Joy laughed at the story. 'I bet he
mentioned the alpacas,' she said.

'You know about that?'

'Everyone knows about that!' Joy replied. 'It was all over
the internet. The man was literally running for his life while

sneezing his head off, eyes all puffy and red.' Joy chuckled a bit to herself. 'The memes were hilarious. May he rest in peace.'

'Wait, that's how he died?!' Lauren gasped.

'Not from that!' Joy laughed. 'Old age. A year later.'

Lauren covered her eyes and sighed. 'I'm beginning to understand why Amelia quit,' she said.

'Oh, buck up,' Joy said. 'These engagements write themselves, you said so yourself. The Duke of Exeter is a handsome man doing a good deed, and everyone wins in the end.'

'Where were you during yesterday's comms meeting, by the way?' Lauren asked.

'Well, I'm glad you asked,' Joy said. 'I was upstairs at the keeper of the privy purse's office waiting for a meeting we had arranged to discuss budget allocations for a number of DEI initiatives I would like to get activated next year, including a potential Pride Day event I proposed in an email that, as of now, only two people have responded to.'

Lauren felt a twinge of guilt. 'I'll respond right now,' she said, opening her mail app.

'No, no, it's fine,' Joy said with a sigh. 'No offence, but I need all the higher-ups to respond. And in any case, ol' keeper never showed for the meeting, so I lost an hour of my very valuable time.'

'I'm sorry,' Lauren said. 'I'm assuming his assistant never reached out to reschedule?'

Joy just tapped her nose before standing up. 'Anyway, go crush it today. Live your dreams! Make your own destiny!'

Lauren smirked as she grabbed her coat. 'Is this the part where you tell me not to do anything that you wouldn't do?'

'You must be joking.' Joy stopped in the doorway. 'Lauren, my love, I am a divorced woman who this year became closer to forty than I am thirty. I have an eight-year-old son whose obsession with Pokémon is taking over my life. You should do *everything* I wouldn't do. Literally everything. Go live life for me, please. I beg you.'

'Pokémon's cute, though,' Lauren said. 'I had Pokémon cards when I was a kid.'

'Yes, it's cute when you're a kid,' Joy replied. 'No woman my age should have as much knowledge about these characters as I do, Lauren. It's not healthy. This one time, when Theo was with his dad, I had a man over and I noticed a rogue Pokémon card had stuck to his back while we were in bed!'

'Oh my God. Okay, I will avoid all Pokémon, thank you for the advice,' Lauren said, then tucked her laptop into her bag and grabbed a long scarf from the back of her door. 'Any other last words before I head out?'

'Just that if you evolve a Shroomish before it reaches level forty-five then Breloom can't learn the Spore attack.'

Lauren laughed as she switched off her office light, leaving Joy in the dark.

'And you *have* to finish the game if you want to catch Dragonite and Charizard.'

'Have a good day, Joy!'

'Safe travels! Watch out for Team Rocket!'

Lauren made it out to the car in the Palace's inner quadrangle, where they were set to meet the duke, and there she saw James engrossed in his phone. 'Good morning,' she said. 'I was hoping you'd be able to change Eugene's mind about this.'

'You're hilarious,' James said without cracking a smile. 'I've worked with Eugene for coming up to ten years, so trust me when I say that there is no changing his mind on anything to do with the Queen or the royal family.'

'Can't someone else come with me? What about Harriet? What's she doing today?'

James snorted as he held the door open for her. 'You don't want to be alone with Harriet.'

'Why? She's harmless.'

'She's sort of known as . . . the Grim Reaper.'

Lauren looked up from her phone, alarmed. 'Harriet?' she said, and James gestured at her to lower her voice. '*Our* Harriet? The woman who wears cardigans that she probably knits herself?'

'Yes, yes, she's quite lovely, but every single royal she has worked closely with over the years has, well, passed away.'

'What?!'

'Of course,' James added hastily, 'bar one, the others were quite old and probably well overdue for their time to come. But it's something that we've all noticed over the years.'

'Have any staffers died?' Lauren asked. 'Like cute young comms directors? Should I be scared?'

'Oh, no, no, of course not.' James laughed like Lauren was the ridiculous one in the conversation. 'And again, they were all fairly ancient. Say what you want about the royals, but they cling to life like a bad ex.'

'Okay,' Lauren said warily. 'I'll, uh, keep an eye out for the scythe.'

'I have to tell you, I feel ridiculous being this dressed up for a hospital.'

Lauren sat next to the duke in the car on their way over to the children's hospital as he straightened his collar and picked a piece of lint off his trousers. James rode shotgun next to the driver–slash–protection officer, tapping a message on his phone, probably telling Eugene that she hadn't started a crisis. Yet.

'Well, you look wonderful,' Lauren said. 'And a suit is very appropriate for this kind of engagement.'

'It's a hospital,' the duke protested. 'A *children's* hospital, as you've pointed out to me more than a few times. Wouldn't jeans be less intimidating for the kids?'

'You are projecting royal confidence,' Lauren replied. 'Or at least you should be. You're a prince *and* a duke, a member of the royal family, and also, these children have probably been raised on Disney princess films. The bar is very high here in terms of their expectations when they're meeting a member of the family. Jeans and sneakers are not what they want to see.'

'My nanny loved playing those films when I was a kid,' he said.

'I watched them, too. I wore a yellow Belle dress until it literally fell apart in the washing machine.'

James turned in his seat and raised an eyebrow at her, shaking his head. She could practically read his mind: *No personal details.*

'Now, did you and Eugene go over all the material that I sent?'

'Yes, I felt like I was studying for an exam – with my teacher breathing down my neck.'

'Great, that means you read it properly.'

'The mural mascot's name is Poppy the Owl. Quite cute, I thought.'

'Absolutely.' Lauren checked her phone and then saw an excited-looking group of staff gathered outside the hospital as they pulled up to the curb in central London's Holborn area. 'Okay, here we go. Remember, there are no enemies here. Just children, parents and staff who are excited to see you. I know you've been away for a long time, but believe it or not, you're kind of a big deal and you're doing a good thing.'

The duke's shoulders relaxed a bit, and when they entered the doors of the hospital, Lauren breathed a quiet sigh of relief when he walked in and immediately cranked up the charisma. He greeted the staff with genuine warmth, nodding kindly at all their words. 'I think I spy Poppy,' he said at one point, gesturing towards the mural, and thankfully Violet was there alongside a TV news camera and producer, capturing it all.

Lauren followed them as they went through the corridors, the ceiling painted with bright characters so that children could see them as they were wheeled towards treatments and surgeries, those same characters playing among flowers and tall grass in murals that lined the hallways. The duke listened attentively as they walked towards some of the children's rooms, even asking questions of the mural's artist.

Lauren mentally high-fived herself and wondered how long she could gloat about this to James.

When they got to one of the children's rooms, though, she sobered up. The child was obviously sick, her small face swollen from treatment, even though she smiled when the duke entered the room. Her mother was standing next to her bed, nearly shaking with nerves, and the duke gently waved at her to sit when she started to curtsy. 'Please, no, none of that,' he said. 'I'm not the guest of honour today, you two are.

'And pay no attention to this lot,' he added, gesturing to the palace team, reporter and photographer behind him. Lauren could see the child – Lily, the operational note she put together had detailed – glancing nervously at them, and the duke positioned himself so that she would have to look at him and only him. 'Just a noisy pack of woodpeckers, they are.'

Lily smiled at that, which made the duke and everyone else in the room smile.

They chatted for a few minutes, the duke asking about her favourite things to do while in the hospital (was Lauren the only person in the world who hadn't seen *Bluey*? she wondered) and if Lily enjoyed the new artwork on the walls. 'Yes,' she said, and then emotionally devastated everyone within earshot when she added, 'but sometimes it's still scary and sad here.'

Lauren felt a lump rise in her throat, and she didn't dare glance at Lily's mother for fear that she would start to cry. The duke just nodded thoughtfully, though, pressing his fingertips together beneath his chin as he took in her words. 'I would imagine that's very true, Lily,' he said. 'You've been through some very sad and scary things lately. So have I, as a matter of fact. I've not been in hospital, but things have gone a bit pear-shaped in my life at times and I've sometimes felt the same way.'

'But you know what?' he continued, and Lauren could see the nearby reporter feverishly scribbling down everything he was saying in shorthand. 'I think it's good that we're able to feel the scary and sad things. It means that we can also feel the happy and wonderful things. It means we've still got fight in us. What do you think?'

Lily nodded, and the duke offered her a wink and a fist bump, which she immediately accepted. 'I'll be thinking of you, Lily,' he said as he started to stand up, then reached for Lily's mother's hand. 'Both of you. And I expect to hear all about your newest exploits when I see you again, okay?'

Lily, whose eyes were shining like she had just met her own real-life prince, just kept nodding. It was amazing to Lauren the effect royal visits like this could have, and she felt excited at the thought of the British public getting to witness more of this over the months ahead.

'I almost lost it right on the spot,' the duke muttered to Lauren as they left the cameras and press behind to continue down the hall for the remainder of the engagement.

'You were wonderful,' Lauren whispered back, handing him a surgical mask to put on. 'Truly. Not even just as the Duke of Exeter, but as a person.'

The duke looked at her, surprised. 'Well, I *am* a person,' he said, his bright blue eyes peering over the fabric of the medical cover. 'I know I've been off the map for a while, but please don't forget that.'

Lauren couldn't respond before he was whisked away into a playroom with about fifteen children, all of them masked. 'Well, hel-lo!' he called out. 'Thank you so much for having me come to visit today. It's wet and miserable outside, so I'm glad to be inside with you all instead!'

Lauren watched for twenty minutes as he levelled every person there – adults and children alike. The room felt too small to hold all his charm, and away from the gazing eyes of millions of people, he truly seemed like royalty, like he was destined to do this. He even read to the children after one of them asked, sitting on a tiny chair while they gathered around him, pointing out things in the pictures and asking them questions that garnered answers all shouted out at once, most of them non sequiturs like, 'I have a dog!' and 'I saw a train once!'

By the time they both collapsed into the waiting car, Lauren felt elated and exhausted, not just because the event had gone as well as she hoped it would but also because James had hopped into his own cab and headed home, confident that all potential crises had been eradicated.

'Christ,' the duke said with a gasp. 'I am *sweating* under

this jacket. I had no idea that reading to children could be so terrifying. All of their little eyes just staring at you. Do I do the voices? Do I not do the voices? How stupid am I about to look reading the lines of a pig that's lost its – What? What's wrong?'

Lauren realised she was staring at him like a lovestruck teenager would stare at her music idol. 'Nothing!' she said. 'Sorry, nothing at all. You were just so good in there. Do you even realise the impact you had on everyone today?'

The duke loosened his tie. 'Just tried to cheer up some sick children and their parents, that's all. Make them forget about their trials and tribulations for a few hours.'

'Well, you did more than that.' Her phone dinged, and she glanced down at a text from Violet. 'THIS IS GOING TO BE INTERNET GOLD,' it read.

'Good,' Lauren texted. 'Go do your thing.'

Violet sent back a heart emoji in response.

'Anyway,' Lauren said. 'You were great, and I think you brought a lot of happiness to a lot of people today.'

'Well, excellent,' the duke said, letting out a nervous breath and wiping his hands on his trousers as the rainy city slipped past their window. 'What else are we good for if not that?'

Lauren's phone buzzed again, and she expected to see another text from Violet.

But it was one from Oscar.

'Any exclusive details you want to share with a member of the press who wasn't allowed to cover the event today?'

Lauren bit back her smile. 'The duke wore a custom Henry Poole suit for the occasion.'

'Must be a day that ends in Y,' Oscar wrote back. 'Anything else?'

'Ormond Street was grateful for his patronage and support today.'

'You're killing me.'

She smirked to herself, but Oscar's question reminded her of something else.

'Do you want to add a quote to the press release?' Lauren asked the duke, opening a new Notes page on her phone. 'We can send it out to all the press.'

The duke thought for a minute. 'No,' he finally said. 'We can let everything stand for today. There will already be plenty of eyes on this.'

Lauren, a little surprised, closed the app before he could see it. 'All right,' she said. 'If anyone has follow-up questions, we can take it from there.'

'That thing you said,' the duke said, turning to her. 'Back at the hospital, about me being a person.'

'That was . . . I chose the wrong words,' Lauren replied.

'No, I don't think you did,' the duke said, sitting back in his seat with a sigh. 'I think everyone forgets that about us, that we're just people born into a strange and unique position.' He paused before speaking again, and this time, his voice was tighter. 'The press back in there, that's partly why I wanted to move so far away, it's why my mum was so desperate for me to go to uni in New Zealand and why I chose to stay. I've seen with other family members how they destroy your happiness and life and then get excited about the clicks they get from it.'

He turned back to Lauren. 'I can't control what the press does, and I assume you know that better than anyone. But in this group, this circle' – he gestured with his hands to the car, the driver, the clothes – 'I don't want anyone here to forget that. All right? I'm not going to be the saviour they want me to be. I can't turn this cruise ship around in a second. And I won't let them use me like they have used so many others in this family.'

Lauren nodded. 'I know,' she said. 'Thank you for – for being here and doing this. I'm sure it wasn't an easy decision.'

The duke let out a laugh that sounded unamused. 'Of course it was easy,' he replied. 'My aunt, who just so happens to be the Queen, called me and asked me. Have you ever tried telling the Queen no?'

'In all honesty, I don't think I'm allowed to speak to her,' Lauren replied, and this time the duke's laugh sounded genuine. 'I'm very serious. I think Eugene would throw himself in between us before I ever got a word out.'

'Ah, Eugene,' Jasper said. 'One day he'll unclench.'

Lauren covered her mouth before she could laugh. 'Maybe,' she said. 'But for what it's worth, I'm glad you're here. People will be happy to see you again.'

'For today, perhaps,' the duke replied, then propped his chin up on his fist as they both looked out the passenger window. 'But good news doesn't sell papers.' He glanced back at Lauren. 'It's the bad news that people always seem to want.'

It turned out that the duke was wrong about one of those things.

'Look at these headlines!' Lauren cried out as Eugene entered the office. She had taken the liberty of pinning all the newspapers' front pages to the rarely used bulletin board in the conference room, where the only other signs warned of a 'serious ant infestation' and that no one should 'EVER' eat food at their desks.

Lauren thought about all her snacks tucked inside her desk drawer – just two metres from doors that led to the Palace gardens – and decided those didn't count.

'I told you, he's magnetic,' Lauren continued, pointing to each newspaper with every word she spoke. James looked somewhat intrigued as he followed close behind, his cheeks flushed from the outside cold air.

Lauren pointed to Violet. 'Violet, can you please show everyone the YouTube play count from the hospital's video promoting his visit?'

'Anything to stop this Stone Age thing you have going on here,' Violet muttered, then turned her phone to show the YouTube clip, which had amassed more than two million views in barely twenty-four hours. 'This is really great, though. The only people who get these kinds of views in a day are, like, K-pop artists and MrBeast.'

Lauren beamed as she turned back to the group. 'Definitely going to be the lead item during this morning's press briefing, I can tell you that! But really, we need to send him on tour,' she said. 'People need to see him.'

'Why do you make him sound like a boy band?' James muttered.

'Excuse me, but I believe I was tasked with helping improve the public's perception of the royal family,' Lauren said, then pointed at the photo of the duke talking to Lily in her hospital bed. 'Everybody loves him. Right, Violet?'

'The only people saying mean things online are the trolls,' Violet agreed.

'Eugene, think of it this way: The Queen's idea has been a spectacular success. Don't you want to run the ball down the field?'

'I suspect this is an American sport reference,' Eugene said drily.

'It's possible,' Lauren said.

He took a deep breath before opening his laptop. 'We can talk after Balmoral,' he said. 'Christmas there will be his *official* royal debut. If it goes well, then . . .' He shrugged and

Lauren realised that was as good of a yes as she was going to get.

'We will definitely be talking after Balmoral,' she said. She still hadn't quite wrapped her head around the fact that she would be spending the holiday at a literal castle. 'You can bet on it.'

'And I await it with bated breath,' Eugene replied. 'By the way, shouldn't you be running a media briefing?'

Lauren glanced at her phone. 'Oh shit,' she muttered, and ran down the hall towards the waiting press pack.

Chapter 5

Alongside overseeing media arrangements for a string of the elderly Earl of Lancaster's engagements in London, including a scintillating ribbon-cutting at a naval club, much of Lauren's November was consumed by planning for the US president's state visit to the United Kingdom the following spring. With the duke's unofficial debut turning out to be a success and her weekly press briefings properly green-lit by James and under control (or at least as under control as she could get them to be when reporters were shouting questions at her about royal clothing budgets or controversies that had most likely emerged from conspiracy theorists on X), she was finally able to turn her attention to the one thing that she had moved across an ocean to avoid:

The Americans.

She had done this before, but never from the non-US side, and never with just her in charge. She had several drafts of the visit's numerous op notes up and running on her screen at all times, trying to coordinate press information, location information, live feeds of the speeches, positions for the reporters at all the major landmarks that she had to liaise with (the president, for example, would be getting a private tour of Westminster Abbey during her visit), arrival and departure times for reporters at every event, contact info for anyone who wasn't her – the list went on and on. At one point, Lauren made a list of all her lists and realised she had basically become a meme.

And when she wasn't doing all that, she was planning for her mum's Thanksgiving trip.

It had happened mostly by accident, somewhat out of sentimentality but mostly because of guilt. Lauren had called her mum to say hi, they mentioned the upcoming holiday, and then Lauren found herself saying, 'You should come out here, I can take the day off work. And all my things finally arrived from DC, so the apartment is all set up for entertaining.'

'Oh, you don't have time to entertain your mum,' she'd said, scoffing at the idea.

'No,' Lauren had said, because the idea was already out in the air and also, she'd suddenly realised that she missed seeing a familiar face that wasn't work- or royal-related. 'You should come! You've never been to London, right? We could be tourists, go to high tea or a museum or shopping . . .'

'Well.' Her mum had hesitated then agreed. 'I'll have to check with work and see if I can get a few days off, but yes, that would be nice.'

It had always been the two of them in the holidays, as Lauren had little recollection of her dad being there. She had seen some old photos of him wearing a Santa hat and holding baby Lauren up to the camera, a smile on his face, but those were just pictures, not a memory. But her mum always made it special and cooked the Thanksgiving meal even if she had worked late the night before. Sometimes some neighbours or college friends joined the two of them, and no matter how big or small their gathering was, it was fun and joyful.

Lauren had spent only one Thanksgiving away from her mum, two years ago, back when Brian's family had invited them to a cabin in Vermont. She had pictured rustic logs, a few deer heads, a roaring fireplace. What she discovered when they arrived was more of a sleek, modern glass-and-marble house, even though *house* didn't seem like the right word to describe it. It was like a penthouse in midtown Manhattan or the Cullen residence in *Twilight*.

And even though she had loved Brian at the time, and even though she felt welcomed by his family, it just felt . . . off. She didn't know the in-jokes or the family lore and found herself spending more and more time smiling instead of talking. It was as if she was doing the cha-cha when everyone around her knew how to waltz. She didn't fit in, and by the time she and Brian got back to DC on Sunday night, she could feel the tension between them. It had felt like a pop quiz that she failed, and Lauren tried not to let herself think too much about whether that was the first crack between them, and if that was when Brooke managed to slip into that empty space, splitting them even further apart.

But anyway. Her mum was on her way to London for Thanksgiving and Lauren was determined to make it fun, to show her mum that she was doing fine. Brian who? Brooke what? Unfortunately, one thing Lauren hadn't considered when inviting her mum to celebrate Thanksgiving in London was that no one celebrated Thanksgiving in London.

'You *did* go to university, yes?' James sarcastically remarked to her when she (foolishly) mentioned this realisation in their weekly meeting the week before Thanksgiving. 'You're not that faux heiress who spent years living in Manhattan hotels and conning those Wall Street businessmen out of millions of dollars?'

'You're going to have to narrow it down for me,' Lauren snarked back. 'That's a very broad category of people in New York.'

Undeterred, though, Lauren spent the Wednesday evening before Thanksgiving in a TK Maxx (why they didn't call it TJ Maxx was something she planned to ask ChatGPT), stocking up on things she didn't need and had no room for. She had only gone in to browse, something she'd been doing a lot lately to keep busy, to distract from the fact she wasn't spending her Saturday morning waking up with someone, grabbing coffee, meeting up with friends for brunch – all the things that she and Brian had done together in DC. The nice thing about being in a relationship, Lauren thought now that she was no longer in one, was that there was always someone to do something with. And she didn't want to admit it, but as she wandered through TK Maxx, adding ceramic pumpkins and an autumn-themed door wreath to her shopping trolley, Lauren realised that London could be very lonely.

She had Joy as a friend, of course, but Joy was often busy with mum life and the staggering amount of after-school and weekend activities that seemed to accompany an eight-year-old boy. She tried to comfort herself with the fact that DC would be lonely, too, her boyfriend and best friend both gone in one fell swoop, but at least it would have been familiar.

'Oh, these are cute,' she said, interrupting her own thoughts, and added fairy lights in the shape of acorns to her cart.

When she got home with four huge TK Maxx bags, she started decorating. She had to admit that the autumnal-themed throw cushions on the tiny sofa that came with the rental may have been a bit much, but her mum – who decorated their family home for even the shortest of holidays or seasonal occasions – would appreciate the effort. She even splurged on two autumnal-scented Diptyque candles to mask the faint smell of cooking that would occasionally seep into the place from one of her neighbours, and as she scanned her eyes around the small apartment, Lauren felt a strange sort of accomplishment.

In the bathroom doing her nighttime routine that evening, Una popped in, a handbag slung over her shoulder. She looked like a model. 'Good morning, Miss America,' Una said jauntily. 'The bathroom sink is leaking, just so you know.'

'Wonderful,' Lauren replied. 'Have a fun night.'

'I always do!' Una sang out as the front door shut behind her, her perfectly messy blowout bouncing with every step.

Lauren was finishing off just as her phone began to ring. 'Hey, Mum,' she said. 'Are you packed and ready for your flight? Oh, before I forget, this Thanksgiving dinner is going to be a little bit, um, creative. I could not for the life of me find cornbread or tinned pumpkin, but I did manage to track down a blueberry pie from this place in Notting Hill I found online that's basically someone's home but—'

'Oh, honey.'

Lauren knew that tone in her mother's voice, and it meant bad news was coming. 'What's wrong?'

'Something's come up with work,' her mum said, and already Lauren could hear the apology in her voice. 'There's been a listeria outbreak at a meatpacking plant down in North Carolina and they need me on-site to help with the messaging,' her mum said, and in the background, Lauren could hear her mum's work phone pinging, her laptop chiming in return. 'What a start to Thanksgiving, huh.' She laughed, but Lauren suspected the joke was for her benefit.

Lauren sank down into a dining chair she'd found on

Facebook Marketplace that wobbled whenever she shifted her weight. 'I can't believe you're cancelling.'

'I'm not cancelling!' her mum insisted. 'Well, I guess I am, but trips can be rescheduled. We can celebrate later. Thanksgiving in February!'

Lauren could hear the forced cheer in her mum's voice as she gazed around her apartment, her ornamental pumpkins now looking silly and stupid. 'I was just excited to see you.'

'Oh, c'mon, you have work, you have your new friend, what's her name?'

'Joy,' Lauren replied, and hoped her mum didn't hear the wobble in her voice.

'Joy! She sounds so great. Plus Christmas is around the corner, so we can just see each other—'

'I have to work over Christmas.'

'Oh. Really?'

'Yes, the royal family goes to Balmoral every year, and I have to be there to handle all the media arrangements.'

'Well, see? That's what I mean! You're so busy.'

Lauren sighed. 'I'm just disappointed. I got us tickets for the Around the World tour at the British Museum. And I made a reservation for tea at Claridge's, which is, like, impossible to get this time of year.'

'Well, I'm sure they will still be there next time,' her mum said. Lauren could hear the relief in her voice, which made her feel sad in a way that she couldn't quite explain. 'Hey, don't be disappointed, okay? It was only for a few days anyway, and like I said, you're—'

'—busy,' Lauren said along with her as she glanced around at her overdecorated apartment, which somehow made it seem even emptier. 'Yep. Soooo busy.'

*

'Don't even start,' Lauren said the next morning when she walked into the office and saw James's look of surprise.

'Didn't think we'd see you today,' he said. 'I thought you were off celebrating your independence from us by eating pumpkin pie and shooting off fireworks and starting wildfires.'

Lauren had spent most of the previous night shoving all of her dumb purchases into shopping bags and digging through the trash to find the receipts. And maybe also crying a little bit. 'Not today,' she replied. 'And you're confusing Thanksgiving with the Fourth of July.'

'Both are deeply traitorous holidays, so you'll have to forgive me for mixing them up.'

Lauren just closed the door to her office. Her sad, lonely, bare little office. She pulled up her Spotify app and went to her go-to 2000s playlist.

'Oh dear,' Joy said when she came in a few minutes later.

Lauren didn't look up from where she had rested her head on her desk, but she held up one finger. 'Hold on,' she said. 'The chorus is the best part.'

'Why on earth are you listening to Nelly and Kelly? Why are you here? I thought your mum was flying in . . .'

'Well, now I have to restart it because we just missed it,' Lauren said, sitting up and reaching for her phone, but Joy got there first and cut 'Dilemma' off mid-chorus.

'You know I adore you,' Joy said, 'but this is pathetic. Spit it out.'

'My mum had to cancel because there was a listeria outbreak in North Carolina.'

Joy paused. 'I thought she lived in Atlanta.'

'No, she doesn't *have* listeria, she just works for the CDC and sometimes she has to go to outbreak sites. But I bought all this stuff at TK Maxx to make the apartment look good for her and now I have to *return* all that stuff to TK Maxx and also I have no life and no friends. Present company excluded, of course.'

'A true honour, thank you,' Joy said. 'Well, we know your dad's not going to come to visit. What about one of your friends from DC? Maybe you could do your turkey celebration over the weekend?'

Lauren glanced down at her shoes before looking back up at Joy. 'My boyfriend cheated on me with my best friend. They both worked at the White House. That's kind of why I left DC and came here.'

Joy's eyes nearly fell out of her head. 'What?!' she screeched. 'Oh my God, you poor thing. You're joking, right?'

Lauren shrugged. 'I wish I was.'

'Well, that is something that we will definitely be unpacking, but not today. We are going *out*. Tonight. You and me.'

'The last thing I feel like doing right now is—'

Joy sat down on the edge of Lauren's desk, cutting her off. 'Let me ask you something. When was the last time you went out?'

'Where?'

'*Out* out,' Joy said, sounding exasperated. 'Dancing, a bar, something social that isn't standing in line waiting to use the bathroom in your own home.'

Lauren winced. 'Probably back in DC,' she admitted.

'Oh dear.' Joy sighed. 'We're fixing that tonight. We are *celebrating.*'

'Celebrating what?' Lauren said, reaching for her laptop again. Joy moved it further away.

'Being thankful!' Joy exclaimed. 'The fact that it's Friday tomorrow. Or that my lovely, beautiful Theo is with his dad this week, thank the Lord. There's always something to celebrate!'

'I don't have anything to wear. I hate everything in my wardrobe.'

'I'm sure you can rustle up something,' Joy said cheerily. 'You basically work in crisis management, you can't track down a single outfit? Hmm?'

Lauren thought for a minute. 'I think I can figure something out.'

'Stand still,' Una said. 'This zip is tricky.'

Lauren looked at herself in the bathroom mirror as Una, her hair in giant Velcro rollers, struggled to lock the zip of her borrowed dress into place. It was a little shorter than Lauren was used to, but the black sequins and colour-blocked flowers down the side were super cute. 'Does it look okay?' she asked, turning to see her reflection.

'Better than okay,' Una said. 'You should honestly just keep it and wear it every day.'

Lauren suspected that was a jab at her professional work attire, but Una wasn't entirely wrong. 'I'm kidding,' Una added. 'Don't keep it, I need it next week.'

'Thank you again,' Lauren said. 'My friend is taking me *out* out tonight.'

'Fun!' Una did a little shimmy. 'Where are you going? Estelle? Arts Club?'

Lauren looked at her and shrugged. 'It's in Mayfair. A woman's name?'

Una clapped her hands together. 'Annabel's! Respectable, I like it. Your friend has good taste. This dress is perfect, then.'

'If you say so!'

'Indeed I do.' Una reached for her fruit-scented vape

stick and offered a hit to Lauren, who shook her head. 'Fair enough. Okay, babe, you look gorge, have fun tonight, don't accept drinks from strangers, even the cute finance boys – especially the cute finance boys – be safe, and if anyone spills booze on that dress, find soda water *immediately*.'

Lauren glanced at herself in the mirror before taking a photo on her phone. She admitted she looked great, and the strappy black Rossi heels were even better. Past Lauren had definitely made the right choice by buying them as a 'Yay, me!' present when she got promoted at the White House two summers ago, even if they had mostly lived in their shoebox ever since.

In the Uber on the way to meet Joy, though, Lauren felt some of her enthusiasm sour a little bit. The last time she had got dressed up for a night out with a girlfriend, the friend had been Brooke. They had spent many Friday and Saturday nights going out, flirting with everyone at the bar to get free drinks, giggling the whole time. When Lauren looked back on that time of her life, it seemed like a film: sparkling lights, noise and voices and laughter, her best friend by her side, but none of it had been real.

Had Brooke been sleeping with Brian then? Had they already started flirting, texting? Those nights when Lauren would come home from a night out and Brian would still be working late, had Brooke just dropped her off and then gone to his office? Thinking about it made Lauren so angry, the kind of anger that makes you cry, which were the sort of tears that she preferred. To be sad would just make her feel pathetic, a sad sack, a third wheel who didn't even know there had been three wheels in the first place. Anger was good. Anger pushed her forward, moved her to London, put her back on her feet to try again.

111

Lauren dabbed at a single tear before it could fall. Una would absolutely kill her if she smudged her perfect winged eyeliner.

Joy, in a corset top, flared trousers and the sexiest heels, was on the steps outside Annabel's when Lauren's Uber pulled up to the curb, chatting and laughing with one of the sharply dressed doormen. With Christmas around the corner, the private members-only club had already put up its famous festive facade on the front of the building, which illuminated the entire section of the street with its bright lights and colourful sculptures. 'Well, hello there!' Joy cried when Lauren stepped out of the car. 'Look at you! Can't get this at TK Maxx, can you? Serge, this is Lauren, and she absolutely demands to be let in. She used to work at the White House, you know.' Joy stage-whispered that last sentence, then gave him a wink.

'Well, guess we'll let her in anyway,' the man said, pulling at the large brass doorknob, the number '46' above the image of a crown. The numbers reminded Lauren of the house where she grew up, one of them always slightly crooked due to the fact that her mum could never hammer them quite—

'Oh, no no no,' Joy said, taking her by the arm and pulling her into a hug. 'No getting all sentimental and mopey tonight. We are here tonight to be thankful and' – she pulled Lauren away from her and held her out at arm's length – 'to have F-U-N.'

Lauren took a deep breath. 'How did you know I was getting all sentimental?!' she said.

'Your face does a thing when you get in your head like that.'

'My face does a thing?'

'Lauren . . .'

'Okay yes, you're right. Let's have fun.'

The place was stunning. There were sculptures everywhere,

including a winged unicorn attached to a hot-air balloon manning the large staircase at the centre of the Palladian building. Each room had its own theme, and florals bloomed in all of them – live ones in giant vases and decorative ones on wallpapers, carpets and the silk furniture.

'So are you a member here?' Lauren said, yelling to be heard over the music. It wasn't clubby or jazzy, sort of a mix between the two, and Lauren liked it a lot.

'Are you asking if I'm an actual member? Because, at those prices? No. But do I *belong*? Oh sweetie, of course I do,' Joy purred, slipping her arm into Lauren's as they walked through the room and towards the back bar. 'Just have a lot of – hey, you! – friends here, and some who like to repay me for favours I did back at Scotland – oh my God, hi! You look *amazing*! – Yard.'

'Favours?' Lauren asked.

'Best not to ask too many questions,' Joy said faux sternly.

Stopping at one of the club's many rooms, Lauren marvelled at the giant pink quartz bar that was seemingly lit from within and cast the most flattering glow on anyone who stood by it. Plush fabric chairs and booths nestled against dark corners, and every single one of them seemed to have someone either very beautiful, very famous or both tucked into them. It almost seemed like the first day of a ritzy, glamourous summer camp: people crying out across the room before rushing to hug one another; others deep in conversation at the bar, making points while poking each other in the shoulders; women going off in twos and threes to the bathroom, heads together as they whispered on their way there. There was a camaraderie that Lauren hadn't felt in a long time, not at the White House and certainly not at the Palace.

She had missed this so much.

'*There* she is,' Joy said as Lauren smiled to herself. 'Just wait until you have a drink. Or two. You'll be positively beaming.' She held up a finger at the bartender, who glided over to her like he was on roller skates and immediately kissed the back of her hand. 'Babe, can we get two gin gimlets, please? With Hendrick's. Don't treat me wrong.'

The bartender winked and gave a knowing smile in response, and Lauren gaped at Joy as he floated away. 'Do you know him?' she asked.

'It's possible,' Joy said with a smile as she pulled her card out of her purse. 'First round is on me. You spent all that money on those sad decorations.'

Lauren did not want to think about her Thanksgiving trinkets at this moment. 'Wait, have you and the bartender hooked up?'

'It's possible,' Joy replied, then burst out laughing when she saw Lauren's face. 'Hugo and I went to law school together, had some fun times together . . .' Joy trailed off with a knowing smile. 'But then I met the man who became my husband, and Hugo chucked it all for acting classes instead. He's one of the good ones.'

Hugo winked at Joy as he started to pull out clean cocktail glasses. 'What about you, Joy? The Palace treating you all right, yeah? DEI and all?'

Joy rolled her eyes a bit. 'Oh, you know, only took them centuries to hire someone. But it's going.'

'Well, if you ever want to bartend . . .' he said, gesturing at the club, his smile clearly indicating that he was joking.

'Oh, this place cannot afford me!' Joy laughed. 'Plus I'd miss this one here.' Joy looked Lauren up and down. 'Where'd you dig this number up, hmm? I love it. You should wear this at the next press briefing.'

'My neighbour, Una,' Lauren said. 'I still don't quite know what she does for a living, and I think maybe I don't want to know, but she has the most amazing wardrobe. She really came through.'

'She did indeed,' Joy said. 'Definitely keep her in your back pocket for future use. Oh, thaaaaaank you,' she said as Hugo expertly slid two perfect gimlets towards them. 'I was just telling Lauren what a gem you are. Hugo, listen.' Joy leant towards the bar to make her point. 'Do you have any single friends? Because this one' – Joy jerked a thumb in Lauren's direction – 'is most definitely looking.'

Normally, Lauren would have wanted to die, but this time, she found herself leaning in as well, eyeing up Hugo's square jaw and perfectly groomed facial hair.

'Let me think on it,' he said with a grin. 'I'm sure I could rustle up one or two.'

'You do that,' Joy said. 'And don't worry, we'll be back, so if you think of anyone . . .' She made a little 'write it down' gesture and then pointed towards Lauren.

'Nice meeting you!' Lauren said as Joy started to drag her away. 'Are you going to introduce me to every potentially single man in this bar?' she asked.

'Do you have a problem with that?'

Lauren thought for three seconds. 'No, I do not.'

Joy raised her gimlet in a toast. 'Let's start with the A's!'

Joy later swore up and down that it was only a coincidence that she introduced Lauren to both Aiden and Albert first, but by then the Hendrick's was starting to settle in her stomach and Lauren found herself laughing along with both of them, leaning against Joy as she talked about her time at the White House and making the leap across the ocean. 'I don't know, I was just ready for something new,' she said, omitting all the ugly parts. 'I think we should do another round,' she said to Joy, who was only too quick to agree.

Hugo set them up with possibly the best Negroni Lauren had ever had, so pretty that it looked like the sun sinking into the ocean, and Joy led her down to the basement level while Lauren carefully balanced her drink. 'You should definitely stay in touch with Hugo,' Lauren said. 'Just in case he ends up not shacked up anymore. Because these drinks are—'

She stopped talking then, though, because standing next to an intricately patterned sofa that resembled peacock feathers was the last person she expected to see – Oscar.

'So I think we've made our way to the O's,' Joy said quietly.

'Did you know he was here?' Lauren whisper-hissed, and wished she was both more sober and more drunk.

'No!' Joy protested. 'I mean, not at *first*. I just saw him when I was talking over there and now he's over . . . here.' She turned Lauren to face her. 'You do realise he's a reporter, yes?'

'Is that a serious question?'

'I know, I know, I just need to know that you know what you're getting into.'

'I have *absolutely* no idea what I'm getting into,' Lauren said, glancing over Joy's shoulder at Oscar again.

'Well, I do,' Joy said, gently poking her in the arm. 'And you need to be careful, all right? If you're going to flirt or hook up or do anything with that man over there, you need to be *careful*. Also, we cannot discuss this at work. After-hours only. I like to keep my professional and personal lines very well-defined.'

''Kay,' Lauren said. 'I thought journalists weren't allowed in here anyway.'

'Well, there's your opening line,' Joy said. 'Now. Shoulders back, stand up straight, and I'm going to pretend I didn't see anything.'

Maybe it was the gin, Campari and vermouth meeting up and deciding to become immediate best friends, but Lauren felt a renewed burst of warmth, of possibility. The club was buzzing and full of energy, and for the first time in what felt like months, she was having fun. Oscar was standing there, the top two buttons of his knitted polo undone, one hand in his pocket at he sipped something dark on the rocks, talking to a male friend. When he glanced up and saw Lauren, she remembered that she was good at a lot of things, and not all of them had to do with work.

Especially not this.

'Well, hello, stranger,' Oscar said as Lauren sidled up to him, and the friend, bless him, got the message and slipped away with a 'Dude, I'll catch up with you in a bit.'

'I didn't know they allowed reporters in here,' Lauren said, taking Joy's advice.

'I have my ways.' Oscar smiled. 'So how did you wind up here? Keeping tabs on a rogue royal?'

'No, I'm off the clock tonight,' she replied, sipping at her drink without taking her eyes off him. 'Happy Thanksgiving and all that.'

'Ah, that's right, the day of gratitude,' Oscar said. 'Where you celebrate your narrow escape from our country and also eat sweet potatoes with marshmallows. Because that makes obvious sense.'

'Naturally,' Lauren said. 'Except I hate marshmallows. We're a savoury family.'

'So you're celebrating in a British supper club?' Oscar took a sip of his own drink, and Lauren didn't miss the fact that his eyes didn't leave hers, either.

117

Damn, these were strong drinks.

'Well, my mum was actually supposed to visit for a long weekend, but she had to work at the last minute, so Joy suggested that we go out instead.'

'Oh, I'm sorry to hear that,' Oscar said, then held up his glass. 'To your mum's next trip, then.'

She clinked her glass delicately against his. 'So why are *you* here? Are *you* the one tracking a rogue royal? Should I be worried?'

He laughed, and his smile had somehow got even better since the last time she had seen him at their press conference last week. 'Not quite,' he replied. 'I was covering an event earlier, and well, it led me here afterwards. And luckily the doorman is a fan of some of my pieces, so he didn't turn me away when he probably should have.'

Lauren held up her glass again. 'To the doorman,' she said, and they clinked again. There was a moment of silence, and the air felt like it was pulsating between them.

'Do you want to go—?' Oscar started to say over the pounding music, gesturing with a thumb over his shoulder.

'Yes,' Lauren said.

She followed him up the stairs as they pushed through what felt like an endless wall of perfectly dressed people, but all she could really focus on was the way Oscar's hand reached back for hers, keeping her close so they didn't get separated in the crowd. His fingers weren't too soft, weren't too rough, and it was definitely the Negroni talking at this point, but Lauren thought that her hand seemed to fit perfectly in his.

They stopped at the club's opulent Southeast Asian–inspired Elephant Room, which was still busy with patrons but much quieter without the presence of a DJ. They made their way to a velvet sofa with soft cushions and sat down, their thighs touching. 'So,' he said. 'We're both off the clock. What a coincidence.'

Lauren smiled despite herself and tried not to think about what James or Eugene would say if they saw her at Annabel's, drinking with a journalist. 'It is indeed, but everything is off the record,' she quickly added. 'Just friends tonight?'

'Just friends,' Oscar agreed, and Lauren hoped she wasn't imagining the way he sounded just a bit disappointed. 'So. Bearnas Lauren Morgan.'

'Oh, not this bullshit again,' Lauren said, leaning into the cushions and tossing back the rest of her drink.

'What?' Oscar said with a grin. 'That's your name! I'm just saying it, that's all.'

'You're baiting me,' she said, 'and goddamnit, it worked.'

'Okay, sorry, sorry. Lauren. Is that better?'

It was.

'Maybe,' she replied. 'So, Oscar. Are you still writing a feature about me?'

He shrugged, regarding her. 'Sometimes.'

'Anything interesting I should know?'

'Hmm.' Oscar pretended to think. 'Your mother lives in Atlanta, Georgia.'

Lauren pretended to gasp. 'Well, that's news to me.'

'You left Washington, DC, and nobody really seems to know why.'

'I feel like you need a magnifying glass and a deerstalker cap when you talk like this.'

'Those are for detectives, not journalists.' Oscar grinned. 'So you don't want to talk about your time at the White House? Off the record?'

'If you want me to talk about that, I'm going to need a few more of these.' Lauren tapped her empty glass.

'On it. Excuse me!' Oscar said, standing up to head to the bar a few metres from their sofa. 'Are you a tequila girl?'

'Hell yes, I am.'

'Excellent.'

Two pours of Don Julio 1942 later, Lauren wasn't sure if the drinks had been a good idea or a very, very bad one.

'So let me get this straight,' Oscar said. He had undone another button on his polo, and at this point Lauren was pretty sure that she was going to make out with him by the end of the night. 'Your ex-boyfriend left you for your best friend, and instead of fistfighting both of them, you came to work at the Palace instead.'

'That's a very tabloid-esque summary,' Lauren said, tracing the rim of her glass with her finger.

'How long were you two together?'

Lauren had to think for a minute. 'Four ...? Yes, four years.'

'Wow.' Oscar shook his head. 'And did he work at the White House, too?'

Lauren narrowed her eyes. 'Oh, come on.'

'What?' He laughed and signalled the bartender again.

'I know you know the answer to this!' she said. 'I bet you still have his *Atlantic* profile in an open tab on both your phone *and* your laptop.'

'Okay, fine, yes, I know that Brian Martinez is a rising star in DC.'

'That's probably because he tells everyone that he is,' Lauren said. 'Only half kidding about that, by the way.'

'But I didn't know that Brooke was your best friend. That one's new.'

'Well, consider it an exclusive from an unnamed source,'

Lauren said. 'You can also have the exclusive that she's a backstabbing betrayer who backstabs and betrays.'

'I . . . would not disagree with you on that point.'

'You know what really sucks?' Lauren said. 'Oh, thank you, you're the GOAT,' she added as a bartender set down two spicy margaritas. 'Do you know Hugo? He's, like, three rooms over. He's great. And so are you.'

'And can we get some water, please,' Oscar said to him.

'Anyway, this is what sucks: They're *happy* together. Like, if they had just fucked behind my back and then broken up once I found out, that'd be one thing. I could live with that. But they're still together. I see them on Insta—'

'You haven't blocked or unfollowed them?' Oscar asked. 'Seriously?'

'I'm petty and have a slight self-destructive streak,' Lauren replied. 'But I see their pics and they just look . . . so happy. They moved in together. They got a dog. His name is Baxter, and I can't even hate him because he's adorable.'

'That is a cute name,' Oscar agreed.

'I feel like . . .' Lauren knew she was definitely drunk at this point because she was about to say the thing out loud, the thing she had only thought in her head for fear of it sounding true. 'Like Brooke is having the life that I was supposed to have, and now that she has it, I don't know what my life is supposed to look like anymore. It's just empty space and I'm filling it in as I go, and I don't know if it's right or wrong.'

'I think that's how everyone feels in their twenties, though,' Oscar said. 'Right? Please tell me I'm right?'

'Do you?' Lauren asked, and then pounced when he nodded. 'Okay, I'm doing a feature on *you* now. Please tell me all about your last girlfriend. Or boyfriend. Or either. Or both. I don't judge.'

121

'Girlfriend,' Oscar said, laughing. 'But thank you, I appreciate that. Her name was Mari.'

'God, that's almost as cute as Baxter. And how'd you meet?'

'At work, of course, because that's practically the only place I go anymore,' Oscar said. 'She worked at the paper. She was a copy editor.'

'Very exacting, I bet.'

'You could say that. Anyway, it didn't work out and she broke up with me because I worked too much.'

'Do you?' Lauren asked.

'No more than you,' Oscar said.

'So that's a yes.' Lauren raised her glass and held it in front of his. 'To the exes for being complete fucking assholes.'

'I will absolutely drink to that,' Oscar said, both of them wincing as they tossed back the tequila remnants.

Lauren felt like things were moving just a little bit more slowly than they had been an hour ago, like she was floating in the ocean and looking up at the sky.

'You know what?' she said.

'What?'

'Still off the record.'

Oscar made a 'cross my heart' motion.

'I don't want to talk about our exes anymore. Or work.'

Oscar quirked an eyebrow at her. 'Oh really? What do you want to talk about, then?'

'I don't want to talk at all.' Lauren held his gaze, their eyes locking together for a few extra beats until Oscar stood up abruptly and took her hand.

'Follow me,' he said.

She walked behind him back through the labyrinth of rooms and hallways until they arrived back in the basement's Jungle Bar, the thumping bass of the DJ's throwback house music instantly reverberating in their bodies as they stepped in. 'Still want to stay off the record?' Oscar raised his voice to ask, pressing up against her until she was flat against the wall, the animal-print damask wallpaper soft against her hands.

'Absolutely.'

'Good.' And then his lips were on hers, and Lauren, for the first time in months, felt her entire body relax.

Fuck, he was good at this.

Oscar had just moved down to the soft spot behind her ear when Lauren saw Joy come over, her eyes widening before immediately doing a 180. A few seconds later she felt her phone buzz in her purse. 'Do you have to get that?' Oscar said, his slight stubble scratching at her cheek. She loved it now and would hate the rash tomorrow.

'It's just Joy,' Lauren said. 'Trust me.'

Oscar didn't ask for further information, which was for the best because he had moved down to the base of her neck, pressing a kiss to the hollow of her throat, and even though it was just a small gesture of intimacy, Lauren knew that she had to either stop it now or not stop at all.

'Oscar,' she panted, pushing at his shoulders. 'Oscar Mason.'

'What?' he asked, putting his mouth back on hers. Lauren could almost taste her perfume.

'We have to stop,' she said. 'Oh, fuck. Wait, no, we have to stop.'

Oscar pulled back, and under the dim lights, his eyes looked hazy and electric. 'Why?'

'Because I'm about to do something really stupid and so are you.' She put her hand on his chest, feeling his pulse racing and heat radiating.

'But,' he said, pulling away a bit, and Lauren instantly

123

missed the weight of him. 'What if ... Fuck. Fuck, okay. You're right.'

Lauren ran her other hand through her hair, breathing heavily. 'I should go home.'

Oscar rested his forehead against hers, nodding. '*We* should go home.'

'I don't enjoy being this responsible all the time, just so you know,' she said to him.

'Clearly,' he replied, a little dejected, before resting his hand on top of her head as he pushed away from her once more. 'You really are a buzzkill.'

She laughed when he couldn't hold back a teasing smile, gently shoving him so he stepped even further away. 'I suppose it wouldn't shock you to know that I was also hall monitor *and* class secretary in middle school.'

'Not in the slightest.'

Lauren pulled the thin strap of her dress up over her shoulder and wondered where her bag was. She hadn't seen it in ... minutes? Hours? 'By any chance do you remember—?' she started to say.

'Joy has it,' Oscar said, then shrugged. 'I'm a journalist. I pay attention to details.'

'Well, I'm glad one of us does, especially at this particular moment.' Lauren took the arm that he offered her, curling her fingers around his bicep. He felt warm under his top, and she once again became annoyed with herself for being responsible. 'Now where is Joy?'

They found Joy in the thick of the dance floor, living it up right in the centre of the crowd, a champagne flute held high above her head as she danced to Robin S's 'Show Me Love,' Hugo the bartender dancing alongside her. When she spotted Lauren, she screamed and pointed to her, holding out her hand, but then she saw Oscar and screamed again, this time whispering something into Hugo's ear before elbowing her way off the dance floor without spilling a single drop of her drink.

'I'm not going to ask questions,' she said, slightly breathless from her dancing.

'I find that very hard to believe,' Lauren said.

'Same,' Oscar added.

Joy turned to Lauren, still not spilling her drink. 'How drunk are you? Very drunk? Do you need me to pour you into an Uber?'

'Well . . . I'm standing,' Lauren said. 'At least, I think I'm standing. I *am* standing, right?'

'You are most definitely upright,' Joy said.

'Is Hugo all over you?' Lauren asked. 'Or am I seeing things?'

'Definitely not seeing things.' Joy grinned.

'Are you being safe?' Lauren asked, and then grabbed on to Joy's arm to steady herself.

'Look at you, adorable when you're wasted. And yes, I'm safe, thank you for being a good friend, but I am doing just fine. Very fine.'

Lauren leant in and whispered-screamed over the music, 'Oh my God. Are you guys going to hook up?'

'Unless my friend here needs me to take her home, that's the plan.' Joy pulled back a little, giggling. 'Are you good to get in a cab, or do you need help?'

'I'm fine,' Lauren replied. She wasn't entirely sure that was true, but there was no way she was going to ruin Joy's fun.

'Okay, Mr Reporter, I've got it from here.' Joy nodded towards a red lipstick mark on Oscar's chin, then took Lauren by the arm. 'I have your bag, don't worry. Hugo put it safely behind his bar.'

'Text me once you arrive home,' Oscar said to Lauren. 'All right? I'm serious. Just so I know you get home safe.'

'I will,' Lauren promised. 'Absolutely. Cross my heart. You can count on me.'

Oscar, it turned out, could not count on her.

Lauren woke up the next morning to a stream of foggy sunshine spilling across her bed. The dress she had borrowed from Una was tangled around her waist, she was still wearing one high heel, and there was a half-eaten Nature Valley granola bar next to her head on the pillow, which was slightly concerning because Lauren had no memory of eating the other half or even buying granola bars.

And why did she eat it *in bed*? The crumbs!

'Shit,' she whispered, pressing the heels of her hands into her eyes and wishing the blinds could just close themselves so she wouldn't have to do it. Had the morning light always been this bright in London? It felt like a laser piercing through her skull, right above her left eye, and when she sat up, she felt like she was on a ship that had suddenly listed to the right and taken her brain along with it.

'Shit,' she said again, because there wasn't a better word for how she felt in that moment, but also because it was her own fault. Mixing her liquor like she was eighteen years old again and hanging out at some frat house party? Why didn't she just toss back a White Claw while she was at it?

She attempted to shift her weight to stand up, then remembered that she had a job and usually that job began quite early in the morning. She fumbled for her phone while trying to not vomit, her hand finally reaching around it under her pillow. Like the Nature Valley bar, she had no memory of putting her phone there, but at least she had it now.

126

And, she discovered as she tapped the screen, she also had fourteen texts and eight missed calls from Oscar.

Shit.

'Hi,' she said as soon as he answered. 'I'm sorry, I'm alive. I mean, I feel like I'm dead, I wish I was dead, but I'm alive.'

'Oh my God,' Oscar said. 'I was about to send Joy over to your apartment. What happened to that whole Girl Scout "cross my heart" promise?!'

'Oscar, you're at an eight and I'm going to need you at a four right now,' Lauren groaned. 'I'm sorry, I really am, I just got home and' – she glanced around the tiny apartment, seeing now the melee she had left in her wake – 'crashed.'

'Next time, I'm taking you home,' Oscar said.

Lauren paused. 'Next time?'

'I mean . . . You know what I mean.'

And despite the throbbing pain in her head, despite the granola pieces lodged between her molars, and despite the fact that she was absolutely going to be late for work, Lauren smiled. 'I had fun last night,' she said. 'I'm not having any fun this morning, but last night was worth it.'

There was a pause on the other end, and Lauren could swear that she heard him smile. 'Me too,' he said. 'Better get to work, though. It's almost 9:00 a.m. We've got your weekly press briefing today.'

'Wait, what?' Lauren pulled her phone away from her ear, switching Oscar to speaker and immediately flicking on her screen to see the time.

And just like that, her headache became much, much worse.

'FUCK!'

Chapter 6

'Well, this is . . . something.' James regarded Lauren as she half sat, half deflated into a chair in the conference room. 'Quite something. Indeed.'

Lauren held up her hand. 'You're being very loud right now.'

'I'm barely murmuring.'

'Ooh, that. That was loud.'

Harriet came into the room next, holding a pile of file folders (what on earth was in those folders? As soon as she stopped wanting to die, Lauren was going to teach Harriet the meaning of digitisation and its benefits in modern society). '*Good morning!*' she cheerfully sang out.

Both Lauren and Joy, who had appeared a moment earlier – and looked, frankly, way too fresh-faced for someone who had been dancing on a table with a bartender a mere six hours earlier – hissed in response. 'Harriet, bless you, but please no,' Joy said, then passed one of the lattes in her hand to Lauren, along with a bag from Leon. 'Here you go. Half of that is mine, don't get any ideas.'

'Well!' James said. 'I see you two had some fun last night.'

Through the fog of her hangover, Lauren thought that he looked a little envious. 'Celebrating being thankful, I assume?'

'Sure,' Lauren mumbled as she blew into the lid of her coffee and took a sip. 'Joy, you're a hero. You had the ability to go get breakfast *and* put on makeup?' She shook her head in appreciation. 'You might be a saint. I'm going to have the pope look into it, but I feel confident about your chances.'

'Oh God, no,' Joy said. 'Uber Eats. Worth every penny. I got sausage muffins, too.'

Lauren whimpered with happiness.

Violet, who was sitting at the end of the table with her ever-present phone in her hands, didn't even look up at them. 'It's like watching your mother be hungover on New Year's Day,' she muttered.

'I'm only like five years older than you!' Lauren started to protest, but then winced and reached for the bag, deciding to take up Violet's misplaced ageism at a later date.

'Good morning, everyone!' Eugene boomed as he came into the room, a suited older man following closely behind him. 'Harold Cockburn is joining our meeting as we discuss logistics of the US state visit. Lauren, I assume you're ready with updates.'

It was definitely not a question, and luckily Lauren was. She nodded. 'It's great to finally meet you in person, Harold. I can email our latest notes to you right now,' she said. Harold was the private secretary to the Strathearns, who are based at Kensington Palace, though he seemed to spend more time at BP than at his own office – usually complaining to Eugene.

He nodded primly as he sat down. He seemed like Eugene's more robust-looking twin, at least in poise and attitude, the kind of person whose waistcoat was buttoned a little bit tighter than it needed to be. Across the table, Lauren could see Violet giving him a less-than-pleased look before she turned back to her phone.

'He's always so rude.' Violet's text pinged through to her laptop.

'Fantastic,' Lauren wrote back.

'Joy,' Harold said, looking at his phone. 'Nice to see you again.'

'And you, Harold,' she replied, giving him a smile that could only be described as 'painful.'

'Joy and I were in touch over a case at Scotland Yard a few years back,' Harold said to Eugene. 'Some of those Occupy protesters got it in their heads that the Strathearns would consider listening to their list of demands and attempted to take matters into their own hands.' He smirked to himself. 'They're gone and the Strathearns are still here, so I suppose we all know how that worked out.'

Of all the mornings. Truly.

Judging from Joy's face, she felt the same way as Lauren and Violet. 'Well, fortunately,' she said, sitting up in her chair so that she was eye to eye with Harold, 'we were able to de-escalate the situation, and of course, this was many years ago.' She sounded sharp, no-nonsense, and Lauren realised that not only was Joy good at her job, she was probably also a great mum, too. 'Now, shall we get started?'

'Plans have been emailed,' Lauren confirmed.

'Then let's begin,' Eugene said, clearly enjoying being in charge of this meeting.

'Right now, we have the Prince and Princess of Strathearn having tea with the president at Kensington Palace on the Thursday of his visit,' Lauren said. 'The press lineup will be one TV camera, one photographer and one photo camera, so it should be a fairly intimate event. Plus most of the other media will be covering the state banquet that night, so they'll be prepping for that and—'

'Will they be watching the speeches live in the room?' Harold interrupted.

'No, we'll have everything set up on a live feed in a separate room here at BP,' she said.

'Good,' he said. 'Keep those jackals in their own pen.'

Lauren thought of Oscar.

'They also of course need to apply to cover the event,' she continued. 'I'll field enquiries until the week before and then will confirm accreditation. There's limited space, so—'

'I'll also be part of choosing that list,' Harold said, and at this point, even Harriet seemed to be frowning at him, which probably didn't bode well for Harold.

Lauren glanced at James, then Eugene. 'Um, I don't feel that—'

'I've been working with the Strathearns for nearly twenty years, and you have, forgive me, been here for approximately twenty minutes.'

Every single pair of eyes in the room shifted to Lauren.

'I may have been here for, as you so kindly put it, twenty minutes, but that doesn't change the fact that I do know what I'm doing with regards to my job. In fact, this isn't the first state visit that I've been involved—'

'From the American perspective—'

'The only perspective that matters right now with re-gards to media arrangements is mine, and yes, in fact, it is American.' Now it was Lauren's turn to interrupt him, and if she was being honest, it felt damn good. 'But it's also a per-spective that's in full service to my job and to my coworkers and to the institution that has trusted me to represent the monarchy to the highest of standards, which I have done and will continue to do.'

Lauren's Messages app flashed up. It was Violet again, this time with just the boxing glove emoji.

'Cockburn,' Eugene said quietly. 'Lauren will handle this. If your assistance is required, rest assured, it will be sought.'

'Fine,' he said. 'What's next on the agenda?'

Lauren was still both smarting from the argument and reeling from Eugene's defence of her when Violet said, 'Coverage of the Duke of Exeter has gone through the roof, he's on every cover. We tried to stop them on the grounds of privacy, but the *National Record* managed to print old photos of him and his ex-wife on a beach, declaring him His, um, "Royal Fineness".'

Joy covered her mouth to keep from spitting out her coffee.

'Well, thank you, Violet, for that important update,' Eugene said.

'He's been so good for engagement,' Violet said. 'Just that one visit Lauren arranged has brought in more traffic than any other member of the family since I started here eighteen months ago.' She looked directly at Mr Cockburn as she said that last bit.

'Well, hopefully this doesn't descend into some sort of competition for clicks. The monarchy has thrived for eleven hundred years without TikTok,' Harold said as he stood to signal the end of the meeting.

'Actually, Harold,' Joy said, 'while I have you here, I wanted to discuss the community outreach opportunity for the Strathearns I emailed you about—'

'Of course,' he said. 'Email my office and we can set up a meeting.'

'Yes, well, your office seems to have some difficulty answering their emails.'

'Everyone has a lot on at the moment,' he replied.

'Of course, who doesn't.' Joy's voice didn't sound like she was asking a question. 'But I really need a response on this if it's to work—'

'As I said previously, contact the office and we can set up a meeting. I'll let them know to look for it. Thank you all for the updates, everyone, varied as they were.'

He seemed to be waiting for someone to reply, but instead they all just looked at him. 'Thank you, Cockburn,' James said. 'I'm sure we'll see each other soon.'

'That man,' Joy said to Lauren after the meeting as they headed down to the BP staff cafeteria. 'Everyone on the team at Scotland Yard hated him, too.'

'I don't want to talk about Harold, I want to talk about Hugo!' Lauren said. 'The fact that Harold delayed this conversation makes me dislike him even more. Tell me everything, or at least everything you're comfortable sharing.'

Joy laughed a little as they walked through the wood-paneled entrance area – complete with its displays of gifts to the Queen from around the world – and into the main canteen. It had been designed to look like a real restaurant, but the harsh lighting and cheap furniture weren't fooling anyone. Underneath a wall of blown-up menus from previous years at Buckingham Palace, Balmoral and Windsor Castle were a stack of trays, and Lauren and Joy each took one as they surveyed their options.

'I'm not a big fan of kiss and tell, but let's just say it was a nostalgic reunion,' Joy said. 'Nothing serious, but it was a lot of fun. I got home, showered and changed, and came into work, so I am both knackered *and* starving.' She asked for the stuffed pepper fajitas.

'I love this for you,' Lauren said. 'This is how we should celebrate Thanksgiving every year from now on, you and me at Annabel's.' She surveyed the cafeteria options, then also took the fajitas and something that kind of resembled a salad.

'Well, if *that's* what your holiday is like, then I can see why everyone would be thankful.' Joy shot a dirty smile at Lauren, who laughed and pretended to punch her in the arm.

'I can say that going from Hugo last night to Harold Cockburn this morning was whiplash I did not need,' Joy added as they progressed down the line. 'A few years ago, we were in a meeting and we all started discussing our Christmas plans, and Harold turns to me – *me*, the only Black woman in the room – and asks if my family follows all the Christmas traditions.' Joy raised an eyebrow. 'I *mean*.'

'What did you say?' Lauren asked.

'I told him we celebrate just like every other family at the holidays: We leave out a mince pie and milk for Santa, eat and drink too much, watch *Home Alone* and fight over the last purple Quality Street.' Joy shook her head then frowned at one of the menu signs. 'What on earth is "Eve's pudding and cream"? Who's Eve?'

'Even Harriet was glaring at Harold during the meeting, did you see?' Lauren asked, passing Joy some silverware wrapped in a napkin.

'Oh thank you,' Joy replied. 'And bless Hattie. Maybe we can put her in charge of him for a bit? Just, you know, see if the whole Grim Reaper thing is true?'

Lauren couldn't help but laugh. 'You're terrible. C'mon, let's find a seat.'

Joy cackled in response. 'I know. No, no, not over there, that's where the garden party ladies sit.' She nodded towards a group of older women who all looked like they were wearing the same flower-printed curtains that Lauren had had in her bedroom when she was six. 'Let's go over here. So what are you going to do with His so-called Royal Fineness, hmm?'

'I'm just going to let the tabloids do their thing,' Lauren said. 'I don't think he's even seen the coverage, and by the time it dies down, it'll be Christmas o'clock and we can re-start the news cycle all over again. No, not over there. That's where the bagpiper who wakes up the Queen each morning sits.'

'Aww, he's harmless, though. Always sits by himself, poor lad.' Still, Joy followed Lauren towards an empty seat. 'Those photos of the duke *were* pretty nice,' Joy said. 'Maybe I want to marry a sheep farmer now.'

'Let's hope the rest of the country is also feeling the same way,' Lauren replied, finally setting her tray down at the empty table. 'Is that man over there wearing a cape?'

Joy didn't even look behind her. 'Probably, that's one of the Royal Collection chaps. They got their PhD in seventeenth-century ceramics or something like that and now they either work here or the checkouts at Tesco's.'

Lauren laughed and then glanced at her phone as a text appeared on the screen. 'Oh God.'

'What?'

Lauren looked at Joy. 'Do you remember the thing we agreed to not discuss at work?'

'Of course I do, it was my idea.'

'It wants to meet for coffee in an hour.'

Oscar was already sitting inside the homey New Acre coffee shop tucked inside Westminster Chapel when Lauren arrived. She waved hello to him as she ordered her own drink, then made her way across the quiet café towards him, feeling a little more awkward with every step. Oscar hadn't been the first drunken hook-up in her life, but he was definitely the first guy who wanted to meet up the day after, and Lauren was secretly grateful that the barista took an exceptionally long time making her oat milk latte.

'Hey,' Oscar said, standing up a little as she sat down. 'Thanks for meeting me so quickly.'

'Of course,' Lauren said. 'Is everything okay? Did you have a story that I have to publicly deny but privately confirm?' She had been joking, but as soon as the words were out of her mouth, she regretted them. 'Wait, please tell me that's not the case.'

'No, no, this isn't work related,' Oscar said. 'I just thought we should . . . talk.'

'Talk,' Lauren repeated.

'You know, about last night,' Oscar said.

'Ah.' She glanced down at the disappearing foam on her latte before looking back at him. The flat patch on the back of his head was giving overslept vibes, but he still looked unfairly handsome and put-together. 'Well, I had a good time,' she finally said. 'Let a little steam out of the kettle, as they say.'

'They do say that.' Oscar nodded as he fiddled with his pain au chocolat. 'And I know we were both drinking, so I also wanted . . .'

A lightbulb went on in Lauren's head.

'Oh!' she said. 'No, I was fine. Well, I mean, I wasn't *fine*, I was pretty toasted, but no regrets at all.' She reached over and put her hand on his. 'Seriously. I'm good. I had fun. We should do it again sometime.'

Oscar grinned. 'We should do a proper date.'

'A date?' Lauren repeated. It was one thing to toss back some tequila and make out with a reporter, but a date? Joy had warned her about this exact thing last night, and Lauren wondered how close to the line she could get without crossing it.

'I took it too far, didn't I?' Oscar said, holding up his hands.

'No, no, I like dates!' Lauren said. 'But I think I need to go a little slow for now. You heard about my last relationship, I told you all about it last night. I think? Sorry about that, by the way.'

'I'm glad you told me,' he said, and something about the sincerity sent another rush of warmth through Lauren. 'The reporter in me loves facts.'

'Well then, the fact is that I got hurt. A lot.' Now it was Oscar's turn to put his hand over hers, his palm both soft and cold. 'I need a lot more runway before my next flight, so to speak. Plus I just started at the Palace barely four weeks ago, and if it got out that I was dating a reporter . . .'

'You'd be the story.' Oscar finished the sentence for her.

'Let me get through Christmas,' Lauren said. 'I feel like I'm restacking blocks into a tower after another kid knocked them down. I need a little bit more of a foundation before I start adding turrets.'

'That's a hell of a metaphor.'

'Thank you.'

'What about a cheeky snog here and there, though?'

Lauren laughed at his question, as did he. 'Look, last night wasn't my worst Thanksgiving,' she said. 'You're good. We're good.' She paused as both of their phones buzzed with identical social media notifications about the Duke of Exeter being spotted biking around London.

'Breaking news,' Oscar said sarcastically. 'I'm telling you, there is nothing happening behind that guy's eyes.'

'Excellent,' Lauren said.

'That wasn't a compliment.'

'I didn't think it was. You have a crumb.' She reached to flick it away from the corner of his mouth just as he did the same, their fingertips brushing before Lauren pulled her hand away.

'I don't care if the only thing in the duke's head is Taylor Swift on a constant loop,' Lauren said. 'We're not asking him to solve the climate crisis. We just need people to like him and want to know more about him and the work he plans to do.'

'So he's making his grand public debut at Balmoral? Can I run that now?'

'He will indeed. And no, you can't. You'll see him at the Christmas Day church service this year and then we're heading down—'

Oscar pointed a finger in the air as he sipped the last of his coffee.

'—up to Balmoral.'

'See, that's an easy one for him, though,' he remarked. 'Christmas is just everyone funneling into the chapel, wearing great coats and smiling and then all the rest of it is completely away from the cameras.'

'Gee, it's almost like I'm good at my job.' Lauren smirked. 'And you can send any complaints, in writing, to Her Majesty the Queen herself.'

'Well, try not to use too many big words when you speak with him. There's a reason he surrounded himself with sheep and not humans in New Zealand this whole time.'

'Everyone loves a second act,' Lauren countered, tapping on the notification just to make sure the paparazzi hadn't been following him around the capital.

'Do they?' Oscar asked, a grin on his face. 'Care to share any personal anecdotes about that?'

Lauren pretended to throw her paper napkin at him, even

though she was smiling. 'You're the reporter,' she said. 'Do your research. Go get those facts you love so much.'

'Oh, I think I've got a pretty good start,' he replied.

His phone buzzed again, and he glanced down, his warm brown eyes scanning over the screen. He was getting the little frown lines he got when trying to take in a lot of information at once – Lauren had seen it happen at their weekly press conferences, and she hated how cute she found it.

She didn't hate it so much now.

'Ah, I've got to go,' he said as his phone pinged again, grabbing his bag from the bench and starting to stand up. 'Just been asked to cover an event.' He held up his phone to show what looked like a PDF invite for a movie premiere in Leicester Square. 'The showbiz editor is out of town, and I have to fill in for them for a few things.'

'Ooh, hold the front page.' Lauren smiled, but then caught her breath when Oscar leant down to kiss her cheek goodbye.

Chapter 7

The second press briefing in December didn't go the way Lauren had planned.

Well, the actual session itself was fine. It was the moments after that were a disaster.

'Lauren,' Adam from the *Daily Dispatch* said after she had wrapped up a briefing that included new details on the royals' upcoming Christmas trip to Balmoral. 'Is there really any point in us coming here if you aren't going to confirm anything?'

'As I have told you a dozen times, Adam,' Lauren said without even lifting her head, 'I am happy to discuss the working lives of the royal family and matters relating to the institution, but personal lives are, and have always been, something that we are not in the habit of commenting on. Questions about a prince's hairline are a waste of everyone's time.'

'That's not what I wanted to ask you about,' Adam said, his voice sounding smug, which was never a good sign, and when Lauren turned around, he looked even more pleased with himself.

Lauren sighed.

Since her first day at the Palace, Lauren had grown to dread the weekends. Or more specifically, the tabloid stories that were scheduled to run on a Sunday. For the British press, the Lord's day was somehow reserved for their most scandalous and lurid tabloid nonsense. Most of them were ridiculous – a royal bought a new car, didn't apply for planning permission before building a pool house, *the horror* – but over the years it had also been when some of the monarchy's biggest scandals were laid bare to the world, like the time a very married Prince of Strathearn was photographed dining with an Australian lingerie model during a 'lads' surfing trip, or the Duke of Cumberland was caught secretly selling gifts from dignitaries on 1stDibs. Lauren usually took turns manning the stream of weekend media inquiries from outlets around the world with Harriet, but not knowing what was happening on Harriet's watch made her nervous.

Not as nervous as the *Dispatch* reporter was making her right now, though.

'We're hearing word about the Duke of Exeter and some pretty serious debts, possibly even an imminent bankruptcy filing,' Adam said.

Lauren went cold.

'I'm sure the British taxpayers would be thrilled to learn that they're funding his escape from bankruptcy. That is why he's back, yes? How is he paying them off if he's not earning?'

Lauren hoped her face looked as calm as she didn't feel. 'And do you have any actual reporting? Because rumours do not really count for much.'

'Working on it.' Adam smiled. 'Just giving you a heads-up, that's all.'

'Always appreciated,' Lauren said breezily, then made sure

to spend a few extra minutes chatting with some of the other reporters and gathering her things before leaving the room.

She went straight into Eugene's office. 'We might have a problem,' she said. 'Tell the duke that we need to meet in my office.'

Eugene, who had been on the phone, hung up mid-sentence. 'What's the matter?'

'Not here. My office. It's about his' – she lowered her voice to almost a whisper – 'finances.'

'Give me five,' Eugene said as he stood up and grabbed his phone and laptop. Lauren sat at her desk frantically searching online and on social media for anything new on the Duke of Exeter, scrolling for anything that could confirm Adam's suspicions. She could breathe a little easier once she saw the same stories that she always saw about the duke – the horseback-riding memes, sightings of him cycling around London, ducking into Waitrose, nothing of consequence.

'This had better be a real emergency,' Eugene said. 'Because I just made the duke practically sprint here.'

The French doors to Lauren's office suddenly swung open, and the duke stood in the doorway, his cheeks flushed from the mid-December air. 'Sorry, forgot to knock again.' He smiled, shutting the door behind him as he stepped into the room. 'What's going on?'

Lauren shut her laptop and stood up to lean against her desk. 'The royal editor at the *Daily Dispatch* approached me after the press conference today and asked about the duke's finances. More specifically, debts. He's gathering reporting.'

'Ah,' Eugene said, putting his clasped hands on top of his head like a hat.

'Exactly,' Lauren said. 'He doesn't seem to have anything concrete yet, I think he's just sniffing around. But it's coming.'

'This isn't really anyone's business, certainly not the press's,' the duke said, raising his voice a bit. 'These are not personal debts. I've done nothing illegal, nothing immoral. My business, which I put blood, sweat and tears into, faced unforeseen difficulties when we lost a major client. And despite what people may assume, I don't have unlimited resources. So, like any other business owner, I went to the banks for help, so I could keep my staff – who I cared deeply about – employed, to keep the one thing I had to my name going . . .'

'With respect, that is precisely the problem,' Eugene said, his tone measured but firm. 'You are not just *any* business owner, nor are you simply another person who has fallen on hard times. Your status – your entire existence within this institution – is predicated on the belief that you represent something greater. Stability. Tradition. Continuity. The public does not want to see their royals struggling as they do. They want to believe in the permanence of the Crown, in its ability to rise above ordinary misfortune. If you admit to being "just like anyone else", you risk proving them right when they ask why they should continue to support you at all.'

'So, what, I'm expected to sit back and watch some scumbag hack try to humiliate me with their twist on it? Another life failure to be mocked over?' the duke said, looking deflated. 'Aren't you going to try to stop this?'

'But it's the truth, one can't stop the truth from running,' Eugene responded. 'With all due respect, this is not a story about the heir or even a spare. I suggest you let them write whatever they want to write and take comfort in the fact it will blow over in the blink of an eye.'

'Oh, thank you, Eugene, for making me feel like I'm the commodity that I apparently am,' the duke said. 'So just so

I'm clear, you're saying that because I don't happen to be higher up the family food chain, I don't deserve the same protection the others get.'

'Okay, please, both of you, could you sit down? You're making me nervous by pacing around like that,' Lauren said, pointing at two stiff-backed chairs in front of her desk. 'I realise you have your opinions, but I'm the one, in fact, running the comms department at the Palace, so I'll take it from here.'

Both men plonked down into the chairs. The duke had the faintest tan line on the finger where his wedding ring used to be, Lauren noticed, which made her wonder if he had continued wearing it long after his divorce was finalised. Just the thought made her feel a little bit more sympathetic towards him.

'Until we see evidence that the *Dispatch* even has actual reporting to run a story, we're not doing anything just yet,' Lauren said. 'Right now you're scheduled to make your first public appearance at Balmoral on Christmas Day. That's the plan we've set in motion, and that's the plan we'll continue to execute.

'If Adam had something, he would have said so. The fact he was trying to weasel intel out of me shows he has very little to go off. The man is not as smart as he thinks. All we need to do for now is make sure we're not caught unaware.'

The duke stared at her, quietly fuming. 'So you'd rather not be on top of this?'

'I *am* on top of this,' Lauren said. 'But Eugene's right. Nobody wants you to be human, they need to see you, as a responsible working member of the royal family, taking an incredibly important job seriously and being here for the right reason.' She thought of their conversation back in the car after the children's hospital, the duke saying, 'Well, I *am*

144

a person' and looking surprised by the idea that he would be seen as anything but that.

'I'll make sure to keep all of you informed if I hear anything else,' Lauren continued. 'And I wanted to tell you as soon as possible just in case this turns into a bigger situation than it currently is, but for now, we just get on with things as normal and stay focused on Balmoral.'

'I knew this was a mistake,' the duke seethed. 'I *knew* it. There's not a drop of goddamn honesty or compassion anywhere in this place.'

'Look, I'm on your side,' Lauren told him. 'And I am being honest with you. But this isn't a decision that you get to make on your own. It's also part of *my* job.'

'And mine,' Eugene added, and Lauren resisted the urge to roll her eyes.

'Fine,' the duke said. 'But do me a favour: Next time you want to bring me into an "urgent" conversation about my own life, please don't.' He left as abruptly as he arrived, although careful to not slam the door, his well-honed manners still in effect as it quietly clicked shut.

'If it runs after Balmoral, we'll have a little more wiggle room,' Lauren said to Eugene, then sighed. 'Did I just manage to upset the only royal I'm allowed to speak to?'

'Yes, but you did your job,' Eugene said as he stood up. 'Well done.'

Lauren did a double take at the compliment. 'Um, thank you.'

'Just don't mess it up,' he added as he reached for his buzzing phone.

'That's more like it,' Lauren said. 'Always a pleasure.'

After he left, she went to lock her French doors – she wasn't looking to have someone else burst through them – when she saw the duke walking across the grounds, hands shoved into his coat pockets, his head down, looking small and glum, just a regular human — a *person*.

Lauren had a little insight into that.

The first couple weeks of December had her feeling especially lonely as the decorations continued to go up around London, and her walks home from the tube at night became festooned with lights that reflected off the rain-soaked streets. Even the Palace was fully dressed up — including three fifteen-foot trees in the grand Marble Hall, covered in twinkling lights, mini embroidered crowns and velvet state carriage ornaments. The decorations didn't quite reach the comms office, of course, but Harriet had put a tiny tinsel tree in the shared kitchen, which honestly felt sadder than if no one had done anything at all.

Lauren, having learnt her lesson from the ill-fated Thanksgiving decor fiasco, didn't buy anything for her apartment. She ran into Una either on her way out or coming home from several Christmas parties, including one Saturday night when she was dressed as a scantily clad Mrs. Claus. 'Gotta go and sit on Santa's lap!' Una laughed as she gave herself one last spritz of Baccarat Rouge 540, then sprayed one in Lauren's direction for good measure. 'You staying in tonight? Again? Want to come?'

'I actually have plans for once,' Lauren said. 'I'm meeting my friend at the South Bank Christmas market and then we're going to dinner.'

'Christmas market,' Una repeated, checking her teeth for any lipstick marks. 'My mum *loves* those.' She smiled in the mirror and shook her butt. 'Okay, wish me luck!'

'Good luck!' Lauren said. 'Wait, for what?'

But Una had already scooted away.

Lauren was not far behind her, her coat and hat and scarf

firmly in place. Winter in London was a mixture of freezing cold outside yet boiling hot on the tube. Lauren pulled her knitted hat a little lower on her forehead as she stepped out, the chill cutting through her coat and heavy layers as she walked a few minutes.

She was just turning the corner towards the market when her phone started buzzing insistently, Joy's smiling photo flashing up on the screen.

'Oh no,' Lauren said when she answered.

'Oh yes, unfortunately,' Joy said with a sigh. 'I have to cancel on you. I'm so sorry. Theo was supposed to go to a sleepover at his friend's house tonight but instead he has a double ear infection. He does nothing by halves, this kid.' Joy almost sounded a little proud about that. 'We just got back from the doctor's, and he's got a fever, which means I'm staying home.'

'Theo!' Lauren groaned. 'I'm sorry. That can't be fun.'

'It's nothing but paracetamol and *Roblox* for us tonight,' Joy said. 'I'm so sorry!'

Lauren looked down the street at the crowds of people already walking through the market, nearly everyone coupled up or walking in small groups. 'I just got here.'

'See, it was meant to be. Go and have some mulled wine for me.'

'Okay,' Lauren said. 'Go and do ... whatever *Roblox* does for me, too.'

'Will do!' Joy said, and then, 'Oh, Theo, darling, let's not—' before disconnecting abruptly.

Lauren took a deep breath and put her hands in her pockets. Everything in her body wanted her to turn around right then and go home, put on cosy joggers, order takeaway and watch Netflix, just like she had been doing most nights since she had landed in London.

But apparently her feet had different ideas and carried her towards the market instead.

Lauren felt so conspicuous at first, the only single in a crowd of couples and families. But then she saw a scarf that she knew her mum would love and started chatting with a stall owner who designed delicate gold jewellery and had lived in California for a year as an exchange student. Lauren bought Joy a pair of earrings and went on to get the mulled wine she had promised herself, and by the time she had the warm paper cup and her first ever mince pie in hand, she realised that while she was alone, she didn't feel lonely anymore. Maybe London, with its drizzle-softened edges and comforting weight of history in every little street, was starting to feel a little bit like home, and the thought warmed Lauren up more than the mulled wine ever could.

The morning of Christmas Eve finally arrived, cold and crisp with a sky the colour of the icy blue topaz that was firmly embedded in the Queen's crown. Lauren had Rent the Runway'd her outfits for the two-night trip to Balmoral. She had never been to an actual castle before, which had basically been her dream as a five-year-old obsessed with Sleeping Beauty, and she had wondered if her younger self would be proud of her for achieving that goal. This job definitely had its perks.

And then she was told about the helicopter.

Though Lauren had been on a helicopter a few times in the past thanks to her six years at the White House, the tiny helicopter in front of her in a windy field in Glasgow looked ... well ... not like the huge twin-engine VH-60s they used in DC.

But with snowfall in Aberdeenshire and the surrounding areas of Scotland hitting record levels overnight, much of the nation's train networks, and even local runways, were no longer options. The Queen and her family members, who would usually travel up by royal train or plane, turned to a fleet of choppers instead to do the job. For Lauren, Harriet and James, who had made it as far as Glasgow by commercial flight from London, the rest of the journey, they were instructed, would continue from a small field nearby.

'Is this how I'm going to die?' she yelled at Harriet as they clambered into the tiny cockpit, her colleague's 'Grim Reaper' nickname suddenly coming to mind. The family members used a much larger helicopter, but this little one was clearly reserved for less important members of the travel party.

'It's perfectly safe!' Harriet yelled, grinning at her as they buckled up their seats and put on their headsets.

Opposite them in his seat, a very quiet James closed his eyes and made the sign of the cross.

Despite the adverse weather, the forty-minute flight was like one big postcard, with sweeping views across the vast stretches of rolling Highland hills and glens, all blanketed in pristine white snow. It was a total pinch-me moment, Lauren thought to herself, until the fairy-tale-like silhouette of Balmoral Castle – complete with its grey granite turrets, steeply pitched roofs and battlements – came into view and she saw what was waiting for them on the estate. She immediately wished they could turn around and go back to London.

Outside the gates, and standing alongside the press, were about thirty protesters, waving banners and placards. As their small helicopter came in closer to a landing space, the group quickly whipped themselves into a frenzy, shaking their fists and waving their banners.

'Not surprised to see that lot,' James said through the headset, pointing down at them. 'They're here every Christmas, yelling at the Queen and the royals about using the royal train, or choppers and "gas-guzzling" Range Rovers,' he explained, making quote signs with his fingers.

Lauren tried to imagine the royal family travelling any other way: lining up at the airport gate to board a budget commercial flight, waiting for the car rental shuttle at the airport or even hailing a cab. 'Are they dangerous?'

'Oh no,' James said as they began exiting the helicopter. 'They just like to yell and make signs.' And indeed, as they got closer, Lauren could see someone holding a sign lettered in red that seemed to drip blood. 'CUT CARBON, NOT RIBBONS!' it read, along with a drawing of a very sad-looking planet wearing a Band-Aid. 'PLANET BEFORE PRIVILEGE!' read another.

'I guess you're right,' Lauren said. 'Not dangerous.'

'Probably best to speak with the press at the front,' James added. 'A run-of-the-mill protest doesn't need to become a story, especially if they're briefed why there was a last-minute change of transport.'

Holding her hair back with one hand so it would stop whapping her in the face, she strode across the long, frosty lawn towards the gates. She could see Oscar in the distance, who seemed to be giving commentary for a TV camera. And one by one she clocked all the other royal reporters, counting them to make sure they had all arrived, and then she turned and saw a man holding a giant sign whose face was both new and oddly familiar. Lauren swept her fringe off her forehead and squinted a little. *Oh my God.*

Lauren immediately felt her heart and stomach and every other internal organ drop out of her body. The Christmas photo, the man in the Santa hat, holding an infant Lauren up to the camera and smiling. He was older and shorter than she remembered him, but she did *remember* him.

150

Even after twenty years, she would still know her dad's face anywhere.

And apparently, he would still know hers.

She could see his brows knitted together, peering towards her with a look somewhere between disbelief and confusion, and Lauren immediately let go of her hair so it could hide her face again, turning back towards her job and away from him.

'Lauren!' she heard him yell, and goddamnit, everyone looked around. 'Lauren!'

Oscar walked over.

'They know you?' he asked with an amused smile. 'Are you a comrade in arms? Did you used to throw paint on people who wore fur?'

'They probably just know me from press coverage,' she said, practically shoving Oscar towards the gates and away from the protesters, who, even though they were small in numbers, seemed especially vitriolic now that they were all eye to eye. Even the sad little earth picture seemed menacing all of a sudden.

'Lauren!' the voice yelled again, but she pretended not to hear it, moving away from her dad's voice, just like he had moved away from hers all those years ago.

Lauren followed Harriet and James, one hand shaking and the other clasped tightly around the handle of her large weekend bag as they got in a car and headed down a narrow private road towards a cluster of tiny guest cottages on the giant estate, all the while thinking of her dad's face and trying to figure out how, of all the places in all the world, her father wound up ten metres away from her in front of a literal castle?

Fuck my life, she thought to herself.

'—and, Lauren, you'll be sharing with Harriet and Violet, who came in yesterday.'

'What?' Lauren's head shot up to look at James, who was definitely avoiding eye contact with her as they left the car.

'Oh this is *lovely*,' Harriet cooed as she walked towards the front door of a grey-stoned cottage. It had two bedrooms – one twin and the other with two double beds. 'I have the best travel humidifier, Lauren. You'll sleep like a baby tonight.'

Lauren very much doubted that spending the night with a person who had such an ominous nickname was going to usher her off into dreamland, but James was already moving on to his own cottage, so she stuffed her complaints down and started to unpack her things in the room. Harriet was fluttering around, setting up all sorts of gadgets by her bed, spritzing some lavender essential oils onto her pillow. Violet briefly poked her head out of her room to say hello before shutting her door again. Lauren sat down on her bed, gripped her phone and frantically texted her mum:

DAD IS HERE.
DID YOU KNOW HE'S A PROTESTER???
I REPEAT, DAD IS HERE. AT
BALMORAL. HE SAW ME.

After waiting for a response, Lauren closed her eyes for a moment. She didn't want to text Joy, she absolutely couldn't tell Oscar and, Lauren realised with a thud, those were her only two friends. Or, in Oscar's case, friends, maybe more, or maybe not.

'Now, I've been told I snore, but I feel that's been greatly exaggerated,' Harriet started to say, but Lauren tuned her out and opened Safari.

If ever there was a time to manage a crisis, it was now.

And Lauren was good at her job.

*

There was definitely a buzz in the air that Christmas morning at Crathie Kirk, the small Scottish parish church a stone's throw away from Balmoral Castle, and that buzz had very little to do with celebrating the birth of Jesus Christ. A few dozen members of the public, who had lined up since 5:00 a.m., all cheered as the Queen and other senior royals made their way into the small granite-walled place of worship. Though she stood alongside members of the public – and still hadn't actually been introduced to the monarch – Lauren felt some nerves being in the presence of the Queen for the first time, who looked much taller than her photos suggested. But the real buzz that morning, and the man the photographers were all hoping would provide their money shot for the day, was only just about to arrive.

When the Duke of Exeter – now looking very much like royalty in an immaculately tailored tartan suit – stepped out of the car and waved towards the watching crowds, Lauren could almost see the ripple in the air. Older people who remembered him as a child with his parents, younger people who were seeing him for the first time, they all seemed excited and curious about having a fresh face on the royal scene.

At the end of the line stood a young girl holding a bouquet, reaching it out to a royal who didn't quite see her. She had one arm wrapped around her mother's legs, and when her mother encouraged her to try again, she just hid her face against her mother's coat.

Lauren wasn't the only one watching. The duke quickly approached, a gentle smile on his face as he knelt down to the girl. He spoke with her for a minute, gesturing towards the intended royal, almost seeming to confirm the little girl's wishes, and then took the bouquet before speaking with her for another minute. When he was done, he quickly ran the bouquet over to the Princess of Strathearn, then turned back and bowed to the girl as if to say, 'As you wish.'

Lauren could tell that this wasn't the average walkabout conversation. She had been around presidents, politicians, diplomats and at least two war criminals, and she could tell when someone was really listening instead of just mindlessly nodding. The duke was genuinely connecting with them, if the slight blush on one woman's cheeks was anything to go by.

The children's hospital hadn't been a one-off. This was true star power, she realised. And the Palace needed all the star power they could get.

It also didn't hurt that against the grey, cloudy skies and austere setting, Jasper's smile was *dazzling*. It was as if he ate Crest Whitestrips for breakfast.

Harriet and Violet were strangely silent behind her, and when Lauren turned to look at them, she saw that they were staring as well, the same fond smiles on their faces. 'He really is handsome,' Violet said, filming his walk up to the church on her phone. 'People are going to be *obsessed*.'

In fact, the only person who seemed not so into spending his Christmas Day working was Oscar, who had his head down, tapping away at his phone, those two little frown lines fully activated again. When he looked up, he was scowling a bit, but his face relaxed a little once he saw her and he smiled.

Lauren looked away. She wasn't so friendly with Harriet and Violet that they could see she was rattled, but she suspected Oscar would notice. Joy definitely would have, too. She was with her own family that Christmas morning, hundreds of miles away and probably surrounded by wrapping paper and new sets of Pokémon cards.

'It's like looking right at the sun,' Lauren agreed with

Violet, then took a deep breath. 'Come on, ladies, let's do our jobs.'

Once the service was over and the royals were en route back to the castle for their Christmas lunch, Lauren filed her final briefing notes of the day to a list of reporters from her phone and then called a local cab company, providing an address she had found online the night before.

Twenty minutes later, the car pulled up, and Lauren walked away from the church to meet it. She had absolutely no idea what she was doing and no one to talk to about it, which was probably for the best. If she did, they probably would have tried to talk her out of seeing her father. But right now, Lauren felt like her entire bloodstream was coursing with anger and hurt.

'Lauren!' someone called behind her, and she turned to see Oscar jogging towards her. 'Are you free later to go for a walk, once I've filed my articles?'

'I, uh, I can't,' she said, trying her best to ignore the cabbie waving over to her at the end of the driveway. 'I . . . I have some distant relatives nearby, I said I'd try to come for Christmas lunch.'

'Your dad's family?' Oscar said, and Lauren froze. 'Just the whole Bearnas thing, you said it was from your dad's side.'

'Yeah,' Lauren said, and tried to turn so he couldn't see her face. 'On my dad's side.'

Oscar put his hand on her arm. 'Lauren,' he said. 'Are you all right? You look . . . a little off.'

She pretended to scoff. 'Thanks. What every girl wants to hear on Christmas Day.'

'No, sorry, I didn't mean you look *bad*. You look lovely, as always. It's just . . . Did something happen?'

155

'I really am fine,' Lauren said again, this time walking over to the cab. 'The holidays are just stressful, you know? I'm fine.'

Oscar paused, waiting for her to get into the cab, then, before she shut the door, said, 'Text me if you need anything?'

'Will do!' she replied, and made sure not to look behind her as the cab drove away.

As much as she hated to admit it, Lauren had often imagined her reunion with her dad, especially when she was a child and still convinced that his absence had all been a huge misunderstanding. She had imagined that he would be sweet and apologetic, regretful over missing all the Father's Days and daddy-daughter dances at school, dozens of holidays and birthdays. As Lauren got older and realised the truth behind his disappearance, that it had been purposeful and intended, she had instead started imagining the only thing she wanted to say to his face, and wow, did it feel good to say it now.

'Are you fucking *kidding* me!'

Her dad stood in the doorway of his small terraced house, which was about an hour away from Balmoral in the city of Aberdeen. He looked somehow both older and younger than she remembered him – his greying beard throwing off her memory of the clean-shaven father she once lived with. Even just seeing him with a beard now made that small recollection feel like a lie.

'Lauren.' He stood back and held the door open, looking at her. 'It *was* you.'

'It was me,' she said. 'Amazing that you remember me after all this time. Dad of the Year right here.'

Callum winced. 'Care to come in?'

'Absolutely not,' Lauren said, even as she marched inside. It smelled faintly of stale cigarettes and more strongly of a roast in the oven. 'So you throw rocks at the celebrity climate criminals and then come back and do a full six-course meal for people other than your family. That's a better life to you than sticking around to be a father and husband?'

Callum looked smaller and shorter than she remembered. How was this really the man who used to toss her into the air after work? He had seemed so strong back then, like he would never have let her fall.

He shrugged. 'I, um, I'm not sure what to say. I've made mistakes, Lauren, I won't lie. You look beautiful, though. Your mum did a great job, it seems.'

'She did an *amazing* job,' Lauren said, and just thinking about her mum working nights, eating off the dollar menu, making sure Lauren had everything so it would never feel like she was missing something, *someone*, made tears come to her eyes. 'Don't talk about Mum. You don't get that privilege.'

Callum held up his hands, calloused and red. 'Fair enough, fair enough. I apologise.'

'Oh, you're apologizing now?' Lauren said. 'Because that's going to take a while. Like, twenty years' worth of apologies. Maybe you have that kind of time, but I don't.' She started to walk through the house, looking at the TV and old books and a newspaper scattered on the kitchen table, its crossword half finished. The sad earth banner was rolled up in a corner, and as she ran a hand across one of the side tables, a small pile of dust gathering on her fingertips, Lauren could feel the lonesomeness in every room. It made her sad when all she wanted to be was angry. 'I don't even know why I'm here,' she continued. 'I don't even know what I want from you.'

'You could stay for supper if you'd like,' Callum said. 'Some of the guys from my activist group are coming over, I could set an extra seat.'

Lauren whirled to look at him, her eyes wide.

'Okay, all right,' Callum said. 'I'm sorry, I just wasn't expecting to see you here. You've . . . you're so grown up, Lauren. I don't know what to say.'

'I know I am,' Lauren said. 'You missed it, remember? The whole thing – me growing up and all. You *left* us.'

'I did,' he said. 'And I am very sorry.'

Lauren walked through the kitchen, opening the fridge before going towards the cabinets. The fridge had a few foil-covered dishes inside, with some cheap plastic glasses in the cabinets. She saw medicine bottles on the counter behind him and wondered what they were for, wondered why she even cared.

Callum paused. 'So you're working at the Palace?'

'I am,' she said. 'You may have noticed that yesterday when you and your friends were screaming at me as I climbed out of a helicopter with the rest of the staff.'

Callum at least had the decency to wince when she said that. 'I think I just about had a heart attack when I saw you. Your face is still the same.'

'Do not do that,' Lauren said, her bottom lip trembling. 'You don't get to say that to me, not after all this time. You had years – *decades* – to see my face.'

Callum took a deep breath as he leant against the door. 'I'm so sorry, Lauren. To both you and your mum. I made a mistake. And once I made it, I didn't know how to go back and fix it. I just ran, and finally I ran so far for so long that I didn't know the way back to you.'

Lauren thought of DC, of the way she had boarded a plane to London with just one suitcase, running from Brian and Brooke, pushing away the hurt, just going as fast as possible before all her feelings could catch up with her.

Fuck.

The smell of a turkey roasting in the oven was starting to make her slightly nauseated, and she found herself wanting some fresh air. 'I have to go back to work. Burn some fossil fuels, you know, maybe pour some oil into a river. Give you something to do next Christmas.'

'I'm glad you came,' Callum said. 'I want you to know that I've deeply regretted my decisions over the years. I should have done more to stay in your life, and I know that all too well now. I know I can't fix the past, but it would be nice to maybe have a fresh start going forward?'

Lauren levelled her gaze at him. 'No.'

'Okay, of course. Well, you're welcome here anytime, Lauren. I mean that.'

'Sure, okay,' she said, knowing that she would never step foot in that house again.

'Merry Christmas,' he added, sounding almost hopeful.

Lauren left without responding, her taxi still waiting outside to take her back.

She was halfway through the car ride when her phone started buzzing, and Lauren glanced down to see her mum's photo looking back at her.

'I'm sorry he showed up at your job.'

'He didn't "show up at my job",' Lauren said. 'He was protesting environmental pollution in this group that apparently demonstrates at Balmoral Castle every year.' She paused before adding, 'So I looked up where he lived and took a taxi to tell him to stay away.'

'You what?'

'I know, it was stupid.'

'No, it wasn't stupid,' her mum said with a sigh. 'I can't say I wouldn't have done the same thing if I were in your shoes. Are you okay?'

'Kinda,' Lauren said. There was something about someone asking if she was okay that always made her feel not okay, and she looked out the window towards the dark woodlands on the grounds of Balmoral. In the light of day, they seemed a lot less intimidating. 'I'll be fine, though. It was just a lot.'

'Well, I think it was very brave of you.'

'I know we don't really talk about Dad that much, but can I ask you a question?'

'Of course.'

'Did you ever try to stay in touch, even though I know he was awful? For me? Or even just for you?'

There was a long pause before her mum spoke again. 'I decided that I wasn't going to let a man – any man, not just your father – dictate my life. If anyone's actions were going to affect my course, they would be *my* actions, my choices. And I wanted you to see me do that so that you wouldn't make the same mistakes that I made.'

Lauren knew that was supposed to make her feel better, that it was supposed to empower her, strengthen her, that she could do whatever she set her mind to. But all it did was make her think about Brian again, how his actions had affected the course of Lauren's life, whether she liked it or not, and she just felt weak and small, not strong like her mother.

That evening at the Balmoral estate, Lauren stayed mostly by herself in the small living room of the guest cottage she was sharing, replying to emails from reporters and producers from overseas morning shows who were only just preparing their royal stories for the following day. By the time she finished, both Harriet and Violet were already asleep and all she wanted to do was take off her shoes, shower and follow suit. However, the wailing sounds of orcas from Harriet's white noise app greeted her as soon as she opened the bedroom door, and Lauren decided that maybe sleep could wait for an hour or so, or until Harriet's phone battery died.

She thought about texting Oscar, but she knew that he was at a B&B an hour away and probably still on deadline, and she also knew that he'd be able to tell that she was agitated after her visit with her dad, and the absolute last thing she felt like doing on Christmas night was accidentally telling a reporter that her long-lost dad's Christmas tradition involved waving hand-painted signs at the Queen and violently screaming about planet Earth before roasting a turkey for a gang of protesters.

A walk was beginning to sound better and better, Lauren decided, just as a whale let out a somewhat orgasmic moan.

Bundled up in a big puffy coat and scarf, she walked around the castle grounds for a while, feeling more and more like Keira Knightley wandering the moors in *Pride and Prejudice*, all moody and messy-haired and waiting for Tom from *Succession* to show up through the morning mist. She had watched the sunset earlier from the living room window, its orange and golden rays descending past the snow-covered tree branches, making them look like they were ready for a long night's sleep.

There was a figure walking towards her as she turned a corner, tall and broad-shouldered, and Lauren sighed. One downside to being at any royal residence was constantly having to prove your right to be there to appease the skittish protection officers.

Lauren pulled off a mitten to dig inside her coat for her laminated badge as the figure got closer. 'Ugh,' she muttered to herself. 'You'll be shocked to know that I *still* work for the family,' she said bluntly. 'Same as when you checked me all of twenty minutes – Oh my God.'

The duke was a few feet away, looking both bemused and tired. 'Well, I'll be sure to make a note of it,' he replied.

'Oh, sorry,' Lauren said. 'I'm sorry, it's dark, I didn't realise it was you, um, Your – Your Highness. I feel like I'm showing this badge every ten seconds these days.'

'I told you when we were first introduced, please call me Jasper,' he replied. He looked at her as she tucked her badge back into her coat pocket. 'I'm glad I ran into you, though. Lauren, I'm afraid it's actually me who owes you an apology.'

'Me?' she said.

'Yes.' He sighed, running a hand through his messy waves of hair that Lauren tried very hard not to look at. 'I've been a bit unsure about taking on this role, as you have probably noticed, and I've taken it out on you, and that's unfair. I'm sorry. I shouldn't have been so riled up in your office the other day or fought you so hard on the event at the children's hospital. You're just doing your job, and quite well, I might add. None of my crankiness is your fault.'

Lauren just stared at him, stunned.

'Was there anything else?' the duke – Jasper – said, laughing a little. 'You look like you just saw two moons.'

'No, no,' Lauren said, pulling the belt of her cream coat tighter around her. It felt like a hug. 'I'm just surprised, that's all. But thank you, I appreciate that. No apologies necessary, but still.' She gave a little shrug. 'I think we're both figuring out new jobs and doing the best we can.'

'That's very generous, thank you.' Jasper smiled. 'How about you? How has your Christmas been?'

'That is a very . . . That's kind of a loaded question right now,' Lauren said. 'You know, the holidays. Always seem to be chaotic.'

Jasper gestured to the grounds around them. 'The holidays,' he echoed. 'Don't I know it.'

'I imagine that Christmas in New Zealand was slightly less protocol-heavy,' Lauren said. 'Definitely fewer photographers.'

'New Zealand was quiet,' Jasper said, and for just a brief second, Lauren could hear real emotion in his voice. 'It was different, peaceful. Definitely not bad. But I never thought I'd be back here doing all of this. What about you? You must be missing your family. I always felt bad that the staff had to work over the holidays. Were you able to chat with them today?'

'Yes,' Lauren said. *You have no idea*, she thought to herself. 'I did, thank you for asking. And it's all right, this is the job I signed up for.'

'Well, still,' Jasper said. 'I'm glad you've had a good Christmas. I suppose I'll see you in the official greeting line tomorrow morning?'

'Yes, you will. And also, if we're apologising, I'm sorry for snapping at you just now. I just thought you were one of the—'

He waved away her comment. 'At least it wasn't the post-man this time.' He chuckled. 'Have a good night, Lauren. Merry Christmas.'

'Merry Christmas, Jasper,' she replied, watching as he walked past her towards the castle. There was a slight pull to his shoulders that made him seem like he was huddled in on himself, and she found herself wanting to press her hand against his back, to straighten out his curled spine, to—

'Jesus Christ, Lauren,' she whispered to herself, and she tightened her coat again before heading back to her cottage. 'What the hell is wrong with you?'

Her phone vibrated in her pocket, and she fumbled for a minute before answering it. Oscar's name was on the screen. 'Hi,' she said. 'What's up?'

'That's actually what I was going to ask you,' he said. 'Everything's fine on my end, but you seemed sort of spooked when you were getting into the taxi today. I can't stop thinking about it.'

'I'm honestly fine,' Lauren said automatically. 'Just, you know, the holidays, family, work.'

'Do you want to talk about it?'

'Not really.'

'Fair enough. What are you doing now? You sound like you're out.'

'I'm walking across the grounds at Balmoral, heading back to my shared cottage with Harriet and Violet. What about you?'

'Glad you asked. I'm in a small bed-and-breakfast with, I believe, every single member of the British press corps. The bar was packed, but I'm about to get in bed now.'

'I'm jealous.'

'Well, wait until you hear about the room. Lace, chintz, doilies on everything.'

'Is there a doll collection?'

'Not yet. It'll probably appear after midnight, though. A bunch of little beady eyes staring at me while I try to sleep.'

Lauren smiled. 'I appreciate that you're trying to make me laugh.'

'I'm not doing any such thing. I'm just telling you about my accommodation. I can't believe you'd mock my pain like that.' She could hear the smile in his voice, though, and she liked it.

'Did you have a good Christmas?' she asked.

'Eh, it is what it is,' he said. 'All work, filing stories, a drink with mostly obnoxious royal correspondents. Just another day, really.'

'Yeah,' she said, opening the door to the cottage and lowering her voice. 'I'm back in my room now so I have to whisper to not wake anyone up.'

'What in the world is that moaning sound?'

'Harriet has to listen to whale noises in order to fall asleep,' Lauren whispered.

'Well, my room situation is sounding better and better by the second.' He paused. 'You sure that's a whale? It sounds obscene.'

'Hard to tell,' she said. 'I better go. Thanks for checking in on me, though. Merry Christmas, Oscar.'

'Happy Christmas, Lauren. I'll see you back home in London.'

Home in London. She sort of liked the sound of that. 'That you will,' she said, and waited for him to be the one to hang up first.

Chapter 8

'I've never been so happy to see you in my life,' Lauren said, setting down her coffee on her desk before throwing her arms around Joy.

'Don't even have my coat off yet,' Joy protested as she hugged Lauren back. 'Oh my God, I'm so glad the holidays are over and I'm back around adults again. Name any *Teen Titans Go!* episode and I can tell you what it's about. Go on, try me.'

'I've never seen it,' Lauren said, still not letting go of her. 'You changed your hair! It looks so good, I love the braids.'

'Oh thanks!' Joy beamed. 'Honestly, the bob was cute, but having to straighten it every morning was killing me. How were your holidays? I didn't hear much from you, wink wink nudge nudge.'

'You can't say that while actually nudging a person!' Lauren said, picking up her coffee again and dodging Joy's hand at the same time.

'So were you making headlines with someone?' Joy asked, waggling her eyebrows.

'That was very cheesy,' Lauren said.

'Wasn't it just.' Joy shrugged out of her long overcoat.

Lauren sat down across from Joy, tossing her phone onto her desk. 'Well, for Christmas I literally stayed in a forest and shared a bedroom with Harriet, which made me feel like I was Harry Potter in the cupboard at his aunt and uncle's house.'

'That sounds both cosy and creepy,' Joy said.

'*And then* I ran into the Duke of Exeter on Christmas night and thought he was a security guard and snapped at him.'

Joy laughed, loud and bright, and Lauren felt a pang for how much she had truly missed her friend. 'What about you? Did you get the last purple Quality Street?'

'Good memory, and yes, I did.' Joy pretended to scoff. 'Can't believe you would even doubt that. And, in equally exciting news, I would like you to know that I went rock climbing. At an indoor rock climbing gym, but still.' Joy flexed a bit. 'Met a guy on the apps and he was the one who suggested it as a first date.'

'Ooh!' Lauren said. 'How was it?'

'The date was handsome but dull as sandwich bread. The rock climbing was fantastic! Well, apart from breaking a nail.' She held up her hand to show Lauren the quick patch-up job she had done on it the night before.

'You can barely tell,' Lauren said. 'Are you going back?'

'To the climbing gym, yes, but not with Sandwich Bread. Where are you off to now?'

'I have to pitch a media opportunity to Eugene that he's going to hate.'

'Happy New Year!' Joy said, and they clinked their Starbucks cups together.

*

'Absolutely not.'

'Just hear me out,' Lauren said, gesturing towards the several days' old newspapers splayed out on the conference table. 'The duke's official debut was a hit. Literally everybody loved him, which is basically impossible in the public eye these days.'

'Well, yes, the press loved him, but behind the scenes, he just looked so awkward.'

'Okay, first of all,' Lauren said, 'I don't know if you two realise this, but this is a *very* intimidating group here.' She gestured towards the entire Palace. 'I can tell you from experience that it's a little challenging to suddenly show up and be completely comfortable and relaxed. And he's been on a farm in New Zealand with a pack of sheep—'

'I believe it's actually a flock of sheep,' Harriet interrupted. 'A pack refers to wolves.'

'Thank you, Harriet,' Lauren said. 'So let's cut him a bit of slack.

'What I saw,' she continued, then reached for one of the papers and pointed at the front page photo, which was the duke kneeling down and taking the flowers from the shy girl, 'and what the press and the rest of the world saw, was this. He's wonderful with people. The way he spoke to that little girl, it was mesmerising. Whatever that "it" thing is that people have, he has it. We need to harness that and use it. I think the Queen was right to want him here back in the fold. It was a very smart move.'

Eugene sat up proudly at that, just as Lauren knew he would. Across the table, Joy hid a smile at Lauren's obvious ploy to win him over.

'It's time that we take it to the next level,' she said. 'We'd be stupid not to leverage this interest people have in him.

And it would be helpful to show that he's good at the actual work itself before stories about bankruptcy knock his image.'

'It's your job to keep that out of the press,' Eugene pointed out.

'That's exactly what I'm trying to do,' Lauren argued. 'So let me do it.'

'What he needs is a good natural disaster – an opportunity to roll up his sleeves,' James mused.

'James!' Lauren cried.

'That's a bit dire,' Eugene added as Harriet frowned at his words.

'Not a big one,' he said to defend himself. 'Just somewhere where the duke can fly in, greet some emergency responders and fly out.'

'That is *not* what I meant,' Lauren said. 'Quick, everyone knock on wood.' They all rapped on the Formica table with the fake wood grain, which would have to do.

'There *is* the visit to Singapore at the end of the month on behalf of the Queen for her Pearly Jubilee, marking thirty years on the throne,' Eugene suggested.

'I like Singapore,' Lauren said with a grin. 'As long as James doesn't try to manifest a hurricane there.'

'There's a higher chance of a hurricane hitting than successfully pulling off plans for something that usually takes the best part of six months to organise,' James remarked.

'The Duke of Cumberland is already attached to the Jubilee,' Eugene said. 'But given his health issues at the moment and' – he lowered his voice – 'the fact that the press rarely cover his engagements, we could perhaps send D.O.E. alongside him? *If* Her Majesty agrees with it.'

Lauren and Joy exchanged a quick glance, and Joy pretended to tip a bottle back towards her mouth.

'I think Jas – the duke would be perfect for this,' Lauren said. 'It's low-hanging fruit, right? A state dinner, some dancing maybe. He would dazzle them.'

'Fine,' Eugene said. 'James is right, we normally have the best part of six months to plan these events. Thankfully most of it is already in place. You have two weeks to figure out the rest once I get the okay from HMQ.' He stood up with his laptop. 'Good luck.'

'Don't need it,' Lauren said. 'But thanks.'

'Knock wood,' Harriet murmured again, and even though she had the utmost confidence in herself, Lauren did so automatically.

Chapter 9

'Okay! If I could have everyone's attention for a few minutes, please!'

Lauren stood in a ballroom at the Marina Bay Sands Hotel in Singapore, her voice getting swallowed up by the loud din from the gathered members of the press – including the royal reporters from back home, dozens of agency photographers, international TV crews and local media outlets.

'Excuse me!' she cried again.

Nothing.

To be fair, it had been a long day of travel, and an even longer twelve days of prep after the Queen signalled her approval. Lauren now understood why it could take more than half a year to set up these sorts of visits, because she barely had time to sleep or eat during the prep for Jasper's additions to the itinerary, and her undereye bags and cranky demeanour proved it.

At least she had had the thirteen-hour flight to rest a little, and she had taken advantage of every single amenity offered to her by business class, including the free champagne, the

Le Labo skincare pouch and the silk pyjamas. At one point, James had popped up over their shared seat divider, but Lauren had pointed at her screen, then back at him, never taking her eyes off the screen. 'I'm watching *Love Island*,' she said, 'and if anyone interrupts me, I will make sure their hotel room is next to the lift.'

James had paused for a minute, then wisely descended back into his seat.

She glanced at her watch while standing behind the podium now, which had a seal on it from whatever business organisation had used it before her, which made her feel like a dictator.

A terrible dictator, because, unlike the foreign press who were also covering the trip, the British press pack still wasn't listening to her.

'As soon as we're done here, we can all go to dinner!' she yelled.

That brought everyone to attention.

'Like I was saying,' she said, 'both the Duke of Cumberland and Duke of Exeter landed safely earlier this evening. They are both happy to be in Singapore and are looking forward to meeting the prime minister and his wife tomorrow ahead of the state dinner at the Istana, the grand official residence of the president of Singapore,' Lauren continued. 'You've all received emails with the updated itinerary, which now includes the Duke of Exeter's movements.'

'I didn't get—' a lone familiar voice yelled from the back.

'Check your spam folder, Nathan. It's been sent to all of you,' Lauren said. 'The duke will also be making a solo visit to the National Stadium to meet with a youth group founded by the Singapore football team, and the following day he will be making a stop at Haji Lane to speak with local artists and shop owners and learn more about some of the mental health initiatives being activated in the area for students.'

There was a pause before another Brit voice shouted from the back, 'So he's going shopping?'

Lauren ignored them. 'Also, I have an update on the travel schedule. The ground transportation for all UK media will be at eight thirty tomorrow morning at the Holiday Inn on Farrer Park Station Road—'

An audible groan rose up from half of the British reporters, specifically the half who were staying at the Novotel a few minutes down the road from the Holiday Inn.

'—and if you're late, then that's a real bummer for you,' Lauren continued. 'Does anyone have any questions?'

At the back, Oscar raised his hand. Lauren could see his slightly bedhead-y hair and his rumpled shirt, and wondered how much he had been working lately. Their time together had been nonexistent ever since he virtually escorted her back to the cabin at Balmoral, and Lauren found herself missing their conversations, missing him. London's January weather had been absolute shit, Lauren had been up to her eyeballs in plans and itineraries for Singapore and Oscar had been chasing down a story.

Still, they'd texted, and Lauren found herself going back and reading through their conversations on nights when she couldn't sleep, smiling to herself in the darkness of her bedroom while listening to Una click-clack down the main staircase, on her way out for another late night.

'Question for you,' Oscar had texted one night while Lauren doomscrolled on her phone and watched a reality show on Netflix about matchmakers. 'Are you so much happier now that you can eat proper British chocolate instead of American imposter chocolate?'

'You can pry my American chocolate out of my cold, dead hands,' she typed back.

'I will, and I'll put Cadbury's in them instead,' he replied.

'Is that a threat or a promise?'

'Dairy Milk. Mini Eggs. Cadbury's Caramel. You'll see.'

'That's not chocolate, that's a grocery list. Can't text anymore, I'm eating a Hershey bar.'

'Hershey's literally smells like vomit. Enjoy!'

It was stupid and silly, something to make up for the endless grey days and the latent gloom that always seemed to make the long January month feel like a holiday hangover. Lauren felt like she always had to be on her toes with Oscar, which was exciting. She wasn't sure if it was because she technically shouldn't be flirting with a member of the press pack or if it was just the witty banter that made her constantly check her phone to see if he had responded, but either way, it was fun.

'Yes, Oscar?' she said, standing at the podium in Singapore.

'The itinerary isn't in Nathan's spam folder.' The slight smirk on his face told her that he was fucking with her, and Lauren resisted the urge to throw the microphone at him. Or maybe just make out with him again.

'Then please tell him to get someone else to forward their copy. Like, perhaps you, Oscar. This isn't exactly encrypted information, you can all share with one another. Now, does anyone have any actual questions that only I can answer?'

There was a murmur of assent through the group, which Lauren took as a no. 'Great,' she said. 'So tomorrow, bright and early, you'll be at the . . . ?'

'Holiday Inn,' everyone responded dutifully.

'Wonderful,' she said. 'Except I won't be there for the first engagement, I'll be travelling with Their Highnesses. Harriet and one of our friends from the British embassy will, however, be on hand.'

There was a smattering of boos, but Lauren just grinned. Not having to start the day on a packed coach bus with the entire press corps was one of the few perks of this visit, and she intended to enjoy every minute of it.

The next day, as Lauren was leaving her hotel room, she stopped to look at herself in the mirror and was surprised that she couldn't remember the last time she had really studied her own reflection. Probably because she didn't have her own bathroom, she realised with a laugh. The navy blue dress she wore fit well, ready to hide any sweat marks from the intense humidity outside, and the overpriced high-tech hairdryer she had borrowed from Brooke right before discovering that she had been sleeping with Brian was the only thing she had kept from that now-dead friendship, and with good reason: Her hair looked fantastic.

She stepped into nude heels before packing up her bag and laptop, and as she was about to open the door, her phone pinged once, twice, three times.

Lauren half expected a series of texts from her mum, but instead it was Norman, the Duke of Cumberland's private secretary, who was also assisting Jasper on this trip. 'His Highness wishes to see you,' it read.

'D.O.C. or D.O.E.?' Lauren murmured as she typed.

'Exeter,' he replied.

'On my way,' she texted. The dukes were staying in the premier suites at the highest end of the hotel, which each had their own 'entertainment den,' linens that cost more than her yearly rent, and expansive views of the Gardens by the Bay.

She gave herself one more glance in the mirror before heading out and up to the fifty-fourth floor, where security immediately greeted her as soon as the doors slid open. 'Oh,' one of the royal protection officers said. 'It's only you.'

Lauren's eyes widened. 'Well, sorry to disappoint, Dan,' she said, just as Norman came jogging down the hallway. She had never seen him jog anywhere, ever, and Lauren's sense of alarm went up by a degree.

'Oh good,' Norman huffed. 'You're here.'

'Is everything okay?' Lauren asked, hurrying down the hall after him, her brain racing ahead to think of all the things that could go wrong, all the reasons that the duke could possibly—

'DON is extremely nervous about the day,' he whispered as he tapped his key card against the door handle and they stepped into the suite. 'I thought you might be able to reassure him.'

Lauren opened her mouth to ask another question, but then she was in the room with Jasper, who was standing by the window in his dark grey linen suit, pocket square tucked perfectly into his pocket, not a hair out of place, his profile illuminated against the entire city of Singapore.

He looked, Lauren thought for a minute, almost too handsome to be real.

And then he turned, and she saw his anxious face.

'Uh-oh,' she said without thinking.

'Something like that,' he replied with a nervous laugh. 'I just ... I wanted to go over my movements one more time, if that's all right.'

'Of course,' Lauren said, even though it was very clear from the worn pieces of paper in his hand that he had gone over them more than she had.

'I just ...' He laughed again, then shook out his sleeves. 'I have to admit something sort of embarrassing.'

176

Lauren, who had maybe read more than her fair share of tabloid magazines while getting pedicures, braced herself for the worst.

'I'm not ... I don't ... My wife, my ex-wife, she was the voice of the operation, so to speak. I'm really not used to having all eyes on me and—'

'—and now you're the man of the moment about to attend two engagements and then a state dinner with a hundred reporters and photographers and TV cameras capturing your every move?' Lauren finished for him. She understood how big a deal this trip was, especially tonight. The state dinner was going to be a meticulously orchestrated evening of diplomacy, elegance and cultural exchange, and both he and the Duke of Cumberland were expected to deliver speeches in front of government officials, diplomats and cultural leaders in a bid to strengthen diplomatic ties with the UK.

Jasper smiled, looking relieved. 'Something like that,' he said again. 'Actually, something exactly like that.'

Lauren glanced over at Norman, who was scrolling through his phone, either busy or pretending to look busy, Lauren couldn't tell.

'Okay,' Lauren said. 'Here are a few things to remember before being seated. First, everyone loves to talk about themselves. If you're struggling, if you don't know what to say, just ask a vague, open-ended question, like "What's something from your culture or work that you wish more people knew about?"'

'Is that what you told American presidents?' Jasper asked.

'I would have,' Lauren replied. 'Because it works. But more importantly, just remember that everyone here – not just the team, but *everyone* – is rooting for you. People are genuinely happy to have someone new in the mix, that you're representing the family, the country, and, on this visit, Her Majesty. They're not out to trip you up, at least not today.'

Jasper nodded again, looking calmer and more thoughtful. 'Quick, ask me a random question.'

Lauren didn't hesitate. 'Which sheep was your favourite?'

Jasper laughed, loud and true. 'What?'

'You owned a sheep farm!' Lauren said, even though she was laughing, too. 'C'mon. This should roll off the tongue.'

'Fine. It was Sweater Weather,' Jasper admitted.

'That's literally the best name I've ever heard for a sheep,' Lauren said. 'Why was she – wait, he? – the best?'

'When I took over the farm, the sheep there were Bluefaced Leicesters and Corriedales. Those breeds usually are responsible for the wool used by decent clothing brands. But the gold standard comes from Merino – the absolute crème de la crème of wool – and Sweater Weather was our first of many. She represented the moment I knew that farm was going to be something special. That I had built something of my own. And she was lucky – a year later we won a contract with one of the biggest clothing manufacturers in the world.'

'Is it normal for a wool farm owner to name their sheep?' Lauren asked.

'Of course! I loved being out there, never shied away from getting my hands dirty. They all had names. Ram-bo, Cottonball, Woolbur. Fleece Witherspoon. I could go on . . .'

'Oh my God.' Lauren giggled.

'But Sweater Weather was stubborn as hel – as heck, and would literally yell at us when it was time to go in for the night. And one time she escaped, ran into the house and ate several pairs of socks before we realised what was happening.'

'Something about a sheep eating socks feels cannibalistic.'

'Sweater Weather played by her own rules,' Jasper replied.

'Well, she would probably be my favourite, too,' Lauren said. 'I like a feisty lady. Okay, are you ready? What would Sweater Weather do?'

'Eat socks,' they both said at the same time, and then Jasper took a deep breath and blew it out slowly. 'Ready,' he said. 'Thank you, Lauren.'

'Just doing my job,' she said. 'And I'll be with you for the first engagement today and then probably wrangling the press into submission after that, but I'll always be around if you need me.'

Jasper paused before saying, 'Thank you,' again.

'I'm sorry, Your Highness, but the cars have arrived,' Norman interrupted. 'We'll take the service lifts down to the garage.'

Jasper glanced at Lauren. 'Are you travelling with . . . ?'

'You? Yes. For the first engagement,' she said, gesturing towards the door. 'But then I'm with comms and the press for the dinner.'

'Noted,' Jasper said. 'Well, off to the races, I guess. Here's to no international incidents.'

Norman laughed nervously as he held the door open for both of them.

Despite Jasper nearly jinxing everything, he managed to remain cool and calm for both engagements during the day. With Lauren's help, of course. After hearing him recite/butcher the names of half the football players they would be meeting from the national team that morning, she had to quickly put an aide from the embassy on loudspeaker in the car to teach him how to pronounce each one properly before their car pulled up at the stadium. Thankfully, he was a fast learner, and when the time arrived, he was ready to impress. Lauren watched proudly as he grabbed the attention of every single person he spoke with. At one point, he stood up to assist a female employee who briefly lost her balance on the pitch, and Lauren was nearly deafened by the rapid fire camera clicks. She could see Oscar out of the corner of her eye, taking notes frantically, and she assumed it to be a good sign that he was too busy reporting to rile her up again.

Still, though. She kind of missed it.

By the time they got to the state dinner at the president's official residence (which was five minutes behind schedule due to a reporter having to stop the bus to throw up from motion sickness), Lauren felt the giddy exhaustion from a hard job that was well done. She and James stood off to the side as the duke greeted the prime minister and his wife, shaking heads and bowing respectfully before posing for photos. His smile never wavered, not a hair was out of place and his shirt (which Lauren knew had been quickly switched out for a sweat-free one in the car on the way to the dinner) was pressed to perfection.

She had made this happen, Lauren realised. She had helped create this moment, and for the first time in a long while, she felt like her old self again, like someone who not only knew how to do her job but how to do it better than everyone else.

Once the actual dinner began, Lauren retreated with the rest of the press corps to a separate space, where they were all given rather unglamourous-looking boxed meals. She glanced around, trying to see if there were any left for her, but then she saw Oscar waving her down with a box in his hand, and the glow from a job well-done transferred into something deeper and warmer.

'I saved one for you,' he said when she sat down next to him. 'The rest of these beasts were acting like hyenas after doing a juice cleanse. It's every man – person, sorry – for themselves.'

Lauren took the disposable box from him. 'Thanks,' she said. 'Is it good?'

'It's gluten-free, organic and high in protein.'

She looked at him excitedly. 'Are you serious?'

'Absolutely not. It's a turkey sandwich, crisps and a slice of pretty unimpressive cake.'

'My favourite.' She popped open the box as Oscar turned back to his laptop. 'Did you get some good stuff today?'

He nodded as he tossed a crisp into his mouth. 'Great stories,' he said. 'Your boy is golden. This will be at least a week of positive headlines and breathless op-eds.'

'And what about the second week?' she asked, taking a bite of her sandwich. It was dry and sort of tasteless and the best thing she had eaten all day.

'Sadly I don't control the media cycle,' he said. 'You know what this lot gets like when they're bored.'

'You one hundred percent control the media cycle!' Lauren pointed out. 'You're a journalist.'

'I'm just a minion,' he protested. 'It all comes down to the editors and the people who click on the stories.'

Lauren rolled her eyes at that, too tired and hungry to argue with him, and when she looked back at him, he was gazing at her with something like . . . fondness? Warmth?

'You did really well today, adding the duke to this,' he told her. 'Seriously. People are actually showing up to see the royals now. They almost look *happy* to see them. My entire TikTok feed is the Duke of Exeter walking in slow motion set to a sped-up Rihanna song. You might be single-handedly saving the monarchy.'

'Well, that's a little dramatic,' Lauren said, rolling her eyes, but inside she buzzed with happiness. 'I just coordinated appointments and got this bunch here.'

Oscar continued to look at her, though. 'Lauren, I know that . . . I think . . .'

His phone suddenly buzzed, and they both looked at their own screens. 'Sorry, I have to file this,' Oscar said. 'My editor is throwing a fit about getting stuff online as soon as possible.'

'Go, file,' she said, standing up with her purse and boxed meal and feeling weirdly like an adult and a little kid at the same time. 'You know where to find me.'

'At Annabel's?' he said, and this time Lauren did pause and turned to look at him.

'You tell me,' she replied with a small smile, then went back to her job.

Once they were all back at the hotel, Lauren took five minutes to wash her hands, refresh her lip gloss and brush her hair before heading back to Jasper's suite to go over his itinerary for the following day. She honestly felt like doing a victory lap, though, running around the hotel and high-fiving the housekeepers and valet and concierge. The early headlines coming out of London were already glowing, with the duke at the centre of it all:

DUKE DELIGHT: JASPER CHARMS SINGAPORE WITH ROYAL FLAIR

EXETER STUNS WITH ROYAL CHARM OFFENSIVE

DASHING DUKE SPARKS ROYAL FEVER IN SINGAPORE

She beamed as she checked her phone in the lift, and once she arrived at Jasper's door, Norman was already there with his own cheerful grin.

This was truly a big day for Norman: first running, and now smiling?

'His Highness is in the entertainment den,' Norman said. 'He just saw some of the headlines. I'm going to go and brief the Duke of Cumberland,' he added.

'Oh, perfect,' Lauren said, but as soon as she saw the duke, she realised that it wasn't perfect, not at all.

He was standing in the room, his tie loosened and the top two buttons of his shirt undone, his jacket tossed onto the sofa. 'Oh, hello, hello,' he said, gesturing towards her. 'Come in. Norman said you'd be stopping by to update me on tomorrow's itinerary.' But despite his words, his face was worried as he picked up a rocks glass. 'Would you like a drink?'

'Um, no, I'm working right now, but thank you,' Lauren said.

'Oh, of course, sorry.' He set the glass back down and gestured towards the sofa as he continued to scroll through his phone. 'Have you seen – well, of course you have – these headlines? I feel like the entire British press might propose marriage to me tomorrow.' He laughed a bit, but it was tight in his throat. 'Sit, please. You must have been on your feet all day.'

She had been, it was true, and her shoes were both very cute and completely unforgiving – as per usual. 'The headlines are wonderful,' Lauren said. 'Truly. Everyone is absolutely enamoured with you. You handled it really well.'

The duke rolled his eyes a bit as he sat down at the other end of the sofa. 'Well, for today,' he said. 'Next week could be a completely different story. I know you're not drinking, but would you like a water? Or something else? There's practically an entire grocery shop over by the wet bar.'

Lauren glanced over his shoulder and saw a glorious display of fruit neatly arranged in a basket. 'Is all that just for you?' She laughed.

'I believe it is,' he said, following her gaze. 'There's even a rare orange dragon fruit in there.'

'Usually it's just berries and some anemic-looking melon chunks,' Lauren said. 'But this looks like a work of art.'

Jasper laughed. 'So you're happy about the coverage, then? Does this make your job easier?'

'It does,' she said. 'But it doesn't make it easier that you don't seem very happy about it.'

He ran a hand through his hair, mussing up the careful style. It looked better that way, she thought. 'I just . . . there's a reason that my parents didn't want me to take on a working role, and why I grew up to agree with them. It was to keep me away from all of this, from all the eyes, the opinions, the inevitable negativity. They wanted me to have a quote-unquote "normal life" because neither of them had one after their marriage until they walked away from it all themselves. And it worked, for the most part.'

'What was the part that didn't work?'

'When it turned out that having a normal life was as complicated as having an abnormal one.' Jasper glanced at her. 'Does that sound like the most privileged statement ever?'

'No, not at all,' Lauren said.

'Despite going away to build my own life elsewhere, I seem to have ended back up where we all started, only this time it's just me, and it's like nothing and everything has changed. And I know I'm the fresh meat for the press, the curiosity, but I also know how fast that bloom can come off the rose, so to speak, and I have *no* idea why I'm telling you any of this, sorry.'

'No, no!' Lauren said, holding up her hand. 'It's good to talk about these things.'

Jasper gave her a dubious look. 'Very American of you.'

'Guilty,' she said with a shrug. 'We like to feel our feelings, what can I say?'

They sat quietly together for a minute, Lauren focused on her hands and Jasper focused on his drink. 'I had a plan and now I have a new plan,' he said quietly. 'And I'm not quite sure how any of that has happened.'

'I know what you mean,' Lauren said before she could stop herself, and he looked up at her. 'I mean, with the plans, especially when those plans are changed by other people and there's nothing you can do about it.'

Jasper watched her for a few seconds, which felt like an hour. 'Sounds like something familiar to you?'

She shrugged. 'I was on a path at the White House, I thought I was going to one day be press secretary, get married, get the guy and the house and the dog and the babies. It was all exactly what I wanted, or what I thought I wanted. And then I found out that the guy got my best friend instead, and now she's the one with the house and the dog. And maybe the babies one day, too.' Lauren blinked hard for a minute, the emotion and jet lag catching up to her in a rush. 'It all went away and now I'm here and I'm trying to figure out if that's even what I wanted in the first place, or if I'm just telling myself that so that losing it doesn't hurt so much.'

Jasper's eyes were soft. 'I'm sorry that happened to you – nobody deserves to be treated that way,' he said, and Lauren felt something inside her shift and start to melt. No one had ever really said that to her before, not about Brian and Brooke and dashed dreams and uncertain futures.

'Thank you,' she said. She wasn't quite sure when they had moved closer to each other on the sofa, but if she moved her leg a fraction of an inch, their knees would be touching. 'It's been hard. I feel—'

'Lost,' they both said at the same time, then smiled in recognition.

'Very lost,' Lauren said. 'But today was the first day in a really long time that I felt like I was good at my job. I felt *proud*, so thank you for that.' She knew that Jasper wasn't her friend, or her therapist or even just a stranger sitting on a barstool next to her. He shouldn't know any of this.

'Well, I'll keep that in mind going forward,' Jasper said. 'Make Lauren proud.'

The weight of his words hit them both at the same time, and now their knees *were* touching, and now something was happening that wasn't on the itinerary or schedule or calendar, and Lauren felt almost outside of her body, Jasper so close that she could feel the warmth radiating from under his shirt, her head buzzing like she was drunk even though she was completely sober, and she wasn't thinking about work or Oscar or Brian or anything else other than the presence of Jasper and how she was pulled to him like a moth to a flame, willing to burn for a mere second of heat, and then his hand was on her leg, gripping her like she was his, and Lauren found herself leaning in towards Jasper just as he leant towards her, and they kissed.

If kissing Oscar at Annabel's had made her pulse race, kissing Jasper in Singapore settled every loose, rattling thing inside of her. He was as warm and steady as his hands on her back and arm, gentle and strong at the same time, and Lauren wrapped her arms around his neck and hung on for however long she would get to enjoy this.

They pulled apart after a minute. 'We can't do this,' she whispered, trying to catch her breath.

'I know,' he replied, then dipped his head towards her again, kissing her again, not nearly as gentle this time.

'Have you read the articles?!' A cheerful voice rang out as the hotel room door clicked open.

The two of them sprang apart like they had been electrocuted, Lauren leaping off the sofa and straightening her dress as Jasper quickly ran a hand through his hair, doing nothing to tame it. They only had a second to glance at each other before Norman came dashing back into the room, waving an iPad as if in victory.

'The papers adore you, Your Highness!' He beamed, and Lauren took advantage of his distraction to tuck her hair behind her ears and grab her phone, pretending to read a text that wasn't on her screen. 'Even *The Sentinel* is calling you a republican destroyer, that's how much people are loving you! And this was all Her Majesty's idea, of course. My goodness, she's just *magnificent*, isn't she.'

Lauren caught Jasper's eye from behind Norman's back – it was obvious that the last thing he wanted to think about in their moment together was his aunt, and well, fair enough. Lauren wouldn't want to think about hers either. 'It's fantastic. Enjoy celebrating,' she said. 'I'm off to bed. Long day and all.'

'Of course, of course,' Norman said. 'Smashing work today, Lauren, truly.'

'Yes, Lauren,' Jasper added, then cleared his throat. 'It was perfect. Thank you for everything.'

She nodded, then turned and left the room before either of them could see the fierce blush spreading up her cheeks.

Chapter 10

'Soooooo,' Lauren said, leaning against the bathroom sink. Una was washing her face after what looked to be a successful night out, if the love bite just below her earlobe was any indicator. The post-Singapore jet lag had been all too real, and this was the first time in three days that Lauren had finally been able to wake up at a civilised hour, which worked out well as it was her first day back in the office.

'Let's say theoretically,' Lauren continued, and Una peeked one soapy eye up from her hands, looking at Lauren in the mirror.

'Well, this sounds like it's going to be juicy,' Una said through a mouthful of foam.

'Definitely not juicy,' Lauren lied. 'Let's say that—'

'Theoretically,' Una said, rubbing at her mascara.

'Always,' Lauren agreed. 'So, let's say you were on a business trip with a, um, a coworker, for example.'

'That is usually who you see on business trips,' Una said. 'But go on.'

'And let's also say that maybe and perhaps possibly,

you and this coworker kissed, even though it would be inappropriate.'

Una peeked her other eye up. 'I'm hoping for your sake that this isn't theoretical after all.'

'It's not about me,' Lauren said quickly. 'I'm just asking for a friend.'

Una looked disappointed. 'Lauren. Try harder.'

'Okay, fine. Let's say you kissed this person but then fortunately you got interrupted and nothing more happened. But then unfortunately, you have to see this person at work.'

'Sounds like a champagne problem,' Una said, splashing water on her face. 'Do you double cleanse?'

'What? No.'

'You should.' Una turned off the water and grabbed a towel. 'Is this theoretical person cute?'

'Yes,' Lauren said, a little too quickly for her liking. 'Very.'

'Hmm, nice. And who exactly would have to know about this if you did hook up?'

The entire world, Lauren thought to herself before saying, 'Possibly no one? But also possibly everyone. At work, I mean.'

Una nodded as she thought, dabbing at her face, and Lauren could see the exact second that it hit her.

'Oh my God,' she said, whirling around. 'Did you fuck the hot duke?'

'What?' Lauren screamed. 'Oh my God, no! What do you think, that this is *Bridgerton* or something?!'

'Because you said you worked at Buckingham Palace. And I saw you in the news in Singapore with the royals.' Una was shaking her finger like a detective who had solved the most impossible mystery. 'And there's exactly one person at Buckingham Palace right now that everyone wants to shag. I have to say, Lauren, I am *impressed*.'

Lauren, for the millionth time since she had arrived in London, wished she had her own bathroom. 'Listen to me. I haven't fucked anyone, which I understand sounds really sad when I say it out loud—'

'Hey, I don't judge,' Una said with a shrug. 'Takes all kinds to make the world go 'round.'

'I'm just saying that a coworker and I became close and I can't stop thinking about it.'

'Well, I am quite proud!' Una said. 'Look at you, working your way through the royal lineage.'

'Oh for the love of – okay.' Lauren covered her face in her hands, possibly smudging the eyeliner she had put on twenty minutes earlier, before Una had come into the bathroom and when her life had been easier. 'I have not done anything with the royal lineage, and please don't think that I did. Or worse, say that I did.'

'Hey, if there's one person who can keep a secret, it's me.' Una turned back to the mirror as she opened a bottle of blue-coloured serum. 'I know where all the bodies are buried.'

Lauren paused before asking, 'Is that a metaphor?'

Una started to dot serum all over her face. 'You can decide.'

'I'm just wondering if it would be bad, if I did something with someone.'

'Is anyone going to die if you do?'

Maybe me, Lauren thought. 'I don't think so?'

'Then go for it. Don't live your life by someone else's rules. This world is hard and if you find someone who keeps your bed warm and also happens to be insanely attractive, then why not.'

Lauren knew that this was *not* the advice she needed, but it was still good to hear. 'Okay,' she said. 'Thanks, Una.'

'One more piece of advice?' Una said, then gestured to

190

Lauren's forehead. 'I know a great Botox lady who can fix that in a second.'

'THANKS, UNA!' Lauren yelled as she left the room. 'Always a pleasure!'

'Hopefully that's what he says as well!' she replied before Lauren decidedly slammed the door behind her.

There was only one reason that Lauren had confided in Una at all, she realised on the tube into work that morning: It was because she could never, ever tell Joy. Even now, she wasn't sure if Joy could read it on her face, and she had enough on her plate without her one friend putting the pieces together.

The truth was, Lauren hadn't stopped thinking about Jasper. Sitting with him on the sofa, their knees touching in a way that made Lauren feel like she was back in high school again. It was like he could see right through her, exposing her in a way that felt even more dangerous than if they had just locked the door and tumbled into those luxurious sheets on his king-size bed. And then there was the sturdiness of his body next to hers, his steady gaze as she had spoken about her past life in DC, the hot press of his mouth on hers.

With Oscar, she had felt incredible tension, the pull to make out with him in the middle of a nightclub and then bicker with him a day later at a press conference. There was the witty banter and the flirty texts, but also the considerate phone call that night at Balmoral. She sometimes didn't know where they stood, which made it exciting. Lauren had never not enjoyed a challenge.

If Oscar felt like her schoolboy crush, then Jasper felt, well, not like a schoolboy at all.

It was thrilling and sparked a specific joy she hadn't felt in so long. But she could not deny the sense of guilt that had also set in. She and Oscar were definitely not exclusive, not really even a thing, but still, she liked him. She knew that if Oscar had kissed someone else, she'd feel jealous and likely pissed off. So she didn't feel great about what had happened with Jasper – even if a relationship with him, or just another kiss, was completely out of the question.

The chill and gloom on her walk from Green Park station to the Palace, along with a quick slushy spray from an errant cabdriver, matched her mood that morning, and by the time she got to work, everyone else was in full work mode, Joy included.

'Hi, my love,' Joy said breathlessly as she brushed past Lauren. 'Look, come with me to this meeting. I want to hear *allll* about Singapore and everything you did, but I have to do this one thing first and it's about this community outreach program we have in the works for the Strathearns, so you should be there as well, as I'm really hoping it finally gets activated.'

'Okay,' Lauren said, and felt the rush of relief that always came from seeing a friend after what felt like a long time apart. 'Did you get more pods for the Nespresso in your office?'

'Of course I did.' Joy looked at her as if she had lost her mind. 'Am I supposed to drink the coffee from the kitchen? Please, Lauren, life is too short.'

Lauren gave her a quick hug. 'I adore you, do you know that?'

'Again, of course I do.' Joy squeezed her arms as they walked towards her office. 'What's got into you?' She glanced around then before mouthing at Lauren, 'Please say Oscar.'

'Sorry to disappoint,' Lauren replied. 'Just happy to see you, that's all.'

The meeting consisted of Joy, Lauren (who had first made herself a double espresso before settling into an office chair) and three members of the Prince and Princess of Strathearn's team, including their private secretary, Harold Cockburn.

'Hello, Harold; hello, all,' Joy said. 'I brought Lauren in as well, since she's currently crushing it as the head of comms, as I'm sure you all are well aware.' The look on Harold's face seemed to say that he did know and he wasn't particularly thrilled about a twenty-eight-year-old American being employee of the month.

'We've been discussing having the Strathearns pilot a community outreach project in the city,' Joy said to Lauren. 'There, now you're caught up.'

'I think it's a wonderful idea,' Lauren said, all too ready to be Joy's hype woman.

'Well, we shall see. The couple already have a few engagements a week in their diaries through to the end of the year,' Harold said. 'Joy did send over a list of community centres in different neighbourhoods, though it appeared to be focused mostly on southeast London.' The way he appeared to say 'southeast London' with a little disdain gave Lauren pause, and judging from the intentionally blank look on Joy's face, she didn't appreciate it either.

'Well, "community outreach" does involve neighbourhoods,' Joy replied. 'Usually in different communities other than Westminster or Kensington, and through research and my conversations with local MPs across the city, there is a need for more youth-focused initiatives and service projects in the likes of Lewisham, Bexley, Southwark and so on – all extremely diverse communities.'

'Hmm.' Harold hummed as he flipped through several of the pamphlets and printed memos. 'Let's do this one in

Lewisham.' He held up a page with the name of a youth centre to the woman sitting next to him, who was apparently low enough on the roster to not even garner an introduction. 'How long will a visit take?' he asked. 'An hour? Less?'

'Ideally this would be a longer commitment than just one visit, with an announcement, an initial visit, a roundtable with local politicians and community leaders, a follow-up visit further down the line,' Joy replied evenly. 'I know they would appreciate as much time as the couple have to offer. Visits like this, they can bring so much attention to the community, and that radiates outwards, of course.'

'I see,' Harold said, sounding less enthused. 'Well, we can look at their schedules and figure out which day is best for bringing the Prince and Princess from the Palace to the ghetto.'

Lauren froze in her seat.

'I'm sorry, what exactly do you mean by that?' Joy asked, her voice suddenly icy in a way that Lauren had never heard before.

'Oh come on,' Harold said with a laugh. 'I'm only joking.'

'Then please explain the joke,' Joy said, folding her arms. 'Nobody here is laughing, so maybe you could walk us through what exactly you meant.'

'Oh lighten up, it was a *joke*,' Harold shot back. 'No need to attack me.'

'You don't get to joke like that, not in my office.' Joy's voice was sharp but measured. 'This is a neighbourhood, a beautiful community, with good people living there. You're not going to disrespect them in front of me or anyone present, am I clear?'

Harold just rolled his eyes, but Lauren could see his knee bouncing up and down underneath the table.

194

Joy stared him down for a few long seconds before going back to her notes. 'Let me know which dates are best for the couple and I'll connect with the community centre to start with next steps.'

'Excellent,' Harold said as he stood up, seemingly ready to beat a hasty retreat. 'I'm sure we all look forward to it.'

Joy's mouth was pinched as she replied, 'I'm sure.'

The second Cockburn and his anonymous lackeys stepped out of Joy's office, Lauren was shutting the door behind them, Joy scribbling a few notes down as she took a deep breath. 'What the hell was that!' Lauren whisper-hissed. 'What he said was so insanely inappropriate!'

Joy just held up a hand as she finished her note, then gestured to Lauren to sit down again. They were both silent for a minute before Joy finally raised her head, looking annoyed. 'Not the first time, not the last time,' she said. 'Unfortunately.'

'He should be fired,' Lauren said.

'Why, so another Harold can pop up to take his place? Someone else who can make me out as the angry Black woman?' She scoffed before sitting back in her chair and sighing. 'Maybe I shouldn't have said all that just now.'

'No,' Lauren said. 'You were right to call him out. Do you want to go to HR? I'll totally back up your story. I'll come with you.'

Joy laughed again. 'You mean file a complaint with the white *Daily Dispatch*—reading lady who runs HR? I'm good, thanks.' She turned towards her laptop and frowned at an incoming email. 'It just never changes, you know? Always the same idiocy.'

'Well, if I see Harold in the halls, I'll trip him up.' It was a childish joke that sounded even more immature out loud, and Lauren regretted it when Joy barely smiled at her. 'I'll be at my desk for most of the day, okay? And let me know the second you're ready to talk comms strategies for the engagement. It's going to be so good.'

'All right, love,' Joy said, then reached for her phone. 'Thanks. I'm going to call the community centre and let them know that they're the *lucky winners* today.'

The office had an air of heaviness to it that day, and Lauren had to stop herself several times from going down to Joy's office to check on her or, worse, going to HR herself and telling them everything. She would never betray Joy like that, though, especially because she knew Joy was right.

Lauren was just starting to pack up to go home when her phone pinged.

'Hey you,' the text from Oscar read. 'Want to get dinner?'

Lauren read the message three times to make sure she had it right. He was asking her out to dinner. Was this for work? Was this so they could get drunk again and make out against another wall? Was it because he had just spent time in Singapore watching her escort Jasper?

She tried several times to write back to him, then gave up and FaceTimed.

'Hello,' he said, his phone pointing almost directly up his nostrils as he sat on a bus. 'Video calling me, I see. You're catching me at my finest angle.'

'I wanted to see you to make sure I have this straight,' Lauren said. 'You want me to get dinner with you tonight.'

'I'll double-check what I wrote, but yes, fairly certain that's what the text said.'

'Hmm, interesting.' Lauren ran a finger along her desk, wiping up dust. 'With barely any notice? How do you know I'm not busy tonight?'

'Well, partly because I know you're still at work and partly because you're calling me. Doesn't exactly imply a hectic evening schedule.'

Once again, Lauren was torn between wanting to reach through the screen and both throttle him and make out with him again. 'Well, I'll have you know that I need at least twenty-four hours' notice before any social commitments. Because I am a professional.'

There was a pause before he said, 'You do realise that I watched you put up your hair with a binder clip last week in Singapore, yes?'

'That's how busy I am,' she replied. 'No time for proper accessories.'

'Or dinner, apparently.'

'Oh, I plan on eating dinner tonight, please don't worry about that.'

Oscar finally laughed. 'Lauren, you're exhausting, and I mean that as a compliment.'

She blushed despite herself. 'What every girl dreams of hearing,' she said. 'Maybe try again tomorrow. I'll check my calendar.'

'Fine,' he said. 'Go eat your mysterious work dinner, then. Probably frozen and microwavable.'

Lauren decided not to acknowledge her Amy's Organics frozen enchiladas that she had hidden in the freezer compartment of the office fridge, just in case anyone got any ideas about stealing her meal. 'I'll see you at the weekly briefing tomorrow, right?'

'Wouldn't dream of missing it,' Oscar replied, and Lauren could see the smile on his face as he spoke. 'The people are breathlessly waiting for the latest news about which group of citizens the Duke of Exeter plans on charming next.'

'Well, we also might be dropping a few titbits about the royal family members' plans for World Book Day. Going to be a big one. Maybe pack a snack so you don't miss anything.'

Oscar laughed. 'Good night, Lauren. Good luck with your busy evening.'

Lauren hung up, then went down the hall to find her freezer dinner. On her way, though, she could see into Joy's office and saw her sitting at her laptop, typing away, her face so smooth and neutral that Lauren knew she was still upset.

And then she had an idea.

'Hey,' she said, sidling into Joy's office, her coat over her arm and her bag over her shoulder. 'How are you?'

Joy shrugged. 'Regretting not signing up for breathwork classes, if I'm being honest,' she said.

'Understandable,' Lauren said. 'Is Theo with his dad this week?'

'Mm-hmm. Thought I'd try to get some extra work done while he's gone.'

Lauren sank down into a chair across from her. 'What food makes you happy when you need cheering up?'

Joy glanced up from her screen. 'Hmmm. My mum's ackee and saltfish with fried dumplings.'

'Well that settles it, then, I'm making that for you,' Lauren declared.

'You can cook Jamaican food?!' Joy said, surprised.

'Well, no, but I'm great at following a recipe,' Lauren said. 'Plus, I want you to have a good end to a crappy day.'

'Babe, no offence, but I've seen those struggle dishes you put in the microwave when you're working late.' Joy laughed, closing the lid of her MacBook. 'And now I'm hungry.'

'Fine. Hot pot in Chinatown?' Lauren suggested. 'Boba afterwards? My treat?'

Joy paused and stood up. 'Yes, *please*,' she said. 'I need to boil some things and eat them. A lot of things. And also drink some things as well.'

'Excellent.' Lauren took Joy's coat and helped her into it. 'So do you want some good gossip?'

'Of course I want some good gossip!' Joy said, turning off the lights as they headed out. 'Do you even know who you're talking to?'

Lauren grinned. 'Got to wait until we're out of the office.'

Joy squealed in anticipation and took Lauren by the arm so they could walk faster.

'Oscar just texted me and asked me out to dinner tonight,' Lauren said as soon as they were outside the Palace walls.

'And you clearly said no, judging by the fact that you're currently on my arm and not his.'

'I didn't say no, exactly.' Lauren sucked her teeth for a second, drawing out Joy's suspense (and secretly relieved that her friend was smiling again). 'I just told him that I need twenty-four hours' notice for any personal events.'

Joy patted her arm. 'That's my girl. I think it's the stupidest thing you've done in some time, but that's my girl.'

'We'll see,' Lauren said. 'To be discussed over a boiling pot of meat.'

'Lead the way,' Joy replied.

Chapter 11

'Okay, Adam,' Lauren said, standing at the podium the next morning for their press briefing. The weekly sessions had been something of a hit with the British media – it was one of the first times there had ever been a sense of having the slightest amount of consistent control over coverage about the royal family. 'As I'm sure you know from your many, many years doing this job, seemingly without a promotion as far as I can tell, we do not comment on any of the family's personal lives. Ever. And that includes the Duke of Exeter.'

'But there are photos of him with a blonde woman—'

'And?' Lauren teased him. 'Were they talking? Breathing the same air? Please, Adam, don't waste our time here. If there's a story, I'll make sure you have the right one, but until then—' She made a 'zip it' motion across her mouth.

Adam glared at her. He had not checked in with her again about his dig for information on Jasper's financial problems, but she had no doubt there would still be some stupid *Dispatch* headline the next morning. She wasn't surprised that everyone was trying to cobble together stories on the duke after his wildly successful Singaporean state dinner and children's hospital visit, and the number of TikTok edits Violet kept sending her was starting to approach harassment. (Not that Lauren didn't watch every single one of them. For work purposes.) One paper even sent a drone out over his old sheep farm in New Zealand to get shots of, perhaps not surprisingly, a huge group of bored-looking sheep. Lauren laughed when she saw the pictures and wondered which one was Sweater Weather.

She hadn't seen Jasper since Singapore. She wasn't sure if that was a conscious decision on his part, but either way, it was probably for the best. She wasn't sure what exactly she felt about him, but she knew that it wasn't nothing.

And it terrified her.

She was positive, though, that the kiss in Singapore had been a moment of terrible judgement on both of their parts, and she needed to put some space between them, which was why she sent Harriet out with the duke on his latest outing to meet volunteers raising money for the London Ambulance Service charity, and then said a quick prayer that Harriet wouldn't accidentally send him to an early grave.

'Okay, final question!' Lauren said. 'Please, if possible, could it be about *any* of the topics I briefed you on at the beginning of this session? That would be much appreciated.'

There was silence, and Lauren sighed. 'Well, I look forward to all of your headlines about our array of World Book Day reading initiatives we have lined up next month. I'm sure they'll be very informative.'

She grabbed her notebook and was about to head back to her office when Oscar stepped in front of her. She had forgotten how much taller he was than her five-foot-four self and found herself looking at the perfect knot in his tie.

'Well, hello,' she said. 'Fancy seeing you here.'

He smiled at her. 'I did have a question for you, actually, but I assumed you wouldn't want me asking it in front of this lot.' He jerked a thumb over his shoulder at the other journalists starting to file out of the room. 'Not sure how you feel about personal questions at work.'

'Not great, actually,' Lauren said. 'The last thing I need is James or Eugene thinking that I'm using work time as personal time.'

'Oh, you know Eugene loves a good strop,' Oscar said. 'It keeps him young.'

'Well, he's going to be Benjamin Button at this rate,' Lauren replied, picking up her bag. 'So, if you had to ask me a personal question at work—'

'Which I am absolutely not going to do, of course.'

'Of course. But if you were?'

Oscar glanced at his watch and pretended to think. 'Well, I did hear something – not from today's press conference, of course, but from a different source – that you need twenty-four hours' notice before making dinner plans.'

'Which you would never do at work,' Lauren added.

'Absolutely not,' Oscar said. 'I'm a rule follower, you know that.'

Lauren snorted to herself, remembering his hand in her hair, the two of them pressed up against the wall at Annabel's back in November. She wasn't quite sure what the rules had been that night, but neither she nor Oscar had been following them, that much she knew.

'Well, even if you were asking me out to dinner tonight, I couldn't go anyway. I have to run some errands, and I've already put them off for way too long.'

'Well, then, maybe you need some help. Is it dry cleaning? Food shopping?' Oscar pretended to shiver in happiness.

Lauren couldn't hide her smile this time. 'You're good,' she said.

'Well, I'm assuming that the twenty-four-hour rule doesn't apply to casual errands,' he said, returning her smile.

'You know,' she said, 'you actually could be a really big help to me tonight.'

'Great,' he said. 'I love helping.'

'No, you don't.'

'No, not really. Did I guess right, though?'

Lauren paused. 'Not exactly.'

'Just for the record,' Oscar said, 'I hate you.'

She turned and grinned at him. 'When was the last time you were in a TK Maxx, anyway?'

'With my mum when I was like seventeen. Why do they have a random section selling suspicious-looking foods?!'

They were standing in an extremely long queue, considering it was 7:00 p.m. on a Friday night, each of them holding a huge bag of autumnal-themed decor from Lauren's failed Thanksgiving celebration.

'Please don't take this the wrong way,' Oscar started to say.

'Oh, this should be fun,' Lauren said.

'But you never struck me as the kind of person to buy an entire load of holiday-themed ... crap.' He glanced into the oversize plastic bag. 'Is that a cushion of a pumpkin wearing sunglasses?'

'Probably,' Lauren said. 'And I'm not that kind of person. I just was super homesick and momentarily panicked about the holidays and spent way too much money as a coping mechanism, which is why we're returning all of this. And I've been putting it off for ages. And then you swooped in and so graciously offered to help me!' She batted her eyes at

203

him. 'My hero. Plus,' she added, 'it would have been a pain to carry all this here by myself.'

'Yes, a real highlight of my day,' Oscar replied, but he looked more bemused than annoyed. That changed, though, when Lauren reached around him towards the clearance section, stocked with post–Valentine's Day goodies, and plucked a headband from the pile. It had two spiral wires connected to shiny pink hearts, like a bug's antennae.

'These are cute!' she said, holding them up so he could see them, and Oscar winced.

'If you put those on my head . . .' he warned her.

'Oh, who do you know in here anyway? I think they're perfect.' She raised them towards him, and when he didn't protest, she slipped them over his head. 'You're adorable.'

'No offence, but no grown man wants to be referred to as "adorable".' He opened his phone and looked at himself in the camera, then groaned.

'Pretty sure there's a pumpkin pair in one of these bags somewhere if you want to swap them.'

'I feel like I'm in one of those stupid made-for-TV movies that my mum watches.'

It was so fun to rile him up, Lauren realised, to catch him off guard from his normal buttoned-up ways, to get him excited. She felt like a kid playing tag on the school playground. 'Fine, fine,' she said. She slipped them off his head and onto hers. 'What do you think? Do they make my eyes pop?'

Oscar looked down at her with something like fondness, his eyes warming up as he reached out to smooth her hair back. 'Okay, you do look adorable,' he said.

Lauren's smile faded into something a little different, a little more vulpine, and she suddenly wished she hadn't tried so hard to be cute and flirty and put her little twenty-four-hour notice rule in place. Because right now, she was pretty sure she would have followed him anywhere and done anything.

'Next!' one of the many cashiers said, holding up a red flag, which Lauren decided was just a coincidence and not a warning from the universe to pump the brakes.

'Hi,' Lauren said as she and Oscar staggered up to her.

'How did you even get this *home* with you?' Oscar asked as he dragged his bag.

'I need to return all of these items, please,' Lauren said, ignoring him, then produced a crumpled receipt from the bottom of her purse, smoothing it out on the counter before handing it over.

'What is the reason for your return?' the cashier said, looking less than thrilled. 'I can only give you credit as it's been well over the return period.'

'Well, I bought it because my mum was supposed to come over and visit me for Thanksgiving, and I was slightly panicked, so I did some stress shopping, but then she ended up cancelling because of a listeria outbreak, so I'm returning them now.'

'I meant, like, are any of these items defective?'

'Depends on who you're asking,' Oscar muttered, and Lauren gave him a gentle kick.

'No,' she said. 'Just need them out of my house. But,' she added, then motioned to her antennae headband, 'I will take these. Somebody I like told me I look adorable in them.'

By the time they left the shop, the sky was dark and the streets were packed with people heading in all directions. 'So much easier to walk without carrying an entire pumpkin patch,' Lauren said. 'But thanks for your help, seriously. I would have had to get an overpriced taxi or something.'

'Well, I'll add it to my list of special skills,' Oscar said, pulling on a pair of gloves. 'Are you heading home?'

'Yeah, just down to High Street Kensington station,' she said, gesturing towards the tube entrance that was a few streets away.

'I'll walk you there,' he said. 'I'm going that way as well.'

The station looked crowded as they tapped their cards at the turnstiles and headed down the steps and to the end of the platform, away from the milling people and Friday-night tourists. 'So,' Oscar said as Lauren glanced down the track to see if she could see the train's headlights.

'So,' she said, turning back to him. 'Thanks again.'

'Of course. I also wanted to ask you, how late do you normally eat dinner?'

'Um, pretty late? I think?'

'Well, it's seven fifty-five now,' he said, tapping at his watch. 'And I have five minutes left to ask you to dinner at eight o'clock tomorrow night. And if you don't want to go, then I have five minutes to try to change your mind.'

That seventh-grade-crush feeling was back in force.

'Well, you better hurry up and ask me,' she said. 'The clock's ticking.'

'Lauren, I would love to take you to dinner tomorrow night at eight p.m.' He paused before adding, 'Why do I feel like I should be down on one knee right now?'

'Bite your tongue,' Lauren said. 'Dinner in an actual restaurant, right? Not, like, Nando's?'

'Lauren, I'm trying to impress you here. Of course we're not going to Nando's. No shame against it, though, I could murder a quarter chicken and Peri-Peri fries right now.'

'And you'll pick the place? I don't have to figure it out?'

Oscar frowned. 'What sort of idiots have you been dating? How low is the bar?'

'Story for another time,' she said. 'Anyway yes, I would love to go to dinner at an actual restaurant of your choosing. With you.' She picked up his wrist and glanced at his watch. 'Two minutes to spare. Anything else you want to ask me?'

Oscar paused, and suddenly his eyes weren't teasing at all, and it felt like they were the only two people on the platform, and Lauren had to catch her breath.

'Just one thing,' he murmured. 'Do you promise that you'll wear these?' He reached up to tweak one heart antenna, and Lauren shrieked.

'I forgot I had them on!' she cried, taking them off her head. 'Why didn't you say anything?'

They were both laughing now, and as the train started to pull in, Oscar reached for her arm and pulled her in close, kissing her cheek. Lauren could feel the stubble on his skin, chilled from the cold night air, and smell his shampoo and his soap. 'I told you,' he said as he pulled away. 'You look adorable.' He squeezed her arm as he started to take a step back. 'Get home safe. I'm not even going to ask you to text me because I know how that'll go.'

'Wait, are you not . . . ?' Lauren gestured towards the train as it stopped at the platform.

'This isn't my station,' he said, then lifted his hand in a wave. 'See you tomorrow. I'll text you the place.'

She watched him even after she was onboard, looking out the condensation-covered window. He didn't leave until the train was pulling away, and Lauren watched as he took the stairs two at a time, a spring in his step, a lightness in him that she had never seen before, but she knew how it felt, because she was feeling that exact same way, too.

Chapter 12

The cab dropped Lauren off at Gloria in Shoreditch at 7:58 p.m., exactly twenty-four hours since she had seen Oscar on the train platform. She was absolutely not wearing her love antennae, choosing instead to leave them propped up on her one potted plant that, if she was being honest, probably wasn't going to make it another four weeks until spring.

She had been texting with Joy while picking out her outfit, making plans for their brunch the next morning while trying on jeans and skirts and heels and blouses, none of which made her feel as good as she had felt when Oscar had asked her out the night before. She tossed them into a pile while agreeing to meet Joy at 10:00 a.m., then reached into the very back of what she not-so-lovingly referred to as her 'capsule closet' and found a dress that she hadn't worn since . . .

Well, since Brian.

It was still in the dry cleaning bag from DC, and Lauren felt a small pang of homesickness when she saw the paper receipt clipped to the top. When she tried the Pacific blue puff-sleeved minidress on, it felt better than it had ever felt in the States, and she liked the idea of it having a renewed life right alongside her.

She was nervous, she realised, as her black cab bounced along some of East London's cobblestone side streets, nearly giddy not just with excitement, but for the potential for good to happen, for all the things she had endured throughout the past year to melt away under the warm haze of something new and promising.

Oscar was waiting outside for her, wearing a cashmere sweater and cream trousers. She suspected he had had a hair-cut that day, he looked so crisp, and her heart pitter-patted a little bit at the thought. He was trying to impress her.

'Hey,' he said when she stepped out of the car, hurrying over to take her hand as she climbed out, praying that she didn't smell like the four pine tree air fresheners that hung from its rearview mirror. 'You look great.'

'Thanks,' she replied, pulling her chain-link handbag over her shoulder. She had had to unpack the small bag from a still-unpacked moving box, realising that her daily work bag wasn't exactly going to complete her outfit. As she dug it out, she had started to wonder how much was left in her moving boxes, how much she hadn't touched, and what exactly she was waiting for.

'You look really good, too,' she said, rubbing the soft fabric of his sweater. 'I like this.'

He held the door open for her as they entered the Italian restaurant. It was packed for a Saturday night, and Lauren – a planner down to her DNA – was about to wonder aloud if they'd be able to get a table without a reservation when the maître d' saw Oscar and immediately lit up.

'Oscar,' he said, doing the half-handshake, half-hug thing that every man seemed to have mastered. 'Hello, hello, it's good to see you. It's been a few.'

'Yes, I know, sorry, work travel,' Oscar said. Lauren had never seen him so relaxed before. Even his shoulders seemed less tight and tense, and when he smiled, his whole face seemed to change. She wondered if he knew that about himself.

'I was in Singapore for a bit,' he continued, then reached for Lauren and guided her forward. 'With Lauren. We work together.' He put his hand on the small of her back, and she felt herself get goosebumps. 'She's a VIP guest tonight, she needs looking after.'

'Of course,' the maître d' said. 'Here, let's get you a booth.'

'That'd be perfect, thank you.' Oscar guided Lauren in front of him. 'Follow him,' he murmured. 'He'll take care of us.'

Their table was nearly in the centre of the noisy, bustling room but still felt intimate, and Lauren and Oscar slid into the booth on opposite sides. 'So why are they so nice to you here?' Lauren asked.

'I'm a very loyal customer,' he said. 'Probably too loyal. I'm in here more often than not. I'm not much of a chef and it feels like . . .' He shrugged and glanced around the room. 'Feels a little bit like home, I guess. Noisy and loud, everyone talking over one another.'

'Do you come from a big family?'

'A big extended family. One brother, but I have a million cousins, aunts and uncles. I can't even keep track.'

Lauren tried to imagine Oscar at a big Christmas table, or Easter brunch, or a wedding, and found that she couldn't. She only knew him as a journalist, she realised, someone poking around for the full story, and the idea of him being more than just that made her heart swell.

'What about you?' he asked.

'Only child,' she said. 'And not a lot of cousins. I think I have ...' Lauren thought fast. 'Three? They're all older than me, we don't really talk.'

She could tell that Oscar wanted to ask more questions, but the menus landed just then, and pretty soon they were deep in discussion about drinks and salad and whether pizza should have shaved truffle on it (which they both agreed it should). Then Lauren shrugged out of her coat, shaking her hair back, and Oscar pushed up his sleeves, and it felt right and warm and normal to be together.

The night raced by as they shared truffle pizza and linguine and chatted over a bottle of wine about their lives, their interests and dreams in life. For the first time since they had met, the subject of the royals didn't even come up. After a shared scoop of pistachio gelato, Oscar picked up the bill and they made their way towards the exit, both of them effusively thanking the maître d,' who just smiled and handed over a doggie bag of leftovers before giving Oscar a thumbs-up.

'I saw that,' Lauren said, nudging Oscar's arm as she waited for her Uber.

'Well, I think he likes you,' Oscar replied. 'Everybody likes you, though.'

Lauren laughed, turning to face him. 'That is factually untrue. You need to check your sources.'

'Oh, do I?' he asked, wrapping his arms around her so that she was locked in against his chest. 'Prove me wrong.'

Lauren hesitated before leaning up to kiss him, but once their lips met, she wasn't hesitant at all. The taste of him was familiar, his mouth warm against hers. There was a different intensity than there had been at Annabel's, their first time hooking up rooted in the immediacy of the moment. This felt like something stronger and deeper.

211

'Well,' he said as they pulled apart. 'Not bad for a first kiss.'

'What?' Lauren said. 'This is like our sixtieth kiss. Remember Annabel's? Oh my God, please say you remember.'

'No, I remember,' he said, and he was brushing the hair off her face again as he looked down into her eyes, and Lauren hated how much she liked it when he did that. 'But this is our first date, so those previous kisses don't count. This one's legit.'

'Prove it,' Lauren whispered, and then he was leaning down to meet her again, and well, Oscar had no problem at all proving it. No problem at all.

'Damn,' she whispered when they pulled apart again. 'You can't just . . . wow. Okay. Give me a minute.'

The Uber pulled up just as she was getting her bearings, Oscar still holding on to her arms. 'Are you sure you want to go? We can grab a drink somewhere around here, or maybe a coffee.'

Coffee was the absolute last thing on Lauren's mind. 'I could grab a drink,' she said. 'At yours, maybe?'

Oscar pulled back to look at her, his eyes slightly dilating. 'I think we can make that happen,' he replied, then opened the car door to speak to the driver. 'Change of plans, my friend,' he said. 'We're going to walk.' Lauren felt his hand reach for hers as they made the four-minute stroll to his place.

Not that Lauren had thought a lot about what Oscar's apartment might look like, but she hadn't been expecting what she found.

'Okay, I'm just going to ask,' she said, setting her handbag down on the stone kitchen island. 'How the hell do you afford this on a newspaper salary?'

Oscar laughed as he swung his coat over a walnut-and-wicker

dining chair. The apartment was neat, but not the sort of clean and organised that suggested he had thought her visit was an inevitability. There was post stacked on one end of the table, a few cups in the sink, a hastily made bed on the mezzanine floor that looked over the living room and several pairs of trainers strewn by the front door. It felt lived in, and Lauren liked it.

'I share it with my housemate, who is fortunately away for the weekend,' he said. 'We've lived here for a few years.' Then he looked her dead in the eyes and said, 'I know when to hold onto a good thing.'

They both paused for a few seconds before bursting out laughing. 'That was terrible!' Lauren cried.

'I was trying to be cool!' he protested, even as he laughed alongside her. 'I know, I have zero game.'

'Game is overrated,' she promised him.

'Do you want something to drink?' he said. 'I have some whiskey tucked away somewhere, some beer.'

Lauren suspected that she was going to want to sober up for whatever happened next. 'Just water,' she said. 'For now.' He had taken off his sweater when they got in, and when he turned towards the fridge and opened the door, she could see the muscles of his back through the plain white T-shirt he had on underneath, and Lauren said a quick thank-you to whatever gods had convinced her to stay on birth control after breaking up with Brian.

'Soooo,' Oscar said, sliding the glass of water over to her before sitting down at the kitchen island. 'Only child, not many cousins.'

Lauren shrugged. 'It is what it is.'

'Is that why you moved here?'

'Because I don't have cousins?' She laughed. 'People have done far more because of far less.'

213

'No, I just meant, like, you're not anchored anywhere.'

Lauren had never thought of it that way, and after hearing it out loud, she had no intentions to do so in the future. 'I moved here after my relationship and life imploded, which I know you know, and I needed a change.'

'Still, it's a big move,' he said, sipping at his own bottle of beer. 'I really admire that about you. That's a huge change, and you just did it, no fear.'

'No, there's a lot of fear,' Lauren admitted. 'I'm always wondering if I just fucked up the next ten years of my life. Or maybe I'll regret not having more time with my mum, I don't know. But yeah.' She gave him a dramatic shrug. 'What's done is done.'

'I'm glad it is,' he said. 'Where do your parents live?'

Lauren decided to pivot. 'Did you *really* invite me back here to talk about my relocation?' she asked.

Oscar smiled as he stood up from his chair. 'Well, if I recall correctly, you were the one who invited yourself back to my place.'

'Hmmm,' Lauren hummed, sitting back in her chair and parting her legs a little so he could stand between them. 'Is that so? I might need a fact-check.'

'I'll get right on that,' he said. 'After this, of course.' And then his mouth was on hers once more, and this time they weren't surrounded by strangers, she wasn't thinking about who would possibly see them together, and she sank into Oscar's arms. She felt herself rise up to him, letting her mind unravel as her body took over, as his hands ran up her thighs and under her dress, as her own hands tugged at the hem of his T-shirt, and for the first time in what seemed like months, if not years, Lauren found herself not having to think at all.

*

'Favourite food?' Lauren asked.

'Easy. Korean barbecue and beer.'

'Respectable, respectable,' she said. Lying next to Oscar in his bed with the sheets pulled up around them, she could not have felt more relaxed. Oscar's hair was rumpled, and she loved how undone he looked, how much more relaxed he looked when he wasn't Oscar the Royal Reporter.

'My turn,' he said. 'Best Christmas present you ever got.'

'The first iPad,' she replied. 'Don't even have to think about it. I sent texts to every single person I ever met in my life that day. Which wasn't that many people because I was only thirteen at the time. Okay, biggest challenge growing up.'

Oscar hesitated this time, glancing down at the bed before looking up at her. 'Dyslexia,' he said. 'I was diagnosed when I was eight. The teacher used to make us go around the room and read out loud and I always dreaded it.'

'Were the other kids mean about it?' she asked.

'Course they were.' He laughed. 'A classroom full of kids is like Romans at the Colosseum. But it was crushing because I always wanted to work for a newspaper or be a writer and it just didn't seem possible. But my mum made me realise it could be a superpower as a journalist. And I think she's right, it forces me to take an extra beat and check that all the information is always accurate. So it didn't end up getting in the way like I thought it would, and well, here I am.' He gestured towards the apartment. 'Nothing but luxury from here on out!'

Lauren smiled as she linked her fingers with his. 'I'm glad you told me that,' she said. 'That must have been really hard.' She thought briefly of her own mum and, more importantly, her dad. She still had dreams of seeing him at Christmas, lost in his small house and unable to find her way out. No one

215

other than her mum knew that she had seen him, and she had planned on keeping it that way, but she wondered now if she should tell Oscar. He had shared something so personal, and it felt like the right time to open up to him.

'Well, I have it on good information that two of my worst tormentors got indicted in a major money laundering scheme a few years ago, so, you know, things have a way of working out.'

And just like that, the moment was gone.

'And did you report the story?' she asked.

'Every single detail.' He grinned and then leant forward to kiss her. 'Okay, my turn. Why did you leave the White House?'

Lauren paused, suddenly aware that she was in bed with a journalist. 'This is off the record, right?'

Oscar groaned and let go of her hand, rolling over onto his back. 'Lauren, I just told you about being teased for dyslexia in primary school! You're literally in my bed. I promise you, everything that's happening here is one hundred percent off the record.'

'Okay, okay,' she said. 'I'm sorry, occupational hazard.' She took a deep breath and wondered if maybe she should just kiss him again to distract him. But he had been vulnerable with her, and it would feel unfair if she didn't meet him in the middle.

'Just so you know, this is an exclusive. Hardly anyone knows about this.'

Oscar crossed his heart. 'Nothing leaves this room.'

'So after Brian and I broke up, I was really upset – Wait, are you sure you want to hear about my ex right now?'

Oscar just made a 'keep it going' motion at her.

'Okay, fine. So I was a hot mess and I wasn't really sleeping, couldn't even talk to my best friend about it, who is also an ex, because they had been having an affair for months in secret. It felt like everyone at work knew about what had happened between them and were whispering behind my back. And at the time I had been handling cleanup after a series of damaging hit pieces one of the US papers was doing on the president, and one day I got this email from a reporter asking for comment on a totally false story they were planning to run the next morning, so I had to act on it pretty quickly.'

Lauren took a deep breath. This was still so embarrassing to admit. It'd be one thing if she had gone out in a blaze of glory, but this was just a stupid amateur mistake. Even an intern could have done better. 'So instead of looping in the relevant person on POTUS's team, I accidentally emailed the request to someone in my contacts under the same name.'

'Wait, I feel like there's way more to this story,' Oscar said.

'You would be correct. So not only did I send it to the wrong person, who, thankfully didn't even use that email address anymore, but then I went home, got drunk by myself, and fell asleep, because that was my pretty much my routine for the previous couple of weeks, and that journalist who was planning on running the piece never got a response from the team. So the next day, this awful, defamatory story ran in full, above the fold, news alerts everywhere, and my boss had to step in and clean it all up.'

Oscar groaned and fell back onto his pillow. 'Nooo.'

'Yes,' Lauren said. 'And then to top it all off, I had to confess to my boss that this email had gone to some random person at a company I had emailed, like, one time in my life. So that was another thing they had to clean up. To stop this confidential email from getting out.'

'*Lauren*,' Oscar said. 'Did you want to die?'

217

'I prayed for two days straight for the ground to swallow me up,' she said. 'And at the end of that week my boss called me into her office and said that maybe it was time to take a leave of absence. Only she didn't say the word "maybe" and she actually said that I had become a liability. She thought I had taken my eyes off the wheel, and she was kind of right. And it was just so humiliating, and I didn't want anyone to find out, so I just handed in my notice. And she didn't stop me.'

'I'm really sorry,' Oscar said. 'Breakups are the worst. They fuck you up so much.'

'You know what made me the angriest?' Lauren said, falling back down on her pillow and rolling onto her side to face him. 'I let them get the best of me. I let them get to my head. I let a man take over, and he didn't even care about me anymore.'

'Men are the worst,' Oscar agreed, but he was smiling.

'Definitely.' She grinned. 'We should probably still keep a few around, though.'

'Do you miss it?' he asked her. 'The White House.'

'I miss the idea of it,' she said. 'And *Air Force One*.'

Oscar laughed out loud. 'What, you don't enjoy England's finest train system, where it can take just five short hours to travel a hundred miles?'

'A literal leaf could fall on the tracks and suddenly every train is delayed!' Lauren cried, laughing along with him. 'Sometimes it's almost faster to walk!'

'Ah, it's one of this country's many charms,' he said, then reached forward and wrapped his arm around her waist.

'Hmm,' she said. 'I'm starting to like many of your charms, it turns out.'

'Oh, really?' Oscar said, rolling her over so that she was on top of his chest. 'Going to need confirmation on that one.'

'Well, twist my arm,' she said, then reached up for him again.

Her alarm went off at 8:00 a.m., which felt particularly cruel until she remembered that she had set it the night before so she wouldn't miss her brunch date with Joy. If there was anyone in the world who would have understood that Lauren had to cancel brunch because she was in bed with Oscar, it was Joy, but Lauren knew Joy had had a hard week, and she didn't want to be the kind of friend who flaked.

She managed to uncover her phone just as Oscar groaned into his pillow. 'Kill it,' he muttered. 'Kill it with fire.'

'I'm trying,' she said, her voice husky with sleep. 'I told you, I'm having brunch with Joy this morning.'

Oscar nodded, his eyes still closed. 'Spare toothbrush in cabinet under sink if you want it,' he said, gesturing vaguely towards the bathroom.

'I'm sorry I have to go,' Lauren said. 'This wasn't my best planning moment.' Her eyes felt gummy and sticky, and she also felt like she had slept for twelve hours straight, even though they had only dozed off around 3:00 a.m. or so.

'No, go,' Oscar said, finally unearthing his face to look at her. 'Joy's your friend. Friends are important.'

Lauren leant close and brushed his hair off his forehead before giving him a kiss. 'Thanks for last night,' she said. 'It was really fun.'

'It certainly was.' He kissed her collarbone.

Lauren reluctantly climbed out of bed before anything happened that would delay her. She went to the bathroom then slipped out the door, opening Google Maps to find the nearest tube station.

When she got home, she was running late and had to hastily pull herself together.

'Well well well,' Una said, sidling into the bathroom as Lauren, fresh out of the shower, was pulling on a pair of jogging bottoms. She had no time to dig through her wardrobe and find a cute brunch outfit, and she hoped wherever they were going wasn't fancy. 'Look at you. I'm very proud.'

'And how do you know that I didn't just go for an early-morning run before getting ready for brunch?' Lauren said, pushing her date night dress to the side of the floor with her foot.

'Um, because I know you?' Una said, moving the dress back into the middle of the room with her own foot. 'Was it with . . .' She gave Lauren a wink.

'It was not,' Lauren said. 'And thank you for your discretion.'

'Well, in any case, the morning after looks good on you.' Una's own mascara was smudged, and for reasons that Lauren didn't have time to ask about, there was a feather in her hair. 'And look at you, racking them up! The student has become the teacher, I'd say. Did you use my primer again?'

Lauren paused. 'It's possible?'

'I'll allow it. I'm too tired to protest. But it's expensive so don't go thinking this can continue.'

'Are you just getting home?' Lauren asked. 'It's nine o'clock.'

Una just looked at her. 'It was Saturday night, Lauren. What am I, a nun? And don't throw stones from your glass house.' She clicked her tongue as she started to pull her hair back from her face. 'Gonna get Maccy D's delivered and hit the hay.' She grinned at Lauren in the mirror. 'Don't you just love the morning after?'

Lauren had to admit, she kind of did.

*

'Oh my God,' Joy said when she saw her. She was wearing a tailored vest top with wide-legged trousers and, alongside everyone in the restaurant, was about 90 percent more dressed up than Lauren.

And she also had a young boy standing next to her, his entire attention focused on an iPad.

'I am so sorry,' Joy said as soon as Lauren ran up. 'Theo's dad had a work emergency, they were supposed to be going to a football game today, and, well . . .' She looked down at the child with both exasperation and obvious fondness. 'Theo, say hello to Lauren.'

'Hi,' Theo said without looking up.

'Eye contact, please, like we've discussed.'

This time Theo glanced up. 'Hi,' he said again.

'Hi,' Lauren replied. 'Your mum is really cool.'

Theo just shrugged and went back to the game on his iPad.

'It's a work in progress,' Joy said, giving Lauren a one-armed hug as they were led to their table. 'And oh my God, where were you last night?'

'I need coffee,' Lauren replied. 'And why do you ask?'

Joy raised an eyebrow at her as Lauren sank into her seat. 'Have you forgotten that I used to work at *Scotland Yard*?' she said, then gestured towards Lauren's outfit. 'Please, give me a little credit.'

'Coffee,' Lauren said again.

Joy immediately caught the attention of the waiter and mouthed 'double espresso' to him, and Lauren turned around and said, 'Americano, please.' She added to Joy, 'I don't need your micro shots. I need something in a big cup.'

'Even more promising!' Joy pressed her hands together and turned back to the waiter. 'And a hot chocolate for the little one, please. Extra whipped cream.' She turned back to Lauren. 'Anything to distract him. *So.*'

'We had a great night,' Lauren said.

'Of course you had a great night!' Joy said, slapping the table. 'And honestly, can I just say that it's about time? I've been watching the two of you dance around each other for months. Those press conferences were starting to get *me* . . . well, you know.'

'Oddly not reassuring,' Lauren said, nearly falling face-first into the cup of coffee delivered to the table.

'Okaaayyy,' Joy said as she tucked a napkin around Theo, who looked up from his iPad long enough to reach for his cocoa. 'It might be hot, darling, just check it first. So do you want to share any details?'

'Maybe not yet,' Lauren said. 'Everything's still sort of new, I guess? I think I just want to keep it to myself for a bit.'

'We love a boundary,' Joy immediately replied, which only made Lauren love her more. Brooke had always been pressing for the juiciest details about Brian, even after Lauren would demur, and of course Lauren had realised why Brooke was so insatiably curious after it all fell apart.

'Thanks,' Lauren said.

Joy hesitated. 'Do you think maybe we could play charades instead?' she asked. 'That way, you don't have to say anything, you can just act it out.'

Lauren burst out laughing, as did Joy. 'If we play charades about last night,' Lauren told her, 'I'll be arrested.'

Joy squealed in delight.

Chapter 13

T he next day, Lauren found herself on the sidelines of the Picture Gallery at Buckingham Palace alongside Eugene while the Queen, the Duke of Exeter and the president of Congo and his entourage took a tour of an art display curated for his visit to the UK.

Her life had become a very strange Mad Lib.

She was listening attentively, hands behind her back, when Joy came into the room, carefully closing the door behind her. 'I didn't know you were going to be here,' Lauren whispered as Joy sidled up next to her.

'It's very last minute,' Joy said. She was flushed and smiling as she straightened her suit jacket. 'I was at the Lewisham youth centre engagement with the Prince and Princess of Strathearn, but traffic was unusually light for some reason, so I was able to make it back in time.'

'And?' Lauren said. 'How was it?'

Joy clenched her fists and hid behind a column so she could do the tiniest victory dance. 'So good!' she squealed under her breath. 'The Strathearns were there and present and they asked excellent questions, and the kids and staff seemed to really enjoy speaking with them.' Joy tucked her hair behind her ears as she continued. 'Everyone there was so excited to have the media covering their efforts, lots of TV cameras, and the pictures going up online now look great. It just made me feel like this job is working, you know? All the struggle was worth it for today.'

'Of course it is!' Lauren said before giving her a quick one-armed hug. 'I'm so happy for you, you worked so hard to make that visit happen.'

'And don't I know it,' Joy said. 'What did I miss here?'

'You're just in time to witness me not actually meeting the Queen again. This is the closest I've come so far.' The Queen, she had been told when she joined, rarely communicated with anyone on the comms team, using Eugene as a conduit. She had been promised, however, that an introduction would happen 'at some point,' though that was starting to feel like a pipe dream.

The Picture Gallery was majestic, with arched skylights stretching throughout the rooms and dusty rose damask wallpaper across every wall. Intricate patterns of leaves and flowers were woven into long Chinese-style rugs, and Lauren half felt like she should have taken her shoes off before stepping on them. It was the duke's first engagement alongside the Queen, so he seemed a little nervous as they toured the room with their guests, discussing the artefacts on display. When he glanced at Lauren, she could see the change in his eyes. He suddenly looked like he had the last time she'd seen him, when they were sitting on the hotel sofa in Singapore: less duke and more Jasper.

She told herself to turn away, but she didn't, and when he gave her the barest hint of a smile, she did the same.

224

She was here to work, she reminded herself, and immediately went to Eugene's side to assist with the receiving line details.

'Dare I ask how the final op notes for the US state visit are looking?' he muttered to her as the Queen and the Congolese president chatted in French, their translators standing alongside them just in case any additional help was needed.

'You can absolutely dare,' Lauren whispered back. 'It's all going just fine. We're two weeks out, and I'm planning to send everything out to the media after the next weekly press briefing.'

'Just doing my job,' he replied. 'I have to say, it is nice having an American handle the Americans.'

'Thank you. I think.'

They continued around the Picture Gallery as Lauren's little comms team trailed behind the two state dignitaries, Harriet looking just thrilled to be there and Violet working with a photographer to make sure he got social media-friendly posts as she captured footage on her phone. It was funny how Lauren had begun to predict their movements, how Harriet would always be fiddling with her sweater sleeve, or how Violet would suddenly move across the room to film from a different angle. She felt like they were in an intricate dance that only they knew, an oddball little family.

It wasn't slick like the White House press office, of course, but it was something.

Jasper suddenly crossed in front of her, and Lauren nodded her head as she got out of the way. 'Your Highness,' she said.

'No curtsy?' he whispered. Lauren hid a smile behind her hand, pretending to cough. 'Pleasure to see you, Your Highness,' she said, then stepped away to admire a painting.

When she glanced up again, he was talking to someone but looking at her, and as they both moved around the room, she could feel that pull to him, could feel his eyes on her again and again. She focused on his hands, her phone, his hands, the paintings, his hands. She remembered how his palm had felt on her leg back in Singapore, so warm and steadying, thrilling and comforting.

'Lauren.' Joy was suddenly next to her. 'Can I speak to you outside for a moment? Something just came up.'

'Oh, of course,' Lauren said, and wondered if she looked as flustered as she felt. She motioned to Eugene that she was going to step out a minute, and as soon as the door shut behind him, Joy was leading her down the hall to an empty room that easily looked like it could be in a museum.

'What in the world are you doing?' Joy said.

Lauren paused. 'Um, taking notes while the Queen and the president of Congo look at a collection of newly restored sculptures?'

'You know that's not what I mean,' Joy replied, and all the happiness that had been in her voice just a few moments earlier was gone.

Shit.

'I'm not doing anything,' Lauren said.

'You and the duke' – Joy lowered her voice to a stern whisper – 'are practically making googly eyes in front of everyone.'

'We are not making googly eyes!' Lauren said.

'Please tell me,' Joy said, pressing her fingers to her temples, 'that the director of royal communications at Buckingham Palace has not gotten entangled with the Duke of Exeter, member of the royal family and the tabloids' number one new obsession.'

Lauren took a deep breath, letting it out slowly. 'There may have been a tiny moment in Singapore between Jasper and—'

Joy didn't let her finish. 'Jasper?!' she whisper-screamed. 'You're calling him Jasper now?'

'The duke—'

'How tiny was this "tiny moment"?'

Lauren paused. 'We might have kissed in the hotel room. But only briefly.'

Joy's eyes widened, and she quickly glanced around the hallway to make sure that no one was in earshot of their conversation. 'And you didn't tell me?!' she said, her voice almost a hiss.

'Nothing has happened since then, I swear!'

'My God, Lauren.' Joy took her own deep breath. 'Okay, I need you to listen to me. I'm sure the Duke of Exeter is a very lovely person. I know that you yourself are a very lovely person, which is why I need you to hear this. You cannot, for any reason whatsoever, get into a situation or anything else, with him.'

'Joy, I was literally just at Oscar's,' Lauren said, trying to laugh it off, but her own voice sounded too high and reedy, like a little kid who had just been handed a recorder.

'And that's great. Go be with Oscar every night of the week, I don't care,' she continued, lowering her hushed voice to an even quieter tone so she couldn't be overheard. 'A reporter is a risk in itself, but that's your choice. A member of the royal family? Lauren, I know you think you know what could happen, but I'm telling you now, you do not. The press will absolutely destroy you. There won't be anything left of you, or your family, by the time they're done. Your privacy, your reputation, everything. They aim to kill, Lauren, and they are *very* good at what they do.'

There was a fear in Joy's face that Lauren had never seen before. It scared her. 'Okay,' she said. 'Nothing's happening with us, and nothing will ever happen again.'

'Are you sure? Do you promise me?'

'I promise. You're so upset, I didn't—'

'You have no idea what I saw at Scotland Yard,' Joy said, and the fight seemed to ebb away from her posture. 'The tabloids and their wiretaps. They were even tapping our own phones at one point. Some of the worst things they did never even saw the light of day. I can't in good conscience stand here and think about anything like that happening to you.'

'I said it's fine!' Lauren snapped. 'You don't need to lecture me. I'm not an idiot.' She felt hurt and embarrassed, being chastised by her best friend, especially because she knew that Joy was right about all of it. 'I'm an adult, I can make my own decisions. You're my friend, not my mother, and I don't need you treating me like I'm a child!'

Lauren regretted the words as soon as they were out of her mouth, and she found herself wanting to claw at the air as if she could take them back and hide them away. 'Joy—'

'So that's how you think friendship works, then,' Joy said, holding up her hands. 'Fine. I warned you, don't say I didn't. I'm looking out for you, and I'll be damned if I watch you screw up this opportunity and hurt yourself even more. But I'm also not going to roll over and let you speak to me that way.' Joy's voice was stern.

'I need to go back inside,' Lauren said, smoothing down her skirt and trying to calm her racing heart. Fighting with a friend was so much more disorienting than fighting with a boyfriend, something that she knew all too well. 'I have a job to do right now, which I can do very well and take seriously, thank you.'

'Then go,' Joy said, holding up her hands once again. She looked frazzled as well, and when Lauren turned to leave the room, Joy didn't immediately follow her.

Lauren paused for a few seconds before going back into the Picture Gallery. If she had worried about looking flushed when she had left the room a few minutes ago, she knew she looked even worse upon reentry. Part of her wanted to go to the bathroom and cry in a cubicle, a rite of passage for all workplaces, but she didn't have that luxury right now.

Back in the room, she stayed far away from the duke (just thinking the name 'Jasper' made her feel guilty now), her head down as she politely listened to the conversation between the Queen and the Congolese delegation. Eugene raised an eyebrow at her once she slipped back into place, and she nodded before pretending to read a message on her phone.

She could feel another pair of eyes on her, though, but she didn't dare look up to meet them.

As soon as she could leave the room, she did, rushing back to her office so she could shut the door and be alone for a minute, but Eugene managed to intercept her before she could get there.

'This is absolutely ridiculous, Eugene!' a voice shouted.

'Lauren, can you come in here, please?' Eugene said, poking his head out of his door.

Lauren froze for a second before stepping into his office, where a furious-looking Harold Cockburn was seated. 'Was this your idea?' he demanded as soon as Lauren entered the room.

'Cockburn, calm down,' Eugene said.

Lauren glanced between the two men. 'What exactly is happening right now?'

'Eugene has decided to go ahead with *your* suggestion to pair the Prince of Strathearn with the Duke of Exeter for the visit to Skipton. With two days' notice.'

Lauren had shoved that visit to the back of her mind after putting the idea forward a few weeks earlier, too occupied with the upcoming US state visit and also the mess she was making of her personal life. She had finalised all the details, though: Skipton was a few hours' train ride away, just north of Leeds, and the royal visit was to help promote the town's upcoming food and drink festival. Lauren hadn't been looking forward to travelling with the Prince of Strathearn or Harold, but she hadn't been too worried about it.

'You did?' she said to Eugene.

'It's really not open for discussion,' he said to Cockburn. 'This decision comes from Her Majesty herself.'

Lauren smiled internally, knowing the Queen was aware of one of her ideas and had even given it the royal thumbs-up. Or something more graceful than that, probably.

'So what would you like me to tell the prince, then?' Harold fumed. 'That the heir to the throne is not good enough to carry out an engagement on his own?'

'Oh, for God's sake,' Eugene muttered. 'It's one visit to one town, one time. You're making this a much bigger deal than it is. Especially considering this trip was originally for the Duke of Cumberland, until his hip problems got worse.'

Lauren stayed silent, trying to calm her own racing brain. Oscar was among the accredited reporters for that trip, and now with the duke attending as well, the breezy day trip out to Yorkshire felt monumental, and it had nothing to do with the Skipton food and drink festival.

'Plus it's only a good thing for the prince to be seen generously showing the royal ropes to his cousin, who is still new to all of this,' Eugene added.

'Eugene is right,' Lauren said. Sending the duke on this trip would be smart, would bring him back to his English roots and reward all the love and attention that had been thrown his way in the last several months.

Even if the idea of shepherding him on this trip with Oscar, taking notes at every moment, filled her with anxiety.

'Well, that's it, then,' Harold said, standing up and storming towards the door. 'But we are not making a habit of this. These engagements are planned months in advance for a reason, you can't just mess around in the final hour.' He stomped off before either of them could reply.

'You could have told me that it was actually happening before you told Harold,' Lauren pointed out.

'Well, you're caught up now,' Eugene said, looking annoyed and flustered by the outburst. 'Just make sure it goes well, otherwise I'll have to hear about it from that man until the end of time.'

'I always make sure it goes well,' she said, but then she paused. 'Eugene?'

'Hmm?'

'Does Harold know about the duke's money issues?'

'No,' Eugene said shortly. 'Absolutely not.'

Lauren remembered the duke's words from months ago all too well: They bring *you in, build you up, then offer you as a sacrifice when someone with a higher rank makes a mistake.*

'I'm worried that the Strathearns' office is going to leak the bankruptcy story,' Lauren admitted. 'They have had a reputation in the past of leaking things to distract from their own bad press.'

'And that's why they don't know about it and why it's going to stay that way. Any other questions?'

Lauren shook her head then left, heading for her office, where she sat at her desk for a long time, dizzy from her fight with Joy and the Skipton updates. She had always known deep down that Jasper's and Oscar's paths would align again at some point after Singapore, but this trip felt a little too close and personal. Would Oscar be able to tell that she had kissed Jasper? And would Jasper know what was going on between she and Oscar? The guilt still stirred in Lauren's stomach.

Lauren stared at the French doors. Jesus Christ, what had she got herself into?

Chapter 14

Lauren was at King's Cross station early on Wednesday morning, even though she wasn't looking forward to the trip at all, even though she only slept in thirty-minute bursts the night before, tossing and turning with anxiety.

She was double-checking the itinerary when James came over to her, holding out his hand. 'Fine,' he said, looking annoyed. 'I'll do it.'

Lauren glanced up, a little confused. James had never offered to do anything for her. 'Do what?'

He gestured across the station to the famous Platform 9 ¾ sign and the luggage cart halfway embedded in the brick wall below it. 'Take your photo,' James said. 'You've been staring at it for the past ten minutes.'

Lauren just sighed. 'Twelve-year-old me would have said yes in a heartbeat but I can't support that anymore,' she said. 'But wait! You can take one here!' She gestured toward the station's arched ceiling and a train pulling in at the platform behind her. 'To commemorate my first away day.'

James looked even less thrilled by this option. 'We're not

even getting on that train. Violet can take it for you when she's back.'

'Violet's still in line at Starbucks.' Lauren handed him her phone, then took a few steps back and fluffed her hair a bit. 'Take it on zero-point-five so you can see the ceiling,' she said. 'Wait, why are you holding the phone like that? Turn it to portrait.'

James lowered the phone just long enough to glare at her.

'What! Landscape doesn't post well.' Lauren straightened the collar on her coat, then tilted her head to the side and smiled.

James lowered the phone again. 'I already took it. That's enough.'

'C'mon, James, one more. This is my tourist era.'

'The word 'tourist' implies that you'll be leaving soon, so fine.'

Violet and Harriet rejoined them, and the group headed towards the train track. Despite the early start, the others all seemed raring to begin the journey up north, but Lauren had a sinking feeling in her stomach she couldn't quite shake off.

She had been up most of the night before thinking about her fight with Joy, just as she had done for the past several nights. They weren't speaking to each other, their frostiness evident in the hallways as they passed each other and as they sat at opposite ends of the conference table. Even Violet had looked up from her phone long enough to glance between them, one eyebrow raised and the other frowning down as she tried to suss out the situation.

Lauren knew she had to apologise. Joy was a great friend, always looking out for her. She was the friend Lauren wanted to emulate, but now that the ball was in her court to fix what she had broken, Lauren found herself unable to do just that.

The last time she had lost a friendship, she had lost her relationship as well, and her job, and now she was too paralysed by shame and uncertainty to make amends with the one person who mattered most to her.

The train whistle blew, and Lauren jumped, shattering her reverie.

On board in the first-class carriage, Lauren and James sat in their reserved seats in front of a table, while Harriet and Violet sat on the other side of it, facing them. 'Prince Alexander, God rest his soul,' Harriet was saying, oblivious to the fact that Violet had her AirPods firmly jammed into her ears and was only hearing the playlist she had made, not Harriet's wistful speech. 'He often travelled to his estate in Pembrokeshire and would invite the entire team to join him for a weekend at the start of the summer break. We would take the royal train there most times, as he always got carsick, ever since he was a young boy ...'

James caught Lauren's eye and very gently shook his head. 'Do not engage,' he quietly whispered, pulling on his own headphones, which were large and bulky and made his head look slightly like a chickpea. 'Unless you want four hours of personal royal trivia.'

Lauren most definitely had zero plans to engage, so she quickly put in her own AirPods, her go-to 2010s playlist at the ready. James had settled back into his seat and closed his eyes, but Lauren knew there was no way she was sleeping on this train, even after waking up at 4:00 a.m. to triple-check her bag and confirm that she had packed not one but two power banks. She had learnt that from her past travels escorting press on *Air Force One*. (She also missed the unlimited personalised boxes of presidential M&M's on board the plane, which felt like an especially sharp dig now that she

235

was hurtling into the English countryside on an understaffed train with no snack trolley in sight.)

Lauren always felt unmoored on trains, like home could have been any one of the towns that they passed through, like she could have had any sort of life. At first the skyline was still dark before fading into dusky pink and then light blue, the surroundings brown and grey matching the train tracks on the ground. But once they went through a series of tunnels, they emerged into a small town, green grass racing alongside the train as it sped through, and Lauren found herself feeling oddly sentimental for a place she had never seen before, much less visited. They flew through town centres and places with names that felt made up before they quickly faded back into rolling hills and wide-open fields dotted with bare trees. At one point, they passed the back of a long row of red-brick houses and Lauren peeked into their gardens before catching sight of a young woman hoisting up a toddler who waved gleefully at the passing train. Lauren waved back, even though she knew the child could not have seen her.

Any sort of life.

The pregnancy scare with Brian had been just that, a scare, but Lauren still had a hard time understanding what exactly had been the scary part. Had it been her late period, Lauren visiting the bathroom twelve times a day, holding her breath each time and feeling her anxiety rise up a bit more every time the trip revealed nothing? Had it been the realisation that she could be a parent, could be responsible for another life, another tiny human, when she rarely came home from work before ten at night and mostly used her fridge to store her leftover takeaway and her expensive night cream?

Or was it thinking that what she had with Brian could be permanent, that they would officially be tied together in a way that couldn't be severed? Eventually she started her period a week later in a staff bathroom at the White House, crying for reasons that she still didn't understand, Brian five metres away and none the wiser. She never told him. There was nothing to tell. And probably for the best, considering that six months later she found out about him and her best friend and all her worlds, real and imagined, crumbled around her, the rubble unable to support her, much less an imagined baby.

It had been a relief, she told herself now, and turned away from the window so she could go over the op note again, double-checking the names of the people Jasper would meet that day. There was a set that was shared with members of the press and a more detailed document for the team that had short bios for every person they would be interacting with that day. Everything had been planned to the tiniest detail.

They changed trains in Leeds, their little group huddled to-gether on the (non-magical, non-Hogwarts-bound) platform, Harriet telling a lengthy story about the day some now-dead earl (Lauren widened her eyes at James, who pretended not to notice) had struggled to cut a ceremonial ribbon on an engagement due to blunt scissors and how she saved the day with a small sewing kit she had kept in her handbag, the rest of them either listening out of politeness or pretending not to hear her at all. Violet tapped away at her phone the entire time like she was covering breaking news, her thumbs flying, though when Lauren checked the official royal channels, she saw no new social updates. But then she saw the little smirk that only came when you were sharing something private with another person, and Lauren felt a pain in her chest as she once again thought of her argument with Joy.

Four hours after their departure, their train finally rolled into Skipton, a town that seemed to be entirely made out of stone walls and cobblestones. There were several people standing on the platform, and Lauren could see their cloudy breath come out in puffs in the near-freezing morning air. It was much colder here than in London. She wrapped her scarf around her neck a little tighter, wishing she had remembered her hat.

'I don't think I've been in Skipton since Thatcher was in office,' Harriet said brightly as she nearly stumbled into Lauren. 'Oops, sorry, dear.' She glanced around the train platform. 'It hasn't changed a bit.' She stumbled into Lauren again, and when Lauren turned around to figure out why exactly Harriet seemed to not understand the concept of personal space, she realised that Harriet was grinning and pointing towards something.

Or, as it turned out, someone: Oscar walking towards her, two coffee cups in hand.

'Morning,' he said.

'Hi,' she said. 'Um, hello. Were you on the train with us?'

'Of course. Though at the back with the commoners. We don't get first class on expenses at the *Tribune*,' he said. 'Got you this.'

He held out the cup to her, which was smaller than the other one. 'Double espresso,' he said. 'You ordered it at the restaurant back when you tried to kill me with the seafood tower.'

Lauren froze. 'Wait, you were only kidding about the shell-fish allergy, right? Right?'

Oscar smirked a little. 'You'll find out one day,' he replied as she took the cup from him. 'See you at the pen.'

It took Lauren a couple of seconds to figure out that the pen was the press pen at the 'fixed point press position' detailed in

238

her op note, and by the time she found her words again, he had sidled away, meeting up with a few other reporters she recognised from past press conferences at the Palace.

'Rizz alert,' Violet said under her breath, and Lauren whirled around.

'Don't even,' Lauren whispered to her. 'He is a *professional* and I am a *professional* and he brought me a very *professional* coffee as a way of saying—'

'That you're his espresso.' Violet grinned, and this time, even Harriet was trying to hide a smile.

The truth was, of course, that normally she would have texted Joy with the news. 'Um, excuse me!' James called, clapping his hands together like he was trying to herd up a litter of puppies. 'I'm over here and you all are still over *there*, and I'm just curious why that is.'

'If you make a thing of me and Oscar to James, I will change all of your social media passwords,' Lauren whispered under her breath. Violet didn't exactly look threatened.

'Coming!' Harriet said. 'Come on, you two. The work begins.'

'Okay,' Lauren said as a small pack of reporters and photographers and someone with a very unwieldy-looking video camera followed her every gesture. She held her hand up to a pushy cameraman. '*Off* the record, please.' She continued. 'This is where the prince and the duke will come in, they're going to talk to the pub owners about the food and beer festival, they'll probably pull pints together—'

'But just have one sip, of course,' James interjected.

'Of course,' Lauren replied. 'Because it is eleven thirty in the morning. Thank you, James, very helpful. Anyway, Their Royal Highnesses will chat with the pub's landlord as well as four local business owners before we make our way through the rear exit to the town hall for a civic lunch, which will be attended by over twenty-four local politicians and civic dignitaries from Skipton Town Council. They will be greeted by the Lord Mayor before sitting for lunch, details of which you will receive from Harriet as soon as they're inside. After that, we're back outside for a walkabout, where Their Royal Highnesses are looking forward to meeting as many locals as possible before departing.'

Lauren could see Oscar in the very back, credentials on a lanyard around his neck, nodding along as he made notes on his phone. He was both handsome and familiar, and when he glanced up at Lauren, he gave her a small wink that only she noticed.

'Lauren?' Harriet murmured.

'What?' She looked up to see Celia Parker from the *Sentinel* pursing her lips like she was sucking a sour plum.

'I asked,' Celia said, the irritation clear in her voice, 'if the prince would be addressing the rumours about the twins deferring their university entries by a year.'

'Given that Prince Thomas and Princess Helena are minors entitled to privacy, the answer is obviously not.' Lauren smiled at her, and in the corner of her eye, she could see Oscar smiling, too. 'Today's focus is on the engagements here and the Prince of Strathearn and Duke of Exeter's efforts to highlight the Skipton Food and Drink Festival, as well as talk with local townspeople, while also promoting the importance of supporting local tourism efforts in small towns throughout England and how they add to both our culture and economy.'

'You mean *our* culture,' the reporter muttered as she slunk away to scribble something in shorthand on her notebook.

'Any other questions that I can answer?' Lauren called.

'Do we get lunch?' someone yelled out.

'Not my problem,' Lauren replied, then gestured towards the pub owners, who were almost beaming at the fact that journalists from every major newspaper were in their restaurant.

'Thank you again for having us,' Lauren said to them. 'I know Their Highnesses will be so thrilled to meet you.'

Just as she was about to step away and go wait for the duke, James came up to her. 'Well, I'll let you handle the rest of this,' he said. 'I'm off for the afternoon.'

Lauren blinked. 'You're not here to watch my every move and report back to Eugene?'

'No, you know what you're doing at this point. And I have plans.' James smiled.

'Plans?' Lauren repeated.

'Yes, I'm going to visit my mother.'

'Your mum lives here?' Lauren said. 'In Skipton?'

James nodded, and for the first time since Lauren had met him, he actually looked somewhat pleased. 'It's been a while since I was able to come see her, so I thought today might be a good opportunity to do just that.'

'I agree, it is,' Lauren said. 'Go, go, we've got this locked down.' She gestured towards Harriet and Violet. 'I have a good team.'

'Well, let's keep it that way,' James said. 'Please don't destroy the monarchy while I'm eating lunch with my mum.'

'I'll do my best,' Lauren assured him.

A few minutes later, a black car carrying the prince and the duke glided up to the curb, and when they stepped out, the royal charm was in full effect, and Lauren was once again no exception to it. The local citizens burst into spontaneous applause, cameras began clicking and Lauren was pretty sure she saw one older woman start to cry happy tears.

A local brass band started playing an upbeat ditty as soon as they exited the car, which Lauren had feared would be cheesy but was actually quite touching, and when the duke stepped into the pub two steps behind the prince, Lauren saw him search the crowd before his eyes landed on her for just a second.

Nothing is happening between us, she told herself, taking a deep breath as she walked over to him.

'Your Highness,' she said. 'It's great to have the both of you together for this.'

'Of course. Anything to get Cockburn all riled up,' he said with a chuckle. 'How are you?'

By this point, Lauren had worked with enough politicians and royal figures to know that none of them had ever, ever asked how she was doing, and she hated how the simple question went right to her gut. 'Just fine, thank you,' she said, and turned away before he could ask her anything else.

The visit continued to their next stop, the town hall, which had an overwhelming smell of fresh paint. Lauren had to stop herself from wrinkling her nose as soon as she walked in, lest one of the agency photographers get a shot and put it on the front page of the UK tabloids: 'Rude Sass from US Lass.'

Instead, she and Harriet stood back as the prince and the duke both greeted the mayor and began to chat. Lauren thought that if she ever threw a party, a royal family member would be an amazing guest. They could talk to everyone, knew how to make conversation without straying into any offensive territory and also knew how to make a polite exit.

Not that she was throwing a party any time soon, of course. You needed friends to host a party, and Lauren was all too aware of the fact that she lacked them.

Harriet crept up next to her as across the room Violet was

taking video. 'This has gone quite well,' Harriet trilled under her breath, and by this point, Lauren had learnt enough about Palace employees to understand that she was being paid the highest of compliments.

'Thank you,' Lauren replied. 'Amelia did most of the leg-work on this one before she left, I have to say.'

Harriet reached into her handbag and pulled out a tin of mints, holding one out to Lauren. 'Helps with the paint smell.'

'How did you know?' Lauren asked, helping herself, and wow, if Harriet wasn't right.

'All of these stops smell like paint,' Harriet replied. 'They get so excited for a royal visit that they spend weeks getting ready. When the Princess of Strathearn was pregnant, one village hall even built an entirely new bathroom in case she needed to use it.'

Lauren turned to look at Harriet. 'You are joking.'

'I am not,' Harriet said, taking two mints before tucking them away. 'These trips can really invigorate small towns. It means so much to people. I know it's easy to mock or brush off, especially if you didn't grow up with it, but it matters. *They* matter,' she added, gesturing towards the duke chatting to the manager of the local library as they laughed together.

After the visit, the duke and the prince stepped outside, where there were dozens of, if not maybe a hundred, people surrounding the town square, cheering and waving, their children shoved towards the front of the crowds to give them a view. Lauren could see the top of Oscar's head moving behind one group of very giddy, blushing women, phone and notebook in hand, and she felt a rush of happiness to see him followed by a sharp nervousness that just behind him, the duke was greeting the crowd. Lauren buttoned up the top of her coat and wiped down her clammy hands. She had once sat next to Oprah herself at a Presidential Medal of Freedom ceremony and managed to keep her dignity, but now she felt like she was about to climb out of her skin. Still, she kept her face steady as she watched Jasper mingle with the local residents as Oscar took notes on everything that he said. Everything was fine, she said to herself. Oscar didn't know about her kiss with Jasper, and he didn't need to. Her relationship with Jasper was purely work-related at this point, even if their shared glances made Lauren feel like there were hamsters tap dancing in her tummy. Her friendship with Joy was another problem entirely, of course, but Lauren could fix that because that was what she did – she *fixed* things. And even though she had no idea how to do that, she would figure it out because—

'Hey,' Oscar said as he came up next to her, and Lauren just about fell out of her Louboutin ankle boots, which she had purchased preloved on Poshmark. 'Great job today. Nobody was assassinated.'

Lauren felt all the colour drain from her face.

'Oh no, I'm *kidding*,' Oscar said, starting to laugh a little. 'I'm only kidding, I promise. Sorry, I shouldn't have said anything while we're all still working.'

'I grew up in the United States, Oscar,' Lauren said, trying to settle her nervous system. 'They pretty much give you a gun when you're born. No assassination jokes, please.'

Oscar held up his hands in surrender. 'Noted. All right, got to get back to work. See you on the train, yeah?'

'Right behind you,' Lauren said. A few steps away Harriet was nodding at a young child who was talking to her like they were old friends, all of them fielding gifts and flowers and notes meant for the royals.

'Your Highness,' one older woman piped up to the Prince of Strathearn. 'How are your twins doing? Ready for uni yet?'

It was like someone had blown a whistle meant to summon reporters: Every single one of them within a three-metre radius suddenly closed in, Oscar included.

'Well, I imagine they're taking their time to decide what's next.' The prince chuckled, now passing a child's drawing to Lauren, who took care not to crease it. 'Whatever they do, we're always extremely proud.'

'I waited outside the hospital when they were born,' the woman said. 'It was such a special day.'

The reporters were furiously tapping into their phones, and Lauren suspected that within fifteen minutes, she'd start receiving news notifications on her phone about Prince Thomas's and Princess Helena's next moves.

It never failed to startle her, how fast the speed of news could be. And it blew her mind that no matter how many guards and fences and walls protected the people she had worked for, they couldn't stop the flow of information seeping into every corner of the globe, wild as a weed, moving too fast for anyone to cut it back or rein it in.

At the end of the walk, Jasper came upon a woman who was holding a framed photo of the Queen, one of her portraits from when she was a newly minted monarch thirty years ago, and she was visibly shaking, her eyes filled with tears. 'This used to hang in my mother's house,' the woman said when the duke approached. 'She passed in August, today would have meant the absolute world to her.'

The duke nodded reverently before clasping the woman's hand between both of his. 'I'm sure she was a wonderful woman,' he said, and Lauren had a sudden image of her own mother's house, the framed baby and childhood photos of Lauren that lined the upstairs hallway, and almost four thousand miles away from home, away from her own mum, Lauren felt the homesickness burning her throat and eyes.

Lauren managed to escort him back to his waiting car. 'Almost wish I could take the train with you lot instead,' he said. 'No snacks in the car.'

'Well, I would trade with you in a second,' Lauren said. 'Trust me.'

He was turned away from the press and royal watchers so they couldn't see his expression, but Lauren could, and she didn't miss the look of wanting that crossed his face. He opened his mouth to say something, then thought better of it, and Lauren felt a tightness in her throat that hadn't been there a moment ago.

'Well,' he said. 'Thank you again for a job well done, as always.'

'Of course, Your Highness,' she replied. 'Safe travels back to London.'

The banal words they were saying to each other didn't do a thing to cut the tension between them, and Lauren saw Jasper's knuckles turn white as he gripped the open car door. There was no room for mistakes or whispers or regrets or emotions, not with the press pack steps away, and Lauren stood back as he climbed into the car and felt herself sag a little once the door was firmly shut behind him.

By the time the crowds had dispersed, the metal barricades had been dismantled, and the pub the duke had visited earlier that day found itself packed to the walls with revellers all wanting to take pictures with the two pints the royals had pulled, Lauren and her team practically crawled onto the train, all too ready for a four-hour break from the hectic day. 'I would like a very strong drink,' Harriet announced. 'But a tea will suffice.'

James made his way onto the train just minutes before it was scheduled to leave, breathing a little heavily from the exertion. 'I take it all went well,' he said to Lauren, who gave him a thumbs-up in response.

'How was your mum?' she asked.

James hesitated. 'Annoying,' he finally said, and laughed. 'But I love her to bits.'

Lauren spent the first hour of her ride catching up on texts and emails as James and Harriet sat across from her, working on a short press release summarising the successful visit. Three rows down, Violet slumped against a window as she sent them links to all the trending social media posts, including a clip of Jasper jokingly waving to the sheep on the hill. 'Hello, old friends!' he boomed, which made the crowd chuckle.

As soon as the press release was updated and approved, Lauren sent it to the Buckingham Palace media list and then stood up to stretch. Although she had been on her feet most of the day, she was restless, wanting to just move and let her brain slowly unspool. If she had been back in the States, she would have driven home with the windows down, probably singing along with some party playlist from her college days. She suspected such a thing would not be appreciated by the rest of the train's passengers, though, and instead got up to make her way into the aisle.

'Just going for a walk,' she told James when he glanced up at her, and he nodded. Even he looked a bit tired and rumpled, not as neat and pressed as he normally did.

She recognised several of the reporters as she passed, all of whom nodded or gave a tired wave. 'Does anyone have a Wi-Fi hotspot?' one of them was muttering. 'The train's keeps going dead and I need to get this story filed now.'

'Violet does,' Lauren said, gesturing over her shoulder. 'She might share if you ask nicely.'

The reporter looked dubious but stood up to go and find her. 'Better than nothing,' he said as he left.

Lauren kept moving, walking through two more carriages, and as she went to open the door to step into a third, it suddenly opened for her.

Or rather, Oscar had opened it.

'Oh, hi,' he said, freezing in place.

'Are those *potato chips*?' Lauren gasped, and he quickly slammed the door behind him, trapping them both in the small area.

'Shhh!' Oscar said. 'Keep it down! This lot will go absolutely feral if they find out I have these.'

'*I'm* about to go feral!' Lauren said. 'All I've had to eat today were Harriet's mints.'

Oscar held them up just out of her reach. 'Well, these are British-flavoured, you know. You probably won't like them.'

'I'm assuming by "British flavoured",' you mean they have no seasoning,' Lauren teased, trying to reach for the bag as he held it further away from her.

'I *mean*, these are cheese and onion,' Oscar said.

'That doesn't exactly scare me off. Plus, if you don't share, I'm going to tell the whole press pack that you're hiding out here with these.' She held up her phone. 'One group WhatsApp text, and it's all over for you.'

Oscar hesitated, then held out the bag with a grumble. 'So good,' Lauren said as she took a handful. 'Thanks. You saved a life today. First coffee and now chips.'

'Crisps.'

'You know what I mean.'

'You fight dirty.'

'I do what I can to survive.' Lauren helped herself to another handful. 'Hey, seriously, thanks again for the coffee. That was sweet of you.'

Oscar shrugged then took more chips from the bag. 'Not a problem. Anything for you.'

Lauren waited for the sarcastic follow-up, but he didn't say anything, and after a minute, she leant against him, grateful for the warmth of him in the small space between the train cars as the two of them stood munching for a minute in silence.

'It really is quite wild, isn't it?' Lauren finally said, standing up straight. 'How excited people get. Like the woman with the framed photo, it just meant so much to her.'

'Royal visits tend to bring out the sentimental nature in people.'

'Do they still do that for you?' she asked. 'A veteran reporter like yourself?'

'Depends on the people I'm with,' he said, looking down at her before giving her a quick kiss on the lips. 'You taste like cheese and onion.'

'That's the nicest thing you've ever said to me,' Lauren said, wanting to kiss him back for longer but not willing to do so on a train filled with reporters. 'By any chance, is your roommate out of town again this weekend?'

'Sadly, he is not,' Oscar said. 'I imagine he'll spend most of it at home watching Formula 1, screaming at the television.'

'Hmm,' Lauren said. 'Then I guess you're going to have to come to mine.'

'Guess so,' he said. 'Should I bring more crisps?'

'Always,' she replied. His phone started buzzing. 'Why does technology always kill the mood?' she said.

Oscar fished out his phone and squinted at the screen.

'Oh shit,' he said. 'I have to call my editor, I'm getting SOS messages from him.' He looked around before kissing Lauren again quickly. 'I'll text you tonight?'

'Of course,' she said. 'Go report!'

After finishing the crisps he left behind, she stepped into the bathroom to wash the grease and salt from her hands. As she made her way back to her seat, she did a quick social media scroll. 'Great job today, Violet,' she said as she passed her row, but Violet had balled up her jacket against the window and was snoozing peacefully.

It was possibly the first time Lauren had seen her without a phone in hand.

Back at her seat, Harriet was also asleep, but James was still awake, typing something on his iPad. Lauren sat across from him, pulling out a Yuval Noah Harari book that she had been reading for the past five months, going so long in between reading sessions that she had had to go back a couple of chapters each time she resumed.

'You know, Lauren,' James said, and Lauren braced herself. 'I'm not one to give out compliments—'

Lauren looked up from her book.

'—but I have to tell you, I admire the work you're doing at the Palace.'

Her book fell to the table.

'You took a risk just by coming here, after all, and you've risen to the occasion time and time again. I'm almost a little bit envious, I have to admit. You don't hesitate to go after what you want, to push for things even when they're not the norm and when most, including myself, would stick to the rules.'

Lauren wondered if he had had a drink at lunch. Or, given that his mother had been annoying, two. 'Wow, James. I don't even know what to say to that.'

'Well, no need to speak up if you have nothing to say,' he replied. 'God knows you Americans always have to ruin the silence.'

Lauren grinned. 'We all have our gifts,' she said, then picked up her book and enjoyed the silence for the rest of the way home.

Chapter 15

Lauren was knee-deep in final plans for the fast-approaching American state visit. She had coordinated last-minute press accreditation requests, finalised all remaining press releases with their relevant embargo details and even had her first interactions with 10 Downing Street's press office to make sure that anything coming out of the BP comms office aligned with the messaging on their diplomatic priorities.

Today her first duty was to join a Zoom call with the Foreign, Commonwealth and Development Office for a briefing on political sensitivities, relations between the US and UK, and any global issues that could come up over the days ahead. Her phone had been buzzing regularly throughout the call, nothing too important, but when she saw Oscar's name pop up on the screen, she briefly turned off her Zoom camera to read it.

Right away, she knew it was bad.

'Need to talk to you in person. Can we meet at Canada Gate?'

'I'm in a meeting,' she texted back. 'What is it?'

'Can't say over text but it's urgent.'

Lauren sighed and glanced at her schedule. 'I can be there in 30,' she wrote back.

She had barely sent the message before he responded '20,' and then his notifications turned off.

And for some reason, she suddenly felt frightened.

'What is it?' Lauren asked the second she saw him standing across the street from the front of Buckingham Palace. She had left so fast that she had forgotten to grab her coat, and she pulled her cropped cardigan around herself to stay warm.

'Aren't you cold?' Oscar asked.

Lauren stopped in her tracks. 'You just sent me a text making it sound like I had to flee the building ASAP. Are you serious right now!'

'All right, all right, sorry,' he said, touching her arm. 'C'mon, let me get you a hot coffee.'

'I have, like, barely ten minutes,' she replied, letting herself be pulled into Green Park, which was an unfortunate name for early March, given the mostly bare tree branches.

'That's fine,' he said, somewhat abruptly. Despite the park being busy, there wasn't a line at the wooden coffee kiosk, and Oscar quickly ordered two lattes.

'Will you please just tell me what's going on?' she said as they walked to the side of the coffee hut. 'You're freaking me out.'

'Sorry,' he said, looking at her, and all that rumpled softness that she remembered from their night together last weekend was gone. Oscar the Royal Reporter was back in place, and her heart started to beat even faster. 'I'm sorry, I just . . . There's something going on at the paper.'

Lauren waited for him to continue.

'Something about you.'

'Are you running a piece on me?' Lauren paused for a second. 'You said back at our first lunch that that was just a joke! We slept together and now you're doing a story on me?!'

'No, no, nothing like that. It's . . .' Oscar paused again.

'Oh my God, Oscar, *please*. Just spit it out.'

'I'm *trying*.' He pulled his phone out of his pocket, swiped a few times, then showed her a video. 'Here,' he said, turning the sound up.

Lauren recognised the scene immediately: Balmoral Castle at Christmas. She watched as the comms team's helicopter touched down on the ground as the protesters waved their signs and shouted.

Her blood went cold.

'Lauren!' one of the protesters shouted, and the camera saw her head whip around, her face going from surprised to shocked to horrified before she and the rest of her team went through the castle gates.

Lauren paused the video and looked directly at Oscar. 'Every single thing I say from hereon in is absolutely off the record.'

'I know,' he said. 'I'm not here as a reporter, I'm here as . . . well, whatever we are.'

'How much do you know?' Lauren asked him. 'Is this going online?'

'Not yet,' Oscar said. 'But the paper has it as an exclusive, and my editor wants to run it on Sunday. We have a new investigative reporter on staff, and he's aggressive. He's been watching all the B-roll from recent engagements for weeks, and well, he found this and put it together.'

Lauren nodded and bit the inside of her cheek. 'So you know that . . .'

'It's your father,' he said, sounding almost regretful. 'Callum McConnell. He and your mother lived together in the States and divorced more than twenty years ago, which is when he moved back to Scotland. He has a hard time keeping a job but always pays his rent on time. And he protests around the country, including every single Christmas at Balmoral Castle, rain or shine.'

'So who cares about that?' Lauren said, even though she knew that many people would, in fact, care. 'He shows up once a year and waves a sad little homemade sign.'

'It goes beyond that,' Oscar said, and Lauren could tell from his tone of voice that he was trying to cushion the blow for her. 'He's been involved with Extinction Rebellion to protest climate change. Not a bad cause, but that group instigated chaos in the UK for a while,' he added when Lauren just looked at him blankly. 'He's also protested against Big Oil, against Brexit many years ago, against Britain funding wars in various countries and so on. Again, none of these are bad things, but given where you work ... The press is going to love, and twist, every single detail.' He stopped and looked at her.

Lauren narrowed her eyes. 'Well, congratulations. Now you know more about my dad than I do.'

'Did you know he would be at Balmoral?'

'Are you still asking as "whatever we are"?' she said, making finger quotes around the phrase.

'Yes.' His eyes looked so sad, which almost made her even angrier. How dare he look so upset when it was her family – her *life* – that seemed to be falling apart, all because of *his* paper.

'No, I didn't. I didn't know any of that. I hadn't seen my dad in twenty years. My parents didn't just divorce, he left us.

You know this, Oscar. And I know even as I'm talking that nothing I say is going to matter, is it?'

'Probably not,' Oscar admitted. 'I'm trying to kill it, Lauren, but this goes over my head. The editor in chief really wants to run it.'

Her chin wobbled so she lifted her coffee and took a sip.

'Especially with the state visit from the US president next week,' Oscar added. 'The timing isn't good.'

'Well, not for me,' she said. 'It's great for you, though. And your paper. My God, I can't believe you can't kill this.'

'I told you, it's not me!' he said. 'I swear—'

'I laid in your bed, Oscar, and we talked. We talked. About our lives, our families!'

'No,' he said bluntly. '*I* talked about my family. *You* talked about your mum. That's all. You never brought up your dad. You hid him from me.'

If she had been a cartoon character, Lauren's head would have blown clear off her body and into orbit.

'Really!' she cried. 'Hey, I wonder why! Maybe because telling a reporter about my ecoterrorist father who abandoned our family before I could barely tie my shoes wouldn't have been a great idea. And it looks like I was right because here you are, with *this*.'

'Did you tell anyone about this?' Oscar shot back. 'James? Eugene? Joy?'

'Joy and I aren't exactly talking much right now.'

'What!' Oscar looked shocked. 'Since when? You two are joined at the hip.'

'Look, I'll decide who I talk to and what about,' Lauren said.

'Well, great,' Oscar said, 'because that's exactly how you got here. You kept all of this to yourself and now it's about to blow up, and you're going to get hurt and I can't stop it!'

'I am so sorry to inconvenience you,' she said, turning around to walk away. 'My mistake. I'll make sure it doesn't happen again.'

'Lauren!' Oscar called after her, and she spun around on her heel and went back to him.

'The last boyfriend I had only stole my best friend,' she told him. 'But you're coming after my family. Guess I really know how to pick them.'

This time when he called after her, she kept walking, her head held high even as she could feel tears gathering at the backs of her eyes, her mind spinning with all the possibilities: Reporters showing up at her dad's house, or worse, her mum's duplex in Atlanta, banging on the door for hours. Earlier that week Joy had put the fear of God into her about the tabloid news media, and now Lauren was terrified for an entirely different reason.

And what made her so mad was that Oscar was right about one thing: She should have told someone about that day. There were cameras everywhere, the press pack, and she had thought that she could just ignore it and it would go away.

She walked back through the side entrance into the Palace, showing her credentials for the millionth time, only this time her hands were shaking. She bypassed her own office and went further into the room towards James, who was sitting in his office tapping away at his laptop.

'Hey,' Lauren said, hearing the wobble in her own voice, and James went from looking mildly interested to very concerned, all in the space of three seconds.

'Are you okay?' he asked, and if it hadn't been such a terrible moment, Lauren would have felt touched by his concern.

They had come such a long way from their first meeting, and now she was about to blow it all to smithereens.

'Can you ask Eugene to come in here, too? It's important,' she asked.

James raised an eyebrow but quickly sent a message, and a few minutes later Eugene arrived in the room. He took one look at Lauren's face and said, 'What on earth is going on?'

She pressed her hands together so that they wouldn't see them shaking.

'I need to tell you something,' she said. 'And it's not good.'

The conversation went about as well as Lauren thought it would go.

'So, yeah, the *London Tribune* has the video and every detail about my family,' Lauren said. 'Oscar says they're still working on it, that it's not scheduled to run—'

'Yet.' James filled in the last word for her.

'Exactly.'

Eugene slipped off his glasses and rubbed at his face for a second. 'So let me make sure I have this straight,' he said in the kind of calm voice that only meant yelling was about to commence. 'Your father, your biological father, is an eco-terrorist who protests our monarch every single Christmas, and when you saw him there last year, and when he yelled your name out loud, you didn't think to tell anyone. Do I have that straight?'

'He would never hurt anyone,' Lauren started to say, but Eugene held up a hand.

'That is absolutely not the point right now,' he said, still eerily calm. 'What is the point is that now we have our acting director of communications, an American who worked at the *White House*, about to be pilloried across every single

UK newspaper just days before a state visit by the American president.'

Lauren was too scared to say anything.

'Well, you're wrong about one thing, Lauren. Actually many things, but one thing in particular. The people your father chooses to associate himself with could absolutely hurt someone, and his actions are about to hurt many people. Mostly you.'

Then he started to laugh as he turned to James, who didn't look like he found any of this funny. 'I told you,' Eugene said, giggling maniacally to himself. 'I told you, didn't I? That we shouldn't hire her, that she'd never fit into a place like this. But everyone else wanted something "new" and "different" and now look where we are. Right in a pile of shit!'

'Eugene, please,' James started to say, but Eugene held up his hand.

'No,' he said, then turned back to Lauren. 'Lauren, you are literally – this is not an exaggeration – our director of communications. That means that you are supposed to *communicate*. Things about the Palace, the Queen, the family or perhaps things about your *own* family that could complicate matters here!'

'Why didn't you tell us?' James said to her. Eugene was furious, but James didn't seem mad, just disappointed, which, after the compliment he had given her last night on the train, made her feel ten times worse.

'Because, like I told you, I haven't talked to my dad in twenty years. Our only connection is biological. I barely know what he does. I'm not responsible for him or his actions.'

'Of course you're not, but that is not the point!' Eugene said. 'You *knew* about his actions! We could have cut this off at the knees if you had just said something. We could

259

have issued a letter to editors through the Press Standards Organisation, got ahead of it with a statement, and why am I even saying any of this to you? All of this is *your* job! And quite frankly, you're really rather incompetent at it.'

Lauren sat back in her seat, stunned. 'If I had told you,' she said, 'and we had got ahead of it, as you said, then that means every single newspaper in the UK would be camped outside my parents' front doors. Getting ahead of it would just mean sacrificing my parents to the tabloids so you didn't have to worry about any of it.'

Eugene turned to James. 'This is why,' he said, pointing at Lauren, 'she doesn't get it. She never will.'

'What don't I get, Eugene?' she cried.

'That this job means not prioritising anything – not even our own families – over the Crown. Something you know absolutely nothing about and never will.'

'Should she be taken off the state visit?' James murmured, like Lauren wasn't in the room.

'No, because there's no one to take over at this late stage,' Eugene said, now starting to pace back and forth in the small office. 'She's been overseeing the bulk of the comms strategy, plus it might look suspicious.'

'I'm sitting right here,' Lauren said. 'You can speak directly to me.'

'Trust me, you don't want me to do that right now,' Eugene said, glowering at her, then took a deep breath and ran a hand over his hair. It had become slightly thinner since she started back in October, and Lauren wondered if that was because of her.

'All right, here's what we'll do for now,' Eugene said. 'You'll stay on the state visit since that's already too far in motion, but Harriet will take over communications with the White

House comms team. James and I are going to work together and try to find a solution to this problem. You're going to send us Oscar's contact information so someone can stay in touch with him directly in case there are any developments. And also, you are off any other work for now. Harriet will take over the press briefing next Friday and the engagements following.'

Lauren watched as James's eyebrow twitched at that last sentence. She tried to imagine Harriet, sweet, innocent Harriet, wrangling the press pack, and it made her think of those nature documentaries that showed a limping gazelle on the savanna.

'Okay,' was all Lauren said, though.

'Is there anything else we need to know?' James said, and he sounded marginally kinder than Eugene, which made her feel even worse.

Well, she was dating the journalist whose paper was about to break the story, kissed the Duke of Exeter in a heated moment, ruined the best friendship she had ever had and was about to deal with a slew of Americans arriving for the state visit.

One thing at a time, she told herself.

'No,' she replied, standing up. 'You've been very clear.'

'At least one of us has,' Eugene muttered, turning his back as she left the room.

Lauren had thought she wanted nothing more that night than to go home, take a shower, order food and hide away in front of her laptop with old episodes of *Modern Family*, but then once she was there, she only wanted to leave. It didn't even feel like a home, she realised, more like a hostel or hotel room. She still had unpacked boxes lining one wall, some of them hastily yanked open so she could find one thing or another.

Even the sofa felt uncomfortable once she sank down on it to eat the Thai food she had just ordered in, realising that she actually hadn't spent much time sitting on it. Her days had been work, work, work, sleep, repeat, and now work was, at least for the moment, nearly gone.

If this was a home, it was certainly the loneliest one she had known in a while.

So she reached out to the one she did know.

'Lauren!' Her mum's voice rang through the phone. 'It's late for you!'

Lauren glanced at the clock on her oven. 'It's barely eight o'clock.'

'Well, that's definitely late for me! How are you?' She could hear sizzling in the background, her mum probably making a late lunch. 'How's work?'

Lauren moved over to a dining chair, literally the only chair at her tiny bistro table. 'Oh, you know. Work.'

'No, I don't know.' Her mother laughed. 'I haven't ever worked at a palace. Tell me something good.'

Lauren's long pause seemed to trigger something, because she could hear she was taken off speakerphone and her mum was now speaking into the handset. 'Laur?' her mum said. 'What's wrong?'

'Just . . .' Her voice trembled. 'Just a really bad day, that's all.'

'That's all? A really bad day sounds like a lot.'

'I don't know if this is going to work out,' Lauren replied, and it was the first time she had said it out loud. 'I don't know if I'm going to last here.'

'Oh, honey,' her mum said. 'Well, whatever happens, you can always come home. Your room is still here, just like you left it.'

Lauren could picture her childhood bedroom in her mind,

and what should have been a comforting image left her feeling cold. It had been a wonderful room when she was twelve, but now that she was twenty-eight, the idea of going to sleep every night under the chintzy Target bedding, the faded Laura Ashley wallpaper and her old One Direction posters just seemed . . .

Well, really fucking sad.

'Yeah, maybe,' Lauren said. 'I don't know.'

'Tomorrow is a fresh day,' her mum said. 'Things can get better. They always do.'

Lauren had imagined a scenario where she could cry on the phone to her mum, finally let out her frustration and fear and annoyance with herself, but hearing that made her retreat back inside herself. She couldn't admit that her work had been less than wonderful, that her *life* was currently feeling much, much less than wonderful, not to the one person who thought she was still great, still strong.

She wanted to be the person her mum believed her to be, so after they said goodbye and ended the call, she got dressed, put her laptop in her bag and grabbed her phone again.

Half an hour later, her Uber pulled up at Buckingham Palace, her now-boxed takeaway in hand. Her job responsibilities may have been put on hold, but there were always emails to organise, files to go through and shred, something that could make her feel productive instead of just sad and angry at herself. And work was where she felt most comfortable.

She turned on her small desk lamp, in no mood for the bracing fluorescent light strip overhead, and sat down at her desk, pulling her laptop out of her bag. She had got through three emails and a quarter of her reheated pad Thai when her work phone pinged.

'Everything all right? I saw you rush out of James's office today. You seemed upset.'

It was Jasper. He had never texted her before.

Lauren dropped her iPhone like it had burned her, then picked it back up.

'All fine here thanks. Not something I'd like to discuss via text.'

She watched as the three bubbles appeared, then disappeared before the next sentence popped up. 'Well, if you don't want to discuss via text, then you probably don't want to discuss via phone either.'

Two minutes later, and for the first time, there was a gentle knock.

Lauren turned towards her office's French doors, pushed back the drapes, and saw Jasper standing just outside.

'How did you even know I was here?' Lauren gasped, stepping outside and pulling the door shut behind her (and saying a quick prayer that she hadn't just locked herself out).

He gestured towards the doors, which were lit from the inside. 'I saw your light on,' he said. 'I hope you don't mind, I was out for a walk.'

'You tend to do that, don't you,' she said. 'Go for walks.'

'Guilty,' he replied. 'I prefer being outdoors. Too cooped up indoors, especially at this place.'

'Do you regret it?' Lauren asked him. 'Coming here, moving back?'

He looked surprised by the question. 'I don't think so,' he said. 'At least not yet. Maybe ask again later.' He smiled, trying to make her smile, too, but his own faded when he saw her sombre face.

'Do you want to walk with me for a bit?' he said. 'Fresh air does you good.'

She glanced back at her office, at the job that no longer needed her, no longer wanted her. 'Okay,' she said. She knew it was risky to be alone with him, especially when she was feeling so low, but the risk felt less awful than the loneliness and anxiety that had been consuming her. 'That would be nice. I've never actually been out here.'

They strolled in silence for a while, past the freshly cut lawn and towards the gardens. In the distance, she could hear frogs at the pond. 'This was always my favourite place when I was a boy,' Jasper said. 'Lots of places to hide out here, avoid everyone and everything.'

'You're not avoiding me,' Lauren pointed out.

'Well, you're not a pinch-faced nanny who always made us eat boiled vegetables,' he replied. 'And I'm very glad about that.'

Lauren smiled.

'Any reason you're back at work so late?' he asked.

'Oh, just the . . . the state visit next week,' she stammered.

'That's all?' He was teasing her again, but Lauren kept looking down, suddenly feeling the weight of her day crash over her.

'Sorry,' she said. 'It's just been a terrible day. I'm sorry, I should get back to work—'

She started to turn around, but Jasper caught her arm, holding it so lightly in his hand.

'Hey,' he said. 'Don't go back. Talk to me.'

Lauren hesitated, then thought of all the times she should have talked to someone: She should have told Oscar about her dad. She should have told James and Eugene about his sudden reappearance. She should have told Joy about kissing Jasper sooner.

Maybe it was time for her to finally start talking.

'I screwed everything up today,' she whispered. 'I thought I was good at my job, and now I don't even know if I have a job anymore.'

'Wait, all right, just a minute.' Jasper stopped walking and came to stand in front of her. 'What are you talking about, you don't have a job?'

'I used to be so good at this, too,' she said, ignoring his question. 'And ever since I landed at Heathrow almost five months ago, it's like I can't do it anymore. I don't know if it's this place or me, but I can't . . . actually, no. It's me. It's because of me.'

And then she started to cry.

Jasper paused, then took her arm again and led her over to a bench under a willow tree. 'Someone very royal and important probably once sat and cried on this very bench,' he told her gently. 'So you're in good company.'

'I *am* in good company,' she sniffled, and started to wipe at her eyes before he put a handkerchief in her hands. 'Thank you.'

'Well, here's another fun fact for you,' he said. 'I have been carrying a handkerchief around for at least fifteen years now, and this is the first time I've been able to give it to a crying woman.' He pretended to sigh with relief. 'Thank you for letting me cross that off my bucket list. I mean, I know you're sad, but this is quite the victory for me personally.'

This time, Lauren did laugh a bit. 'Was it worth the wait?' she asked.

'Absolutely,' he murmured, then nudged her leg with his. 'C'mon, tell me what's wrong.'

She gave him the broad strokes of her week, mentioning her fight with Joy (and even though she left out the details about what it was over, it still made her cry again), her conversation

266

with Oscar and the video of her dad. 'Eugene's furious,' she said.

'Well, it doesn't take much to get Eugene going,' Jasper pointed out. His hand was on her back now, and it was as warm and strong as she remembered it being in Singapore.

'But this story is going to come out, Oscar can't stop it, and it's all going to implode right before the state visit, and I'll never get hired anywhere again.'

'Well, that's definitely not true,' Jasper said, moving his hand up and down her spine in long, slow strokes. 'I happen to know a sheep farm in New Zealand that is in desperate need of a house manager. Are you allergic to wool, by any chance?'

She gave him a brief, shaky smile. 'I don't know how it's possible I lost the respect of my best friend and potentially my job all in the same week.' She wiped at her eyes again, letting out a sigh.

'Okay,' Jasper said. 'Do you want advice or just for me to listen?'

'Wow,' Lauren replied. 'Nobody has ever asked me that before.'

'Well, look, yes, it did end in divorce, but I *was* married for a good amount of time. I learnt a few things about women, and trust me, unsolicited advice is not something that is always appreciated. Or telling them to calm down when they're upset. Also a catastrophic thing to do.'

'That's the worst,' she agreed.

'Okay, so, dealer's choice.'

'Advice,' she said. 'Because clearly the one thing that I'm not good at fixing is myself.'

'Everybody's family is fucked-up,' he said.

'Are you allowed to swear?'

'I never said that word, and you couldn't prove it anyway. But it's true. Everybody's family is fucked, and everybody screws up at work a few times in their lives. Look at me. I share *actual* DNA with William the Conqueror, my marriage imploded, I went to Eton but still ended up running a farm and am basically bankrupt, to my family's utter mortification. Even without the royal duties for so long, there are still expectations. And I can't meet all of them. Neither can you.' He paused and then continued. 'I think that's why it caught me so off guard at the children's hospital, when you said I seemed like a person—'

'God, that was such a stupid thing to say.'

'No, it wasn't, not at all. I'm sure you hear it all the time here, but it's about duty, first and foremost. Which is a very good value to have, but when it supersedes your humanity, that's when things get dicey and tend to go off the rails. And what are we if not human?'

'Have you considered maybe doing a TED Talk?' Lauren asked. 'Because that was really good.'

Jasper chuckled. 'Well, luckily I happen to know the director of communications at Buckingham Palace. Maybe she could put in a good word for me.'

'*Acting* director. And maybe. If I don't get fired after next week.' Lauren pressed the handkerchief against her eyes again. 'You know what I keep thinking about?'

'What?' His voice was softer now, closer.

'Eugene and James, they both said the same thing: Why didn't I tell them things? Why didn't I come to them with this information? And I don't know why I didn't. I'm supposed to be a good communicator – it's literally in my job title! I was trying to protect my parents, but otherwise . . .' She shrugged. 'I don't know why I didn't trust them when they've put so much trust in me.'

'Well,' Jasper said. 'I'm not a psychiatrist, of course, but perhaps having a father who fucks off to Scotland for most of your life and an ex-boyfriend who cheated on you with your best friend would make it a *little* bit difficult to trust people. Also, there's plenty of people you *shouldn't* trust around here.'

Lauren looked up at him now. 'Seriously. TED Talk.'

He smiled at her again, but this time it faded until they were both looking at each other. The trees rustled overhead, the hum of London's evening traffic floated through the air and Lauren leant into his side, grateful for the silence.

'I know I shouldn't have,' Jasper said quietly, 'but I don't regret what happened in Singapore.'

'I don't either,' Lauren admitted. 'It can't happen again, but I'm glad it happened once.'

'I'm sorry it can't happen again. I'm sorry about so many things I can't do for you, *with* you, Lauren.'

'I know,' she whispered back.

'I would never bring you into this kind of chaos. I couldn't do that to you.'

'I know,' she said again. 'But thank you for saying it anyway.'

They sat together on the bench for a while, Lauren's head on his shoulder. 'So what are you going to do?' he asked.

Lauren thought for a minute. 'Probably hand in my notice,' she admitted. 'See if I can get out of my lease, go back home and crash at my mum's house. Figure out what's next.'

'Well, that is the absolute worst plan I've heard in a very long time.'

She raised her head from his shoulder. 'What?! I changed my mind. I don't want advice, I only want you to listen now.'

'Sorry, no going back. Do you really want to go home? You've got too much grit. Anyone who can take on the snakes

269

in that press pack *and* James *and* Eugene *and* me has some fight in them. Get a plan together, one that doesn't involve your mother's house, for God's sake.'

'It's like you've been to my mother's house,' she said.

'I've been to *my* mother's house, and trust me, it is always enlightening and infantilising.' He gave her the gentlest shove. 'You're in the fight now, might as well try to win it.'

Lauren slowly nodded. To be honest, she was so tired from her day, her call with her mom and crying that fighting sounded like the last thing she wanted to do.

But Jasper wasn't wrong.

He walked her back to her office, holding one of the French doors open for her as she stepped inside, the spring air creating a cold draft. 'Anytime you want to go for a walk,' he said, 'you know where to find me.'

'Thank you. For everything. The good advice and the, well, you know.'

'Oh, I do know,' he said with a wink, but then his face grew solemn. 'I meant what I said. If things were different than they are now . . .'

She reached out and squeezed his hand, not trusting herself to say anything too serious. 'See you around,' she replied.

'Without a doubt,' he said pointedly, before slipping away and shutting the door behind him.

Lauren looked at her office, at her now cold and limp pad Thai, and wondered how it could look so different from just an hour or so earlier, when it had felt like her world was crumbling. Her laptop was still open, and Lauren sat down, opened a new document and got to work.

She stayed up all night at her desk, coming up with idea after idea of what stories the press could run instead of the video of her dad. Once the sun rose, she went to the Palace's pool house, quickly showered and changed into the spare outfit she kept in her office, carefully avoiding the eyes of two of the Queen's rather intimidating ladies-in-waiting who were swimming slow lengths back and forth, circling like swim-capped sharks.

And as soon as she heard them come into the office, she went down the hall towards James and Eugene.

Chapter 16

'No.' Eugene's voice was low and steady. 'Not on your life.'

'I have at least fifteen good ideas here,' Lauren said, gesturing towards her phone.

'Wonderful news, but we've already decided how to deal with the *Tribune*.' He glanced at James, who nodded. 'Instead of running a story about your anarchist father, they're going to get exclusive details about how the Queen will be privately helping the duke clear his debts. You and your family get off scot-free, despite the chaos you've created, and we finally get to end speculation and control the narrative about the duke's finances. Two birds, one stone.'

Lauren felt her insides go cold. 'You can't,' she said. 'Eugene, you *cannot*.'

'It's not ideal, but at a time when the relationship between the US and the UK is more important than ever, a story about a traitorous American inside the Palace has the potential to cause far more damage,' Eugene replied. 'You have no say in this, Lauren. Every single member of the family has a duty to protect country and Crown, regardless of the cost to themselves. The duke came back into the fold partly, if not mostly, to help negate his personal and business debts, and that's what happened. And now he has to pay the price for that by helping the family avoid this . . . mishap you created. I'm being kind with my word choice here.'

Lauren glanced down at her phone, dozens of ideas mapped out that now looked childish and foolish.

'I've asked someone on the Strathearn team to brief directly to the paper's royal correspondent,' James said.

'You're welcome, by the way,' Eugene added.

Lauren bristled but said nothing.

'Does the duke know?' she asked instead.

Eugene looked her right in the eyes. 'He agreed to it right away. He understands the importance of duty.'

Lauren flashed back to their conversation the night before, to Jasper talking about duty and humanity.

'We already know that the *Dispatch* royal editor has been sniffing around this story so it's only a matter of time before it comes out,' Eugene continued. 'And God knows that Cockburn would foam at the mouth if he got wind of it first. This way we get ahead of both of them and are able to control the narrative. And if the Duke of Exeter wants his aunt, Her Majesty the Queen, to use her own personal funds to pay off his debts, this is the least he could do.' He glanced down at the newspapers scattered across his desk. 'Don't you have a state visit to get ready for? I know you have nothing else on your docket right now, that's for sure.'

Lauren balled her hands into fists but then turned away, too afraid of what she would say if she stayed any longer in that room. She retreated to her office and shut the door, fuming like a chimney in winter, trying to figure out how she could solve the problem instead of making it worse. It all felt so fucked up.

Finally, she texted Oscar.

'I just talked to James and Eugene. I know you're going to run the piece about the duke's financial problems instead.' She paused before adding, 'If that runs, it will destroy him.'

She watched the three bubbles go in and out for a few minutes (and who exactly designed those three bubbles?! They were almost mocking her at this point), before Oscar responded.

'I'm trying something,' he said. 'Sit tight.'

Sitting tight was not exactly Lauren's forte, and she knew Oscar knew that. Instead, she paced around her office for a while, brushing invisible dust from her desk and checking her phone every three seconds to see if Oscar had anything else to say like, 'I'm sorry, you were right, I owe you a gigantic apology.'

Instead, there was only silence.

Finally she texted him back: 'How long am I supposed to sit tight?'

'Until you hear from me,' he replied, then set his phone to Do Not Disturb mode.

Petty, Lauren thought. But still, she had to admit that she felt a tiny bit better knowing that he may come back with good news.

She just wished she knew what exactly that meant.

The following week passed in an anxious blur of schedules, itineraries, confirmation numbers and not a single sighting of Jasper nor even a whisper of information from Oscar, despite her texts to him. Lauren stayed late at the office most nights, always wondering if there'd be another rap at her French doors, but instead all she got were the incessant buzzes and chimes of her emails. There were no fun texts from Oscar, no slightly humorous but mostly testy banter with James and Eugene, and even Violet had retreated to focus on social activations for the state visit. And perhaps worst of all – no, definitely worst of all – there was no Joy.

She and Lauren had run into each other a few times in the kitchenette, all awkward stutters and 'sorry, excuse me's' as they tried to move through the space. She missed their raucous conversations after-hours, both of them slumped around the office as they recovered from the brutal pace of the day, their secret shared eye rolls whenever a visitor to the Palace seemed just a bit too high and mighty. And that loss was only made worse by the fact that Joy's absence was Lauren's own fault. She had no one to blame but herself and the stupid outburst that had caused her to lose one of the best friends she had had in a long time, and the guilt she felt was even more painful than the loneliness.

The only person who was really speaking to her was, alas, Harriet, who had taken over most comms-related duties until further notice. Harriet, who had the biggest heart but, quite frankly, absolutely zero ability to conduct a press briefing, which both she and Lauren knew full well.

On Friday morning, amid a flurry of back-and-forth emails with a White House official about the necessary additional security sweeps required for the media present at the BP state banquet, Harriet came into Lauren's office and shut the door behind her. 'Uh-oh,' Lauren said.

'I can't do the press briefing,' Harriet said. 'My nerves won't handle it. I even mouth the words when I sing at church.'

Lauren sighed. 'I mean this in the nicest way possible, but yes, I agree with you. That being said, I can walk you through the basics, so you at least know who to call on, who to never call on, that sort of thing.'

Harriet shook her head. 'No, no, I've already decided. Either you do it or we should cancel. It's in the best interest of the institution.'

'I don't even get to make this decision,' Lauren told her. 'You need to talk to James and Eugene if that's what you want.'

Harriet paused before tilting her head to the side, curious. 'And why exactly aren't you doing the press briefing?'

Lauren hesitated. She didn't doubt for a second that there was some fast and furious gossip flying around about why she hadn't been at meetings, why she was spending so much time in her office and, of course, why she and Joy weren't speaking to each other.

'Because I'm working on some things right now that are . . . of a clandestine nature,' she said, sounding slightly unsure of her own statement. 'Yes. That's why.'

'Of course,' Harriet replied, her side-eye clearly indicating that she was not buying anything that Lauren was saying. 'I'll go talk to Eugene right now.'

Ten minutes later, Harriet was back in Lauren's office. 'Eugene wants to talk to you.'

Lauren closed her eyes and sighed. 'Okay,' she said. 'Thanks.'

When she arrived at Eugene's plush office on the first floor, James was also standing there, waiting for her. 'Harriet can't do the briefing,' Eugene said.

'Trust me, I am very aware of that,' Lauren replied. 'She's shaking like a leaf in my office right now.'

Eugene ignored her. 'We're going to put you on this morning for a very brief, very abbreviated conference. You talk

276

about the state visit and only call on the people who you know will have unchallenging questions.'

'So, you want me to do my job?' Lauren asked. 'Done.'

'Excellent.' Eugene glanced at his phone. 'I have to take this.' Lauren doubted that there was a call, but she wasn't sorry to go.

Lauren left, and James followed. 'Lauren,' he said quietly, 'you might want to contact Oscar before the press conference.'

Lauren froze. 'Why?'

'Just what I said.'

Lauren hesitated, then turned and started running down the hall to her office. Halfway there, she passed Harriet in the hall. 'How did it go?' Harriet asked.

'You're off the hook!' Lauren said, giving her a thumbs-up as she ran past.

Out of the corner of her eye, she saw Harriet practically wilt with relief.

She nearly slammed her office door shut before grabbing her phone and calling Oscar.

And of course, it went to voicemail.

'Hi,' she said breathlessly. 'James just told me to talk to you, so this is me talking to you. What's happen—?'

As she was speaking, a message popped up. 'Park in 30 mins,' Oscar typed. 'Can't talk right now.'

She ended the call and thumbs-upped the text, then immediately grabbed her bag and went to the park early to get a coffee and wait for him.

One latte and a brownie down, Oscar finally strolled up almost an hour later. He was dressed smartly in a blue-checked gingham collared shirt under a navy jacket, with flat-front khaki trousers that made him look taller.

She still felt that buzz of attraction when she saw him, but she knew that their relationship had gone past the fun, flirty stage. They were now knee-deep in real life, with real consequences. If they were ever going to make this work, Lauren realised, they would have to swim instead of sink.

'Hi,' she said, relieved to see him after days of silence. 'How are you?'

'Well, it's been kind of a crazy week,' he said. 'But I'm okay. Sorry I'm so late. How are you?'

She shrugged. 'Same. Eugene didn't murder me, so I can put that in the plus column.'

'That is positive,' he agreed. 'Um, I was waiting to reach out to you until it was done, but I just finished interviewing the Duke of Exeter this morning.'

Lauren tried to keep her face neutral when really, it felt like someone had planted a firecracker into her heart. 'An interview?!' she asked. *Did you talk about me?* was what she thought.

'Not the article you think it is,' he said. 'I convinced my editor, and your man at the Palace, to run a different exclusive instead.'

'About . . . ?'

'About the duke's life in New Zealand and his return to the royal fold, how his relationship with his aunt, the Queen, has been the one thing that has sustained him through his divorce, and general stuff like being in the public eye and how much he's missed Britain and its people.' His voice was so rote that it sounded like he was reading off a dry press release, one that even Lauren would have punched up.

Lauren blinked, then felt the relief sag through her bones. 'Nothing about his finances?'

'We discussed the rumours around his situation,' Oscar

said. 'But we spun it. I have to get back to the office and write it up, but my editors are looking at images now for the piece. We'll have everything online at midnight on Saturday before the paper is out in the morning, and before the state visit begins.'

'I don't even know what to say.' Lauren felt breathless, still processing the huge 180 in this crisis and the fact she had no idea that this had even taken place. 'Oscar, seriously, *thank you.*'

He shrugged. 'Gotcha journalism isn't really my thing, anyway.'

Lauren folded her hands together on the park picnic table. 'I'm very sorry about what – No, no, let me say this,' she added as Oscar started to wave away her apology. 'I need to say it because you deserve to hear it. I'm sorry I got so upset and yelled at you. And I'm sorry I didn't tell you about my dad. You were vulnerable with me, and I didn't meet you there. I was just worried about my dad and mum – and myself, for that matter – and I panicked, and I'm sorry. You didn't deserve any of that; you were just trying to warn me.'

Oscar blew out a breath, looking over her head. 'You Americans and your overly effusive apologies,' he teased. 'Now I have to match that.'

Lauren smiled at him. 'You don't,' she said.

'No, I – I shouldn't have accused you of holding things back from me. What we have is . . .'

'Complicated?'

'Well, I had been about to say "special", but also complicated, yes. You weren't wrong to protect your family, at least from the press. You always try to do the right thing.' Then he paused before adding, 'Even when you completely fuck it up in the process.'

Lauren laughed, feeling a little lighter than she had in days. 'Was the duke okay with doing the interview?' she asked. 'Was he snippy about it?'

'He doesn't have a snippy bone in his body,' Oscar replied. 'Honestly, he was fine. He did that whole gentlemanly charm thing that seems to work.'

'And did it?'

'Definitely. Even I was swooning by the end of it.'

'Doesn't take much,' Lauren said, then laughed when he threw his paper straw wrapper at her. 'And what about the video of my dad?'

'Dead for now,' he said. 'That doesn't mean it might not resurface again, but at least you can get your talking points ready with the comms team in case it does.'

'Thank you,' she said again.

'I do what I can,' he replied. 'Oh, and you're definitely buying me dinner. Sushi. Omakase. Lots of it. Maybe two dinners, now that I think about it.'

'Deal,' she said.

'And the next time you buy a bunch of seasonally themed house stuff, you're returning it by yourself.'

'Done.'

'And—'

'Whatever you want,' she said. 'You really helped me out today. All the sushi for you.'

'One last request.' He caught her gaze. 'Fix things with Joy.'

Lauren tried to stop the rush of tears to her eyes but was only marginally successful. 'I will,' she said. 'I have to. I know.'

Oscar looked at her for a minute, his eyes both soft and sharp, making Lauren's pulse start to beat just a bit faster. 'I can't tell if you're good for this place or not,' he said, 'but I'm really looking forward to finding out.'

'Me too,' she said, and when he reached for her hand, she wrapped her fingers around his, grateful for the anchor, and even more grateful for him.

Chapter 17

The first morning of the state visit, the power went out on Lauren's floor of her building.

'Oh, for fuck's sake!' she screamed, looking at her wet hair and the lifeless hair dryer in her hand. 'Today?! Really?'

Una popped her head into the bathroom a minute later. 'The power's gone,' she said.

'You think!? I have – the banquet and – Gah!' Lauren gestured towards her hair. 'I have to look presentable at the very least.'

'Well, I know just the person who can help—' Una started to say, but Lauren held up her hand.

'First, does this person work in a job where they're required to wear tights every single day at work?'

Una paused. 'I don't even think they wear pants that often, really.'

'Then thank you very much, but I can figure this out.'

Una looked at her with some doubt. 'Are you sure about that?'

'Not really, but that's what I have to tell myself, otherwise I'm going to start screaming.'

'Fair play,' Una said. 'I'll manifest good things for you. And your hair.'

Lauren went back to her room, her hair dripping all over her dressing gown, and thought fast. She had prepared for every single emergency related to the state banquet: extra cars for staff on backup in case one of them had engine troubles, a bag filled with everything from Tylenol to Imodium A-D, and she had even arranged for a coffee trolley to be in the media room instead of just the usual pots of tea – because a room full of under-caffeinated journalists for six hours was a far greater crisis than a fire alarm going off.

But the power going out at home was not something that had been on her bingo card.

Not wanting to waste any time, she grabbed her phone.

'Hey, boomer.' Violet's dry tone came through loud and clear.

'Violet, once again, you and I were born in the same *decade*.' Focus, Lauren, she thought to herself.

'Well, you're the one who's *calling* me. Even my grandmother texts.'

'It's an emergency, texting would take too long,' Lauren replied. 'The power's out at my building, can I come to yours and get ready?'

'Sure,' Violet said, and Lauren could practically hear her shrugging. 'We have power.'

'Sounds like heaven,' Lauren said. 'Give me the address, please!'

She knew Violet also lived in Hampstead, but Lauren didn't quite expect her to be in *this* part of Hampstead, right by the heath, in one of the most beautiful houses on the street. The window boxes were filled with lush hydrangeas, the front door was a glossy obsidian black and even the brass door knocker and house numbers were completely untarnished.

'Does she squat here?' Lauren wondered out loud, and before she could even knock, Violet opened the front door. She had AirPods in but pulled one out and said, 'Sorry, editing,' before holding the door open for Lauren, who was now fairly certain that she was on a prank show because there was absolutely no way that this was where Violet lived.

'How long have you—?' she started to ask.

'My whole life,' Violet said, then rolled her eyes. 'It's my parents' house. So annoying.'

'Yeaaaaah,' Lauren said, pretty sure that she was looking at an original Basquiat on the wall in front of her. 'So annoying. Really.'

The guest bathroom she followed Violet to was as lush as a five-star spa, with stacks of fluffy white towels and even a mini-fridge filled with bottled still and sparkling waters. 'I can't believe you live like this!' Lauren said, raising her voice over the sound of her hair dryer.

'What?' Violet yelled back.

'Nothing!'

After she'd dried and styled her hair, she pulled on a navy midi dress from Reformation and a cropped jacket. Lauren looked at herself in Violet's full-length mirror. Not terrible, she thought to herself, then did a little pose for an imaginary photo before dropping her arms down to her sides and sighing at her reflection. She had imagined this night as sort of a victory dance, proving once and for all that she belonged in London, at the Palace, that she could triumph over adversity and show everyone that Lauren Morgan was back! But the truth was just that it was weird and sad and lonely standing all alone in one of Violet's many marble-covered guest bathrooms, and she didn't feel triumphant at all.

She just wanted the state visit to be over. And everything to go back to normal. Or whatever version of normal she'd got used to before her life imploded thanks to her dad.

'Do you want to share an Uber?' Lauren asked Violet when she went downstairs. 'We all have to be at BP five hours before the banquet starts, remember.'

'Well, I was just going to use my parents' driver,' Violet replied, as blasé as ever. She herself was wearing a black cotton dress and looked a little like she was dressed up for her family's Christmas card photo. Lauren knew that she hated it.

'Your parents' driver,' Lauren repeated slowly.

'Yeah, he takes me to work every morning. George is pretty chill.'

Lauren bowed her head for a minute before regrouping. 'That would be lovely,' she said, and wondered if Violet's parents would be open to adopting a twenty-eight-year-old woman from America.

Lauren had attended state banquets at the White House before, back when she had a lot less responsibility and therefore a lot more fun, but seeing one at Buckingham Palace really took the event to an entirely new level.

Set in Buckingham Palace's Ballroom, its walls adorned with grand portraits of historical figures and ornate tapestries, the dinner was a level of regal she didn't know existed. At the centre of the room was a network of connected dining tables for 160 guests, all covered with pristine white linens and glittering silverware and crystalware. Lauren had sent Violet in the day before to capture some of the meticulous planning and polishing that went into each of the place settings – including

285

video clips of household staff putting out huge floral arrangements and using rulers to ensure that every piece of polished silver cutlery was precisely aligned and spaced. It took a military-style operation to achieve this level of perfection.

Before the president, the First Gentleman, the Queen and members of the royal family processed into the room, the rest of the presidential team arrived at the dinner alongside the other guests. Lauren felt like a rabbit in the crosshairs, tense and ready for anything. She stood and smiled in the distance as people greeted one another, the entire American team looking, well, like they had been styled and polished within an inch of their lives: trousers pressed, shirts starched and dresses worth more than a month of her Palace salary.

Violet wrinkled her nose when members of the White House comms team arrived in the pressroom nearby. 'Are they all wearing the same perfume?' she whispered to Lauren. 'What's that smell?'

Lauren sighed. 'Drybar,' she said wistfully.

Since no photographers were allowed inside the actual dinner, the impromptu pressroom, which was really just one of the smaller rooms near the ballroom, quickly filled with at least forty accredited reporters, international correspondents and other Palace and White House aides who didn't have seats in the dinner. Lauren couldn't help but feel nostalgic seeing her fellow Americans get so excited about being in a Palace. She had felt that same way once before, so intrigued by all the mystique shrouded behind ornate gates, leafy gardens and stone walls.

And now they were about to learn what she had also discovered: Stone walls and old wiring equalled *terrible* internet service.

'Why are these upload speeds so bad?' someone asked.

'It keeps bumping me off the Wi-Fi.'

'It's just a little slow,' Lauren said to a new White House correspondent she hadn't met before. 'And there's a lot of people using it.'

'By the time I get this footage out, it'll be time for the next state banquet,' he muttered in response.

'Oh, c'mon, man,' a voice said, and Lauren looked over to see Oscar typing furiously on his laptop. 'Just do what the rest of us do: Upload from the Starbucks down the road.'

'Great,' the reporter said, turning back to his laptop with a groan, and Oscar caught Lauren's eye and smiled.

'Is that true?' she mouthed.

'No,' he mouthed back, making a face as if to say, *Who would actually believe that?*

Lauren sent him a quick text: 'Please do not antagonise the Americans.'

'But it's so fun,' he replied.

She sent back three angry-face emojis.

'Are we going to get a live stream of the dinner?' a member of the American team asked Lauren. She didn't recognise her, but to be honest, none of them looked familiar. Turnover was high, with most people getting promoted or going to different teams and administrations. DC was nothing if not a highly ambitious town, and just watching them work behind the scenes made something inside of Lauren start to twitch. She had that ambition once, that desire to always be doing more, going further, working harder and smarter. The money had been good and the perks were fun, but at the end of the day, Lauren had loved how the job had made her feel.

It had made her feel like herself.

And standing in the pressroom, Lauren realised that it had been a very long time since she had felt that way.

'Sorry, what?' Lauren said.

'A live stream? Of the event? Should I talk to someone else about it?'

'No, you should talk to me. I'm Lauren Morgan, I'm the head of communications. Unfortunately we're having some issues with the screen here, but a lot of people here are watching the arrivals feed through the Sky News app until our own is working for the dinner itself.'

'I have to download an app?'

Lauren pointed at a laminated QR code that had just been taped to the table. 'This will take you there,' she said. 'We have a member of the IT team coming as soon as possible.'

A minute later, Harriet pulled her aside. 'Do we actually have someone coming?' she asked. 'No one's answering my emails.'

'Supposedly,' Lauren whispered nervously.

Harriet hid a smile. 'I also wanted to ask you, where did you set up a desk for Brian Martinez?'

It felt as if all the blood had drained from her body.

'I'm sorry, what?'

Lauren's face must have gone completely white, because Harriet suddenly looked alarmed. 'Yes, um, I confirmed with the White House last week while I was filling in for you that he would have a desk set up here.' She started going through her phone, looking for the email. 'He was just promoted to digital director in the—'

'Communications office,' Lauren finished for her. The job she had wanted before everything went to hell.

'Sorry, I should have told you sooner.'

Lauren didn't know how much Harriet had heard over the past several months, but clearly she had heard enough. 'So he's here now?' Lauren confirmed.

'He's been with the president throughout the day, but he'll be at the Palace any minute.'

'I see. Well, make sure to seat him over there,' she said, pointing to a foldout desk with a power strip taped to it in the corner of the room. 'I'll handle anything else that comes up.'

Lauren spun around and started to head in the direction of where she thought the IT crew might be, but she stopped short. There, for the first time in six months, was Brian, standing three metres away from her.

She always thought that if she saw him again, she'd scream or sob or throw the nearest object at his head, but instead she stood perfectly still, like any bodily motion would force her brain to shut down. He was shorter than she remembered, which she found to be very satisfying. He was still handsome, though, a walking Ralph Lauren ad in his navy suit, white dress shirt and deep burgundy tie.

'Hey,' Brian said nervously. 'Lauren. Hi.'

'Hi,' she replied, then immediately hated herself for doing so.

'I figured you'd be here,' he said. She may have looked completely put together, but it was clear that she was nervous.

Lauren wasn't exactly upset about that.

'I am definitely here,' Lauren said.

'Yeah, director of communications at Buckingham Palace! That's so cool! I always knew you'd do great things.' Brian smiled. 'And London's awesome.'

'Uh-huh,' Lauren said, her mouth and brain stuttering just like the Palace Wi-Fi. 'What are – Is everything going well so far?' *Stay professional*, she told herself. *Do not pick up a steak knife and threaten him with it. Do not yell. Do not cry.*

'Oh, yeah, really great,' he said. He sounded so American! Had she sounded like that when she first got to London? 'Thanks, yeah,' he awkwardly added.

289

'Sure,' she said. 'Well, if you need anything, you can let someone else know.'

'Hey, Laur.' He exhaled and adjusted his tie. 'I also … I also wanted to apologise. To you.'

At the word *apologise*, Lauren felt her brain suddenly click back online.

'Stop,' she said. 'Brian, just *stop*. Not here, not right now. I need to work, and so do you.'

'Okay. Of course. But do you … Can we just talk at some point?'

Lauren glanced over at a reporter's iPad live-streaming the arrivals at the dinner. The camera panned to a tuxedo-clad Jasper, who was taking his seat next to the daughter of the Lord Mayor of London, a very single and fashionable woman who was often in the headlines for her charity work. (And definitely not her long list of celebrity exes.) The papers would love seeing them together.

'After dessert is served,' Lauren said. 'Maybe then. I'll be around.'

Brian blinked a few times. 'Sure, I'll find you.'

Lauren said nothing as she walked away.

This would have been, she thought to herself with a re-newed sense of sadness, a perfect time to text Joy. She almost laughed thinking about the emojis Joy would have sent back upon hearing that Brian was in the building, which cheered her up for a moment.

But mostly, Lauren spent the evening looking at a life that could have been hers.

Lauren thought she would feel an immense sense of relief as soon as the dinner concluded, but instead she just felt nervous and edgy, knowing that Brian was somewhere out there, lurking like Jaws underwater, waiting to take Lauren by surprise yet again.

But in the meantime, she had journalists to wrangle and two press memos to finish writing. One of the members of the US press pack had brought their own power strip to plug into the wall so that more people had the ability to charge their devices. It was a great idea in theory, but not so much when plugging into the Palace's somewhat antiquated electric system. It immediately shorted out the entire strip, along with some of the charging devices plugged into it, and after Lauren determined that the smoky smell was only from the initial spark and they weren't about to burn the place down, she ran back to her office to grab her phone charger, yanking it out of the wall. She almost made it back to the pressroom when she glanced up in the corridor just outside it.

Brian was standing there. 'Hey,' he said, looking even more nervous this time. 'Sorry, I hope you don't mind.'

'I do, actually, I have to get this to—'

'Lauren.' Brian didn't move from his spot. 'I just wanted to say that I'm sorry.'

'Great,' Lauren said. 'Good for you.'

'No, I mean it. Truly. What I did to you was . . .'

'Horrible?' Lauren said. 'Fucked up? The kind of thing that happens on Bravo reality shows?'

'Yes,' Brian said. 'All of that.'

'You literally upended my entire life!' she cried. Lauren held her arms open, gesturing to the Palace. 'I left everything behind to come here, and while I'm not sorry I'm here, I hate the fact that I was the one who ended up leaving when you were the one who was in the wrong!'

Fuck the press. They could wait for her charger.

'You know what else I hate?' she said. 'That we were

291

building a life together, Brian. I told you so many things that I hadn't told anyone else about my dad, how it felt when he left me! And you *knew* that that was my biggest fear, being abandoned, and somehow it still seemed easy for you to do exactly that to me.'

'It wasn't easy—'

'Sure looked easy to me.' Lauren crossed her arms, stood her ground. 'You've taken up so much space in my brain for all these months and you don't deserve any of it. You've controlled my life even though you're not even in it anymore, and I am done. You wanted to leave so you can just stay gone. And how dare you come up to me here, on one of the biggest days of my job, and try to smooth things over. You're smug as hell, and I bet you're not even that sorry at all. You're only apologising now because we're in the same space and you feel awkward about it.'

'No, I meant it!' Brian protested.

'Then why are you still with Brooke?'

Brian fell silent, just like Lauren knew he would. 'Like I said, you just do whatever you want and you don't care about the collateral damage. I don't accept your apology, and I won't accept the way you treated me. Go fuck yourself, Brian.'

And then Lauren went past him and raced down the corridor back to the media room.

The pressroom had emptied out, stories filed, reporters departed, dignitaries tucked safely back into town cars, limousines and private planes. No one had choked or seized up, and when Lauren glanced at some of the early front pages already online for the next day's newspapers, it looked like it had been a spectacular event, with all the stories talking about the reinvigorated relationship between Britain and America.

And Lauren was now slumped in a chair, a hand over her eyes, willing the painful headache to go away, when she saw Norman, the Duke of Cumberland's private secretary who was still looking after Jasper until his own was hired, come into the room.

'Yes?' she said, sitting up.

'DON would like to speak with you for a moment,' said Norman. 'He's waiting in the 1844 Room.'

'Of course,' Lauren said, running her hands through the ends of her hair before following behind him.

The duke was standing behind a blue and gold silk armchair, which he had rested his jacket on, and he turned around when Lauren entered the room. He always looked good, but the white starched shirt and white bow tie he was wearing were something else, and Lauren found it extremely unfair that some people just looked incredible in every single piece of clothing they wore.

'Your Highness,' she said, curtsying. 'How can I help you?'

'Lauren, hello.' He sounded so formal, so royal. 'Thank you, I'm sure you've had quite a long few days.'

She picked up the undertone of his words: They both knew that she had.

'I was just wondering what you thought of the interview and if you were happy with the reaction.'

'Oh yes, absolutely,' she said. 'People seemed to love it, our social media feeds were flooded with positive comments.'

'Good, good, I'm so glad, truly.' He glanced up as Norman answered his phone and left the room to talk outside. 'Oh, thank goodness, we can speak normally now.'

Lauren smiled.

'Did the piece do its job?'

'Yes, absolutely. I'm just deeply, deeply grateful that you

even agreed to do the interview in the first place. It would have been fine if you didn't want—'

'It would very much not have been fine, and you and I both know it,' he replied. 'Plus, let's be honest, it helped me steer the conversation away from the money stuff as well. At least for now. I hope this helped you get ahead of your situation. I know a little something about damaged family ties, and I'd hate to see you and your father's relationship be damaged even further.'

Lauren nodded, waiting for the lump in her throat to smooth itself out. 'Thank you again. I know that you don't love press attention.'

'Well, *good* press attention isn't the worst thing. And this is my reality now – the trade-off for reclaiming my position here with the family.' He looked a bit sad, then added with a smile, 'Plus Sweater Weather always appreciates some nice news stories about her. She got an entire picture caption of her own.'

'I know the team is very grateful—'

'I'm just glad it all worked out.' Jasper paused, and when he spoke again, his voice was rough and serious. 'But I didn't do it for the team, Lauren. I did it for you.'

'But you didn't have to.' Now her eyes were watering, damn it.

'I did,' he murmured. 'You've been by my side every step of this journey, including the time that I came into your office and scared the hell out of you—'

'I'm still really sorry about—'

'It's fine, of course,' Jasper said. 'I did in fact look scary. But you were there at the children's hospital when I was a complete grump, and then in Singapore . . .' He trailed off as they both remembered the hotel suite that night. 'Well, yes, Singapore.'

He reached for Lauren's hand then, gripping it tightly. 'I

told you the other night in the gardens, there are so many things I'd like to do with you, but I can't. It would be throwing you to the rabid press wolves, and I couldn't protect you if that happened. But this story was something I *could* do to protect you. So please, let me have this one.'

They looked at each other for a long minute before Norman came bustling back into the room, interrupting the moment as Jasper quickly shook her hand as if it was the end of a business meeting, and they stepped apart. 'Well, thank you, Your Highness,' Lauren said. 'I appreciate all that you've done. For everyone.'

'Of course,' he said. 'Have a good evening.'

Lauren's head was spinning as she made her way back to the media room to collect her belongings. But with the arrival of Eugene just a couple of minutes later, it only spun more.

'Lauren!' he said, standing in front of her, still in his white-tie attire. 'Good, they said I could find you back here.'

'I'm here,' she said. 'What is it? What's wrong?'

'Did you get into a *fight* with a digital director of the American communications team?' He seemed absolutely aghast.

Here we go, Lauren thought.

'I had a personal disagreement with someone who used to be a close, um, friend—'

'Who now works for the president of the United States of America, one of our greatest allies.'

'—and I was taken by surprise in my office.'

'On the night of the state banquet at Buckingham Palace.'

'Believe me, Eugene, I didn't want this conversation to happen any more than you did. He accosted me. How do you even know about this? Did you have me followed or something?'

It was hard to imagine Eugene looking any more offended, but he did. '*Excuse* me!' he said. 'Cockburn mentioned he saw you and the American arguing.'

'Well, I hope he enjoyed the show,' Lauren said.

'After all the events over the past few weeks, that you would have the nerve to—'

Lauren felt the pain behind her eyes explode into a supernova.

'Eugene, enough. Please!' she said, her voice more fearsome than it had ever been with Brian. 'I told you, it was *personal.*'

Eugene froze, but only for a second. 'We will discuss further on Monday,' he said. 'In my office. Ten a.m. sharp.'

'Fine,' Lauren said.

After he left, she glanced around the media room at the empty camping-style pop-up tables, coffee cups and saucers, and crumpled-up napkins strewn around. Someone else would clean it up, she realised. There was always someone to clean up the mess.

This time, though, she suspected that her time cleaning up after everyone else was about to come to an end.

Chapter 18

Lauren spent the remainder of the weekend eating over-priced Uber Eats orders that she really couldn't afford anymore, streaming bad reality TV on her laptop and rotting in bed. Normally that would have felt like a perfect way to spend her time after something as demanding as the state visit, but she felt only restless and somehow even more tired by Sunday night.

She hadn't been able to stop thinking about Brian, about how she was probably about to be fired, about how she'd have to explain to Oscar that she sucked at her job and they couldn't date anymore because she had to go back to Atlanta and live with her mum and probably do things like get excited about the Double Ad Wednesday deals at Sprouts. (She didn't even know what that was, but she knew her mum *loved* Double Ad Wednesdays.)

She'd never see Jasper again, either, except on TV or online, or probably in the sexy fan edits that hadn't slowed down at all, especially after he had been photographed in his tailcoat at the state banquet. His interview with Oscar had been all fluff and sunshine, charming smile and sun-dappled photos.

It basically read like a fawning film star profile, which had made her grateful to Oscar. She had sent him a text afterwards: 'Great work.'

'Right back at you,' came the reply, alongside a winking emoji.

But worse than Oscar or the duke, Lauren found that she couldn't even think about saying goodbye to Joy without starting to cry.

In fact, she was crying in the bathroom that Sunday night when Una waltzed in followed by a cloud of Baccarat Rouge 540. 'Uh-oh,' Una said breezily. 'Do you need a minute for a good sob-fest? I can wait out in the hallway, but I absolutely *cannot* be late tonight. I have to be on a flight at nine p.m., no exceptions.'

'No, I'm fine,' Lauren said as she hastily wiped at her eyes.

'You don't look fine, babe,' Una said, pulling her makeup bag out of her purse and going towards the mirror. 'Want to come with? I'm sure we can squeeze one more on his plane. That's right, his *plane*.'

Lauren suspected that there were rules regarding private jets and weight limits, but she didn't want to get into it. 'No, it's fine. I'm actually glad I saw you. You're about to have this bathroom all to yourself.'

'Oh, really? Are you moving to a new apartment?' Una widened her eyes and started applying another layer of mascara to her already-spidery lashes.

'Kind of?' Lauren said, and Una glanced up at her in the mirror. 'I'm going back to America. I don't think the job at the Palace is working out.'

'Ooh, say more,' Una said, moving to her other eye.

'I've just screwed up basically every relationship I have there,' Lauren said.

'Did things not work out with the fuckable royal?' Una said, then glanced at her mascara tube. 'Wait, is this waterproof?'

'Things were never going to go anywhere with the duke,' Lauren said. 'But it's everyone. My boss, his boss, my best friend.' Just thinking about Joy made her tear up again, and she reached for a tissue. 'I think I'm toxic. I ruin everything.'

Una made a boo-hoo face. 'Hun, don't you fix things for a living?'

'Yes, but not, like, *my* problems. I fix everyone else's.'

'Oh, because you get paid to do it.' Una nodded wisely. 'Makes sense. Never do what you're good at for free. Me too.'

'No, I just . . .' Lauren trailed off, thinking about Una's comment. She *did* fix things. She had fixed the very first problem she had discovered at Buckingham Palace, walking into a room and solving the racist vase scandal before she even had the job. She had helped transform Jasper from a broke sasquatch into the world's most talked-about and desired royal. She had won over the lord chamberlain by talking (well, lying) about Irish setters, a dog she had never encountered in real life. She had finally told her absentee father how she felt about him and held her own with Harold Cockburn even as he repeatedly tried to knock her down. Eugene – well, Eugene was probably a lost cause, but James, the world's most buttoned-up man, had even admitted he admired her.

And if she could do all that for near-strangers, then surely she could fix a few things in her own life, right?

'Una?' Lauren said.

'Hmm? Change your mind about the flight? I'm not sure where it's landing, but I know it'll be grand.'

'No, I'll pass. But did anyone ever tell you that you're a genius?'

299

'Course. Everyone in my Mensa club. We meet the last Tuesday of the month.'

Lauren's brain was humming again, her tears forgotten, and she gave Una a quick, fierce hug from behind. 'You're the best!' she said.

'Watch the body makeup!' Una cried, but Lauren was already back in her apartment, a plan starting to form. 'Does this mean you're not leaving anymore?' Una yelled after her. 'Can I have your cabinet space?'

'Sure!' Lauren said. 'Whatever you want!'

She could hear the clatter of products being moved as she slammed her front door.

At 8:15 on Monday morning, Lauren came into work with a banker's box under her arm and Starbucks in her hand. She had been expecting a pretty empty and quiet office, especially after the state visit, when everyone had been pushed to the brink of their abilities, but she knew there was one person who nearly always showed up bright and early.

And sure enough, Joy was in her office, a croissant on top of a white paper bag and a steaming cup of coffee next to it. She was typing away on her laptop, and when Lauren knocked on the half-open door, she looked genuinely surprised to see her.

'Oh!' she said. 'Hello.'

'Hi,' Lauren replied. 'Um, sorry, didn't mean to scare you.'

'No, it's fine, it's fine.' Joy paused. 'What's in the box?'

'Oh, this. Yes. I'm' – she decided to rip the Band-Aid right off – 'I'm going to hand in my notice.'

Joy blinked. 'I'm sorry, you're what?'

'I'm quitting,' Lauren said. 'I'm going back to DC and figuring out my next steps.'

'What?!' Joy said again. 'Why?'

'Because.' Lauren took a deep breath. She hadn't slept at all the night before, trying to figure out what she was going to say, and she still didn't feel like it was right. 'I ran away from my problems in DC instead of facing them. There are some things I just can't fix here. But one thing I know I can fix – the one thing I *need* to fix – is my friendship with you.'

Joy just blinked at her, but Lauren was fairly certain she could see tears gathering in the corners of her eyes.

'Joy, I am so, so sorry,' Lauren said. 'You were trying to protect me from doing something really stupid, and I was embarrassed and I lashed out, and you are the absolute last person who deserves to be treated that way. You've been this amazing friend to me ever since that day I tried to suck up to everyone with doughnuts—'

Joy chuckled a little in remembrance.

'—and every single day after that. You work so hard, even when people act like absolute assholes, and you bring me food from Pret and you took me out dancing when you knew I was homesick and . . .' Lauren looked up at the ceiling and took a deep breath. 'You helped me remember what it was like to have a good friend, and I'm sorry that I wasn't a good enough friend back to you. And I don't know if I can fix what we had, but I want to try to make it up to you in the future.'

Joy was quiet for a few seconds too long, which made Lauren's stomach swoop with anxiety. 'I was gutted, babes,' she finally said.

'I know,' Lauren replied.

'The way you spoke to me really hurt.'

Lauren looked down at her shoes, dabbing at her eyes.

'And I forgive you. But!' Joy quickly added as Lauren's head jerked up. 'This can never, ever happen again. I give second chances, not thirds. No matter how much I love you.'

Lauren just flung her arms around her.

'It's too early for all of this!' Joy protested, even as she hugged Lauren back. 'Look at you, coming into my office and performing a dramatic monologue like you're in the West End.'

She stood back and held Lauren out at arm's length. 'You better be joking about going back to DC, though.'

Lauren pulled away. 'I'm not,' she said. 'I think my time here at the Palace is up.'

'Okay, hold on,' Joy said, then went to shut her office door. 'You're quitting?' she said.

'Um, yes?' Lauren said.

'*You're* quitting.'

'I'm going to quit before Eugene fires me. I screwed up a bunch of things and I don't know if I can stay here because of that. I'll go back and stay with my mum to figure things out first. Maybe I'll look into law school.'

Joy was silent at that, and when Lauren finally looked up at her, she seemed disgusted. 'Oh *no*,' she said. 'What, are you going to live in your childhood *bedroom*?'

Lauren's guilty silence was all the answer Joy needed.

Joy pressed her fingers to her temples. 'Lauren,' she finally said. 'I truly enjoyed your little soliloquy, so let me deliver one myself. We've both been here for exactly the same amount of time. How much progress do you think I've made here at the Palace compared to how much I wanted to? I'll tell you, you don't even have to guess.' Joy rolled her eyes. 'Barely any. Most of my initiatives have been shot down, Pride at the Palace probably won't happen until 2028 because, as you quite rightly pointed out, I cannot get anyone to respond to an email about it. My biggest win was getting the Strathearns to actually interact with real people for longer than thirty seconds. So now you're telling me that you're seriously just going to leave me here by myself? How badly did you fuck up, Lauren?'

And for three minutes straight, Lauren unfurled the entire story for Joy: her dad at Balmoral and the ensuing video, James's and Eugene's reactions to it possibly leaking, Oscar working overtime to keep the duke out of the crosshairs, Jasper taking the fall for her and Brian showing up at the state banquet.

'What?!' Joy said again as soon as Lauren said Brian's name. Her eyes had been getting bigger and bigger as Lauren spoke, but this shocked her out of it. 'As in, *Brian* Brian?'

'Brian Brian,' Lauren said.

'The nerve of that little shit,' Joy said. 'Oh, I wish I had been there.'

'I wish you had been there, too,' Lauren admitted. 'I've really missed you.'

'I've missed you, too,' Joy said. 'And we're *still* friends, which is why I'm telling you how stupid you're being by quitting. Do you think Scotland Yard was a romp in the park for me? I had to deal with so many idiots and unnecessary battles there, to prove that I wasn't a token hire—'

'You've never been!' Lauren protested.

'I know. People still say it, though, even here. Maybe not to my face, but they think it. But I'm not going to give them the satisfaction of making me leave. I came to the Palace because it was a better position and I believed that if I could make just the slightest change to this place, it would be a step in the right direction, but my God, it has not been easy. I want to quit at least once a week, but I'm not going to because I'm really fucking great at my job, and so are you. So let's stick together and see what we can do.'

Lauren sank down into the chair next to Joy's desk and ran

a hand over her eyes. 'Everything just feels so messy all the time,' she said. 'Everything I've done seems to create absolute chaos behind the scenes. I don't know enough, I'm not polished enough, my ideas are too different, all of it.'

'Who cares if it's chaos behind the scenes? It's *supposed* to be chaos behind the scenes so that everything is nice and smooth in front of the rest of the world. Isn't that how the royal family have survived for so many centuries? And that's what you're doing. You're fantastic at this job. Yes, you've had some hiccups, but you worked with your team to fix them.'

'Eugene said—'

'Oh, Eugene's always upset about something. He'll be upset about something else tomorrow. He's probably one of those people who brings a healthy snack from home when he goes to the cinema. Just ignore him. That's what the rest of us do.'

'I really do think I'm going to be fired, though.'

'Well, then, go out swinging,' Joy said. 'Make 'em fight. Don't go in there with your sad little empty box, all pitiful and mopey. Show them who they hired and fight for the job like you *should* have done back at the White House. DC is behind you, Lauren, but this is something you can fix now.'

Lauren wiped at her eyes. Joy was right. She was so right. 'We're such a strange group of people,' she said with a laugh.

'Well, yes,' Joy said, laughing along with her. 'A bunch of weirdos who work and eat and fight and make up and have one another's backs. We're a *family*, like it or not. And neither one of us are leaving.

'Now go tell Eugene that, and if he doesn't like it, tell him to come and see me.'

Lauren didn't doubt for a second that Joy meant it, too.

'And leave that stupid box here,' Joy added, motioning to the floor. 'I'll put it out for recycling.'

Lauren paused then stood up and threw her arms around her friend. 'You're my favourite part of London,' she said. 'Thank you, Joy.'

Joy hugged her back tight. 'I'm always here to give you a kick up the bum,' she said. 'That's what best friends do.'

Lauren laughed again. 'Okay, how do I look?'

Joy gave her a quick up-and-down glance. 'Honestly? Meh. But that's fine. You had a long weekend.'

And Lauren was fairly certain that Joy was right about that, too.

At 10:00 a.m., Lauren was in Eugene's office, James close behind as he shut the door after them. She had practised her speech in her office, freshly powered by Joy's call to action and a flat white, which seemed especially strong that morning.

And just when she opened her mouth and was about to explain all the reasons she should stay, Eugene spoke first.

'Lauren,' he said, 'I want to say something to you.'

Lauren looked up at Eugene, who seemed almost . . . sheepish? Contrite? *Apologetic?*

She hadn't been at work for even two hours but already the day was off to an unprecedented start.

'I – I may have overstepped after the banquet,' he said.

If Lauren hadn't been hearing it with her own ears, she wouldn't have believed it.

James looked over at Eugene, waiting for him to continue.

'I know that while work can demand so much of our time, sometimes our personal life collides, and I understand that that can't always be controlled.'

'Did you rehearse this?' Lauren asked.

'Yes, he did,' James replied.

Eugene shot him a look. 'And I would like to also apologise

for confronting you in such a hostile manner after what we all know was a very long and complex evening. My concerns could have waited until today to be expressed in a more professional style.'

James looked pleased.

'Wait, wait.' Lauren held up her hands. 'Am I being fired or not?'

'Let's just consider these next few months as an extension of your probationary period,' James said. 'There have been some missteps, I think we can all agree, but at the end of the day, the coverage has been solid. You've done what we hired you to do.'

When Lauren burst into tears again, both James and Eugene looked horrified. 'She's going to try to hug us, isn't she?' James said with mild horror.

'I'm sorry, I'm sorry,' she said. 'I'm fine. I'm just glad I'm staying, is all.' She pulled it together as fast as she could. 'I know I may not be your first choice to run the comms team, but I do like it. Plus I really don't want to move back in with my mum again.'

'Well then,' James said. 'Shall we get back to work?'

'Yes, please,' Eugene said, straightening his jacket as he stood up. 'This operation is not going to run itself, as you both well know.' He held the door open for Lauren, pointedly waiting for her to exit and shutting it behind her as she did.

On her way back to the office, Lauren felt her phone buzz, and she glanced down to see a face and a name that made her heart pick up speed. 'Lunch?' the message read. 'Top of Primrose Hill?'

'See you at 1,' she wrote back, then went down the hall to tell Joy.

*

306

London was busier than usual on that gorgeous spring day, as it seemed nearly every single office worker and uni student had escaped outside to enjoy the mild weather. Lauren expertly dodged a cab as she crossed the street towards the daffodil-scattered park, her hastily grabbed coat now slung over her arm.

The city skyline was sparkling now that the morning rain shower had passed, and Lauren could see St. Paul's Cathedral and the London Eye out in the distance when she got closer to the summit of the hill. Her shoes weren't exactly ideal for the incline, but she trudged on anyway.

And as she got to the top, she saw Oscar, a tartan blanket thrown down on a park bench and a couple of grocery bags on the floor next to him. He was unpacking food containers, and when he saw her, he stood up and waved.

Lauren waved back, and for the first time since she had set foot on English soil, she felt like she was truly home.

Acknowledgements

Omid Scobie

I can't start this without thanking my literary agent and friend Albert Lee, who – just one day after I turned in the final edits for *Endgame* – was already encouraging me to start work on the book of *Royal Spin*. I planned to take a month off, but in true fashion of our working relationship, we were already deep into planning the next steps within twenty-four hours. As is so often the case with Albert, when there's a good idea he wastes no time bringing the right people together.

Robin, every step of writing this book with you has been both fun and inspiring. I've learnt so much from your exceptional talent as an author. Your ability to infuse scenes with meaning and bring heart and life to characters is truly remarkable. You've helped me become a better writer, and I can't wait to do more!

I'm deeply grateful to the wonderful team at HarperCollins and William Morrow, especially Liate Stehlik and Jennifer Hart. Liz Stein, your keen editorial eye and thoughtful guidance were instrumental in shaping

Royal Spin. Thank you to the phenomenal marketing and publicity teams – an impressively well-oiled machine that helped put this book into so many hands right out of the gate. Big thanks to Rachel Weinick and Andrea Monagle for keeping everything on track and the manuscript spotless, respectively. And to Vi-An Nguyen, who created our beautiful cover – thank you for your talent (and your patience with my fiddly requests!).

To David Shelley, Charlie King, Rebecca Roy, Elisha Lundin and the entire team at Hachette UK and Little, Brown Book Group: your early vision for the title in Britain and across the Commonwealth won us over from the first meeting.

Endless thanks to the incredible *Royal Spin* squad at UTA – Albert, Lisa Grupka, Talia Myers, Mary Pender and Geoff Morley – as well as Sam Solomons, Harry Sherer, Sophia Saker and Rukia Magege, whose efforts behind the scenes helped bring this book and television adaptation to life. Melissa Chinchillo and Meredith Miller – thank you once again for expanding the book's global reach even further.

Elena Grieco – navigating new territory with you has been a joy, and I'm excited for all that's still to come.

As the world of *Royal Spin* expands into television, I feel beyond lucky to have showrunner extraordinaire Emily Fox by my side. From the commemorative thimble that brought us together in 2022 to now, it's been an unforgettable ride.

To the dream team at Universal Television – Erin Underhill, Vivian Canon, Adam Giagni, Montserrat Gomez and Bryana Stern – thank you for championing the development of *Royal Spin*'s TV adaption from day one. Your belief in its potential means everything. And to the amazing team at NBC Peacock – Donna Langley, Lisa Katz, Cara Dellaverson, Christina Lehmann, Deepak Jesrani and Jake

Castiglioni – bringing Lauren and this wonderful cast of characters to life on screen continues to be a dream come true.

I'm endlessly thankful for the love and support of my dear family and friends back at home. Even from 5,500 miles away, I feel it constantly and miss you more than I can say. To the old and new friends in L.A. who have made this place feel like a second home – thank you.

Finally, and most importantly, thank you to everyone who's supported me over the years by reading or watching my work, sharing it and standing by me through the craziest moments. For those who've been around since the beginning: your belief in truthful, honest and fearless storytelling gave me the courage to tell the hard stories. And now, your continued support has helped open the door to a new chapter – one where creative freedom leads the way. I hope you enjoy where it takes us.

Robin Benway
Thank you to the dream team of Lisa Grubka and Albert Lee at United Talent Agency for putting this project in motion and for doing what they do best. Thank you also to Meredith Miller and Melissa Chinchillo, with extra gratitude towards the assistants at UTA for all of their hard work on our book's behalf.

An extra-special thank you to our editor Liz Stein and the team at William Morrow: Rachel Weinwick, Andrea Monagle, Liate Stehlik, Jennifer Hart and the publicity and marketing departments, all of whom have put so much time and effort into this project.

Thank you to Rebecca Roy for being our first editor at Sphere and Hachette UK, and to Elisha Lundin and the Sphere team for shepherding this book along its way with such care.

Thank you to Mary Pender for being an absolute rock star and for answering all of my questions and texts about how film and TV deals work, and for making the job look so easy. (It is not easy!) Thank you also to Erin Underhill, Adam Giagni, Vivian Cannon, Montserrat Gómez and Bryana Stern at Universal Television, and to Emily Fox, for helping bring *Royal Spin* to life in an entirely new medium.

Much gratitude to my friend Steve, who read this manuscript in one day and gave fantastic notes about life in Washington, D.C. and at the White House. Any mistakes in this book are solely ours, not his.

Thank you to my friends and family who have always been steadfast in their support of my career, even when (and especially when) things haven't always gone the way I hoped they would. Thanks for the gifs, text messages, taco dates, funny dog photos, handwritten notes and love. I love you all right back.

A perennial thank you to the people who have let me have this job for so long: the readers. I love writing books, but being able to share them with you is the real joy.

And the best for last: Thank you to Omid. I had no idea what I was stepping into when we started writing this book, and I'm so glad to say that it's gone above and beyond my expectations. Working with you has been a dream, and my admiration for your talent and knowledge is only surpassed by my gratitude for our friendship. Let's go to Chili's soon.

About the Authors

During his twelve years covering the royal beat for major outlets including *Good Morning America*, *ABC News* and *Harper's Bazaar*, **Omid Scobie** became the most talked-about royal correspondent of his generation and is the author of two non-fiction bestsellers which have been published in over twenty countries. His debut title, *Finding Freedom*, an instant no. 1 Sunday Times bestseller is one of the fastest-selling royal books of all time, and his follow-up 2023 release, *Endgame*, was his second instant *New York Times* bestseller. He is the founder of the production and development company Box Room Entertainment and serves as co-creator, executive producer and writer on the TV adaptation of *Royal Spin*.

Omid grew up in Oxfordshire, England, and graduated in journalism at the University of Arts London. He currently lives in Los Angeles.

Robin Benway is a National Book Award-winning and *New York Times*-bestselling author of nine novels for young adults. Her books have received numerous awards and recognition, including the PEN America Literary Award, the Blue Ribbon Award from the Bulletin for the Center of Children's Books, ALA's Best Books for Young Adults and ALA's Popular Paperbacks for Young Adults. In addition, her novels have received starred reviews from *Bookpage*, *Kirkus*, *Booklist* and *Publishers Weekly*, and have been published in more than twenty-five countries. Her sixth novel, *Far From the Tree*, won the National Book Award for Young People's Literature, the PEN America Literary Award and was named one of the best books of the year by the *New York Times*, the *Los Angeles Times*, NPR, PBS, *Entertainment Weekly* and the *Boston Globe*. In addition to her fictional work, her non-fiction work has appeared in the *Los Angeles Times*, *Bustle*, *Elle* and more. *Royal Spin*, written in collaboration with Omid Scobie, is her first adult novel.

Robin grew up in Orange County, California; attended NYU, where she was a recipient of the Seth Barkas Prize for Creative Writing; and is a graduate of UCLA. She currently lives in Los Angeles with her dog, Marnie Chicken.